BOOK TWO

WICKED SOULS

KATIE WISMER

WICKED SOULS

Copyright © 2021 by Katie Wismer

For more information visit: www.katiewismer.com

Cover design by Seventhstar Art
Proofreading by Beth Attwood

ISBN: 978-1-7346115-6-4

First Edition: December 2021

10 9 8 7 6 5 4 3 2 1

To the readers who share the books they love with anyone who will listen. You are the best kind of people.

THE ESTATES

New York City, United States
Carrington Estate

Prince Rupert, Canada
Auclair Estate

São Joaquim, Brazil
Queirós Estate

Stockholm, Sweden
Olofsson Estate

Rjukan, Norway
Botner Estate

Dikson, Russia
Vasiliev Estate

Utqiagvik, United States
Locklear Estate

Chongqing, China
Wénběn Estate

Tórshavn, Faroe Islands
Jógvan Estate

Hat Yai, Thailand
Suksai Estate

PLAYLIST

Listen on Spotify: shorturl.at/luFO9

Graveyard — Halsey
I Want My Life Back Now — The Wrecks
i can't get high — Royal & the Serpent
And So It Went — The Pretty Reckless
Zombie — Miley Cyrus
Dead Weight — PVRIS
The Underground — Meg Myers
Make It Naked — DYLYN
why are you here — Machine Gun Kelly
1 Last Cigarette — The Band CAMINO
Blondes — Peach PRC
A Thousand Ways — Phoebe Ryan
Dirty — grandson
Go Fuck Yourself — Two Feet
Sticky — The Maine
M.C.K. — Group Project
LIVE ONCE — John the Ghost
It's Alright — Motel 7
Medicine — Robinson
Afterglow — Taylor Swift
Somebody's Gonna Love You —The Wldlfe
Never Learn — Good Boy Daisy, The Wrecks
Once in a Lifetime — All Time Low
Still Not Dead — DREAMERS
chocolate — Ziggy Alberts

IN A DREAM — Troye Sivan

broken people — almost monday

Forever & Always (Piano Version) (Taylor's Version) —
Taylor Swift

Teeth — 5 Seconds of Summer

Crumble — Fairlane

April 7th — The Maine

Bodybag — chloe moriondo

good 4 u — Olivia Rodrigo

Hate Myself — dodge

Two Nights — Javailin

love race — Machine Gun Kelly, Kellin Quinn

Let Me Down Slowly — Alec Benjamin, Alessia Cara

Ice Cave — The Maine

i hope ur miserable until ur dead — Nessa Barrett

split a pill — Machine Gun Kelly

searching for freedom - Alternative Version — Ziggy
Alberts

getting low — Ziggy Alberts

Song About You — The Band CAMINO

Bad Girls — M.I.A.

honey — Halsey

Know It All — The Band CAMINO

Fallout — Marianas Trench

CHAPTER ONE

I NEVER THOUGHT my blood would get added to the queen's collection. Now it sinks into the glass floor, drop by drop, joining the swirling pool of victims past. I barely feel the bite, not after the venom floods my system, and the chaos of the room dims. Shouts and footsteps muffle around me like I'm underwater. My body fills with warmth, and it sparkles and glows inside of my veins. Connor's tongue laps at my neck, and I sigh, hoping he'll bite again and I'll get another rush.

A second figure materializes above me, but my vision is too hazy to make out much more than his towering build and dark hair. He grabs Connor's shoulders and tries to rip him off me. Connor's fangs dig deeper into my skin as a few others join and haul him away. I tilt my head enough to see my blood gushing over my shoulder and into the floor.

A shout cuts through the room. One second passes, then two, and the wound in my neck burns as it heals itself.

The prince's face comes into view as he leans over me and braces a hand where the bite had been. "Valerie?"

The contact sends a jolt through me. All I see when I look into his eyes is the fog of his glamour. My mind might be free of it now, but the weight in my stomach is just as heavy. I jerk away. "Don't touch me."

My mother's head appears beside his, her features set in a deep scowl. The sight of her sends seething hot rage through my veins, so strong I have to clench my teeth against it. *She* did this. She *did this.* I flinch away from her outstretched hands. "*Don't* touch me."

She turns and murmurs to the prince, but I push back against the floor before he can reach for me again. A flash of something I don't understand crosses his face, and we stare at each other. He nods at whoever is behind me, and they help me to my feet. I turn to look at them—a man in a guard's uniform. Someone I don't know.

Apparently that's better than anyone I *do* know in this room.

I sway but refuse when the stranger tries to carry me. He lets me lean on him as I limp toward the door. The venom continues to burn through my blood, blurring everything around me, but a tug of the bond breaks through the haze. A small, searching pull that feels like a question.

I keep walking.

EVERYTHING in my room is the same when I step inside, but I feel like I'm in a stranger's home. Everything belongs to me, and yet, I feel nothing when I look at it.

I feel absolutely nothing at all.

The wooden floor creaks beneath my feet as I pace across the room and glance in the mirror on the wall. The entire left side of my shirt is stained with blood, and the material is stiff against my skin. I yank my hair into a pony-tail, ignoring the crunchy strands also coated in blood, then throw off my clothes and pull on the closest alternatives I can find—sweatpants and an oversize sweater.

I catch a second glimpse of myself in the mirror, then I start to laugh. Once I've started, I can't stop. I laugh until my ribs cramp and my cheeks ache, then I slide down until I'm sitting on the floor, my back propped against my bed.

The entire estate I'd grown up in had been conspiring for God knows how long to make killing my boyfriend my final task to get into the Marionettes, the one person I'd started to trust here took away my choice and glamoured me, and it all turned out to be for nothing anyway because Connor came back as a *vampire* and attacked me.

And my first priority was to…change my clothes?

Another fit of laughter consumes me, and I hug my arms around my abdomen, trying to make it stop. But the harder I resist, the harder it comes out, until tears are streaming down my face.

There's a knock at the door, but I'm too preoccupied trying to catch my breath between laughs to answer.

The door creaks open, and Reid steps inside. A splatter of blood runs down the length of his white shirt. The sight of him is finally enough to snap me out of it, and I push to my feet.

"Get out," I say through my teeth.

"Valerie—"

"I don't want you here."

"I know." He takes another step and closes the door behind him anyway.

"*Leave.*"

"Valerie—"

"I said *get out!*" I pick up my bloody shirt from the bed and throw it at him.

"Valerie."

I search my immediate surroundings for something else to throw.

He takes another step.

"The funny thing is, I was actually starting to trust you."

"You *can* trust me." He closes the rest of the distance between us, and I swing.

"You *glamoured me.*" My fists connect with his chest, but he doesn't stop me. He lets me hit and punch and shove him until he's back against the wall.

"I tried to warn you," he says, but I don't stop. My fists ache with each hit, but that only makes me want to punch harder. "And I tried to fix it."

"By *turning* him?"

"Would you rather he be dead?" he demands.

I shove him again, even though he's already against the wall and there's nowhere for him to go. "That's not up to us! Connor never would have wanted—"

"He agreed to it, Valerie!" Reid grabs my arms before I can hit him again and spins us around, pinning me against the wall, both of us breathing hard. His hands tighten around my wrists, trapping my arms between us. "You think I would've done it if he hadn't?"

I suddenly feel so very, very tired. Every time I close my eyes, I see Connor lying there, broken. Until that moment, I'd thought that was the worst thing that could ever happen to me.

As his teeth sunk into my neck, I realized maybe I was wrong.

I try to swallow the lump in my throat, and tears burn in my eyes again. "Just go."

"Valerie, look at me."

"Why?" I snap. "So you can glamour me again?"

He takes a step back. "Valerie—"

"Just *get out!*"

When he doesn't move, I dig my nails into my palms until hot blood runs down my skin. I focus on his legs, his muscles, then force them toward the door. He doesn't fight it as my magic shoves him into the hall. He catches himself on the opposite wall, but I pause before slamming the door.

"Where is Connor?" I demand, my voice not sounding like my own.

"I don't know—"

Something snaps inside of me, and I flip the blade out of my ring and have it against his throat in the next second. "*Stop lying to me.* Where is he?"

Despite the blade pressing into his skin hard enough to break the surface, he doesn't flinch. Very calmly, he says, "I'm assuming one of the cells in the basement until he calms down and they can figure out what to do next. My guess is they'll keep him there until after the ceremony to be safe." His eyes flick from me to the blade. "Are you done?"

I step back and turn to head down the hallway, but then Reid is in front of me again, so fast I didn't see him move.

"Get out of my way," I growl.

"You can't go down there."

"Like hell I can't." I step around him, and he grabs my shoulders, holding me in place. I yank out of his grasp and pivot, only for his arms to circle my waist and pull me back against his chest. I struggle, kicking at his legs and throwing my arms out, but he tightens his grip.

His lips hover right behind my ear, his voice low and rough. "You think given the emphasis on loyalty they wanted to see from you, immediately going to check on him is going to do you any favors?"

"I don't *care*."

Connor is probably scared and confused. He might not remember what happened. Or worse, he *does*, and he's hurt —*angry*—with me for what I've done. Let alone he's a *vampire* now and probably starving. Are they feeding him? Explaining things to him? Is he all alone?

"You don't care now," Reid says, "but after you've calmed down, you'll see if I let you go, this would all be for nothing."

"You're really telling me to calm down right now?" I thrash in his arms. "If you don't let me go, Reid, I swear to God, I will hurt you."

"You need to hate me for this? Then fine. But you're being unreasonable and letting your emotions cloud your judgment. And I'm not going to let you get yourself killed for it."

"Oh, I'm being unreasonable? *I'm* the one being unreasonable?"

"I will take you to see him, but not tonight. *I* will check on him, okay? But you can't go down there." I try to break free from his arms, and his grip tightens so much I can barely breathe. "I am not above knocking you unconscious and locking you in your room."

"Get the fuck off me."

"Swear to me you won't go down there."

I pull against his arms, my blood running hot.

"*Swear to me.*"

"Fine! I won't go see Connor. Now *get the fuck off me.*"

He releases me, and I stumble forward a step, breathing hard. His eyes sweep my face, his jaw tight. But then he turns and wordlessly strides from the hall, leaving me alone in the quiet. In his absence, the rage simmers, which leaves me with nothing left to do but cry.

I SPEND a lot of time that night running through imaginary arguments in my head, trying to figure out the perfect thing to say to my mother when I see her. But it ends up being a waste of time because she never comes.

Despite this not being particularly unusual, a heaviness settles in my chest all the same. We've never been ones to check up on each other. We've never been outwardly affectionate or emotional at all, but given what happened today, I thought maybe she would at least try to talk to me. Come by, even if not to apologize, to congratulate me on passing the final trial. On doing what needed to be done. On jumping through the sick little hoop she set up for me.

But she never shows.

And now that hours have passed, and the adrenaline from the final task has faded, everything else trickles back in. Wendigo claws tearing into my chest. The Russians drugging me in the hospital. Knives in my stomach. The snake—

A full-body shudder rolls through me, and I realize how exhausted I am. My entire body feels raw and bruised.

Texts and missed calls from Kirby and Monroe litter my phone screen. I don't know if they're asking about the final trial or worried about me going missing from school. I can't bring myself to listen to their voice mails or call them back. Even though I wouldn't be able to tell them exactly what happened, all it would take is a few words for them to know something was wrong. Then they would have a million questions and want to talk about it and be there for me.

Though that's probably exactly what I need, I don't have the energy for it right now. I send them a quick text to let them know I'm okay and I'll talk to them later, then turn off my phone and climb into the shower.

The water is hot enough to turn my skin bright red, and I stand under the spray until it goes cold. It takes several minutes of scrubbing my skin raw to rinse off the blood and grime.

I change into some sweats, crawl under the covers of my bed, and curl in on myself. The room feels too big around me, so I slip one hand free from the blankets and brace it against the wall like I used to do when I was younger. It helped me feel anchored enough to fall asleep. It reminded me of where I was, that I was safe, that I was alone.

But tonight, it doesn't bring me as much comfort as it once did. Because I know tomorrow I'm going to have to wake up, get ready, drag myself into the throne room, and pretend the events of tonight never happened—or at least that they didn't affect me. I'll stand there for the initiation ceremony, smiling at the queen and my mother in gratitude, and pledge my undying allegiance and loyalty to them, all the while choking back the bile in my throat.

I guess that's assuming what just happened with Connor won't change things. What if they find out about the glamour and decide I don't pass after all? Or they think I somehow was involved in turning him? Then this was all for nothing. This thing I've worked my entire life for, the only outcome I've ever been allowed to entertain, is over?

I can't muster the energy to worry about it. To care. The Marionettes was always expected of me, sure, but it was also supposed to give me some sort of protection. More than witches on the outside have, at least. But this? *This* is their idea of protection? This is the group of people I'm going to pledge my life to? The ones who ripped my heart straight out of my chest and enjoyed watching it bleed into the floor?

God, I just want Connor. I want to curl up against his chest and feel his arms around me. To hear him tell me it's going to be okay.

I let out a choked sob and press my face into the pillow. *I* did this to him. I'm the reason he's in this position, that he's locked up God knows where now, that he's now the thing he hated the most. Loving me has only put him in danger. There's no way he could know about the glamour too. So he must think I did it. That I really chose them over him.

How could he ever forgive me for that?

And to think, this is all I've ever wanted.

CHAPTER TWO

A HUMAN SERVANT shows up the next morning with a dress. He stands stiffly in the hall when I open the door. I offer a weak smile, but he doesn't return it. He looks familiar. I think I've seen him talking with Connor before. Judging by the way he looks me up and down with obvious disdain, he knows who I am.

So. Word has spread already. And apparently I'm to blame.

I hold out my arms. He hesitates a moment before dropping the dress into my hands, then turns on his heel and leaves the hall. The plastic garment bag crinkles as I carry it inside and lay it on the bed. So all of the vampires and witches would have blamed me for *not* killing him, but now the humans blame me for going through with it.

I can't even fault them for it. Working in the Carrington estate was supposed to grant them protection other humans don't have. The queen practically spit in all of their faces with this task. Of course, they can't be angry with her.

But they can be angry with me.

How they know, I have no idea. The details of the final tasks are always kept under lock and key, everyone in the room getting spelled to secrecy. Either they got sloppy because of the chaos, or people have put two and two together.

The invitation to the ceremony sits on my desk—the official announcement I'd passed my initiation. They'd slipped it under my door while I slept. At one point, I probably would've framed the stupid thing or put it on display somewhere.

I grab the thick piece of stationery, rip it in half, then shove it in the trashcan.

The same headache I've had since the moment I woke up pounds against my temples, intense enough the room feels wobbly around me. I brace myself against my desk and let out a slow breath through my nose. Once the dizziness subsides, I prick my finger and rub the blood between my eyebrows. The tension eases, but not completely.

I startle at a knock on the door. Adrienne pokes her head inside. She's already dressed for the ceremony, and she suddenly looks much older than seventeen. The silk red dress hugs her body, the neckline dipping down in a sharp V, exposing the thin, gold necklace that hangs all the way down her sternum. The hair, though, is the same as always. Straight and smooth, perfectly in line with her chin. Her eyes dart from the dress on the bed to me, and she purses her lips.

"I thought you might need help getting ready," she says.

I stare at her for a moment, the surprise likely evident on my face, then nod. There'd been a time when I couldn't picture this moment without her, but given our track record these past few months, I'd figured a casual glance across the room would be the best I'd get tonight.

She closes the door behind her and heads to the bathroom. I clear my throat, the quiet weighing between us. When she reappears, her arms are full of makeup products, and she juts her chin toward the bed. "Sit down."

I do, and she pulls the desk chair up to the edge so she can face me. Neither of us says anything at first. She gets to work, meticulously painting the ceremonial look. She starts with the red tint, blending it from my hair to my eyes, the color getting progressively lighter the farther it goes down my face. She smudges and blurs it out along my lower lashes. The small white dots that run in a straight line over my brow are next, and she presses her lips together and leans in close to concentrate.

As she moves on to blending the dark kohl around my eyes, I manage to find my voice. "Did you hear about…?"

Her hand stops moving. We sit like that for a minute, but then she clears her throat and pulls back to find the product to fill in my brows. A small line appears on her forehead. "They shouldn't have done that."

There's something she isn't saying. Before I can respond, she tilts my chin up and pulls out the red pencil for my lips. I sit quietly as she finishes, wondering if she's thinking about the same thing I am. Two years ago, it was Calliope sitting here, and we were both giggling and gossiping as we helped her get ready. She'd put on a brave face, forcing smiles and laughing along with us, but she'd been off that day. She hadn't said much. We couldn't talk about her final task, of course, but I'd always thought whatever had been bothering her must have happened in that room.

"You should put your dress on," says Adrienne. "Then we'll do your hair."

The full black skirt billows out around me as we pull it on. The sleeves are intricately embroidered with golden vines and red roses, if they can be called sleeves. The dress is designed like it's meant to be strapless, the neckline cutting straight across my chest. The flowers and vines branch up over my shoulders and across the back of my ribs as if the flowers had just floated down and landed there, suspended in the empty space.

I sit back down as I pull on the gold heels, and Adrienne gets started with my hair. She twists back strands from my face and piles them at the crown of my head, leaving half of it down as she weaves in black and red flowers, then finishes it off with a gold comb.

"There," she breathes.

I stare at my reflection for a moment, barely recognizing the girl looking back. Adrienne appears at my side, and a jolt goes through me as she grabs my hand. She keeps her gaze on the mirror, and her voice is barely audible when she says, "I never blamed you, Valerie. For Calliope. Or maybe I did, for a while. But I know it wasn't your fault."

I swallow hard, refusing to let the burning in the backs of my eyes show.

"You should probably get downstairs," I murmur. "It'll be starting soon."

"You don't want me to wait with you?"

I squeeze her hand. "I'll be okay. Thank you. For your help."

She nods, and I stare at the door long after she closes it. *I know it wasn't your fault.* Instead of lifting any kind of weight off my chest, it just makes the silence of the room ring louder, Calliope's absence today taking up twice as much space. She would've known just the right thing to say before I headed down.

My hands shake as I slip my earrings from my desk— simple gold chains that hang nearly to my shoulders—and put them in. The same ones Calla had worn for her cere- mony. Maybe it's silly, but it makes me feel like she's here with me in some way. The matching necklace—a thin, gold chain—doesn't go on as easily. I wrestle with the clasp and let out a frustrated breath through my nose. I roll my eyes, irritated with myself as tears blur my vision.

I will not cry tonight. I will not—

A second, softer knock sounds on the door behind me, and my pulse jumps. Nerves dance across my skin, raising the hairs on my arms, and they don't feel like they're all coming from me.

I lower the necklace, giving up, and brace myself before I open the door. Reid stands in the hallway, his head down. His black suit is a perfect match to my dress, the gold embroidery along his jacket a mirror to the vines along my arms. His crown is properly in the center of his dark, wavy hair today, and when he looks up, his blue eyes are piercing against the thick, black band painted across his face.

He looks…

I don't let myself finish the thought.

He looks like the man who glamoured me last night. *That's* what he looks like.

He wets his lips and lets out a soft breath as his eyes travel the length of me. I try to loosen the knot sitting in my chest like a rock. The faintest trace of music trickles up from below, and my eyes dart toward the stairs.

Reid looks at the necklace in my hands. "Can I help?"

I want to say no for the principle of the matter, but it's either that, let him watch me struggle with it some more, or go without it. I hand it to him wordlessly and turn around.

He takes a step closer, and the heat of his presence lights up every nerve across the bare skin of my back, even without him touching me. He pushes my hair over one shoulder, and his fingers brush my spine as he secures the clasp. A shiver dances across my skin as his breath hits my neck, but I step away as soon as he's done.

Reid extends his arm as I turn around to face him, his expression perfectly neutral. "Shall we?"

I ignore his arm but follow him into the hall. He drops it and leaves a foot of distance between us as we start to walk. Honestly, with how shaky my legs are right now, I could probably use the anchor, but I sure as hell am not taking it from him.

"There's nothing to be nervous about," he murmurs. "You already did the hard part."

I glance at him sideways. "All of this is the hard part."

He smirks as he leads me to the service staircase on the other end of the hall—presumably to avoid running into any of the guests before we're announced. The door is hidden in the wall behind a large painting of the Carrington estate back when it was originally built. The brushstrokes are harsh, angry against the canvas, the surrounding trees painted red and orange, and they look like they're encroaching on the structure, threatening to swallow it whole. Reid takes the picture by the frame and swings it aside, revealing a well-lit staircase.

"After you."

I teeter on the stairs in my heels, and Reid reappears at my side, closing the wall behind us.

I catch him looking at me again and raise a single eyebrow. "What?"

He shakes his head. "Nothing. I like the dress. It suits you."

I roll my eyes but find the anger in my chest a little harder to hold on to as we reach the main floor. The clamor of the crowd seeps through the door, probably all gathered in the throne room already.

"I went to see Connor," he adds, and I whip my head to the side, hanging on to his every word now. "He's fine. I made sure he had enough blood. They're letting him out tomorrow."

I nod, the relief that courses through me heavy and immediate. *Connor is okay.* That doesn't resolve all of the issues at hand, not even close, but he's alive. He's fed. And they're letting him out. They wouldn't let him out now just to kill him later, would they?

"There aren't going to be any other surprises tonight, are there?" I ask, freezing in place before he can open the door. "Like suddenly I get paired with someone random?"

His eyebrows lift. "Are you saying you actually *want* to be paired with me now?"

I stare at him but can't seem to muster a reply. My stomach is too tight, and my mind is too busy, and there's too much *noise*. With all of the surprises lately, I don't think I could take another one.

His expression softens. "Nothing to worry about, Darkmore. I won't give you up to someone else that easily."

The door opens to the back hallway behind the throne room, where the other initiates wait to be announced. Torches along the walls flicker and reflect off the glossy floors. Only about a dozen pairs seem to be here so far, and I scan the crowd, trying to see who made it in. The conversation among the group quiets at our arrival as people turn and straighten at the sight of Reid.

Daniel stands toward the front of the group and waves when he catches my eye. Wes is next to him, unsurprisingly, and Beth is on his other side. I stretch my neck, trying to find Kirby or Monroe, my heart steadily beating faster in my chest with every moment that passes and I don't see them.

They can't have not gotten in. I'd thought they'd been calling to see how my task had gone, but their tasks were later that day too. What if they'd been calling to say they hadn't made it? I'm a horrible friend. I've been so absorbed in my own problems—

Reid tugs me back a step and juts his chin toward the end of the hall. The tension in my shoulders eases as Kirby swims into view, a powder pink, floor-length dress swishing along behind her as she struts into the hall. The vampire beside her is the same size as she is. In fact, their blond hair is the exact same shade too. They almost look related.

Kirby notices me a moment later, and her entire face lights up, the red paint around her eyes crinkling as she beams. She quickens her pace, crossing the rest of the distance between us, then throws her arms around my neck.

"Kirby—" I laugh and hug her back, stumbling under her weight.

She pulls back and holds me at arm's length as she studies every inch of me. "I've been so worried about you. Are you okay? You look okay."

"I'm okay," I say. The genuine concern in her eyes makes my throat tighten, but I force a smile. I don't want to get into it, and definitely not with so many people around. All I care about right now is getting through tonight.

She tightens her grip on my shoulders for a second before finally releasing me, then grins, all the tension gone as she looks from Reid to me. Her cheeks flush a bit. "Okay, you two look amazing. I don't think we've officially met, *Your Highness*. I'm—"

"Kirby La Doux," Reid says.

I stare at him, trying to remember if I'd ever spoken of my friends with him, or if he just pays more attention than I realized. Maybe I've shown him more through the bond than I'd meant to.

Kirby's eyes practically fall out of her head, and she whips around to grin at me. "So you've talked about me. Figures. I *am* the most interesting person in her life."

"I'll try not to take that personally." Monroe appears on Kirby's other side, her hair done up in an intricate bun.

She's in a sleek red dress with off-the-shoulder straps, the color perfectly matching the streaks in her hair.

Her eyes rake over me, just like Kirby's had, and she opens her mouth to say something else, but whatever she sees on my face stops her. She gives me a small smile instead and says, "Leave it to you to look *that good* after all the shit the past few days. Criminally unfair, Val."

I glance behind her head, and my stomach drops to my feet. The vampire lingering behind Monroe meets my eyes and nods.

Nathan.

Avery's old partner.

Avery had said he'd probably get paired with someone in our class once she left, but Monroe? Her pair for initiation had been someone temporary, so she must have just found out Nathan would be her final pair, maybe even earlier tonight. And she probably has no idea what she's getting into. No idea about his history.

Hell, I don't know exactly myself, but I know it can't be good. Monroe's expression is as unbothered as ever as Kirby reaches over and smooths out a smudge in the red makeup on her cheek.

There's a faint tug on the bond, and I look over to see Reid staring at me. I try to smooth out whatever was on my face.

"Don't they usually do it alphabetically?" Kirby is saying. "So Val should be one of the firsts."

"I just hope they have drinks," mutters Monroe.

"Do we know how many initiates there are?" asks Kirby.

"Twenty-five," says Reid. "As far as I know. But she's

right." He looks over at me. "You'll be one of the first called. We should probably get near the front."

I nod and squeeze Kirby's and Monroe's hands as I pass. "I'll see you guys inside."

Heads turn as Reid and I head for the large golden doors at the front of the group. I let out a shuddering breath. Every inch of my skin feels hot, like it's trying to escape from my body. I shake my head, trying to clear the dizziness. I don't know where this disorientation came from or why it's clinging to me like fog. I feel like I'm floating through a dream, like nothing around me is real.

Maybe I'm just exhausted, and everything that's happened in the past few days is all catching up with me at once. Maybe I should have fed after losing so much blood when Connor attacked me. Or maybe it's all in my head.

Reid opens his mouth to say something, but stops as someone gasps beside me. All of the conversation in the hall dies as the queen makes her way toward us, two guards following closely behind.

The crowd parts, clearing a path to the throne room door. She stands in a lavish silver gown that glows beneath the lights, and a veil hangs down from her crown, though the lines of teeth arranged among the gold spikes are still on full display. Somehow even with her face covered, I can still tell her expression beneath is amused.

She turns toward where Reid and I stand, and I stiffen, but her gaze continues to sweep the rest of the group. She inclines her head a fraction of an inch.

"Congratulations," she says. Her voice comes out smooth and low. I'm half expecting some kind of speech, but she turns to the door, and the guards follow on either side of her. The noise coming from the other side of the wall dims until it becomes so quiet, even my vampire hearing can't pick up anything distinct. Both guards reach forward at the same time, and light floods the hall as they open the doors. A deep voice announces the queen's arrival, and she steps into the room.

CHAPTER THREE

A HUSH FALLS over the room as the queen slowly makes her way to the throne. Flames flicker in torches along the walls, casting shadows over the hundreds of vampire and witch guests all waiting in the outskirts, wearing suits and dresses as extravagant as those of the initiates. Human servants linger by the opposite door in white uniforms.

The center of the floor is clear, save for a line of tall men in all black, their faces covered in masks. Twenty-five of them, I would guess. They each hold a small, golden cup with red inset stones.

The tapping of high heels against the glossy floor breaks through the silence as my mother comes down from the dais and stands among the men at the center of the room.

Every muscle in my body tenses as her red lips curve into a smile. She's in a black dress similar to my own, though hers has long sleeves and glitters when she moves.

"Today we welcome twenty-five new witches to the Carrington estate's Marionettes," says the queen. She stands in front of her throne, face still covered by her veil. "These twenty-five witches have shown great strength and discipline, and it is an honor to welcome them home. Just as we know they will protect and serve us, we now vow to protect them as our own."

The guests murmur their agreement and bow their heads.

"And it is our honor to witness their pairings. Rosemarie?"

My mother smiles again and steps up beside the man at the end of the line. "Daniel Abney," she calls. "To be paired with Warren Harding."

Daniel squares his shoulders and shoots me a wink before stepping into the room, a man with dark skin and darker hair following a few paces behind—Warren, apparently. My mother instructs them where to stand, facing each other, with the man in black behind them.

"Bethany Coldwell, to be paired with Valentina Reyes."

Beth lets out a nervous giggle but composes herself before walking forward and finding her place in the center of the room. I stare at the torches over their heads until my eyes start to burn.

"Valerie Darkmore," calls my mother. "To be paired with Prince Reginald Carrington."

I don't move at first, and Reid gives me a small nudge between my shoulders. My footsteps seem to echo in the room, and the expression my mother gives me as I pass is entirely emotionless. Beth smiles at me as I step up beside her, and I force myself to smile back as Reid finds his place across from me. I can feel him staring at me, and indeed, when I look up, he's studying my face.

We stand silently as more names are called, and the spaces beside me are filled one by one. The air feels warmer here than it did in the hallway, and sweat starts to form in my hairline.

"Kirby La Doux," calls my mother. "To be paired with Alice McCoy."

My vision blurs in and out for a moment, and I blink a few times, trying to force myself to focus.

"Monroe Macavei, to be paired with Nathan Van Doren."

A tug on the bond makes me look up. Reid's gaze is probing, unblinking. I force a small nod to show I'm fine, though I guess I'm not entirely sure if that's true.

Once we're all in line, my mother slowly makes her way back to Daniel and takes the cup from the man behind him.

"Daniel Abney, do you swear to uphold your duties as a Marionette and pledge your loyalty to your partner, Warren Harding?"

"I do," says Daniel.

"Hold out your arm."

He does, and my mother carves a deep line in his skin with the razor on her nails. The blood pools in the golden cup, and once there's enough, my mother lets a single drop of her own blood fall onto Daniel's arm so it will heal. She then adds a second drop of her blood to the cup as she says the pairing incantation under her breath. Once Warren drinks, she takes back the cup and carves a line in his arm.

"Do you, Warren Harding, swear to uphold your duties

as a paired member of the Carrington estate and pledge your loyalty to your partner, Daniel Abney?"

His voice comes out rough and low as he says, "I do."

Once the exchange is complete, my mother returns the cup to the man in black and moves on to the next pair. The room remains unnervingly silent as they proceed, as if everyone is holding their breath. The cups must already have a drop of the queen's blood inside them, meant to signify tethering us to her estate. My shoulders tense as my mother draws closer, and I clench my jaw in the hopes my thoughts won't show on my face.

It was only yesterday we were in this room, and not only did she sit and watch my entire world fall apart, I have a feeling she orchestrated it.

And now, as she steps up between me and Reid, the look on her face is still utterly impassive. She jabs her nail into my arm with more force than necessary and stares at me as my blood fills the cup, but I refuse to give her a reaction. Her eyes flick down to my arm before casting the spell over the blood—is she expecting the wound not to heal? When it does, her expression doesn't change. She hands the cup to Reid.

"Do you, Your Highness, Prince Reginald Carrington, swear to uphold your duties as a paired member of the Carrington estate and pledge your loyalty to your partner, Valerie Darkmore?"

Something burns behind his eyes as he says, "I do."

"Valerie Darkmore, do you swear to uphold your duties as a Marionette and pledge your loyalty to your partner, Prince Reginald Carrington?"

Reid holds my gaze, and I can't look away. "I do," I whisper.

My hand shakes as I take the cup with his blood, my mind flashing back to the last time we did this. But there's no immediate effect as it coats the back of my throat. Nothing except maybe some relief. It's been a while since I've fed, and the warmth of the blood as it trickles down my throat is welcome. My vision clears as my mother moves on.

The blood goes straight to my center, circling and warming around the bond that's already there. It seems most of the others in line have stayed with the same vampires they'd been paired with for the initiation, but some are new pairings. I wonder what it feels like to have that first bond severed and replaced with another. As annoying as it had been at first, I've grown used to its presence, and it's hard to imagine what it would be like without it now.

See? Reid's voice appears in my head. He's watching me again, a bemused smile on his lips. *Hard part is over.*

I roll my eyes, but for the first time all night, I smile back.

THE PARTY WASTES no time getting started once the pairing ceremony concludes. The room livens as guests flood the space again, and waiters carry flutes of champagne back and forth—some plain for the witches, some laced with blood for the vampires. Orchestra music plays from the corner, and the room brightens with the lighting of additional torches and chandeliers.

I hesitate by the tables of food near the back, picking through the different platters and adding a few fruits and cheeses to my plate. My eyes flit over the human servants as they float through the room, taking away empty trays and bringing out new food and drinks before anything can get too low. They're blurs of white uniforms, making eye contact with no one. Speaking to no one.

A sharp stab of pain emanates in the middle of my chest as I realize I'm looking for someone I won't find. Of course Connor won't be here tonight. But every time I'd envisioned this night, he'd been here. Even if we couldn't spend much time together, just the looks across the room, maybe stealing a brief conversation in the corner, would have been enough.

He's okay, I remind myself. But that does nothing to help the guilt still eating away at the pit of my stomach as I picture him on his knees in front of me. How still he'd been on the floor—

Trying to brush off the thoughts, I turn toward the dance floor, where Monroe and Kirby have abandoned their pairs and are dancing with each other. They spot me a moment later and wave for me to join them. I shake my head and hold up the plate of food I still haven't touched as an excuse. Glancing through the crowd again, I wonder where Adrienne is. I don't see Reid either. He disappeared shortly after the ceremony, swept away by the queen to talk with some visitors from the other regions.

A blond human appears beside me with a tray of champagne. He bows his head as he offers them to me, and I slip one off.

"Thank you," I murmur.

He nods and disappears back into the crowd.

"Everyone who feels like they just joined a cult, say *aye*."

I snort as Daniel leans against the table next to me, a glass of champagne in each hand.

A girl in a short silver dress breezes past us, and Daniel's eyes dart from me to her retreating form. He lifts one of his glasses to me, then hurries after her. "See you around, Darkmore!"

In his absence, Adrienne swims into view across the room. She's standing in a corner with a few other girls her age, dancing along to the music. She gives me a hesitant wave when she notices me watching.

A hand brushes the back of my elbow, and as I turn, Reid slides in beside me. The sight of him immediately makes my stomach drop.

"Dance with me," he says.

I sip my drink. "I'll pass."

He reaches over, takes the glass and plate from my hands, and sets them on the table. When he turns back around, he's so close I have to tilt my head back. His blue eyes burn into mine. "It's tradition."

Sighing, I let him take my hand and lead me into the center of the floor, though only a few other people are dancing right now. Bracing one hand on my hip, he takes my hand with the other, his grasp firm. The orchestra music swells as we sway side to side, and a few more people trickle onto the floor around us. I catch sight of Kirby and Monroe over Reid's shoulder.

A second image appears in my mind—a memory. Ten years ago, back when Monroe first arrived at the estate.

She'd somehow immediately fit in with the dynamic between me and Kirby, even though she didn't talk much at first. Her parents had been two of over a dozen victims of an antiwitch group in the city, but for some reason, the queen had found her promising enough to bring her to the estate until she was old enough for the academy.

It wasn't that unusual; the estate has a program to teach and house kids who otherwise wouldn't have had a chance at the Marionettes. Kirby and I spent that whole first week trying to get her to talk, smile, *something*. The thing that finally did it was sneaking into the throne room while the rest of the estate slept. We'd danced around, laughing and daydreaming about what our initiation celebration would be like. Kirby had tried to teach Monroe to slow dance, but the two kept stepping on each other until, eventually, they fell over. It was the first time I'd ever heard Monroe laugh.

I blink back to the room in front of me as Monroe and Kirby twirl onto the dance floor, giggling. They find a spot a few feet away from us and fall into an easy rhythm, alternating spinning and dipping each other.

This is all we ever wanted. A day we've been dreaming about since we were kids. I used to curl into bed with Calla and muse about what color my dress would be, how I'd do my hair. As I reached my teen years and my friendship with Connor shifted into something more, I let myself picture dancing with him under the lights, even though I knew it would never happen. But as I look around the room at all of the dancers, the lights, the food, and the glamour, suddenly I want to be anywhere but here.

How can I possibly enjoy a second of this after what I

did to Connor? While he's sitting down in some cell all alone?

"You have scars on your fingers," Reid says.

My head snaps back to him. His gaze is trained on our interlaced hands, and he runs the pad of his thumb along my fingertips.

"The violin, right?"

I don't respond.

He sighs. "You ever going to talk to me again?"

I glare up at him.

He shakes his head. "I think you may be the most stubborn person I've ever met."

When I still don't respond, Reid tightens his hand on my waist and bends down until his lips are beside my ear. "At least pretend like you're having a good time. Your mother is looking."

I glance out of the corner of my eye. Sure enough, *both* of our mothers are looking straight at us—the queen at her throne, my mother beside her. My mother gives me what almost looks like a smile. Maybe I'd been imagining the weird mood between us earlier, or maybe she hadn't wanted to show favoritism during the ceremony. But that doesn't change what happened. All I'm ever going to see when I look at her now is the blankness of her face as they dropped Connor in front of me.

"Then that's the last thing I should do," I mumble. "She hates it when I'm happy."

He turns us so his back is to them, blocking me from their view. He meets my eyes but doesn't say anything else. Neither of us do. We move along with the music, watching each other, and something about it makes my stomach knot and heat rise to the surface of my skin.

One song blurs into another, and halfway through the third, his eyes flit over my face. "You want to get out of here?"

I raise an eyebrow. "It sounds like you're propositioning me."

"It's a yes or no question, Darkmore."

I sigh, glancing at our mothers still by the throne. Not only are my thoughts probably written all over my face, but I'm willing to bet he's getting some of them through the bond too. "More than anything, yes," I breathe.

His hold tightens on my waist, then he pulls back and offers me his hand. I can feel eyes on us as I take it, and he heads for the door. But I don't look. I just tighten my grip and follow.

———

THE AIR BITES the moment we step outside, but my body barely reacts to it. At least, not the way it once would. No goosebumps rise on my arms; no chills run down my spine. It's like I can feel the cold, but it's fleeting. As soon as I register the sensation, it moves on. Reid closes the door to the patio, muffling the music still pouring out from the party. The sky is overcast, few stars managing to squeeze through.

He comes to stand at my side and leans against the railing. Neither of us says anything, and the breeze picks up, sending his hair into his eyes.

God, I want to hate him. I want to scream and throw

things and let all of this rage inside of me pour out at him. Tears rise up again, and I have to look away. Because as much as I want to direct all of my anger at him…all the people in this estate who knew about the trial—all of the people who know me and watched me grow up—they all stood by and let this happen.

And he was the only one who tried to help.

"Will you get in trouble for turning him?" I whisper.

A corner of his mouth lifts. "Nothing I can't handle. No matter how angry they are, I don't think they'll hurt him. Not now that he's one of their own. I'll keep an eye on him to be sure."

I nod slowly and wrap my arms around myself. "Who spelled your blood for you?"

Finally, he turns to me, a troubled expression on his face now. "Adrienne."

My eyebrows lift, and I sway a little on my feet. I guess that would explain her weird behavior earlier, but why hadn't she told me? Something wet hits my cheeks, and it takes me a second to realize I'm crying.

"Valerie."

I sniff and turn away again, looking out at the grounds.

"Valerie."

I don't respond.

"Look at me." He takes my chin between his fingers and forces me to meet his eyes. I'm struck for a moment by the intensity, the hardness there. "I'm sorry. No matter the reason, I shouldn't have done it. But if you hadn't killed him in there, they would have done it anyway—possibly somewhere I wouldn't have been able to give him my blood and complete the process. Then you'd be out of the running for the Marionettes, and he would be dead. I thought it was the best option at the time."

He releases me, and my skin feels cold.

I don't—can't—respond. Tears burn in the back of my throat, and I worry if I tried to speak, my voice would break. Because as much as I wish it were, the feeling inside of my chest isn't hatred. It's sharper. Darker. Now that some time has passed and my emotions have calmed enough to listen to reason again, his logic makes sense. But no amount of understanding why he did it makes it any easier to trust him again. And I realize it's not what happened with Connor that's pulling at me. It's the glamour. The *violation* of it all.

He digs in his eyebrows and lets out a slow breath. "It won't *ever* happen again, Valerie," he says, voice low. "You have my word."

I hold his gaze for a moment, then turn back to the railing. My fingers rub at the spot Connor's teeth had dug in, the skin mostly healed now, but still tender. The aftereffects of the venom have worn off, but their memory is just as sharp. How easily I'd given in to it. The moment it flooded my veins, there was no reasoning. I just wanted more.

Reid's eyes follow the movement, and the lines in his forehead deepen. "He didn't know what he was doing."

My words come out barely louder than a whisper. "I know."

"Just like when you first turned—he probably didn't even see your face, Valerie. He couldn't help it."

I nod, too many times, too fast. Logically, I know exactly what he went through. The tunnel vision. The thirst. The instincts taking over everything.

But a quiet voice in the back of my mind still can't help but whisper, *He knew*. He knew about what happened to Calla. He *saw* it. He knew how I felt about venom, how I'd never tried it, not even once.

Reid meets my eyes.

I swallow hard, realizing I was probably advertising all of my thoughts down the bond, and a flush of heat fills my cheeks. "I'll be fine."

"I know. But if you end up needing anything, I'm… here. I've seen a lot of rough final trials. But this…this was cruel, Valerie. You didn't deserve this."

I stare at him, the word *cruel* hurdling around in my chest. When he looks up, I can tell he means it. When I'd looked into the queen's and my mother's eyes in the throne room, there hadn't been a hint of regret. No compassion. Nothing. Reid's eyes are heavy. Not with pity, exactly. Just understanding.

His expression shifts, almost into a wince. "I didn't get a chance to ask you before. How are you feeling?" There's no mistaking his gaze drifting down to my stomach, then quickly away.

"I'm fine." I curse my voice for shaking around the words and turn to the gardens. "Are they…?"

He sighs. "No one's seen them since they dropped you off at my room. No sign of them in the region at all. We have a team looking for them, but…" He trails off. "We're not going to let this go, Valerie. We *will* find them. I swear to you."

But they're still unaccounted for. Which means they could be anywhere. Doing anything. They could come back at any time and finish what they started with me…or worse.

Which is probably exactly what they want, for me to be afraid. Whatever they're playing at, this is some kind of game to them. And the anticipation, the fear, it's adding to whatever they're actually after.

Reid's words from yesterday echo in the back of my mind. *I don't know if they want revenge, if this was just for fun…if this was just the start.*

I shiver. The music swells behind the door, and I glance over my shoulder, trying to shake off the heaviness that's settled between us. "You don't mind missing the party?"

He lets out a low laugh. "I am very okay missing the party. But we can go back if you change your mind."

"It wasn't as much fun as I'd imagined it would be," I say, almost to myself.

"Things rarely are." He clears his throat and looks at me out of the corner of his eye. "Don't make any plans for tomorrow, okay?"

I blink, and it takes me a minute to process the change in subject. The very idea of *making plans* almost sounds like a foreign concept. Every minute of my days has been planned out for I can't even remember how long. With initiation over, the semester has officially reached its end for juniors. The underclassmen still have a few weeks left, but for the next couple of months, I'm…free. All incoming seniors are required to participate in the summer program, so I do have one class, but that still leaves me with an unprecedented amount of free time compared to the last few months.

I raise my eyebrows. "Why?"

"I was thinking it would be a good idea for you and me to practice feeding."

"Feeding," I repeat.

He presses his lips together and nods, his expression suddenly serious. "Now that you're spending the summer at the estate, you can't very well go downstairs and grab some blood like the rest of us, or have a human sent to your rooms. We'll try to get you blood bags when we can, but I think it's best you learn how to feed properly, just in case."

I stare at him. "You want me to learn to feed on humans."

"Would you rather put yourself in a situation where you can't get any bags and you're so hungry you snap and don't know how to stop?"

He has a point. I hate that he has a point. But the idea of drinking directly from someone makes me feel like I'm going to throw up.

"It doesn't have to be as bad as you're probably making it out to be in your head," he says quietly. "Plenty of humans are willing, or you can glamour them, or use a spell to make them forget. You don't take much, not enough to cause them any harm. But it's something all vampires have to learn to do when they're young. And I don't think never teaching you is a good idea."

I try to imagine it. Try to imagine taking a human and sinking my teeth into their neck. Someone like Madison.

Someone like Connor.

"We'll try it tomorrow," he decides. "They'll have let Connor out by then, and he'll need to learn too. We'll go into the city."

A small jolt goes through my body at Connor's name. Despite everything I've seen—despite feeling his fangs in my own neck—in my mind, he's still human.

I say nothing, even though I want to argue. Because the only thing worse than learning how to do this is the alternative. If I hurt someone, if I got to that point and didn't know how to stop, I don't think I'd ever be able to forgive myself.

CHAPTER FOUR

THE TEARS and the shock from the initiation ceremony are long gone now. The second the sun goes down and people at the estate start to rise, my feet take me where I need to go before I realize where I'm heading. My jaw aches from clenching it so tightly, and I force my hands to relax out of the fists I've been holding at my sides. I'm not looking for another argument. Just, for once, I want actual answers.

I end up at the gym at the back of the estate. The outside door faces the pool, and I hesitate a moment, steeling myself with a breath before yanking it open. It's mostly empty since it's first thing in the evening, so he isn't hard to find.

Reid's in the corner with the free weights, along with two guys I don't recognize. Other vampires, I'm assuming, based on the smell of them. One says something to Reid, and he smiles, genuine laughter in his eyes. He's in nothing but a pair of black shorts, and the muscles in his back flex as he sets the dumbbells back on the rack and runs a hand through his sweaty hair. He straightens suddenly and glances over his shoulder—probably sensing me in the doorway—and tugs the headphones out of his ears.

I still don't know how exactly this bond works, but hopefully if he doesn't get the *I need to talk to you* I send his way, he'll assume as much. I turn around and head back out the door.

He's following me—I can feel him getting closer. I sink onto one of the stone steps and pull a cigarette out of my bag. My hands shake as I prick my finger to light it. The night air is so warm it's almost muggy out here. I feel like I'm choking on it.

Reid's wearing a shirt when he steps outside, and he lifts the hem and uses it to wipe the sweat from his face, revealing the flat planes of his stomach. The muscles flex as he catches his breath. I don't know why the sight makes my face burn, why I'm even noticing in the first place. I shake my head and look away before he can drop his shirt and catch me looking.

He nods and takes a seat beside me, a flicker of uncertainty passing over his face as he braces his arms on his legs. "Hey."

I glance at him out of the corner of my eye and blow out a cloud of smoke. No use beating around the bush. He probably already knows why I'm here. "I need you to tell me exactly what happened. From the beginning."

He nods slowly. "I'll tell you anything you want to know."

"How long did you know? About my final trial?"

"I found out the day you were attacked at the school."

I swallow, my gaze trained on the end of my cigarette.

"I tried to reach you through the bond," he continues. "But I couldn't. I didn't know if you were purposefully blocking me out. Then I heard about what happened. I went to the academy to try to talk to you, but by then, you'd already been taken. And everything got so chaotic. We were trying to find you. I'd just barely gotten back to the estate when they…" He presses his lips together. "When they brought you back."

I startle as his hand brushes mine. He extracts the cigarette from my fingers and puts it between his own lips. I stare at him as he takes a drag then hands it back to me.

"I didn't know you smoked."

He gives me a humorless smile. "I don't. Anyway. You got back. Even after all of that, I couldn't convince you not to go, so I had about thirty minutes before your trial started to figure something out. Your friends were all busy with their trials—obviously I wasn't going to your mother—"

"She knew," I cut in. "How long did she know? Did she…?"

"It wasn't her idea," he sighs. "But she agreed to it, yes."

I guess that shouldn't surprise me. I'd assumed as much. But it feels like someone is twisting a knife in my stomach all the same.

"So I went to the only witch I thought I could trust with this." He glances at me sideways. "Your sister. She didn't know why she was doing it, but she agreed. As did Connor. But then…" He shakes his head, his gaze unfocused now, as if he's watching it all back in his head. "I could see it in your eyes the moment you decided not to do it. I *never* planned to—I panicked."

We stare at each other in silence for several long moments before I nod and stub out the cigarette on the concrete.

"Adrienne, she didn't know…?"

"About what the trial was? No, she didn't know. I think she connected the dots though once I went to see her."

I keep my gaze trained on the smear of ash between us. "Where was he? Before the trial?"

He runs a hand along the back of his neck. "In the cells in the basement."

My chest squeezes like someone is tightening a fist around my heart. When I manage to respond, my voice comes out tight and small. "How long was he down there?"

"I don't know. They weren't hurting him. And he had food and water—I know that doesn't make it any better."

"When you went to see him, how did he seem? What did he say?"

Reid's shoulders slump a little, like he was hoping I wouldn't ask that. "All he cared about was you. He'd heard what happened at the school and that you were missing. He was…upset. All I had to say was this was for you, and he agreed immediately."

Tears fill my eyes. I lean forward and cover my face with my hands. Even sitting in a cell, knowing he was probably about to *die*, he was still worried about me. *Me* being the reason he was down there in the first place. God, this is all my fault. And all that time…I'd thought he'd been ignoring me and…

Fuck. I'm *so* stupid. I feel like I'm going to throw up.

"Valerie," Reid says quietly.

I shake my head. "Is there anything else?" I ask, my voice muffled by my hands.

"No. That's it."

I pull in a deep breath and turn away from him as I wipe at the tears. When I face him again, he frowns and searches my face.

"Do you…wish I hadn't done it?"

With the alternative being Connor would really be dead? Of course I don't want that. But he never would've chosen this for himself. He did it for *me*, which isn't fair to him at all. He never should've been put in that position in the first place. But selfishly, all I care about is him still being alive.

"No. I don't wish you hadn't done it." I study Reid's face, wondering if maybe *he* wishes he hadn't. He'd told me that night in my dorm room he'd never turned anyone before me. Had never wanted to. Now in just a few weeks' time, he has the responsibility of both me and Connor on his shoulders. "Do you?" I whisper. "I mean, all of this. Getting paired with me…and everything that's come with it."

He jerks his head back. "Of course not."

I sigh and tuck my hair behind my ears. "I wouldn't blame you—"

"Valerie, no. I don't at all."

I hold his gaze for a moment, then clear my throat and face forward again. "Where is he now?"

"His room, I think. He…uh…wanted to be alone for a bit."

I narrow my eyes. "I can tell when you aren't telling me something."

Reid sighs and braces his arms on his legs. "He's having trouble adjusting. He just needs some space."

"So you think it's a bad idea if I go see him?"

A muscle in his jaw works. "I wouldn't. I think he needs some time to process. But I'm not going to tell you what to do."

"But you still think he'll come with us tonight?"

"Yeah, I'll make sure he's there. I think you and I should go separately though, so we don't draw any attention. I'll text you a time and an address, okay?"

I nod. The wind picks up and small ripples appear on the pool's surface. Strangely, the thing I can't get out of my head is Connor will never turn twenty-one. He's not quite a year younger than me, but it's something I've always teased him about. I was hoping to get some of his human friends around the estate to agree to a night out in the city once he finally turned twenty-one. The drinking laws are different for vampires, so it's not like it matters, but now he's going to be twenty forever.

I'm going to keep getting older, and he's going to be twenty forever.

"I know it doesn't mean much," Reid adds quietly, "but I'm sorry about how all of this turned out."

I clear my throat and turn my head so he can't see the tears building again. "Yeah. Me too."

"How does this even work for you?" Kirby asks. "Won't it just heal?"

The city noise doubles as I throw the car door open and

step onto the sidewalk. People hurry past us as Kirby climbs out next to me, and I crane my neck back to take in the building. Apartments line the top floors, but in front of me is a bright red door, *Memphis Tattoos* drawn on the windows in swirling letters. The neon sign below that clearly says Closed.

"I think they have a special ink for blood witches," I say, distracted as more black cars from the estate pull up behind us and the rest of the new Marionettes spill out onto the sidewalk.

I haven't been able to stop thinking about Connor since talking to Reid. Even before that, my dreams had been nothing but a cruel montage of memories, and now all I want to do is go see him. I can't stop picturing him sitting all alone in his room, hoping I'll come see him, wondering why I haven't…

"How are you holding up?"

I blink back to Kirby chewing on her lip.

"I'm fine," I say immediately.

The worry in her expression doesn't let up. "Val…"

"I don't want to talk about it."

"Val—"

"Just not right now, okay? Let's just have a normal night."

Kirby narrows her eyes for a moment, then grabs my arm and pulls me toward the door. "Let's hurry. I don't want to get stuck at the end of the line."

Bells ring above the door as we step into the empty lobby, the entire place closed down for the next few hours for our group. A woman with a shaved head and a slice through her eyebrow glances up at us from the front desk.

"Marionettes?" she asks.

Kirby grins. "That's us!"

The bells clang together as more people file in behind us. The shop is a decent size, but as twenty-five of us accumulate between the leather couches and coffee tables, it quickly feels much smaller.

"*There* you guys are." Monroe pops up beside Kirby, a little out of breath. "Way to ditch me."

Kirby shrugs. "You snooze, you lose."

We *had* all planned on taking a car here together, but in the battle between Kirby's desire to be the first ones here and waiting for Monroe, who slept in…well, Monroe took a different car.

A tall, slender man steps through the curtains sectioning off the workstations in the back. He barely glances up as he calls, "I can take the blood witch."

All eyes turn to me.

Kirby makes an excited little squeak and rushes forward with me, Monroe close behind. The man considers the three of us, expressionless.

"I know there's only one of you," he says.

"Oh, it's her." Kirby points to me. "We're just the moral support."

The man makes an unintelligible noise in the back of his throat and turns away, disappearing behind the curtain. The three of us hurry after him as another artist, this one a woman in a bright red wig, steps out to grab the next person. The man leads us to the last workstation in the corner and pulls the curtain shut as we step inside. There isn't much space—just a large padded chair in the center, a desk against the wall, and a few feet of standing room.

"Lucky you." The man pulls on some latex gloves and juts his chin for me to sit. "Yours is going to hurt the worst."

"Way to sugarcoat it," Monroe mutters.

The man arches an eyebrow but doesn't look up as he fishes something in a plastic container out of his drawers—something red. Probably the ink. "Didn't know the Marionettes believed in sugarcoating. Roll up your sleeve."

I situate myself on the chair and do as he says, trying to decode the tone of his voice as he says *Marionettes*. It's not distaste, exactly, but it's something. Kind of odd for him to work at the single tattoo shop that's worked with the Marionettes for decades if he has a problem with us.

"Lie down."

I do, my heart rate skipping higher. I've never been afraid of pain before. Especially not with how often I have to cut myself. But my throat runs dry as I focus on the needle in his hand.

"What's in it?" I ask.

He rolls his chair over so he's near my head and props my arm on the table. "You don't want to know."

I try to relax, but all I can think about is how the Vexillium had felt getting shoved into my skin by the Russians. How every inch of my body had been consumed—tiny insects and teeth crawling and biting along the insides of my veins—as they carved letter after letter into my stomach.

What if this feels like that?

"How long does it usually take?" Kirby asks, drifting over to the other side of the table. She slides her fingers through mine and squeezes my hand.

"Just a few minutes. Now stay still."

Buzzing fills the room as he brings the needle toward my skin, and it occurs to me he didn't apply any kind of stencil. I suppose a thin line around a bicep isn't overly complicated, and he's probably done a million and one of these.

Heat permeates my veins as he starts. The needle pinches and stings, which is what I imagine the others will feel. As he moves across my skin, however, a bone-deep ache spreads down my arm like a sickness sinking into my blood. I exhale slowly through my nose and tighten my hand around Kirby's, but it's not as bad as the Vexillium had been. He has me roll onto my stomach as he completes the circle around my arm. After a few seconds of touching up any issues in the band, as quickly as he'd started, he's done. I hop off the table, my arm still aching, and he rifles through his drawers again, probably to find the normal ink.

"Whoa," Monroe says softly as I stand in front of the mirror. My skin is flushed and inflamed, but the thin, red line is plainly visible. I twist back and forth, inspecting my arm. Even without a stencil, it looks perfectly straight to me.

Kirby climbs onto the table next, immediately holding her hand out for someone to take. Monroe smirks and rolls her eyes, but grabs it in both of hers.

"Oh!" Kirby giggles as the man starts, and he shoots her a glare. "Sorry." She repositions herself on the table and presses her lips together. "Just tickles a little."

Monroe rolls her eyes again, but she's fighting back a grin.

He has all three of us done in a matter of minutes, then he can't shoo us out fast enough. Three elemental girls hurry in next, the place now a mess of voices as bodies fill all of the workstations.

Daniel, Beth, Wes, and Andie are out in the waiting room, lounging on the leather couches. Beth jumps up when she sees us come out, her sleeve still shoved up to expose the new line around her arm.

"Let me see!" she exclaims.

Kirby grins, showing hers off as if it isn't the exact same thing we all got.

"We were just making plans to head to the Blood Lounge tomorrow night," Wes says behind her. "You know, before everyone takes off for their summer programs. You guys in?"

"Hell yeah," Monroe says. "I've been dying to go there."

"I can't drink too much," says Kirby. "I leave first thing the next day."

"Oh!" says Andie. "Are you on the Suksai trip? Me too!"

Kirby nods and hurries over to sit next to her.

"You two are headed back to York, right?" Daniel points at Wes and Monroe. They nod.

Beth sighs. "I feel like I'm the only one going to Locklear." She frowns at me and Daniel. "What about you two?"

I shrug. "Staying put."

Daniel reaches out a fist for me to pound. "Like all the cool kids are doing."

I roll my eyes, but humor him. "Pretty sure it's just the two of us."

"Well, yeah."

Kirby hops back up from the couch and throws her

arms around me and Monroe, pulling us to her. I let out a surprised grunt. "Don't have too much fun without me, okay?"

Monroe glances at me behind her back. "We're totally going to have to carry her home drunk tomorrow."

I nod.

"I heard that!"

I laugh along with the others, and for a moment, everything feels normal. It's just an exciting day with friends. A day we've been looking forward to for so long. No one is in immediate danger. No one is missing or getting attacked. And for the briefest moment, I can forget about how not normal everything has become.

At least, until I remember what waits for me after this.

CHAPTER FIVE

As MUCH AS I'm dreading tonight, the burning in the back of my throat reminds me it's necessary and I can't avoid it for much longer. It's colder than it had been while getting the tattoos several hours earlier, so I pull on leggings and a sweatshirt out of habit before realizing the cold probably won't affect me either way.

A buzzing sort of nerves creep up my skin. I'm going to see Connor tonight for the first time since it happened. What the hell am I supposed to say to him? Nothing could possibly make up for everything I've put him through. He's probably overwhelmed, scared. New vampire senses and everything aside, he *died* back there. I should've tried harder to see him before now. To be there for him. Reid had said he needed space, but what if he'd just said that, and he'd been expecting me to come see him?

Or worse, what if he doesn't want to see me? In the moment, sure, he'd said it was okay. But now? What if he thinks I chose them over him, and that's why I haven't sought him out? Or does he think *I'm* mad? The longer I let the thoughts spiral, the more I feel like I'm going to be sick.

I need to suck it up. Whatever he needs from me right now, he's going to get.

I take one of the estate's cars, but after they drop me off, I wave the driver on, figuring I'll either catch a ride with Reid or find my own way home. If nothing else, my magic has been working consistently enough again that a teleportation spell wouldn't be too hard.

I hesitate at the entrance to the waterpark as I wait for Reid and Connor. I must have gotten here first. Rust and overgrown vines cover the gate, and the park itself doesn't look much better. The wind picks up and rustles the leaves and trash scattered across the concrete. Almost every surface that's visible from this angle is covered in graffiti, and even that looks weathered and aged.

This place must have been abandoned for a while. Not that it's particularly surprising. A lot of human businesses have struggled over the years, especially once more humans switched to the night schedule, some for vampire jobs, some just because they wanted to be more immersed in the vampires' side of society. I guess not many people wanted to go to a waterpark at night.

I peer through the iron bars of the gate again and cross my arms over my chest. There are obviously no humans around, so why would Reid choose to meet *here*, of all places? Though I guess it is a good in-between from the estate and downtown, and kind of in the middle of nowhere. The trains don't even come this way anymore. Queen Carrington has eyes all over the city. If he chose this, it must be a safe spot.

Headlights cut through the dark, and I raise a hand to block my eyes as a black SUV pulls up. The engine hums as it idles by the curb, and three doors open. Reid climbs out of the front passenger seat first, and I hold my breath, preparing myself. I keep my eyes on the car as he heads toward me, but the person to appear from the back seat isn't Connor. A tall, red-haired woman steps out, followed by a skinny dark-haired man, both middle-aged and... human. At least Reid planned ahead. My eyes dart from them to Reid as they approach us, but then the final figure steps out of the car.

Connor slams the door. The headlights surround him as he makes his way toward us, and my heart squeezes in my chest as I brace myself for whatever I'll find on his face.

But he doesn't look at me.

He doesn't look at anyone. He keeps his gaze on his feet, even after he reaches us. I can't read him at all, but just the sight of him standing here nearly brings tears to my eyes. I keep picturing him broken and still on the floor. But here he is. Breathing. Walking. *Alive.*

Alive, but not looking at me.

"This is Quinn and Sebastian." Reid gestures to the two humans. "They very graciously agreed to help tonight."

The woman—Quinn—beams and steps forward to offer me her hand. I've seen her before. Where have I seen her before? I shake it, and her smile widens. "So happy we can be of service."

Sebastian nods along and takes my hand next, as smiling and happy as his companion.

"Thank you," I murmur, a little uncomfortable under all of the attention.

"They agreed to help with feeding, but also practicing glamouring, if you want to," says Reid.

I immediately shake my head. Reid meets my eyes but doesn't push the subject.

"Are we going inside?" Connor says suddenly, and I whip my head around. He lifts his eyebrows and nods at the park behind us. "Or are we just gonna hang out by the gates like some bad drug deal and wait for someone to call us in?"

I stare at him, frozen by the harsh quality of his voice. Usually, he sounds so calm when he talks.

Okay, so, angry. He's angry. That's okay. We can work with this.

"We can go inside," says Reid.

He steps aside to let Connor pass. I swallow hard as Connor strides forward, ignoring the rest of us, and grabs hold of the gate. It lets out an ear-splitting shriek as he yanks it open, the muscles in his arms bulging as he does. I know it must be difficult to move, but he throws it open like it's nothing, then continues into the park without looking back.

I meet Reid's eyes and fight to keep my voice steady. "He's angry."

He tilts his head to the side like, maybe, but he's not entirely convinced, then nods at the two humans behind me. They head into the park after Connor, and he doesn't speak again until we're alone. "Not in the way you're thinking. I've spoken to him. He doesn't blame you, Valerie. But turned vampires are unpredictable when they first turn. It's not uncommon for their personalities to be drastically different. They tend to be cold and hard at first. With you,

you still had your witch half to hold on to your humanity. Connor doesn't have that. Everything just changed for him overnight."

I blink, momentarily thrown. Angry at the situation, I could handle. We could work through that. He would have every right to be upset with me. But if this isn't about that... "Are you telling me he's just going to be like this from now on?"

I want him to laugh and say *Of course not*, but his expression doesn't change.

His gaze travels the length of my face, from my eyes to my chin and back again. "There's no way of knowing," he says, then turns and follows the rest of them into the park.

I stand by the gates for another few moments, my heart feeling twice as heavy in my chest. Connor wasn't just a little different. He didn't even look at me. It was like I wasn't here. I had been prepared for him to be upset. We've had fights and disagreements before, but even then, he was unfailingly kind. Understanding. He's never just ignored me.

The way he looked around, the way he acted—I could have been anyone, not someone he's known for twenty years, or someone he's loved for the past six.

I shove down the thoughts and tears threatening to rise. I just need to talk to him. We'll figure this out. We always figure it out. And this is something to deal with another time. My throat burns, as if agreeing with me. I need to focus on the task at hand.

I take off into the park, passing a pirate-themed slide and a sign in the ground. It's tilted to one side with half a dozen arrows pointing to other rides. I catch sight of the others up ahead at some kind of bar. The barstools are in a pool, though there's no water now, with the bar area lower and beneath a wooden awning.

Connor is sitting in one of the stools, Sebastian facing him. Reid stands beside them, gesturing with his hands as he talks. I look around for Quinn and spot her a moment later. She's on the ride behind them, arms held out to her sides as she tries to balance and walk along the top of a round slide.

Connor is listening to whatever Reid's saying, so I don't want to interrupt them. I head over to Quinn and walk along the pavement beside her.

"Hi!" she says without looking at me.

"Thanks for doing this," I say, because what else am I supposed to say to some person I don't know who seems oddly cheery about the idea of me biting them?

"I'm not a venom junkie, if that's what you're thinking," she says.

"I wasn't thinking that."

She shrugs. "I wouldn't be insulted if you were. It wouldn't be an unfair assumption." She spins herself around, waving her arms to keep her balance, then starts walking the other way.

"Do you work at the estate?"

"As of a few weeks ago, yes!" She stops and looks over at Reid and the others. A small smile crosses her face, and she sits down and hangs her legs over the side of the slide. "I first got a job there when I was eighteen, almost twenty years ago now. They said they were looking for more servants for the estate, but really what they wanted were some babysitters." She nods at Reid.

My gaze slowly pans between the two of them. And it clicks where I've seen her before—that day I'd met Reid outside at the estate to practice with our bond…before the Russians had showed up. He'd been talking to a woman. Quinn. I guess now it makes sense how familiar she'd seemed with him. "You worked with Reid as a kid?"

The smile returns, and she nods. "He was about five or six at the time. But then after the queen sent him away—I think he must have been thirteen at that point?—they let me go."

"Oh." I frown. "I'm sorry."

She shrugs again. "At least this is a good city if you want to get into the vampire industries. I ended up finding a position at a vampire childcare center down in Queens. Which is where I'd been until Reid showed up a few weeks ago. Offered me a new job. Not looking after him anymore, obviously. I think he told them he wanted me as a feeder."

I stare at Reid as she talks. He's still facing Connor and Sebastian, his arms crossed over his chest as Connor leans in and sinks his teeth into Sebastian's neck.

"You're his feeder?" I ask.

"Oh no." She laughs. "He doesn't feed from me. Never has. Even as a kid, we couldn't get him to drink from humans. He always preferred the bags."

"So then why did he bring you back to the estate?"

She shrugs again, but her smile is softer now. "I think he just likes having someone familiar around. He was always a good kid." She nods at Sebastian as Connor leans back and wipes the blood from his mouth. "I met Sebastian a few years ago at my other job, and we've been together ever since. So he got him a job too."

"If you don't like feeding, we don't have to—"

"Honey." She reaches over and squeezes my shoulder. "I'm happy to help. If this is important to Reid, it's important to me." The intensity of her gaze makes my face heat. But even once I look away, I can still feel her watching me. "He turned that boy for you, didn't he?"

I press my lips together and nod. "How much do you know?"

"Well, you're a Marionette and his partner, but you also need to learn how to feed. I was able to put it together." I glance at her out of the corner of my eye, and she offers me a small smile. "This must be difficult for you. The change, but also…" She looks at Connor. He and Sebastian rise up from their chairs, and Reid looks over at us. I keep waiting for Connor to look at me, but he doesn't.

"He's been my best friend my entire life," I say softly. "I can't remember a time I didn't love him." I don't know what makes me say it. Maybe it's easier to talk to a stranger than see the pity in my friends' eyes.

Quinn hops down from the slide as Reid makes his way toward us. She pats my shoulder. "It can be hard to let people go."

Something about the way she says it makes me clench my jaw, as if letting him go is inevitable and my only option. As if he's not still here and standing right there and *alive*. The rough adjustment period won't last forever. We'll get through this like we've gotten through everything else.

Reid blows out a breath and raises his eyebrows as he reaches us. "Ready to get started?"

His words draw me back, and a hint of unease warms the pit of my stomach. God, now I'm even more nervous.

This isn't some random human he picked up off the street. This is someone important to him. She gives me a reassuring smile.

He comes to stand beside me as Quinn pushes her hair behind her shoulders, exposing her neck.

"You'll be able to feel when you need to stop," he says. "You'll feel her heart rate slow. If you're really hungry, I'd suggest finding a couple of humans, if you can, and taking a little from each of them. But if it comes down to it, humans are resilient. Just don't let the heart rate get too slow."

"Reid—"

"It's okay. I won't let it get too far."

I turn around to face him and throw my hands up. "I don't even know if my teeth are sharp enough for this."

He presses his lips together in a bemused smile, then waves his hand at me. "Let me see."

I sigh and open my mouth. He leans in and pushes my top lip up.

"This is so weird," I mutter.

He runs a finger along the bottom of my canine and nods to himself before pulling back. "You'll be fine. Now stop stalling."

I turn back to Quinn, but then turn around again just as fast. "What if I don't have any venom and it just hurts her?" Typically, vampire bites only hurt the human for a second until the venom gets into their system, but if I don't have any, there won't be anything to dampen it.

Reid pinches the bridge of his nose. "Darkmore."

"You could always glamour them to not feel any pain, if that ends up being the case," Quinn offers behind me.

Great. Another thing I don't know how to do.

Reid raises an eyebrow.

Okay, so the glamour thing is my own fault for not wanting to learn. But I hate the very idea of it and would feel so uncomfortable doing that to someone. But I guess if it was to help someone else not feel pain…

Maybe I'm being stupid. Stupid and stubborn.

"Come on, Valerie," says Quinn behind me. "I don't bite."

She laughs at her own joke, and Reid presses his lips together like he's trying not to laugh.

"I'm glad this is amusing for you," I mumble and turn back to Quinn.

She stands with her head slightly tilted to one side, waiting for me. I can see her pulse throbbing at her neck from here, and my mouth waters.

"Just trust your instincts," Reid says.

I meet Quinn's eyes, then place one hand on her shoulder and lower my mouth to her skin. The smell of her sweat and perfume momentarily overwhelms me. I sink my teeth into her neck before I can talk myself out of it, and she lets out a soft sound that quickly gives way to a moan. So, that answers the venom question. Her blood fills my mouth, but instead of getting lost in it, I force myself to swallow. It dulls the burning in the back of my throat, but I have to fight a gag as I feel it go down. It's thick and…sour.

I take a step back, and Quinn sways on her feet. Reid appears at her side, steadying her, and stares at me with his brows pulled together.

"You can take more than that. She'll be fine——"

"I'm good." I wipe my mouth with the back of my

hand and take another step away from them. The blood roils in my stomach. Quinn is still too out of it to notice. "Does her blood taste a little…odd to you?"

He wipes the remaining blood from her neck with his thumb and brings it to his mouth, frowning. "No, I don't think so. Why?"

"Oh." I wave my hand. "I must have imagined it." I jab my thumb over my shoulder. "I'm going to try to talk to Connor for a second. Okay?"

The tension in Reid's expression doesn't let up, but he nods.

Sebastian is splayed out on top of the bar, arms spread wide, clearly enjoying the aftereffects of the venom. I glance around, trying to find Connor. Something taps softly to my left, and I follow the sound. On the other side of the bar is a wide, empty pool. Connor stands at the end, flicking rocks as if trying to skip them across a surface that isn't there.

I steel myself, my heart hammering in my chest. I don't know if I've ever been this nervous around him—if I've ever been nervous around him at all. But eventually, we have to have this conversation. It might as well be now. *I can do this.*

I clear my throat and try to keep my voice light. "That would probably work better with actual water."

He glances at me over his shoulder, and for the first time all night, he meets my eyes. They're the same blue eyes I remember, but somehow not. There's no warmth there. They don't soften at the sight of me like they used to. Instead, he looks me up and down and snorts.

"You look like you're about to hurl," he says, then turns way and throws another rock.

I stand there, stunned for a moment. "I—I was hoping we could talk."

"We are talking," he says without looking at me.

I can't read his face or his voice. Usually, all it would take is seeing him across the room to know exactly what he was thinking. But now...I have no idea. Maybe that's the point. Maybe he's trying to hide how upset he is from me. "Connor, I—God, I'm so sorry—"

He lets out a heavy sigh, as if exasperated by the subject. "If that's all you wanted to talk about, we don't have to do this. Really."

I stare at his back. I'd been prepared for angry. Honestly, a part of me *wanted* him to yell. But this? This... indifference? The shock in my chest quickly gives way to anger as I step up beside him. "Connor, can you just look at me?"

He raises a single eyebrow and glances at me sideways. "What do you want, Valerie?"

"What do I...?" I break off, a hysterical laugh getting caught in my throat. "Look, I get it if you're angry with me. And you're a vampire now, so I know you feel different. But... it's me, Connor. It's *us*. I'm sorry I didn't come find you sooner. I wanted to. I just—I just need to know we're going to be okay. I just want to understand. Tell me what you're feeling."

"Right now I just feel irritated," he mutters. "Might be the new senses, but man, your voice is grating."

I suck in a sharp breath and stumble back a step like he physically hit me.

Don't get upset, I remind myself. This isn't him. He doesn't mean it. This won't last.

"Connor," I say evenly.

"Valerie," he mimics, mock-serious.

My eyes sting, and I clench my jaw. How can he not want to talk about what happened? "Connor, I—"

"If you're going to cry, can you go do it somewhere else? I was kind of enjoying the peace and quiet over here." He leans down, picks up another handful of rocks, and starts throwing again.

I stare at his profile, trying to find even a hint of the man I know, but he's not there. Of all the ways I'd played out this conversation in my head, I'd never considered this.

My stomach twists again, and I turn away and head for the park's entrance. I make it past the gates and into the trees before the contents of my stomach surge up. Blood splatters across the bushes, and I retch again. It burns in my throat, and I cough, trying to spit the taste out of my mouth. I don't know if it was the conversation with Connor that did it, or if the blood really was bad. It had tasted off, but Reid said it was fine.

Maybe I'm just being pathetic.

I wipe the back of my hand across my mouth and yank the rubber band off my wrist to tie up my hair, the hunger already starting to creep back in. The parking lot is empty, the car nowhere in sight, so I'm not sure how Reid was planning on getting back. He'll probably call the driver when he's ready.

All I know is I'm not going back in there, no matter how hungry I am. I'm not walking past not-Connor or facing Reid, who probably already knows everything I'm feeling right now through the bond. Suddenly everything is too much.

Something rustles behind me, and I whip around, scanning the trees. Did someone follow me? My shoulders tense, but no one appears.

I flip the blade out of my ring and carve a line in my palm, deeper than I need to, and squeeze my hand into a fist. I let the blood fall onto the grass in front of me as I close my eyes.

My pulse roars in my ears, then I'm back in my room at the estate, alone. Reid and I have talked about the possibility of cutting each other off from the bond, putting up a wall, so to speak. I don't have much practice with it yet, but I imagine the bond in a black space—a small, glowing ball. Then one by one, I build metal walls around it until it's completely boxed in.

When I open my eyes, my chest feels lighter, like I can breathe again.

And I don't feel anything from Reid for the rest of the night.

———

I CAN'T BREATHE. My lungs ache for air as something jolts deep in my stomach. I feel the pressure all the way up to my throat, filling every inch of me. It thrashes against my insides, and I look down to see it moving under my skin.

The snake.

It's back inside of me.

I claw my hands at my stomach like I can pull it out myself, nails tearing through skin and drawing blood. I choke and gasp for air as its tail presses down on my wind-pipe. Tears leak out of the corners of my eyes, and my vision blackens at the edges.

I roll over, and a different pain spikes through me, something sharp against my stomach. It moves, carving a line into my skin.

A knife. A word. A message.

I gasp and jolt up in my bed, the sheets soaked in sweat. My chest heaves as I try to catch my breath, and I push the sweaty hair out of my face with shaking hands. I fall back against the pillow, still breathing hard.

It was just a dream. I run my hand over my stomach and the smooth skin there. I thought maybe some of it would scar, but there's not even a trace of what happened. Like I imagined it. I roll onto my side and curl into a ball, wrapping my arms around my knees and waiting until I fall back asleep.

The next dream, I can't quite make sense of. Streams of red and black surround me, something like smoke, or maybe water. I'm standing in darkness, nothing tangible. Just colors.

My throat burns and aches so fiercely I can barely breathe around it. My gums throb, and I dig my nails into my temples to try to distract me from the other pain.

And then it all disappears.

Cold presses into my back. As I blink my eyes awake, something tickles the side of my face.

I push myself up with one arm and startle when I realize I'm touching grass, damp and rough against my palm. I shoot into a seated position and look around.

I'm no longer in my bed.

I'm in the middle of a field, city lights glowing in the distance.

What the fuck?

A cold breeze picks up, rustling the trees around me and tangling my hair. I shove it out of my eyes, then go still.

I'm not alone.

When I pull my hands away from my face, they're covered in blood. I bring my fingers back to my head, looking for an injury, but then I smell it.

That is definitely not mine.

I pull in a shaky breath and push myself to my feet, too afraid to look. My heart races in my chest, pounding so hard against my ribs I can feel the vibrations throughout my entire body. Slowly, I turn.

There are three of them. They're scattered carelessly through the grass, blood and gore spilling onto the ground. Two women and one man, all seeming about the same age.

All seeming about *my* age.

I look around again, but we're alone. I can't hear the noise of anyone remotely close by, the dull hum of the city in the distance barely pricking my ears.

The smell is fresh. Fresh enough I'm willing to bet if I went to touch them, the bodies would still be warm. The woman closest to me—close enough that her extended hand nearly brushes my shoe—is almost completely beheaded. There are distinct teeth marks in her throat and tears along the skin, so her head hangs on by a few intact muscles. The breeze picks up, carrying the scent of her blood with it.

It smells exactly the same as the blood all over me.

I try to comb through my memory, try to figure out how

I got here. Part of me wants to believe I'm having another dream, but no dream has ever felt this real.

Finally, the delayed panic sets in.

My body trembles, and I cover my mouth with my hands, unable to tear my gaze away from the bodies.

Oh God. *Oh God.*

I don't want to believe it. I want to stand here and pretend I have no idea what happened to them. But even if I can't remember it, deep down, I know.

Because suddenly, my throat isn't hurting anymore.

How did we get out here? Did someone see? If someone saw me…

Forcing down a deep breath, I try to clear the fog of panic in my mind. One thing at a time. Stay calm. Make a plan.

I can't leave them here, but I can't ask for help for too many reasons to count. I focus on the bond, making sure I build as strong of a box around it as I can.

Reid can't know about this.

No one can.

I glance back at the woman at my feet, and my body goes still. Her long sleeve is tucked up on the extended arm, revealing the pale skin of her forearm. Right on the inside of her wrist is a smudge of black ink. The tattoo is barely the size of a coin, but even from here, I know what it is. An intricate star inside a circle, containing all of the different elements.

The alchemist symbol.

And if the three of them were together, I'm willing to bet they're all alchemists, if not some other kind of witch.

I lean down, still covering my mouth with my hand.

Whether it's from the shock or the smell, I'm not sure. Slowly, I unzip the jacket and slide it down her shoulders to see the upper half of her arm, searching her bicep for the red mark.

But there's nothing there.

This doesn't bring me as much comfort as I'd been hoping for. I may not have killed three Marionettes, but I still killed three witches.

I still killed three people.

And I can't even remember doing it.

I need to get back to the estate. How did I get here? Did I take a car? Walk? Teleport? Was I followed? Was I seen? How did I find these witches? Were they already here? Did I *lure* them here? Kill them somewhere else and then moved the bodies?

How could this have happened?

I force down another breath and try to think logically, rationally. The guilt gnawing at my chest like a wild animal wants me to report this. If someone else had done it, that's what I would do.

But if I report this, I won't just go down for killing them. They'll see the bite marks. The way the bodies are completely drained of blood. Then they'll know about me. I don't let myself think about what would happen after that.

The trees in front of me rustle, and I stiffen. I need to get this cleaned up before someone finds me like this. I need to get out of here *now*.

I pull the blade out of my ring and slice a line in my forearm. Before I make the conscious decision to, I walk a circle around the bodies. All three of their faces are pointed toward the sky, and it feels like their eyes are watching me.

But as my shoes crunch along the hard grass and I complete the circle, the guilt, confusion, worry, and undistinguishable tangle of emotions in my chest twists into something else.

Fire consumes the bodies, and the heat brushes against my skin as I stare, unblinking, as they burn and turn to dust.

I can't remember doing this. But with the smell of their blood so thick in the air, a part of me can remember what it had tasted like. And even though the blood is still warm against my skin and soaking through my clothes, I already want to do it again.

CHAPTER SIX

THE ESTATE IS ALWAYS BUSTLING with activity the first week of summer. Students from the academy are moving back in, some getting ready for their trips to the other estates. It's also the most popular time of year for members of other regions to visit, leaving the estate at maximum capacity, every guest room filled.

Reid's in some meeting downstairs. I don't know how I know, exactly. I can't see or hear anything through the bond, but if I started walking to find him, I know I'd end up at the right room. I think he's trying to block me out, but still, there's the faintest undercurrent of...*stress* running from him to me. Whatever the meeting is about, it can't be good.

I almost laugh. So many disastrous things have happened lately that I can't even venture a guess. I'm not sure which would be worse. Is it about him turning Connor? Candace going missing? Me? Something else entirely? They couldn't possibly already know about last night…

I pace the length of my room over and over again as the buzz of activity grows outside my door. It sounds like someone new is moving in across the hall. Whoever it is, their heartbeat is abnormally high, and whenever they laugh, it pierces my brain like tiny knives.

I shouldn't already be hungry again, but somehow, I am. It's been less than twelve hours since I cleaned up the bodies in the field and teleported myself back here. Just thinking about it has my gums throbbing. The scent of their blood in the air, the warmth of it as it dripped down my skin…

I have to get it together. I scrub my hands over my face.

I drained *three* people. That should've kept me satisfied for a couple of days, at least.

What is happening?

At least I kept the blood down this time.

God, I killed three people. I *killed* three people. How am I any better than the Russians who left those witches in the parking garage? These are just yet more deaths I covered up. The thought knocks the wind clear from my lungs.

Sweat breaks out across my forehead as the ache in the back of my throat intensifies, snapping me back to the present. With all of the activity around the estate, no one will even notice me. Probably.

I slip out into the hall, not making eye contact with anyone as I head for the stairs. Humans and witches alike stream by, but their pulses all sound the same. Slightly elevated, strong, and *mouth-watering.*

I've never been inside the blood bank before. No one

but the vampires at the estate have any reason to, but I know where it is. With every person I pass—with every thud of someone else's pulse in my ears, with every whiff of their skin and sweat—the muscles in my jaw clench harder and harder until it feels like the bone might break through skin.

I keep my head held high. No one asks questions if you look like you know what you're doing.

There are two sectors for the blood banks, separated by large, wooden pocket doors. I've heard they have more of a clinical appearance in other estates, but the Carringtons claim to value comfort and *ambiance*. The rooms are dimly lit and full of warm tones—dark wood, plush red furniture, a roaring fireplace in the corner. There are dividers available for privacy, but you can also take your blood on the go.

The first room is for blood that's already packaged. Bagged or bottled. Behind the wooden doors on the far wall is where you go if you prefer to drink directly from the vein.

A slender, dark-skinned vampire looks up from the monstrous wooden desk in the corner when I step into the room. Her head cocks to the side at the sight of me, but her expression remains blank.

"Valerie Darkmore. What can I help you with?"

Mercifully, all of the surrounding seats are empty, though I can hear a faint slurping noise coming from the other room.

"I'm here to pick up a bag for my partner, Prince Reginald," I say without missing a beat. "He's…occupied and sent me to pick it up for him."

She doesn't blink. "Of course. Warmed?"

"Please."

She reaches for a wooden panel in the wall beside her. A wave of heat wafts into the room as she opens it and pulls out a bag.

"Thank you," I say, all but snatching the thing from her hands.

A crack in her demeanor appears, just the slightest raise of her eyebrows. I walk as calmly as I can manage as I hear the vampire from behind the doors finish up, and the human lets out a small sigh. The corridors are full of people swarming back and forth as I step out of the room. The bag is too big to fit in a pocket, and shoving it under my shirt or hiding it behind my back seems far too obvious. I veer left and slip into the closest bathroom—a rustic, wooden room with three stalls and flat sinks. No one else is inside, but I go into one of the stalls anyway.

The moment I pull the stopper from the bag, I cover my mouth with my hand. The smell is overwhelming. It seems to stretch and expand until it fills the entire room, and I hold back a gag. Putrid and rotting. It just smells *dead*.

It smells like Quinn's blood had tasted.

I tentatively bring the bag to my nose and sniff again, my eyes watering. Surely the vampires in charge of the blood exchange would have noticed something so strong. They must have procedures to make sure there's nothing wrong with the blood before distribution, right? And what are the odds I got the blood of two sick humans in a row?

Maybe it's me, and there's something off with my senses. Pinching my nose shut with two fingers, I bring the bag to my mouth and swallow as much as I can.

My stomach roils, and I fall to the ground on my knees and lean over the toilet, heaving. The blood splatters across the white porcelain. Wiping my mouth with the back of my hand, I slump against the stall's wall. The hunger seems to rest for now, though I doubt I managed to keep any of the blood down. My body must be too preoccupied with the nausea.

I should tell Reid. I can't go on not feeding. Not unless I want a repeat of last night.

I force the thoughts away, burying the memory as far back in my mind as I can manage. Then I climb to my feet, shove the blood bag in the trash, and head back into the hall.

A few other people stream past, not sparing me a glance. Wherever they're going, it looks like they're in a hurry. I frown and follow their progress down the hall. Is something going on today that I don't know about?

My heart plummets into my stomach as I lock eyes with the man standing at the end of the hall. If I'd managed to keep any of the blood down, it would definitely be coming back up now. Connor's expression is unreadable as he takes me in.

He cut his hair. The blond curls are cropped closely to his head now. It suits him. He stands stiffly, not his usual comfortable, relaxed posture. Coming out of my shock, I lift a hand and give him a small wave. He doesn't return it. Then without a word, he turns and disappears around the corner.

My arm awkwardly falls to my side, and I keep staring at the place he'd been standing long after he's gone.

"*There* you are. Hey! Valerie!"

I turn to see Monroe and Kirby hurrying toward me in nearly identical outfits—black leggings and white athletic tank tops. They both have their hair yanked up in high ponytails and are covered in a fine layer of sweat like they came from the gym.

"We've been looking all over for you," says Kirby, slightly out of breath.

"You're still coming tonight, aren't you?" adds Monroe.

I stare at them, the gears slowly turning in my head. "Of course," I say, because I know that's what I'm supposed to say, but I still can't remember what *tonight* is supposed to mean.

"Okay good." Kirby puts her hands on her hips. "I would've been really bummed without a last hurrah. We were thinking of leaving around 5:00 a.m.? We're just going to meet the others there. Does that work?"

I nod.

Monroe squints, scrutinizing my face, and I try to relax whatever expression is left over from seeing Connor.

"How are you holding up?" she asks.

"I'm fine," I say a little too quickly and wave my hands for them to continue on. "I'll see you guys later."

Monroe doesn't look entirely convinced, but she gives my arm a little squeeze, then the two of them hurry off down the hall. My head spins until I remember the conversation at the tattoo shop yesterday. *Of course.* I guess I had agreed to Wes's plans for a group night out.

Who knows? Maybe I'll actually be able to find something to eat there.

THE LINE to the Blood Lounge is so long it stretches down the street and disappears around the corner. It seems to be mostly vampires and witches in attendance tonight, with the occasional human companion.

Kirby shifts in her heels beside me, adjusting her outfit —a corset-style red top and matching miniskirt. Monroe throws her head back and lets out a long sigh, her dark hair flowing down her back. She and I both opted for an easy bodysuit-and-jeans combo, but it's her throat I can't stop staring at. Her skin is tan, smooth. I can smell her ambery perfume from here, mixed with her sweat and the faintest trace of blood pumping beneath the surface.

I blink and force myself to look away.

My fingers itch for a cigarette, but my throat burns for blood more.

"When do you leave?" asks Monroe.

Kirby perks up. "I'm heading out with a group tomorrow around midnight. They've got a private plane and everything."

Monroe shakes her head. "I'm so jealous. I've always wanted to see Thailand. I'm expecting daily picture updates."

"Of course." Kirby's smile dims. "I'm going to miss you guys though. This is our last summer break, and I'm missing it."

"Yeah, well, Monroe's ditching me too, so it's not just you," I say.

"I'll be in York!" Monroe protests. "I'll probably still come home and hang out with you, like, every weekend. *She's* going halfway around the world."

We inch forward with the line, and they both fall silent for a moment as they exchange a look, then glance at me.

"What?" I ask.

"Nothing," Kirby says in a voice that tells me it's definitely not nothing.

"You're looking at me like a kicked puppy."

"We're just worried about you being stuck here all alone all summer," says Monroe. "With your mom, and with everything...*you know*...going on." She coughs. "Plus, we heard about Connor."

"I'll be fine," I say, the sound of Connor's name cutting through me like a knife, hard enough that all of the buzzing conversations and pulsing blood around me disappears altogether. Ever since the waterpark, that conversation has been playing over in my head on a loop. The distance in his eyes. The harsh quality of his voice. The way he'd completely ignored me in the hall earlier.

I need one night where I'm not thinking about him, otherwise, I very well might have a breakdown.

I clear my throat. "I'm taking that foreign affairs class at the estate anyway. That'll keep me busy."

Not like I have a choice. The class is mandatory for anyone who got paired with someone in a royal family. Now that I'll be sitting in on meetings and traveling with Reid, there's a whole world of information I have to memorize. Names, families, laws, histories, treaties... Considering I paid the least amount of attention to my history and policy classes over the past few years, I'm expecting this one to be rough.

Kirby presses her lips together like she's fighting back her next words, but they come out just the same. "How are things with Connor anyway? I saw him in the hall today, and he seemed…"

Kirby and Monroe exchange another look.

"You can say it," I sigh.

"Cold," Monroe finishes.

"It was like it wasn't even him," Kirby adds quietly.

A group of humans ducks into the pub across the street. A small stage is set up inside the window—an open mic night, it looks like. Now would be a good time for us to run into the others and end this conversation, but there's no sign of any of them in line. Maybe they're already inside.

"I'm trying to give him space for a little bit. Reid says it could be temporary," I say. "That it's just an adjustment period."

When I look back at them, they're staring at me like I've spontaneously sprouted an extra head. The line moves forward again, this time bringing the front door in sight. The moment the neon sign swims into view, it brings me back to the last time I was here—food weighing down my bag, a deserted house. Wherever Madison and her family ended up, hopefully it's somewhere better than here.

"*Reid?*" Monroe sputters.

I realize my mistake a moment too late. Kirby's mouth is already hung wide.

"Don't," I say.

"You've been holding out on us," Kirby whines.

We finally make it to the front of the line, and the wall of music that hits us as we duck through the doors saves me from responding. Black velvet curtains hang over the end of the hallway, and two lanky men pull them open as we approach. They open to an enormous circular space drenched in red and purple lights. The dance floor is lower than the rest of the room, with stairs leading down to it and metal rails cutting it off from the bar and seating areas. Curtains line the far back wall as well, leading to who knows where.

"I say we start with shots!" Monroe calls over the music.

Kirby nods vigorously and loops her arm through mine as we weave our way through the crowd and toward the bar. The EDM pounding through the room is so loud the floor vibrates beneath my feet, but it's still not as loud as the blood pulsing through each neck we pass. My mouth waters, and I dig my fingers into Kirby's arm, trying to anchor myself.

There are dozens of people already waiting at the bar, but as the bartender turns and sees Monroe waving at him, he straightens and heads straight toward her.

He's nearly a full foot taller than she is, further accentuated by his bright red Mohawk, the color a perfect match to the streaks in Monroe's hair. She says something I don't catch, but the man nods and ducks to grab something from below the bar.

Kirby pulls on my arm. "I'm *so* glad you came out with us. I feel like we haven't seen you much. But you know what?" She waves her hands. "Tonight, we're not talking about any of that. We are getting trashed and embarrassing ourselves, and I will happily carry you home afterward. Deal?"

"Here we are, ladies!" Monroe reappears with six shot glasses balanced against her chest.

Kirby and I each grab two before she drops them. Judging by the smell, it's vodka.

"How did you get him to serve you so fast?" asks Kirby. "Did you...?" She wiggles her eyebrows.

Monroe shrugs a shoulder. "I may have sent some very specific pheromones his way."

I raise one of the shots. "Last hurrah?"

"Last hurrah!" they cheer, clanking their glasses against mine. We throw them back, perfectly in sync, then immediately down the second shots.

The burn of the alcohol as it travels down my throat is a welcome reprieve from the hunger, and I already want another one.

"Oh! There's Beth and Andie!" Kirby points to Beth swaying her hips in a short, silk dress on the dance floor. Her blond hair looks as white the dress under the lights. It takes me a moment to recognize Andie beside her, now at least a full foot shorter than Beth in the heels. Daniel and Wes are still unaccounted for. "Let's go dance!" says Kirby, already pulling my arm.

I twist out of her grasp and wave the two of them on. "Go ahead! I'll catch up. I want to grab another drink first."

Kirby beams and points at me. "That's what I like to see!"

The bartender isn't in nearly as much of a hurry to serve me this time as I brace myself against the bar and drum my fingers against the top.

I haven't felt much from Reid through the bond for most of the day. Something that felt intentional from his end. It wasn't *quiet*, exactly, but somehow I knew he'd put up a wall. I can feel him now though, the slightest trace of heat traveling along the thread between us. Something like static or holding your breath. Frustration, maybe?

As the vodka works its way through my system, the bond grows more and more numb. I wonder if I keep drinking if it would cut me off from the hunger *and* Reid. Who would've thought? All of these problems, and all I'd needed to do was get drunk.

Finally, the bartender finishes his rounds and juts his chin at me.

"Two vodka sodas!" I call.

Something like judgment passes through his eyes, but he turns away wordlessly. Okay, alcohol snob.

"Aha! There's my favorite blood witch." Wes slides in on my right and plants a sloppy kiss on my cheek, his lip piercing digging into my skin.

"No, she's *my* favorite." Daniel steps up on my other side and throws his arm around my shoulders. The smell of alcohol pours off him in waves, and his skin is already sticky with sweat.

"Oh my God." I shimmy out from under his arm. "How are you guys this drunk already?"

"Pregame," they say at the same time and shrug.

I cock an eyebrow. "Well, clearly I'm not the favorite if I wasn't invited."

"I'll make it up to you," says Wes. "Drinks on me!"

A few people turn toward us like maybe that means them too. Wes grins, but Daniel snatches the credit card out of his hand before he can get too drink-happy and buy shots for the entire bar.

"And I've got *all* summer to make it up to you," says Daniel. "Just you and me for three months, Darkmore."

"I'm so thrilled," I deadpan.

By the time I get the drinks, the dance floor is twice as crowded as it was before. The song blares through the speakers, something upbeat and clearly a fan favorite. Daniel and Wes order another round of beers and wave me on as they wait for them. I work my way toward the center of the room, trying to pick out the rest of our group in the crowd, but there are so many dancing people and random, flailing body parts swimming in and out of my vision, I can barely see a few feet in front of me.

God, it's so hot in here. Sweat accumulates on the back of my neck and down my cleavage. I eagerly suck down one of the drinks, feeling the edge of the hunger drift away with it, then press the cold glass against the side of my neck and let out a small sigh of relief.

A man touches my waist and squeezes by, putting his throat mere inches from my mouth. I stare at his skin, momentarily mesmerized—the vein throbbing beneath the surface, the sweat collecting in his hairline. I can imagine exactly how it would feel for his hot blood to pour into my mouth. The way his body would go limp with pleasure—

He disappears back into the crowd, and the connection breaks.

I blink, yank the straw out of my drink, and tilt the cup back until the rest of it pours down my throat.

Maybe coming out tonight hadn't been the best idea.

I set the empty cup on one of the bar tables and start on the second one. The crowd parts, just enough for me to catch a glimpse of pink hair.

I shuffle forward, twisting my body to squeeze between people. *There* they are. I see Monroe first, her head thrown back in a laugh. Kirby grabs Monroe's shoulders before she can fall over. They both laugh, and Monroe's hands find the sides of Kirby's face. Kirby's the first to lean in, and judging by the way Monroe's body immediately folds into her, it isn't the first time.

It's not a quick kiss either. I stop moving forward as Kirby's hands trail down Monroe's arms. They hold each other closely, intimately. Like this is some kind of goodbye.

Oh. *Oh.*

I turn away, suddenly feeling like I'm intruding on something private.

Looks like Andie and Beth took off somewhere else too.

The curtains on the back wall rustle like they're caught in a breeze. A back door? Fresh air sounds *amazing* right now. And it'll give Kirby and Monroe some…space. I head that way.

How long has *that* been going on?

How had I not *known?*

The crowd thins as I exit the dance floor and weave my way through the people mingling by the bar. No one pays me any mind as I shove the curtain aside and push out the metal door into an alley. I glance around for something to prop open the door and settle for a beer bottle lying near the dumpster. I bend down to grab it, still holding the door open with one foot, and that's when I see him.

A small cloud of smoke winds through the air off the tip of his cigarette as he blows out a breath and leans his head against the brick building. He's sitting on the concrete, his knees pulled up to his chest. I recognize him immediately from the red Mohawk. He hardly spares me a glance as I approach, just sucks on his cigarette again.

I sit down next to him, and he slowly turns to face me.

"Have a light?" I ask, pulling a cigarette from my bag.

He sighs, apparently inconvenienced by this, and offers me the end of his own. I lean in, cigarette between my lips, but then my gaze falls to the hollow of his throat. His pulse thuds beneath the surface, his skin slightly flushed.

My cup shatters as it hits the concrete. Pieces of glass scatter around us as I grab the bartender by his ridiculous red hair and throw his head to the side. He lets out a choked, surprised sound as I sink my teeth into his neck. His cigarette falls against the bare skin of my leg, but I hardly feel it.

Blood gushes into my mouth, and he stops struggling after a moment. The taste isn't as bad this time, dulled by the alcohol already thrumming through my system. His body slackens against me as more and more blood pours down my throat. I manage to pull myself away as I feel his heart rate slow, shoving his limp body aside to make sure I don't keep going and kill him. He hits the concrete hard but curls into a ball beside the dumpster, a stupid smile on his face as the venom runs its course.

I stand on wobbly legs, the alley slanting around me as I rise. I steady myself against the rough brick of the building behind me. The door to the club flies open and rap music floods the alley. I squint as Kirby's head pokes out, looking this way and that. She spots me a moment later and straightens.

"She's out here!" she calls over her shoulder.

Monroe appears, and they both step toward me.

"Sorry," I say. "Just needed some air."

Their eyes fall to the bartender lying in the fetal position beside me.

"And...that," I add.

"Is he...?" starts Monroe.

"He'll be fine," I say quickly, the alcohol slurring my speech. "Right?" I nudge the guy in the ribs with my foot.

His smile widens, and he flashes Kirby and Monroe a thumbs-up.

"Um, you've got a little..." Kirby motions to her face.

I rub my thumb along my bottom lip, wiping off the remaining blood. As I lower my fingers, a wave of the smell crashes into me. I clamp a hand over my mouth.

Monroe surges forward to grab my hair as I bend over and empty the contents of my stomach in the middle of the alley. I heave a few more times before catching my breath and bracing my weight on my knees.

"How much did you drink without us?" Monroe demands.

I don't bother correcting her, and thankfully it's too dark for her to see exactly what my vomit looks like.

Kirby, however, lets out a small *whoop* from the doorway. "That's what I like to see!"

CHAPTER SEVEN

THE SUN LOOKS like it's threatening to rise by the time we make it back to the estate. With the energy of the club around us, I hadn't noticed the alcohol's effects other than it numbing the bond and the hunger. Now, standing in a near-silent estate, the entire world looks different. My feet pound against the marble foyer as Kirby and Monroe lead me inside, each holding one of my arms. My head lolls against Kirby's shoulder as I struggle to keep my eyes open.

What little relief I'd found from the drinks and the blood in the alley is long gone now. My entire body thrums with need, and it takes every ounce of my concentration not to sink my teeth into Kirby's neck.

"I've got her. You go on," says Kirby.

"You sure?" asks Monroe.

"Yeah. She's on my way."

Monroe extracts herself from under my arm, and Kirby adjusts as more of my weight falls on her.

"I'll find you before you leave tomorrow," says Monroe before taking off toward her room on the opposite side of the estate.

"All right, kid," says Kirby once she's gone. "Let's get you to bed, yeah?"

The world spins as she turns us toward the stairs, and suddenly my legs feel like Jell-O. They fold underneath me, taking us both to the floor. Kirby lets out a grunt, trying to catch me, but we both know she's a fraction of my size. We hit the ground on our backs, momentarily knocking the wind from my lungs.

"Ow," Kirby complains, hitting me in the face with her vodka-laced breath.

"I can take her from here."

A figure paces into view, blocking the light from the chandelier above us.

"Prince—Prince Reginald," Kirby sputters. "I'm sorry. I was just taking her—"

"I've got her."

I squint through a single eye, hoping it will help my vision focus, to no avail. Then I'm moving, two hands planted around my arms. I blink, now in a seated position, and Kirby staggers to her feet beside me.

"Thanks for coming out, Val," she says.

"Congrats on Suksai, Kirbs," I say—well, I try to say. My lips feel numb and stumble around the words. "You've always been the smartest of us."

She leans down and kisses the top of my head before taking off up the stairs. When she's gone, Reid turns to me, but his face is too blurry to make out his expression.

"What are you—doing here?" I ask.

"What are you doing blackout drunk?"

I purse my lips. "Touché."

"Can I help you up?"

I glance at the floor beside me. "I want to say—no. But I don't think I can stand."

"That's what I thought."

I close my eyes, the room spinning again, then I'm on my feet. Reid's hands steady my hips as I sway, and I grab his arm to keep myself upright.

"Just please don't carry me," I mumble.

"Wouldn't dream of it."

He says nothing as I teeter toward the stairs. It's slow going, and I have to lean against the banister or Reid every few steps, but still, he doesn't say anything. We're nearly to the second floor when my shoe catches on the edge of the stair and I pitch forward. Reid's arms circle my waist, but it's too late. He goes down with me, and we land in a tangle of limbs on the stairs.

"Ow," I complain.

"You say that like it's my fault." Reid props himself on the stair beside me as I lean against the wall.

He reaches as if to help me back to my feet, but I shake my head—immediately regretting doing so, because it makes the spinning in my head worse.

"I need a minute."

"You're not going to be sick, are you?"

"I make no promises." I press my lips together, willing the nausea to pass. "You should just go," I groan. "This is so embarrassing."

"I don't have enough faith you won't fall right off the side of the stairs."

My head droops against my chest, and I reach my hands forward, trying to find his arms to haul myself back up. The sudden change in my center of gravity makes the rest of my body slump forward until I fall against his chest.

He lets out a soft grunt, and his hands rest on my waist.

Oh. He smells good.

"No offense, but I can't say the same. I can *smell* how much you had."

"I don't usually drink like this," I mumble.

"Okay."

"It just made everything...turn off for a bit."

"Valerie," he says, his voice softer now. "I'm glad you had fun with your friends. And I will continue to be glad as long as you don't throw up on me. Now here we go." His hands on me tighten, and then we're standing again. I sway, but he's prepared this time, his arms coming around me like a bracket.

We make it up a few more stairs before I manage to say, "Reid?"

He stabilizes me as I start to tip backward again. "Yeah?"

"I need blood."

He hesitates a second, then pulls me into the second-floor corridor, toward the vampire suites. "Come on."

The halls are wider than on the higher floors, winding lazily throughout the entire length of the estate. Each room could probably fit three of the witch rooms inside of them. The corridor branches off halfway through the estate, leading to the separate wing for the royal accommodations.

By the time we make it to Reid's room, I have to close

my eyes against the spinning walls around me. The backs of my legs hit something soft, then I'm sitting on a bed.

"Here."

Plastic brushes my hands, and I blink to see Reid handing me a blood bag. I look from it to his face, my stomach sinking.

"What's wrong?" he asks.

"I—" My heart pumps a little harder in my chest, but the panic I'd felt earlier at the thought of telling him feels more distant now. Probably yet another thing numbed by everything I've had to drink tonight. My tongue moves of its own accord, though my next words come out barely above a whisper. "I won't be able to keep it down."

He kneels in front of me, ducking his head until he can see my face. "What do you mean?"

I sigh and flop backward onto the bed. The ceiling bobs up and down above me. I close my eyes, hoping that'll make the dizziness subside, but all that accomplishes is summoning up images I don't want to see—the bodies in the field. The bartender in the alley.

The snakes and knives that wait for me when I go to bed.

I squeeze my eyes tighter. "I don't want to go to sleep."

There's a pause, and then, quietly: "Why not?"

"I always have bad dreams," I whisper. I frown at Reid's face looking down at me, a harsh line between his eyebrows. "Am I not trustworthy?"

He blinks. "What?"

I run my hands along the soft comforter and stretch them out over my head. His eyes follow the movement, tracing over the length of my body before quickly looking away. "If you had a secret, would you tell me? Do I look like I can't keep a secret?"

"Valerie—what? Focus. What do you mean about the blood?"

The moving ceiling makes my stomach twist again, and I close my eyes. Instead of seeing bodies, this time I'm greeted by the memory of Kirby and Monroe on the dance floor. "I can't believe they didn't tell me. *I* would tell me. You would tell me, right?"

Reid's face swims into view again as he leans over me. "I don't think it's coming out the same way it's going on in your head right now."

I hit his chest with the back of my hand. "Would you trust me with a secret, yes or no?"

His eyes scan my face, and whatever he sees there makes his lips wobble like he's fighting back a smile. "Valerie, you're in my head half the time whether I want you there or not. I don't think I get a choice in the matter."

I frown a little. "Does that bother you?"

His face softens as he adjusts his weight and braces one hand beside my head. "No. It doesn't bother me."

Neither of us says anything for a moment, and I wonder how much of tonight he'd felt. The more I drank, the less I could feel the bond. Could he feel that happening? The dampening of the connection as the night wore on? There's still so much about it that I don't understand. I don't even know if he's experiencing it the same way I am.

I meet his eyes. "You didn't answer the question."

A real smile breaks through, and his hair falls into his face as he shakes his head. "How about you just tell me where you're going with this?"

I frown, picturing Kirby and Monroe again. Am I allowed to be upset? I feel like I'm not allowed to. But...we were a group. It's always been the three of us over everything. And now it's the two of them and their secret on one side of the line, and me over here all alone. Did I make them feel like they couldn't come to me? Maybe I did something wrong. Maybe I'm a shitty friend.

Reid sighs and collapses onto his back on the bed beside me. "Darkmore, you've gotta give me something to go off of."

"Kirby and Monroe are together," I say. "Like, *together* together. And they just...never told me. We've been friends since we were kids. And they didn't tell me." I can feel him looking at me now. God, this must sound so stupid to him. I press the heels of my hands into my eyes. "Forget it."

"I'm willing to bet them not telling you has nothing to do with whether they trust you or not," he says. "Everyone has their reasons."

I turn my head to look at him. "Do you believe in karma?"

His lips quirk up.

"Are you laughing at me? Is that a no?"

"No, I'm not laughing at you." He laughs as he says it and shakes his head.

"You're laughing."

"I just can't keep up with your brain right now." He takes a deep breath, then his expression turns thoughtful. "To answer your question, I don't know if I believe in karma."

"I do." I turn back to the ceiling. "Which would mean

bad things happen to bad people. And bad things keep happening to me, so—"

"No," he cuts me off, his voice suddenly hard. "None of this has been because of anything you've done, Valerie. None of this has been your fault."

The bed shifts beside me, then his hands circle my wrists.

"What are you—oh."

Suddenly, I'm sitting up again. It takes a few blinks for my vision to clear. He holds the blood in front of my face. "Now tell me what you meant about not being able to keep the blood down."

Oh God. I'd forgotten about the blood, but now that my attention is on it, the hunger growls inside of me. I look at the bag in his hands and shiver, the taste of that bartender still in my mouth. "I keep trying, but I just throw it up. It tastes...*wrong*."

"Wrong?"

"Rotten," I explain. His expression is blank, unreadable, but he says nothing, so I continue. "Even the smell makes me gag. At first, I thought it was some bad blood, like the person was sick or something. But it's all the same."

"How long?"

"Since...the initiation ceremony, I guess."

His eyes widen. "You should be starving right now. Are you saying you haven't had anything since then?"

I pull in a deep breath. Slowly, I shake my head, and tears start to burn at the back of my throat.

He doesn't respond for what feels like a long time, until finally, very quietly, he says, "Tell me."

I lie back down, somehow finding it easier to say it if

I'm looking at the ceiling instead of his face. "I can't remember doing it. I just woke up in a field, and they were dead."

"How many?" he asks, voice still entirely calm.

"Three."

"But you kept that blood down?"

I hesitate. "They weren't...human."

When he doesn't respond, I twist my head to look at him, but his gaze is trained somewhere near the door, his jaw set in a hard line. "You cleaned it up?"

I nod, sitting back up.

"You were keeping down human blood before, right?"

"Yes."

He paces and runs a hand along his jaw. "When was the last time?"

I try to think back, but so much has happened in the past few days. It makes everything feel like a lifetime ago. It was back at school. I'd been carrying around blood bags with me everywhere I went. Before the final trial. Before the Russians kidnapped me. Before the hospital. Before...

I let out a small, choked sound and cover my mouth with my hand.

"What?" Reid turns back to me.

The tears break free and roll down my cheeks. My mind frantically spirals through every moment since, every sign, everything I missed.

"What is it?" Reid demands.

"I—" I pull in a shaky breath. "Before the attack at school with the wendigos."

But I was fine. I'd been *fine*. It couldn't be—I can't be—

Reid comes back over and sits beside me. The silence

grows thick between us until, finally, he says, "Wendigo Psychosis. Being half vampire and half witch, you've been able to keep both types of blood down, yes?"

"Yes," I whisper.

"But not human."

It isn't a question.

I cover my face with my hands again. "Oh my God."

Of all the research Kirby and I had done, we'd never come across a cure. The last documented cases were nearly a century ago, but the victims were always put down so they couldn't hurt anyone else.

Because they did. They hurt so many people—so many bodies—and they couldn't control it. And if someone doesn't stop me, those three witches in the field will just be the beginning.

"You have to turn me in," I whisper.

"No."

"Reid, I don't want to hurt anyone else."

"No," he repeats, voice firm. "Here's what we're going to do. We know you can keep my blood down. I think as long as we make sure your hunger doesn't get too bad, you shouldn't have any more blackouts. When you're hungry, even the slightest bit, you come to me, do you understand?"

I shake my head. "I—"

"It's a temporary solution," he adds, not seeming to be talking to me anymore. "In the meantime, I'll see what I can find out about reversing this. Okay?"

I wipe the tears from my cheeks and let out a slow breath. My mind spins, and my heart steadily beats faster in my chest.

"Valerie."

When I still don't look at him, he reaches over and takes my chin in his fingers, forcing my head to turn. He meets my eyes, his gaze unwavering.

"I meant what I said before," he says. "You're my responsibility. And we are going to fix this." He drops his hand, stands, and starts rolling up his shirtsleeve.

He sounds so confident. So sure. But how can he be? How can he possibly be so calm right now?

"Have there been any updates on the wendigos?" I ask. "Has the school found anything with their investigation?"

"I don't believe so. But I have my own theories."

I raise my eyebrows.

He finishes rolling up his sleeve and sighs. "The undocumented vampire attacks in town, that kid in your class getting sick, the wendigos, I believe someone is orchestrating all of this. Using the wendigos to turn vampires—or in your case, half vampires—mad. To what end, I'm not sure. But it follows a pattern. Something similar has happened before."

I sit up a little straighter. "When?"

He shakes his head. "Decades ago. But it happened just like this. The vampire attacks. The survivors getting sick."

His words slowly churn in my head, and my breath gets caught in my throat. "That vampire who attacked Daniel on campus." An image of him flashes in my mind—the crazed eyes, black veins, blood dripping out of his ears. There had been no humanity left when he'd looked in my eyes. No logic at all. Just acting on pure hunger and instinct. "You think that's going to happen to me?" I whisper.

He holds his arm out to me, to drink from, presumably. But he doesn't answer my question.

"Do you know who was behind the attacks all of those years ago?"

He hesitates as I bring his wrist to my mouth. "Yes."

My insides tighten at the look on his face. "What was their name?"

Slowly, he meets my eyes. "James Westcott."

CHAPTER EIGHT

A VERY HUNGOVER-LOOKING Monroe and I send off Kirby the following night as she climbs into a sleek black car along with a few other Marionettes—Andie and Tomás—as well as some vampires from the estate. Andie looks even rougher than I feel, an oversize white sweatshirt drowning her, the hood pulled up over her head and covering half her face.

"Call us when you get there!" Monroe says before Kirby closes the door.

"Will do!"

"And we want regular updates," I say.

"And pictures!" adds Monroe.

"Oh my God, Mom, Dad, you're embarrassing me." Kirby rolls her eyes, grinning, then waves at us through the window as they pull off down the estate's drive. We keep standing there on the front lawn long after she disappears into the dark.

Monroe doesn't mention what happened in the alley, and I don't mention what I saw happen between her and

Kirby on the dance floor. If they don't want me to know, I'm not going to bring it up. It also seems incredibly hypocritical of me to be angry about them keeping secrets considering all of the ones I've kept from them.

"I'm going back to the academy this weekend to get settled," Monroe says. "I know you didn't have a chance to clear out your stuff at the end of the semester with everything that happened. Want to come with?"

There isn't much at my dorm I would miss having for the summer, but I smile and nod anyway. "Yeah, Roe. That sounds great."

She heads back inside, but I linger on the lawn, the slight breeze picking up my hair and scattering it around my face. There are a few guards out here patrolling the grounds, but none of them acknowledge me.

I wrap my arms around myself and stare off at the barest sliver of moon hanging in the sky. I hadn't woken up somewhere other than my bed today, thankfully. And after filling up on Reid's blood, my night had been completely dreamless—and more importantly, nightmareless.

It doesn't feel pressing yet, the hunger. But I can already feel it building, growing. I'll probably need to feed again before the end of the night. It seems to be coming back faster each time. How long do I have until no amount of blood will satisfy me at all?

Reid thinks he can find a cure, something to make this stop. I'm willing to give him a bit of time to try, but if he can't...

I won't turn out like that vampire who attacked Daniel. I can't.

I know Reid's got some baggage with his other partners

dying, so now he feels personally responsible for me, but I don't want to be his pet project either.

I don't want him as an audience if I start to spiral out of control.

The estate has its own library—maybe that's where I'll spend the rest of the night. But with how much research Kirby and I have already done on Wendigo Psychosis, I'm not getting my hopes up. And I'm not sure if I want to waste whatever time I have left flipping through books, basking in disappointment.

The thought almost makes me laugh, but it gets caught somewhere in the back of my throat. *Whatever time I have left.* Days ago, I was so focused on my initiation into the Marionettes, the moment that was supposed to set me up for the rest of my life. And now all of that training and studying and working was…for what?

To get turned into some kind of bloodthirsty husk of a being by whoever the hell this James Westcott person is? Maybe that's what I should be putting my energy into. Finding him. If he's the one causing this, surely he must know a way to reverse it. I'd been too drunk to push Reid for more answers last night, but he sure as hell isn't going to get away with it today. He must know *something* that can help us find him.

And, stupidly, the one thing I keep getting hung up on is how much I wish I could talk to Connor about all of this. He wouldn't know how to help, but he'd sit there with me until I felt better, like he always did.

I have no idea where Connor is, what he's been doing since I saw him last, how he's feeling about his transition. If he's not talking to me about it…who is he talking to? As much as the thought of him confiding in someone else feels like a knife twisting in my stomach, I hope he has *someone* he wants around right now. Because it's clearly not me. And the thought of him going through this all alone...

"You're scaring the servants," someone murmurs by my ear.

I startle.

Reid steps up beside me, hands in the pockets of his black pants. He glances at me sideways. "You've been standing here for nearly an hour, not moving. Don't think you've even blinked."

"Oh." I don't say anything else, because what's the point? He knows what's going on.

The breeze picks up again, carrying the scents of the nearby human guards with it, a mixture of sweat, body odor, and that same rotten tang in their blood.

"Your Highness?" A petite redhead in a white servant's uniform hesitantly steps up beside us, head bowed. "You're wanted in the throne room."

Reid glances at me out of the corner of his eye, then nods. I linger on the grass as the two head inside, but the girl freezes when she notices I'm not following.

"Oh," she squeaks. "You too, Miss Darkmore."

Reid's expression noticeably sours. Something hot and tight trickles through the bond, but I can't make out what it means. The redhead scurries around the corner, and I shoot him a questioning look, but he just shakes his head.

The room is empty, save for the queen on her throne. The redhead closes the large, golden doors behind us, and our footsteps echo around the room as we make our way to the center. There aren't any guards behind her on the dais, not even my mother.

A small shiver runs down my spine, and my stomach tightens.

What is this about?

The queen's eyes flicker from me to her son and back again. "I believe we have some matters to discuss."

Reid stands a little taller and folds his hands in front of him. On the outside, he's the perfect picture of calm, but the smallest trace of his nerves breaks through the bond, like a line of static electricity running between us.

"Three more witches have been reported missing in the region," the queen says in a way that makes me think this has been an ongoing discussion between the two of them. "And a vampire from our own estate is still unaccounted for."

"And you're sure they're not related to the ongoing vampire attacks—" Reid starts.

The queen holds up a hand to silence him. "Don't insult me. We both know the answer to that."

"Two of your *guests* have been keeping quite busy since they got here," Reid adds.

My spine straightens, my stomach burning at the mention.

"We have no reason to believe they're behind these attacks either," she says. "They haven't been spotted in the region since their previous...indiscretion."

Indiscretion. Interesting word choice. I'd probably go with *kidnapping.* Or perhaps *fucked-up-torture-extravaganza.*

But she's right. It wasn't them.

I try to keep my expression neutral, but a cold sweat

breaks out across my skin. If she already knows something, why am I still standing here?

Her eyes flicker between us again, and my heart stops in my chest. But there's nothing *accusing* about it, per se. She looks…exhausted.

"This will be our busiest summer in decades. We're expecting a constant cycle of representatives from nearly all of the other estates, with a very important upcoming meeting to discuss policy amendments. I can't afford for news of this to get out, or for the disappearances to continue." She levels her gaze on her son. "Do you understand?"

"We'll look into it," he says, voice even.

Her harsh gaze doesn't let up.

"Quietly," he adds.

She relaxes back in her throne. "Bring me results, and *your* previous indiscretion will be forgiven. Otherwise, this is your final warning, Reginald."

"I understand."

She waves a hand to dismiss us, and Reid waits for me to head for the door before following.

"Previous indiscretion?" I ask once we're in the hall.

He glances at me but says nothing.

It takes a moment for realization to dawn. "Connor," I breathe.

He nods.

"That's where you were the other day." That feeling of nerves I'd felt the night before heading to the Blood Lounge with Monroe and Kirby…it had been my fault.

Another nod.

I open my mouth, but he holds up a hand to stop me and glances around us. "Not here." The halls seem empty, but that doesn't lessen the tension in his shoulders. "I have someplace we can go." Finally, a small crack appears in his stoic expression. "But you'll probably want to change."

I glance at my leggings and sweatshirt and raise an eyebrow. "Into what?"

His smile grows. "Something you don't care about getting ruined."

THE CITY LOOKS different this time of night—barely 7:00 p.m. on a weekend. People on our timetable are just starting to rise, and some of the humans in the city are heading home for the day. Traffic is light as Reid's driver navigates through Midtown. A comfortable silence settles over the car, and for once, I feel no desire to ask where we're going. I watch out the window as the city lights reflect off the damp pavement and lean my forehead against the glass.

We end up at an alley behind a squat building with crumbling brick and a faded sign out front. I don't catch the text written across the surface in cursive before we turn the corner.

Reid says nothing, but there's something different about the set of his features now that we're here. There's less tension weighing on him, his edges softer as he takes in the building through the window. The car comes to a stop right behind a metal door, and Reid hops out. I follow along silently, trying to figure out where we are from the outside, but the back of the building doesn't have any distinctions— just another section in the endless sea of brick.

Somehow in the time getting here from the estate, the

103

hunger has already started itching in the back of my throat again. It hasn't even been half a day. At this rate, I'm going to bleed Reid dry.

"I'll put some in a bag when we get back," he says.

I whip my head to the side.

"My blood," he clarifies.

"Oh—I—I'm not that hungry yet. It's fine."

He smirks. "I can feel it, Valerie."

"Oh."

Reid holds the door and waits for me to step inside as Alexander pulls the car back onto the street. Despite Reid's apparent ease, I brace myself for whatever I'll find inside. But when I step through the door, I'm greeted by...pottery.

Wooden shelves line all of the surrounding walls, stocked full of bowls, pots, cups, and other creations, and a large, circular machine sits in the corner. The surrounding silence stops me from asking what we're doing here. Reid's quiet footsteps on the concrete make the only noise in the room as he closes the door behind him and heads for the olive-green curtain across the room. Despite telling me to change earlier, he's still in the same black slacks and button-up shirt. I switched out of my sweatshirt into an old T-shirt, but left the leggings.

He pushes aside the curtain, revealing the rest of the studio. The place is teeming with the earthy smell of fresh clay, the air in here much warmer than it was outside. Half a dozen stations are scattered throughout the small space, with wooden stools and metal cups full of utensils surrounding the potter's wheels. There's a desk on the far wall by the front door, but no one's there. Are they even open yet?

Hugging my arms to myself, I glance around. Abstract art hangs on the walls, the canvases swallowing the space, the vibrant streaks of red and orange somehow making the place feel warmer. I turn around to find Reid watching me.

Wordlessly, he pulls over a stool, sets it across from another at one of the low tables, and sits on the other side.

"*This* was your place we could talk?" I ask, but take the stool across from him.

A small smile crosses his lips as he pulls out a plastic bag full of clay. He takes some kind of wire and sections the block off. "Not suitable for you, Darkmore?"

"I—" I roll my eyes. "That's not what I'm saying. But why here?"

He shrugs as he molds the clay into a ball and drops it onto the center of the wheel. "Why not?" He unbuttons the cuffs of his sleeves and rolls them up to his elbows before taking a sponge and squeezing water over the clay. The veins in his hand stand out as he tightens his fist. "I know the owner. She lets me slip in before they open sometimes."

The wheel starts to spin as he pumps his leg against a pedal on his side, and he braces his hands across the clay, pushing in and down. His movements are practiced, precise. His brow furrows as the clay starts to move beneath his hands, his attention zeroed in, and it's quickly apparent this is not a new thing for him at all.

"What did your mom mean about this being your final warning?" I ask.

He sighs, his hands applying more pressure to the clay. "They weren't happy about Connor. Not surprising, but they held a hearing. Just her and few others who had been in the room. They're trying to keep the exact details of what happened quiet, naturally. They let me off with a warning since I didn't technically break any laws other than not getting approval for turning beforehand." He meets my eyes briefly over the wheel. "But I made her look bad. Which, for her, is worse."

Once the clay is in a satisfactory shape, he pulls one of the metal tools from the nearby cup. The water runs down his hands and arms, already stained brown, but he bows his head as he smooths out the edges, and slowly, the clay starts to form into some kind of pot.

"She and I already weren't on good terms," he continues. "She wasn't exactly happy with the circumstances around me coming back. And she's looking for the perfect excuse to ship me off."

"I don't understand," I admit. The queen is not an affectionate person. That much is clear. But Reid is her *son*. And the crown prince, no less. Surely that would offer him some kind of advantage at the estate. Or protection, at the very least.

A single corner of his lips curls, as if he knows what I'm thinking. "Don't for a second think I'm any less expendable to her than anyone else." He glances up at me again. "It's not widely talked about, but she has at least one or two children at each of the other estates. I'm the only son she's claimed in this territory. But she has plenty of other children to choose from should she need to replace me."

"I—I didn't know you had siblings." I try to do the math in my head. How old must they be now? The queen had one of the Marionettes freeze her aging decades ago, before my mother was her right hand, so I don't even know how old *she* is.

He shrugs and smooths out the edges on the clay again. "Half. I haven't met most of them. The two I *did* know growing up—at the Alaskan estate—died under *mysterious* circumstances. After one too many indiscretions."

I jerk my head back. "You mean she *killed* them? Her own children?"

"That word doesn't hold the same meaning for her as it does for you," he murmurs.

I stare at him. I can't look away. I can't even blink. She said this was his final warning. Does that mean if any of the secrets he's wrapped up in because of me come out... she'll...?

He meets my eyes again, his expression still perfectly calm. "Like I said, she hadn't claimed them. I'm the most public of her kids. Though I don't doubt she'd do the same to me if it came down to it, I do think appearances matter too much for her to make a decision like that lightly. So, there's nothing to worry about." He tilts his head to the side. "Probably."

I don't—can't—respond. The way he talks about his own potential murder so calmly, so disconnected. He's clearly thought about this before, grown up with the threat hanging over his head to the point where it's no longer unusual to him.

I shake my head, my mind spinning, as he continues to work. It's mesmerizing—the spin of the wheel, the soft bend of the clay beneath his hands, the flex of the muscles in his forearms as he applies more pressure. Once the walls are thin enough, the entire lower half of his arm disappears into the pot as he uses his fist to pull up and shape the inside.

I sit back in my stool, gaze traveling from his hands to his face. He's focused, intent, but there's something in his expression that I haven't seen before. He looks at peace despite the conversation at hand. A sense of calm washes through me from the bond, and it almost makes me sigh.

I smile a little. Reginald Carrington, vicious vampire and crown prince of the first region is...an artist.

"I spent a little over two years at Suksai when I was younger," he says suddenly, focus still on his work. "It was one of the first estates I went to. They offered different amenities than the estate here. They value art a lot more." A soft, rueful smile pulls at his lips. "I showed up at Suksai as an angry, angsty fifteen-year-old. They assigned me a mentor to look after me while I was there, since I wasn't technically old enough to be a diplomat. Poor guy didn't know what to do with me. So he pawned me off on every class he could. I took to pottery right away."

He pulls his hand out of the pot and lets the wheel come to a stop. After he finishes examining his work, slowly, the wheel starts to spin again, and he pulls out a different tool.

"It was the first time I hadn't been angry in what felt like years. I could just zone out and focus on what was in my hands."

His fingers work at the mouth of the pot, pinching in quick succession until the rim looks scalloped. I hold my breath, not wanting him to stop talking.

"And it was nice, you know," he adds, voice quieter now. "If it didn't turn out the first time, clay is easy to reuse. You just break it down and start over. No matter how bad things were, it never seemed that way anymore when I was doing this."

Apparently finished now, he lets the wheel stop and sits up straight. Silence falls between us as we stare at each other. Then he pulls out the same wire as before and extracts his pot from the wheel.

He glances at me again as he runs a sponge across the surface to clean it off. "You want to try?"

I don't think I've ever done a single artistic thing in my life, and I definitely don't know how to do this. And yet...

"Yes," I breathe.

He gestures for me to switch spots with him as he cuts off another piece of clay. I take it from him and try to form it into a ball the way he'd done. Taking the seat across from me, he leans forward, pulling a bowl of water closer.

"You'll want to center it first," he says. "Then wet your hands."

I do as he says, and he reaches forward, laying his hands over mine to secure the clay to the wheel. He pumps the foot pedal for me but doesn't release my hands.

"You'll want to make a kind of cone shape first," he explains, pushing my hands into the clay. "Then push down and flatten it out a bit."

We work in silence, his hands showing mine what to do. The clay slowly forms into a small, round pot, and he guides my fingers to the center to smooth out the opening. I try to focus on what I'm doing instead of the way his hands fit around mine, but for some reason, I'm hyperaware of the contact.

"So," I say without looking at him. "Are you ever going to tell me what you know about James Westcott, or am I going to have to drag it out of you? Why were you looking into him in the first place?"

The night before is all a blur, everything after the drive home. I vaguely remember having a conversation with Reid, though I can't recall any of the specifics.

None except for the very end.

Do you know who was behind the attacks all of those years ago?
James Westcott.

Silence stretches between us for so long I think he's ignoring me again, but when I peer up at him, he has a strange look on his face. He stares at the clay between our hands.

"Reid?" I prompt.

"I haven't been avoiding your questions on purpose," he says. "And I know this is going to sound strange, but I don't know."

He lets up on the foot pedal until the wheel stops spinning between us.

"You don't know?" I repeat.

He sighs. "I actually didn't realize I didn't know until you started asking so many questions."

What does that even mean? "You're not making any sense."

He shakes his head and lets out a humorless laugh. "I know. I don't know why I was looking into James Westcott. I don't know how, but I think someone planted the idea in my head. But it *felt* like my idea. And I had this unexplainable urgency about it. All I knew was I needed to find him. That was about a week before I came back from Vasiliev. And then everything with you—and the attacks at York that sounded *just like* what I'd been researching—I didn't know what to make of it."

"So you're saying someone else wanted you to look into him before the attacks even started," I say slowly. "But you don't know who. And you don't know why."

His frown deepens. "Yes."

Another beat of silence passes between us, and trying to process his words makes me light-headed. But for some reason, I believe him immediately. I can see it in his eyes. Feel it in the string connecting us, the truth of his words. But I can't wrap my head around the implications, not with everything else already going on.

"What did you find in your research then?" I ask.

He nods, almost as if to himself, and starts the wheel again. I press my fingers back into the clay, thankful to have something to do with my hands.

"There have been a few periods of similar attacks. One a few decades ago, one about a century ago. Vampires going mad and attacking other vampires. The victims—if they survived—falling mysteriously ill. There was an attack on one of the estates about twenty years ago." He hesitates, then meets my eyes. "Wendigos."

I sit up straighter. *Wendigos?* How have I never heard of his before? "Which estate?"

"Wénběn in China." He chews on his bottom lip. "And then less than a year later, they pulled out of the alliance. Anyway. There was a man caught during that second wave of attacks. He was accused of being involved, though the evidence wasn't strong. My mother sentenced him to death anyway. He was executed in front of the court, right here at the estate."

"Wait, then why would you think he'd still be alive?"

"That's the thing. After his execution, he disappeared. And no one has ever been able to find his body."

"Why don't I know about this?" I ask. "The attacks, Wénběn, we've never learned about that."

"I'd never heard of it either before I started looking into it, and the information wasn't easy to find. Nothing in the estate's or academy's library. It seems like someone wanted to keep it quiet. But this time, with these attacks now, it's been on a far grander scale than the previous two times, from what I can tell. We've been getting reports from the other estates of similar cases, and more have happened in York since you left. Last time, there was only around a dozen documented attacks. We've had a dozen just in the last week."

I glance down, startled to find the clay is now completely caved in on one side from the pressure I'd been putting against it, and I pull back. "So, your mother, she was looking into this the last time it happened?"

He nods.

"Have you discussed any of this with her?"

"Ironically, I'd been researching for a few weeks already, and then with everything that happened at the academy during your initiation, she requested I start looking into it."

"Does she have other people looking into it too then?"

"A few, I think. She's still been trying to keep things pretty quiet. To avoid panic, maybe. I'm not sure."

Or if she was the one to order his execution all of those years ago, maybe she's still trying to save face and doesn't want to believe he somehow got away from her.

I blow out a slow breath, feeling dizzy, then something occurs to me. "Madison?"

He nods like he'd been expecting this question. "I'd been going through all of the humans at the estate." He swallows hard and doesn't meet my eyes. "Glamouring them to see if they knew anything. I never would've given her a second thought if I hadn't run into that block in her mind. It was the only thing remotely close to a lead that I'd found since coming back."

I frown, trying to remember what she'd written on the piece of paper I'd give him during initiation.

"It was a name," he says. "On the paper. Camden Farley. Madison seemed to believe he was doing a lot of the work for James Westcott. Recruiting, that kind of thing."

"Recruiting? You mean with the humans?"

Reid shrugs. "That's what I thought, at first. But then I did some digging. He's the pack master for some wolves near the Pine Barrens."

"Where's that?"

"New Jersey. And he has quite the reputation."

My eyebrows lift. "For?"

Reid's expression darkens. "Cruelty. But he's also been off the map for years. His whole pack, actually."

I squeeze my eyes shut for a moment. "This is all giving me a headache."

"Trust me, I know."

"There was a girl," I say. "I'd been doing my own research on blood witches, trying to figure out what was going on with my magic before I found out about the poison. She died about a hundred years ago, but she looked sick. A lot like Daniel. I don't know if it's related, but we kind of…summoned her ghost to ask her about it."

Reid sits up straighter. "When was this?"

"During initiation. She asked if it was 'happening again.' Does the name Samantha Hawthorne mean anything to you?"

"Yes," he says immediately. "She died during one of the early attacks."

We stare at each other.

"I don't know what to make of all of this," I admit.

"Neither do I. I wasn't trying to keep things from you, Valerie. I was just——"

"Hoping to have some actual answers first?"

He gives me a rueful smile.

I sigh and glance around the empty shop again. "Why did you bring me here?"

"Well," he says. "It seems like the only times I see you are when something disastrous has happened. I thought it might be nice to do something normal. Coming here helps me when I'm overwhelmed. I thought maybe it would help you too." He hands me a sponge and gestures for me to hold it against the outside of the pot to smooth out the ridges. "I know we're partners, and it's complicated with everything going on," he continues, "but I'd like to think we could be…friends."

He sits back and leaves me to finish it off, and I slowly raise my gaze to meet his. There's something off about the way he says it, like he's not quite sure, and for some reason, my cheeks feel hot when he stares back at me.

I drop my eyes to the wheel between us.

"Anyway," he says. "If you want to see Connor, I'm meeting with him tomorrow to go over a few more things before his assessment. But it's up to you."

Connor's name hits me like a punch to the gut. "How's he doing?" I ask, my voice tight.

"I think he's coming to terms with things."

I peer up at him, but neither his expression nor his voice gives anything away. "When's his review?"

"Three days."

My hands press harder against the pot. "Should I be worried?"

"I don't think so."

We lapse into silence as the wheel spins between us, the clay forcing its way beneath my nails. "He probably won't want to see me," I say.

"I don't think that's true."

I meet his eyes again. "He wouldn't care one way or another if I'm there, and that's worse."

Reid presses his lips together, but he doesn't say anything. Probably because he knows I'm right. The worst part is, it's not Connor's fault. I want to be angry with him, but I can't. *I* did this to him.

"It could get better," Reid says.

Great, he probably just heard all of that through the bond.

"Well, we'll be in the gardens around midnight tomorrow if you change your mind," he adds when I don't respond. "And I called in some favors to see if anyone has any answers about this psychosis. Nothing's come of it yet, but…"

"Thanks." I sit back, looking down at the finished piece. The pot is wonky and lopsided, but it's better than I'd been expecting.

"You want to keep it?" he asks, pulling out the wire

again. "We can put it in the next batch for the kiln and come pick it up in a few days."

I look down at the poor, ugly thing. "Can I smash it instead?"

He lets out a low laugh and nods. I stand so I can put my full weight into it, then bring both of my fists down. The wet, slimy clay squishes between my fingers, and I grin.

"I think that was my favorite part."

CHAPTER NINE

I DON'T KNOW who decided the only class I'm taking this summer needed to start at the crack of dusk, but it feels like a personal attack. Fading sunlight slides through the windows as I shuffle my way toward the estate's library. Apparently this class is small enough to fit in one of the tiny rooms in the back.

I quickly wipe the back of my hand across my mouth before stepping inside, making sure there's no trace of Reid's blood on my lips. True to his word, he stocked me up on bags. I quickly downed one before heading out this morning, too paranoid to carry it around with me like I'd done at school.

There are far more people here who can't find out. People who are always watching.

I reach for the door handle, but it opens before I have the chance to grab it. I stumble back a step, stunned into silence as Connor steps out, a small stack of books in his hands. They're propped against his chest in a way that I can't see any of the titles, but judging by the thickness of the spines, they're no light reading. He looks equally surprised to see me as he freezes in his tracks and shoves the hair out of his eyes with one hand.

"What are you doing here?" I ask.

He shifts his weight, looking almost uncomfortable. "Do I need a reason?"

"I—no, I guess not."

He sighs and glances down at the books in his hands. "When I was human, I didn't have access." He nods back at the library. "Didn't need to be in here for my job, so that was that. Now." He shrugs.

My heart sinks a little in my chest. He just wanted to… come read some books. Something they wouldn't allow before, probably for no reason other than they could. Something I never would've given a second thought.

There were probably many things in Connor's human life I'd taken for granted.

"I didn't know that was something you wanted," I say quietly.

His eyes cut to mine, harder than they were before. "I don't need you to feel sorry for me, Valerie."

At first, my eyes sting at the harshness in his voice, but then something in my chest hardens, and I clench my jaw. This has been impossibly hard for him, but that doesn't mean it's been any easier for me. And if the roles were reversed, he wouldn't give up on me. He'd keep trying, no matter how much I pushed him away.

"I'm not feeling sorry for you, Connor. I'm *worried* about you. Maybe you feel differently now, but I don't. So snap at me all you want, but I'm still here."

"Maybe I don't want you to be, Valerie." He doesn't even say it coldly. Just matter of fact. And somehow that's worse. His gaze lingers on me for another moment, then he gestures for me to pass and walks away, whistling.

The sound makes me clench my teeth. I will not cry.

Maybe I don't want you to be.

I force my feet forward and shake my arms out as if I can physically shake the interaction off.

It could get better.

That's what Reid had said. And I want so desperately to believe it. But when? How long could this last? Days? Weeks? Months? It's been six days since the final trial, which somehow simultaneously feels like a lifetime and no time at all.

This is never what Connor wanted, to be a vampire. How losing his humanity affected his personality aside, he must also be struggling to process what this will mean for him. The entire trajectory of his life changed overnight. You don't just get over that. Sure, now he has a whole new life and set of opportunities ahead of him, but if he doesn't want them, then what does it matter?

God, I wish he would just *talk to me.* I have no idea what's going on in his head.

With each new day that passes, and the old Connor doesn't come back, it's starting to seem more and more like a delusional fantasy. Maybe my time would be better spent trying to accept this is how things are now. What if he wants a clean break?

Maybe he sees me as a piece of his past life trying to hold him back.

Great, now I really feel like crying.

The library is empty this time of night, except for Daniel leaning against the back wall. It's on the top floor of the west wing, with two stories of dark shelves, rolling ladders, and a small overhang to walk along the second floor of books. Floor-to-ceiling windows cover the far wall, overlooking the back of the grounds where the outdoor pool shimmers beneath the lights, the gardens on the right, the fields on the left.

I frown as I wind my way toward Daniel through the stacks. "You waiting for me?"

He rolls his eyes and yawns. "Door's locked."

I check the clock on the wall. "Are we early?"

He yawns again. "Nope."

Sighing, I lean against the wall across from him and peek through the window on the door. The room's dark. If Daniel wasn't here too, I'd think I got the wrong place.

I quirk an eyebrow at his matching black sweats. "I see you dressed up for the occasion."

He runs a hand through his hair like he's trying to smooth it down, but that makes it stand up more. "At this hour, they're lucky I rolled myself out of bed at all."

I brace myself for him to ask about Connor. If he was already in here, he definitely saw him, and judging by the way his eyes flicker from me to the door, he may have even overheard our conversation. But he just gives me his usual boyish smile. "Wanna be study buddies?"

I roll my eyes and glance around the rest of the library, but no one else is here. There's no way we're the only two in this class.

"Sorry! Sorry!" A spindly woman with a red scarf tied around her hair hurries through the library door, two bags and several books piled precariously in her arms. She blows the blond hair out of her face as she reaches us, struggling to juggle everything and fish out her keys.

"Here." Daniel grabs the books before she drops them.

"Thanks, thanks." She finally finds the keys, then slides them into the lock. It's not until the door's open and we follow her into the room that she actually looks at either of us.

It's a small room with a long table at the front and half a dozen desks facing it. The walls are covered in maps of the different regions, but other than that, it's empty.

The woman—the teacher, I'm assuming—dumps her belongings on the table at the front, then freezes as she takes in the two of us lingering by the desks.

"This is it?" she demands. "Just you two?"

Daniel and I exchange a glance, then shrug. Shouldn't she know?

She lets out a long sigh, then starts digging through her bag again. When neither of us moves, she glances at us over her shoulder. "Well, sit down."

Daniel folds his lips together like he's trying not to laugh as we take the two desks in the back.

The woman yanks a large folder free, then comes over to drop it on my desk. "You're paired with the prince, correct?"

I nod.

She taps the top of the folder. "Lucky you. Extra home-work. You're attending an important meeting with repre-sentatives from the other estates soon, so you have a lot of memorizing to do."

"Holy shit," Daniel breathes as I open it and a mountain of paper greets me. At first, I think it's in a foreign language. That's how little meaning this string of words has for me. But no. It is, in fact, in English.

And I am, in fact, screwed.

"Oh, that's it!" The woman stands back at the front of the room, a piece of paper in hand. She throws her arms up as if she's solved some grand mystery. "First years." She gives me and Daniel an *am I right?* look, then shakes her head to herself. "Idiots are probably lost," she mutters.

Daniel snorts, then quickly covers it with a cough.

"You two bring your textbooks?" she calls.

Daniel and I nod.

"Good." She waves a hand, already collecting her belongings and shoving them back into her bag. "Get reading. Chapter one. I'll be back." With that, she sweeps out of the room as quickly as she'd appeared.

"And here I thought I'd be the biggest train wreck in the class," Daniel mutters.

"Did she say first years? The hell are they doing in this class?"

Daniel shrugs and flips open the textbook on his desk. "Overachievers?"

"You're actually going to read?" I demand.

He smirks, then eyes the folder on my desk. "I'm just counting my blessings that I'm not *you*."

———

THE TEACHER—IF she can even be called that—never returns. Once the hour's up, Daniel announces he's going back to bed and slinks from the library, but I scout out a table by the windows. If I have to be up this early, I might as well make the most of it. Reid's been looking into the wendigos on his own, and though I doubt I'll be able to find much more than he can in these books, it would be stupid not to try.

Which is how I find myself several hours later with three books on wendigos spread out on the table in front of me, my brain not retaining any information. It wouldn't have mattered anyway. There doesn't appear to be anything here I didn't already know. Nothing useful, at least.

Nothing about a cure.

I try to look up what happened years ago with the previous attacks Reid had been talking about. How he found *any* information on it, I have no idea. Because whoever wanted what happened buried did a damn good job.

What I keep getting stuck on is that day in the field. The wendigos hadn't been physically there, and no one saw them but me. All of my research so far has been contradicting. Some sources depict wendigos as literal beasts; some say they're just spirits who possess people.

Does that mean I was *possessed*? And with the psychosis sticking around, is it *still inside of me*?

I shiver and close the book in front of me.

I should probably be spending my time going through this folder anyway, which seems to be full of profiles on important figures from each estate, summaries of treaties, laws, alliances, and whatever the hell else. It's hard to feel like this even *matters* right now. Who cares if I can memorize all of the faces in here if I'm a brain-dead monster in a few weeks?

An illustrated image of a fully emaciated wendigo with blood and gore dripping down its chin sits in my peripheral vision. I close that book too and turn my attention out the window, my gaze trailing over to the garden. The time Reid and Connor are supposed to meet is coming up any minute now. I know Reid offered for me to tag along, but I can't bring myself to go down there.

I can't bring myself to face Connor again yet.

If they're out there already, I can't see them from here. I'm not sure what Reid is going over with him or exactly what the assessment entails. It had always been described to us as a way to ensure the vampire turned successfully and wouldn't go on to be a danger to society. Learning to feed properly, teaching them the rules—that kind of thing.

But stupidly, I can't help but wonder if they're talking about me.

Technically, tomorrow marks one week of Connor being a vampire, but Reid thinks his review will be pushed back a few days since the queen has been busy with all of the new visitors at the estate.

I don't feel anything through the bond right now, but I can't tell if Reid is purposefully keeping me out, or if nothing significant is happening. It seems like the flashes I get from him—and him from me—happen when one of us is feeling something really intensely. The subtle moments don't translate as much.

It's probably cowardly, hiding up here like this. But this whole thing is marginally easier to bear when I'm not around Connor. If I don't see the way he acts around me, I can mold a different version of our reality in my head.

But if earlier today is any indication, that tactic is clearly not doing me any favors.

I sigh as I set the books in a nearby cart to be reshelved. Maybe putting my energy into researching Wendigo Psychosis is pointless when I should be focusing on finding the person behind all of this. Which brings us right back to square one in trying to find James Westcott.

"Valerie?"

I startle and turn to see a familiar face poking out from the stacks.

"Quinn?"

"Sorry, I didn't mean to surprise you." She comes to stand beside me by the windows, her gaze drifting to the gardens below.

"What are you doing in here?" I ask.

"Oh, they were short-staffed. Apparently this isn't a highly sought-after job." She shrugs. "I offered. Always liked it in here anyway." She glances back at the book I'm holding. "I'll take it."

It feels rude to say no, so I hand it over. She glances at the cover and does a single, understanding nod. "Reid told me what happened."

My muscles stiffen, but when she turns back to me, there's no accusation or fear in her expression. Her eyebrows are pinched together, almost in…concern. The attack is public knowledge at this point, I realize. Just not the *side effects*.

"I can't even imagine how terrifying that must have been," she says. "Horrible creatures, wendigos. I'm sure they're taking the investigation seriously."

I manage only a nod.

Movement below catches my eye. Reid and Connor walk out from the thick coverings around the gardens and toward the estate. Connor stalks ahead several paces, his shoulders tense and face tight. Reid stops outside of the garden and rubs his face with one hand.

Quinn follows my gaze.

"He was never like this as a human," I say. "Not even a little difficult. Not ever."

Quinn gives my shoulder a comforting squeeze. "Reid will look after him."

"Is Reid different now from the last time you saw him?" The question is out before I form the conscious choice to ask, but now I can't take it back. I pinch my lips together and glance at Quinn out of the corner of my eye, but she's still staring out the window, a thoughtful expression on her face now. A twinge of something darker, heavier weighs on her brow.

"He's the same in a lot of ways," she says. "But his mother spent his whole life pawning him off on anyone else she could find to raise him. That's bound to change a person." She glances at me sideways. "I'm sure you know a little something about that."

A bit of heat finds my face. "Not a fan of my mother?" I ask, eyes still trained on the window.

"Are you?"

I snort out a harsh laugh. "Maybe Reid's the lucky one. I probably would've been better off if she'd sent me away too."

She doesn't respond, and when I turn my head, I find her staring at me, a curious look on her face.

"What is it?"

"Nothing. I—" She smiles a little and shakes her head. "I'm glad he has you, Valerie." She squeezes my arm again. "I think the two of you might be good for each other."

Before I can ask her what she means, she gives me another tight-lipped smile and disappears back into the stacks.

CHAPTER TEN

"IT'S KIND OF weird without Kirby around, isn't it?" Monroe asks the following night. "Too quiet."

The car hums beneath us as a driver from the estate speeds along the highway back to the academy. Sitting here like this, I can't help but think of Reid. I only ever really travel back to York like this when I'm with him. Otherwise, I take the train or do a teleportation spell.

Monroe chews on her thumbnail beside me. That's the fourth time she's brought up Kirby in the past hour, a fact I probably wouldn't have noticed before. But after that night at the club, I'm seeing it in an entirely different light.

"Have you talked to her since she left?" I ask.

"Oh no." Monroe waves her hand in front of her face. "She's probably busy settling in. Meeting new people. Exploring. You know. She'll call."

I'm caught between wanting to comfort her and not wanting to embarrass her by revealing I know too much. And it also just feels...odd to talk to her about it without

Kirby here, like it's something that should be between the three of us.

"I miss her already," I say instead.

She goes back to chewing on the skin around her nail. "Anyway. How was your first class? As boring as you thought?"

"Don't get me started. I got an encyclopedia of homework on the first day that's not even for class, just for being paired with Reid."

"Well, maybe it's good you were paired with him. I heard he likes to be super involved in the region. Some Marionettes paired with royals basically babysit them all day since they don't do anything."

I glance at her out of the corner of my eye, trying to gauge her expression. She's paired with Nathan, after all. His standing doesn't compare with Reid's, but he's still technically a royal. I have no idea how much time they've spent together since the pairing ceremony, how much she knows about him. About Avery.

She turns and frowns when she catches me staring. "What?"

"How are things going with your new partner?" I ask, my voice light.

"Oh." She shrugs and leans against the door. "Haven't seen him much, to be honest."

I eye her profile again. Monroe and Kirby had never spent much time around Avery, so I guess it shouldn't come as a surprise if she doesn't know. Even *I* don't know what happened. Not really. But that doesn't mean I should keep it to myself. If it were me, I'd want to know.

"Did he tell you about his last partner?" I ask.

She narrows her eyes at me. "I know she transferred to another estate. Whatever it is you're not saying, just spit it out already, Val. For fuck's sake."

"I'm worried."

Monroe's eyebrows pull together.

"Avery—his partner before you—I talked to her the day before she left. She didn't tell me exactly what happened, but it sounded like she was leaving *because* of him, not despite him. I just—I don't know. I thought you should know."

"No, yeah, I'm glad you told me." She shakes her head and looks out the window again as the car veers off the smooth pavement of the road onto the gravel leading up to the academy.

Even though it's only been about a week since I was here last, still, looking up at the towering buildings, the empty paths, and the flowers starting to bloom, it makes something tighten in the pit of my stomach.

The summer session for the students on campus doesn't start for a few more days, so the grounds still seem relatively empty. The car takes us to the dorms and idles beside the curb. A warm breeze picks up as I open the door and step out.

I crane my neck back and take in the buildings in front of us—three identical figures, side by side by side. We've all stayed here the last three years. It hadn't occurred to me before now it would be the last time. The housing for seniors is on the complete opposite side of campus.

The driver pops the trunk behind me, and I jump a little as he hauls two empty suitcases out of the trunk and sets them on the sidewalk.

"Thank you," I say.

"Hopefully this will fit everything," Monroe mumbles, grabbing one and heading for the building. "Come on!" she calls over her shoulder. "Between your packing and my *un*packing, we're gonna need as much time as we can get."

MONROE TACKLES the closet while I focus on the desk. She plays some music on her phone while we work, and Kirby's absence feels twice as big between us now. I imagine her whining about Monroe's rock music and insisting we listen to pop instead, then the two of them fighting over the phone. She'd let Monroe win—she always does—but then she'd go on and pretend to be annoyed for at least another ten minutes, even when we'd catch her singing along to the music.

I watch over my shoulder as Monroe gently fishes the hideous pink cowboy boots from the back of the closet and brushes the dust off. Maybe I had been blind and this had been going on for a while, or at least building that way.

"You going to miss it here?" Monroe asks. "My room this year was so drafty. Good riddance."

I turn before Monroe can catch me staring at her and reach for the violin case propped beside the desk. I sigh as my hand wraps around the metal handle. I don't know why I bother keeping it around anymore if I can't bring myself to open the damn thing.

"I didn't realize you still had that," she says, her voice much quieter now.

Finally breaking out of my trance, I toss it beside the

suitcase on the bed and bend down to continue clearing out the drawers in my desk. "Don't know why I keep holding on to it. I probably don't even know how to play anymore."

"Well, maybe one day you'll find yourself inspired again."

I snort. "You really do miss Kirby. You sound just like her now."

We fall back into silence as we finish packing up the rest of the room, which does not, in fact, all fit in the two suitcases. Monroe finds some old tote bags stashed under the bed and starts filling those next.

"So." She rolls the first suitcase into the hall as I finish clearing the nightstand. "How are things with *Reid?*"

I shoot her a look.

"What? So you can ask about my partner, but I can't ask about yours?"

I sigh and let the nightstand's drawer close with an audible *thunk*. "Everything's fine."

"Is he as intimidating as he seems?"

"He's…" I trail off, not sure how to finish the sentence. Regularly infuriating? Maddeningly mysterious? Kinder than he wants anyone else to know? "…Reid," I finally say.

Monroe's eyebrows creep slowly up her face. "And Connor?"

"It's not like that," I say, my face immediately getting hot. "With Reid, I mean. We're kind of…I don't know. Friends? As for Connor…" I sigh. "He's not the same. At all. And I don't know if I'm supposed to stick it out and wait to see if he gets back to normal—hell, I'd take just a little closer to normal—but right now, it's like he couldn't care less. Like I'm no one to him." My voice cracks, and I quickly clear my throat and stand, pointedly not looking at Monroe now. I've been feeling sorry enough for myself these days. I don't need to see the pity on her face too.

And maybe that's the worst part about all of this. The one person I would usually go to, the one person I desperately want to talk about all of this with Connor is...Connor. And that version of him, the one who would sit with me all through the night, talking through any problem I had, always knowing what to say or when I just needed him to listen, he might not exist anymore.

And if I can't go to him, I don't know where to turn.

"His review must be coming up now," says Monroe.

I swallow the lump in my throat and nod. "Two days."

"I'm sorry. We don't have to talk about this if you don't want to."

She stands in the doorway, wringing her hands together in front of her body like she doesn't know what to do with them. Before I know what I'm doing, I cross the rest of the distance between us and throw my arms around her shoulders. She quickly hugs me back, holding me tightly against her.

"I feel like he died," I whisper. "Reid keeps talking about how he thinks it might wear off, how he might come back more, but I don't. I don't think it's going to get any better. And I feel horrible because a part of me wishes he *had* died, because that would've been easier. How fucked up is that? God, that sounds horrible."

Monroe runs a hand over my hair and squeezes me tighter. "I think it makes complete sense," she says. "I'm so sorry this happened, Val. I'm so, so sorry."

"I've tried to talk to him a few times, and he's just so

cold. Like he wants nothing to do with me. I don't know what to do, Roe."

She rubs my back. "I don't think you should give up on him yet, Val. Keep trying. He's gotta still be in there somewhere."

I want to pull back and shake it off. Laugh. Make a joke. Finish packing and move on with the rest of the day.

But I don't.

I stand there, just grateful to have someone to hold me as I finally let myself cry.

MOVING Monroe in doesn't take as long as I'd expected. Maybe she's trying to spare me after witnessing my breakdown earlier. The senior dorms are twice the size of the other rooms, and Monroe moves her furniture around three times before settling on the best configuration. Once the bed is made and all of the major pieces are in place, I settle myself on her desk chair and pull out one of Reid's blood bags.

"Would it bother you if I…?" I ask.

She glances at me over her shoulder, now having moved on to organizing her closet. "Of course not. Go ahead." Her eyes flick from me to the bag a few times.

"Just ask, whatever it is," I say and swallow a mouthful.

"What does it taste like?"

I take another sip, considering. "They all taste a little different. I'm not sure what it is—blood type, what the person ate, or what. This one's kind of sweet."

Monroe laughs. "Maybe it's from a diabetic."

I pinch my lips together, wondering if I should correct her. I've kept so many things from her and Kirby these past few weeks. I'm not sure if she'll forgive another.

"It's Reid's, actually."

She whips around so fast she nearly loses her footing. "He gives you his blood? Is this some kind of new vampire kink I'm unaware of?"

"Yes, Roe. This is our foreplay," I deadpan.

She throws her hands up. "Well, I don't know!"

I stuff the rest of the blood back in my bag to save for later and sigh. "Honestly? I haven't been able to keep human blood down since the wendigo thing. Reid's helping me look into it, and his blood is all I've been able to stomach in the meantime."

"Wait, what?" She tosses aside the remaining hangers in her hands and takes a seat on the bed. "Are you sick?"

"I don't know," I admit. "Something's definitely not right. We just haven't found any answers yet."

"You try the library?"

I roll my eyes. "Of course. It was the first place I looked."

She thins her lips.

"What are you thinking?"

"I know you probably want to get back for Connor's review and everything, but I think you should stay for the weekend. Or at least until tomorrow."

My eyebrows rise. "Why?"

She gives me a small, satisfied smile. "Because *I* have an idea."

"This is a horrible idea."

I crane my neck back, taking in the hand-painted sign for Magnolia's Magic Shop hanging above our heads. The window displays are covered with neon-bright curtains, strings of beads, and little pedestals displaying different crystals, tarot decks, herbs for sale, and jewelry. A family squeezes past us on the sidewalk, heading for the café Blood and Buzz across the street.

I glance at Monroe beside me. "You know she hates when academy students come in. She feels like we're making fun of her."

"We're not making fun of her! We're asking for her help. She's been around in this town forever. If anyone knows something, it's her."

"And why would she want to help us?"

Monroe hooks her arm through mine and drags me forward. "You should have more faith in people." Bells chime overhead as she opens the door, and a brisk wave of AC and incense wafts over us.

"You really are starting to sound like Kirby," I mutter.

The store is dimly lit, the walls a bright red. Velvet cloths hang over the tables, where various items for sale are on display, seemingly at random. The wood creaks beneath our feet as we pace inside, passing a table with an odd combination of skulls, perfume bottles, candles, and decks of cards. An instrumental song plays in the background, full of bells and low humming noises.

"The door said *open*, right?" I murmur out of the corner of my mouth. I breathe in the heavy scent of sage and old books hanging in the air, a scent I'd usually find calming, but instead of easing my anxiety, it just stokes the flames of my apprehension.

Monroe frowns and glances around the empty shop. It looks exactly the same as it had the first and only time we were in here, when we were freshmen at the academy and painfully arrogant and stupid. Magnolia had taken one look at us in our uniforms, giggling and touching the different knickknacks on display, before spitting at our feet and threatening to put a curse on us unless we left.

We hadn't lasted two minutes in here.

Rumor around the academy is Magnolia had once been a student, but she hadn't made it to her initiation before getting dismissed. Why she'd chosen to stick around in the same small town and set up shop was beyond me. I guess sometimes we don't get to choose what places feel like home. And she probably has far less competition here than if she found someplace in the city.

The curtain of beads covering the door to the back jangles and the floorboards moan as Magnolia slowly steps out.

I have no idea how old she is. She's one of those people who somehow looks simultaneously ancient and timeless. Her hair is dark and threaded through with silver, though it looks more like a stylistic choice than a product of age. She walks slowly and methodically, like she's tired down to her bones, but there are no signs of wear on her skin. Her face probably looks the same as when she was a student.

That alone tells me she's not a scammer. She has some kind of magic.

There's no immediate distaste in her expression when

she sees us. She must not recognize us. At least we're not wearing our uniforms this time.

She looks us up and down in a way that makes me think she's seeing far beyond our appearances. Whatever she sees though must be satisfactory because she hobbles over behind the counter and folds her hands on the glass surface.

"Can I help you find something?" Her voice is raspy and full of gravel, but the look in her eyes is not unkind. Maybe I'd made the first visit here out to be worse than it was in my memory.

"We were hoping we could talk to you," says Monroe. "We have a few questions we thought you might be able to help with, and we'll definitely buy something when we're done! Lots of somethings!"

"Roe."

"Right. I'll just be..." She jabs her thumb over her shoulder and scurries off to the bookshelf in the back.

Magnolia turns her gaze on me, a single eyebrow raised.

"You girls students?" She jerks her chin up toward the academy.

I could lie to her, I suppose, but I have a feeling she'd know. I nod.

"I know you don't have any reason to help us, but I was wondering if you know anything about wendigos. Or maybe have a book on them?"

Her eyebrow lifts another inch, then she looks me up and down. This time when she meets my eyes, there's something behind hers I can't quite read. She nods toward the beaded curtain. "Follow me."

I give her a head start before following, holding my breath as if making any noise might change her mind.

There's a small office on the other side of the door with a large oak desk in the center and vivid red and orange paintings on the walls. She sinks into the leather chair and waves for me to take the seat opposite her.

"Which one of you is it?" she asks.

I pull my gaze away from the nearest painting—some kind of violent scene with a werewolf standing on top of a pile of bodies. "I'm sorry?"

She presses her fingers together into a pyramid and leans her elbows on the desk. "Which one of you has the psychosis?"

My stomach drops, but I don't look away. "Me," I whisper.

She sighs. "Your vampire side probably makes that particularly difficult."

"I—what?"

She waves her hand as the blood drains from my face. "I have no interest in your secrets. How long ago was the contact?"

I rub my palms, now damp with sweat, against my pants. "A little over a week. Do you know how to make it stop?"

She gets up from the desk abruptly and paces to the bookcase on the far wall. "I knew this day would come again."

Again.

A memory flutters in the back of my mind, the ghost of Samantha Hawthorne that day in the cemetery.

It's happening again, isn't it?

"There is nothing you can do to stop it," she continues, then pulls a small, wooden box from the shelf and comes back to the desk. Lifting the lid, she reveals a black velvet interior with small wheat-like herbs lying in a neat row. She picks two up and extends them to me. I scramble forward, reaching my hand out, and they're rough and chalky against my palm. "Crush these and drink them. Only a small amount each time, not even a teaspoon. It will not stop it, but it will help slow down the progression until you find him."

"Find him?" I repeat.

"Must you always have your hand held through things you already know?"

"James Westcott?" I guess.

She tilts her head to the side. "That was the name he was last known as, yes. He has also been Xavier Hearst, Nathaniel Strand, Christian Mazar. Whatever he goes by these days is anyone's guess."

"So, you believe he's still alive?"

Apparently this is too dumb of a question for her to answer because she closes the box and gets up to return it to the shelf.

Something on her arm snags my attention as she pushes the box back into place. Her sleeve rides up, just enough to expose the pale skin on the inside of her wrist. Or rather, the skin there that would be pale, if not for the web of veins, slightly raised and pitch black.

My breath catches, and she turns at the sound, then follows my gaze. She meets my eyes again, a challenge in hers now, like she's daring me to ask.

Only one thing would leave a mark like that—a blood deal. The magic that forms them is so dark, it leaves a visible trace behind. And should either party break the deal, well, that poison in her blood would spread and finish the job.

I look away, swallowing the questions on my tongue. *What deal had she made? With whom? How long ago? Why?*

What could she have possibly needed badly enough?

Instead, I ask, "Why is he doing this? What does he want from me?"

She drops her arm, the sleeve falling back into place. "From you? Not much, I suspect. You are a pawn in a larger story."

"So I'm not the only person he's done this to."

She sighs again and leans against the bookcase as she presses her lips into a tight line. "You are not the first, and I know for certain, you will not be the last."

"Were you here the last time this happened?"

She says nothing and returns to her spot behind the desk.

"Can you tell me how I can find him?" I try.

Still, nothing. I let out a frustrated breath through my nose and rise to my feet. "Can you tell me anything?"

Her eyebrows are dug in, her mouth set in a hard line. She looks a lot like Reid had before my final trial. Like she wishes she could tell me...but she can't.

My gaze drifts back to her wrist, though it's now covered by her sleeve. It could be completely unrelated. But the feeling in my gut tells me it's not.

"Thank you for your help," I say, turning to leave.

I'm almost through the door when she speaks up again. "Good luck, Valerie Darkmore."

It doesn't occur to me until we're back outside that I'd never told her my name.

CHAPTER ELEVEN

I MIX a spoonful of the herbs from Magnolia with a glass of water before going to sleep, hoping it will at least stop me from starving every few hours. It tastes like tar and coats the back of my throat like dust, but I force myself to drink the entire glass. Considering how close I sleep to Monroe's throat as she and I squeeze into her bed that is definitely not built for two people, and I don't have the urge to drain her, they must be working.

After spending the majority of the following night helping her settle in, I have a car from the estate come pick up my things to bring back from the academy. The idea of sitting in a car for another two hours is less than appealing, so I teleport myself back instead.

Now I lie in my bed, staring at the ceiling above me, not desperately hungry like I have been the past few days, but still unable to sleep. The sleeplessness is becoming as familiar as the hunger these days.

Connor's review is tonight. I should swallow my pride

and try to talk to him again. If the review goes poorly, and I don't get another chance, I'll never forgive myself.

I sit up in bed, forcing the thought away.

The review will be fine. Besides seeming to lose all of his humanity, Connor has shown no signs of an unstable vampire. If they're looking for a reason to put him down, it's going to be a stretch.

I kick my legs over the side of the bed. It's barely 4:00 p.m.—no one else is probably awake yet. My hands shake as I pick up my phone and pull up my last text conversation with Connor. My stomach sinks. All of the messages are on one side of the screen from when I couldn't get ahold of him.

When he'd been sitting in a cell somewhere, waiting for my trial.

I force myself to type.

Hey, good luck with your review tonight. I'm sure it'll go well. Would you have a few minutes to talk before?

I stare at the screen after I hit send, though I know he's probably asleep and won't see it for a few hours. The longer I stare at the messages, the more I feel like I'm going to cry, so I toss the phone on the bed and slide my feet into a pair of slippers.

My bags sit accusingly in the corner, still packed, my violin case propped on top. I should've left it behind. Perhaps in a dumpster. Or I could've donated it to the second-hand shop on Main Street once we finished up at Magnolia's. Anywhere I wouldn't have to look at it anymore.

Instead, I wrap an old sweater around my shoulders and tuck the case under my arm, then quickly double back and shove my phone in my pocket in case Connor responds.

The halls are eerily empty as I slip out of my room and head to the main floor. Dim sunlight shines in through the tinted windows as I make my way to the back doors that lead to the garden. A few human servants are scattered about the lawn, but they don't pay me any mind as I head through the grass, my slippers squishing in the mud.

Thick, tall hedges frame the perimeter of the garden, shielding the rest of it from view. The hydrangeas and lavender seem to be in full bloom now, casting a heavy floral scent over the path. A few carved stone benches line the walkway, leading up to a bubbling fountain in the center. I keep walking, plunging farther down the paths until I reach the less frequented areas—this part shadier and quieter.

I sink onto one of the stone benches in the corner, my violin case still in my lap. I had an image of bringing it out here to burn when I first picked it up. Just setting a little fire and watching it turn to ash. Because the thing is, looking at it doesn't make me think of all the times Mom yelled or slapped me when she caught me with it. It doesn't make me think of my bleeding fingers as I taught myself to play, or staying up until the sun rose behind me.

It makes me think of him.

I could be making up his face for all I know, but the only intact memory I seem to have of him is the way he crouched down and set the then-gigantic case in my tiny toddler lap, telling me about how one day, it wouldn't seem so big to me. One day, it would be my first love. One day, I'd need the escape.

He had a mustache, I think. Some stubble around his jaw. A full head of dark hair, the exact color of mine. And perfectly straight white teeth.

I can never remember the color of his eyes though.

He'd had scars on his hands. I'd felt them when he touched me. Crisscrossing lines on his fingers, just like mine.

It would take a lot for me to scar now, but back when I was a kid and learning, I still hadn't fully come into my powers, so the healing was slow, and it left room for the little scars to leave their marks. Even now, they still haven't faded. I have a feeling that's not typical for other musicians. But being a blood witch creates a weird relationship with pain. Sometimes it didn't occur to me to stop, no matter how much it hurt. No matter how much I bled. I wanted to keep practicing, so I did.

I hold my breath as I undo the clasp on the case. I don't know what I'd expected to find when I finally opened it again, but everything is exactly how I left it, albeit it definitely needs tuning now.

I just want to see what it feels like to hold it again. That's all. Gently, I extract it from the case, the bow second, and settle it against my chin. The weight of it is like a familiar hug, and I let my eyes fall shut. I can smell the wood and dust even better now. The surrounding hints of floral mix in too, and I can hear some birds chirping back by the pool, the groan of the mower on the opposite side of the estate, the soft breeze rustling through the trees.

I let out a slow breath, trying to force my concentration back to the instrument in my hands, blocking out all of the other noise as I tune it.

I thought it might feel awkward in my hands now,

clumsy. But the bow finds its place along the strings almost of its own accord, and I play a single note and let it hang in the air. Finally, my shoulders relax. I picture the strings in my head, the placement of my fingers, the notes in the air as if they were tangible things.

I don't try to remember any songs. I never much liked following along with them anyway. Instead, I just play.

The strings bite into my fingers as the music swells around me, fluid and soft and enough to drown out my surroundings. And for a while, I don't even think about him. Where this instrument came from. It's just me and the music and the weight of it in my hands. The muscle memory as my hand carefully glides the bow across the string in slow, precise movements.

I used to come out here to the garden to play when I was a kid. It was the only place my mother wouldn't hear me. I could never get away with it in my room, not with our shared wall. It was only out here or when she was away that I could sneak the violin out of its case and let myself fall into it.

At least, until I started stealing her books to learn spells and came across one for soundproofing the room.

But even then, I preferred to come out here.

My fingers start to ache, no longer used to the pressure, and I sigh and lower the violin back to my lap.

"Don't stop."

My eyes fly open, my breath getting caught in my throat.

The garden is dark now. The sun must have set while I was playing. Reid stands at the break between the bushes, a thoughtful look on his face. How long have I been out here? How long has he been *standing* there?

His lips curl into a bemused smile. "You said you weren't any good."

"I'm not. What are you doing out here?" I ask, already sliding the violin back into its case.

"One of the servants told me where I could find you, then I followed the music."

I snap the latch closed. "Well, you found me. Do you need something?"

"While you were gone, there was another attack in the city. Six vampires dead. The queen has requested you and I investigate…quietly."

Six vampires dead.

I don't look at him. "You're wondering if it was me."

"I didn't say that."

"You didn't have to. Don't worry. I haven't gone on any killing sprees, that I know of. I went to see the witch on Main Street when I was in York. She gave me something to slow down the effects. So far, it seems to be working."

"Ah." He tilts his head back. "Magnolia."

My gaze cuts to him. "You know her?"

He smirks. "Everyone knows her."

"Well, according to her, there's no cure. The only thing to do is find James Westcott. Why didn't you tell me that wasn't even his real name?"

He narrows his eyes, considering me. "The two of you had quite the chat, didn't you? She's not usually so talkative. She must have liked you."

"Or she doesn't want me eating her customers," I mutter.

"Anyway, I'll come find you once I'm done with Connor, and we'll head into the city."

He turns to leave, and I stand too, clutching my violin case to my chest. "Reid?"

He glances at me over his shoulder.

"Have you talked to him today?"

He frowns but nods. "Just to tell him what time to meet me and where his review would be."

My stomach sinks, but I try not to let it show on my face. So, he's awake. I glance at my phone like I'm checking the time, but really, I'm hoping I didn't hear the notification. But no texts from Connor wait on the screen.

"Do I have anything to worry about?" I ask. "With him?"

He presses his lips together and shakes his head. "I don't think so. But if there's cause for concern, you'll know."

ADRIENNE CUT HER HAIR AGAIN. I don't know how I didn't notice before. The blunt bob now looks more like a pixie cut with spiky strands sticking out every which way. She slowly winds through the aisles in the library before coming to one of the study tables in the corner. She pulls out a few textbooks and notebooks, then sits back and drums her pen against the top of her pile like she's waiting for someone.

"Miss Darkmore?"

I snap my attention back to the librarian in front of me. She frowns from behind her desk, then pushes a stack of books toward me with a single sheet of paper on top—

additional reading for our summer class. I hold back my sigh, a headache already creeping in.

Someone coughs behind me, and I realize a line is accumulating. "Thank you," I mutter, quickly collect my things, and head toward Adrienne's table.

She's so lost in whatever she's thinking about she doesn't notice me until I'm standing right in front of her. I set my books on the table, and she jumps at the small *thud.*

"What are you doing here?" she asks.

I drum my fingers on the books. "Summer programs." I glance at the textbooks and study guides set out in front of her, the same ones I'd sat here with three years ago. "Studying for York's entrance exam?"

She nods. "My tutor is meeting me."

"You *know*, I did take that test. I could help, if you wanted."

Her face tightens like she wants to say no, but then she glances back at the pile in front of her, and her shoulders slump around her sigh. "I…might actually take you up on that," she says. "I haven't done well on my practice tests so far." Her gaze drops to my own pile of books. "But I know you're probably super busy right now, so I get it if—"

"Just stop by my room sometime and we'll make a study plan, okay?" I cut in. "I'll see if I can find my old practice tests and stuff too."

We awkwardly stare at each other for a moment.

"Okay," she says.

"Okay." I pick my books up and nod. "I'll…see you around then."

"Yeah."

I turn for the door, shaking my head at myself. I must be

one of the only people incapable of having any semblance of a normal conversation with my own sister.

"Wait, Valerie?"

She stands, chewing on her lower lip. "Do you...do you want to sit for a minute? Connor's review is about to start, isn't it?"

"Yeah, it is," I whisper. I've been trying not to think about it—trying to keep myself busy until the time passed —but that hasn't stopped me from looking at the clock every ten seconds.

She pulls out the chair beside her, and I slowly sink into it.

"Have you seen him much since..." I trail off, not sure I'd be able to say the words without crying right now. "Or talked to him?"

She swallows audibly. "A few times, yeah."

My head whips up. "What did he say? What was he like with you?"

She grimaces.

"Adrienne?"

She lets out a sigh. "He told me to stop staring at him. Then slammed his door."

I slump a little in my chair. "Oh."

"I'm guessing he hasn't been any better with you?"

I shake my head. "I don't know what to do."

Adrienne touches my hand, and I jump at the contact, but she laces her fingers through mine. "I don't believe turning could change someone that much," she says. "You don't just go from being willing to die for someone to feeling nothing for them overnight. You guys will figure it out. I know you will."

"Thanks, Adrienne." I push up from the table before I start crying, give her hand a quick squeeze, then hurry into the hall. I'm not sure where I'm walking until I'm in front of the throne room.

You guys will figure it out.

We have to. We *have* to.

The large, golden doors are still shut. But I don't feel anything negative from Reid through the bond, so hopefully everything is going as expected. So I do the only thing I can do. I find a seat on a bench by the windows and wait.

CHAPTER TWELVE

I PASS the time texting Monroe to see how she's settling in and take a few swigs from the water bottle I mixed with Magnolia's herbs last night. I text Kirby too, but don't get a response. Maybe she's asleep. What even is the time difference between here and Thailand? I make a mental note to look that up later.

The doors crack open, and I quickly shove my phone in my pocket and stand.

Connor walks out first—alive, so that's a good sign. He barely spares me a glance before turning and walking down the hallway. He doesn't seem particularly upset, but he doesn't seem that positive either. Reid comes out next, running a hand through his hair and watching Connor's retreating form.

A few people I don't recognize linger in the throne room behind him, but the doors fall shut again before I can get a good look at any of their faces.

"How did it go?" I ask.

When Reid looks up at me, a shadow of exhaustion passes over his features. "He passed. Everything's fine."

"Well, what did they say? What happened? Why don't you look happy?"

He doesn't deny it. And as usual, he doesn't answer any of my questions. He rubs his eyes and nods for me to follow as he takes off in the same direction as Connor. "I'll let him tell you himself. I'll go grab a car and we can head into the city. Meet me out front."

I open my mouth to protest, but he continues down the hall and disappears around the corner before I can say anything.

AT FIRST I just head upstairs to drop off my books, but I end up taking so long I expect impatience to start flooding through the bond, but there's nothing. I stand in my room in my underwear, staring at the clothes set out on my bed. If we're showing up somewhere in any official capacity, now that I've been initiated, I'll be expected to wear the uniform of the Marionettes. I don't know why I'm hesitating. I guess I thought I'd feel different the first time I put it on. Excited, maybe? But my mind is still caught on Connor as I yank the pants over my hips and secure the top in place. And thinking of Connor means thinking of what happened to him. *Why* it happened.

It fits snugly, which I know it's supposed to, but it's still much more formfitting than anything I usually wear. I glance at myself in the mirror as I tie my hair up. The all-black outfit just makes the rest of my features look even darker and the red tattoo around my arm stand out more.

Reid's leaning against the car when I step outside, scrolling through something on his phone. He glances up as the gravel crunches under my feet and stares at me wordlessly, his expression unreadable.

"What?" I finally ask as I reach him.

He just shakes his head and pops the door open for me.

The car brings us to the shore below the Brooklyn Bridge, and it doesn't take long to find the bodies. They're splayed out on the rocks, some of them partially submerged. The city lights glow behind them, reflecting off the water, as Reid and Alexander pull the bodies up. Reid sets the first one on the ground beside me, frowning, then turns and lifts the arm of another, inspecting it.

"They're drained of blood," he says, moving on to the next. "All of them."

"So it was a vampire," I say.

The woman beside me lies on her back and stares up at the starless sky with empty eyes, half of her throat torn out. Instead of the rotting smell I'd been preparing myself for, she doesn't smell like much of anything. A little like wet dog from the water, and a little stale, but not the way a fresh corpse should smell. Maybe it's a vampire thing.

Reid adds another body beside me, this one an overweight man with a receding hairline.

"Should I start..." I trail off, gesturing to the bodies.

Reid sighs and shakes his head. "We'll have to take them back to the estate. This just got a lot more...complicated."

I help Alexander haul the last of the bodies out of the

water—a boy who couldn't have been older than thirteen. Whoever the killer is, they certainly don't have a type. And draining *six* bodies all at the same time? No one has an appetite that big. And what vampire targets other vampires?

Unless they were practically unconscious when they did the killing…just like me.

You are not the first, and I know for certain, you will not be the last.

A second car pulls up some time later to carry the other bodies back to the estate. Only two can fit in our trunk. We meticulously wrap the bodies in white sheets, and I try not to make eye contact with them. Having them stare at me, even if they can't see anything, makes a shiver run up my spine.

I pause before covering the face of the last girl. She looks about my age. Her mouth hangs open, a piercing still clinging to her lower lip. But it's her eyes that capture me. They're wide and unseeing like the others, but they don't look afraid. Surprised, maybe.

I finish covering her with the sheet and stand.

The water laps against the shore, and a siren wails somewhere in the distance. Reid and Alexander talk in hushed tones as they pile the other bodies into the trunk of the second car. There doesn't seem to be much else around here. The closest apartments and establishments are blocks away. Did the killer happen upon them out here? Drag them here to kill? Dump the bodies after they were done? If they were trying to cover it up, they didn't do a very good job.

So probably a newbie vampire. Someone older would've been smarter about this. Unless they'd still been in the blood-lust haze and didn't realize what they were doing. Maybe the killer woke up covered in blood somewhere else, not even aware of what they'd done.

The back of my neck prickles, like someone's standing right behind me. I whip around, scanning the rocks and concrete pillars beneath the bridge, but there's no one else around. A shadow moves up by the street, and I squint. Is someone up there watching us?

Rocks shift somewhere to my right, and I turn back around, expecting to see Reid coming to get the last body, but he's still over by the car with Alexander. The rocks move again, and I tentatively step forward.

Then I hear a small, strangled whimper.

"Reid!" I shriek, falling to my knees and shoving the rocks aside. A small, pale hand appears, and I keep digging. Reid kneels at my side and joins, our hands frantically throwing the rocks back. There's another whimper, but when I finally manage to find where it's coming from, a brown face appears. Round cheeks and equally round eyes —she can't be older than fifteen. Blood trickles from the corner of her mouth, and she lets out another cry.

"It's not just her," I say through my teeth as we finish digging her out.

"What?"

I nod toward the first hand I found. "There are others buried under here."

He pauses and glances at the girl. Her head lolls against my shoulder, her eyes fluttering. "Take her to Alexander," he decides.

I nod and scoop her into my arms, her body weighing practically nothing. Rocks continue to crack together as

Reid digs for other bodies. I glance back to where the shadow had been, but there's nothing there now. I'm probably being paranoid. The driver of the second car, a silver-haired woman, takes off at a run to help Reid.

"Put her in the back," says Alexander, his voice low. I do as he says, laying her gently across the seat, and he circles to the driver's side. "I'll take her to the estate and come back."

I nod, close the door, and head back to the rocks to keep digging.

———

FORTY-TWO BODIES, including the ones that had been left uncovered. What I'd first seen as a sloppy disposal was… running out of room. But what I find the most curious is, although all of the bodies belonged to vampires, they weren't all drained of blood like the first six. Some of them had black veins webbed across their skin and dried blood coming out of all of their orifices, like they'd died of something else. A sickness.

Like what Daniel had.

But Daniel got better. It took forever for him to heal, but he hadn't died.

Apparently, he's in the minority.

My stomach clenches at the sight of them all laid out along the rocks, taking up the majority of the shore. How have more of them not been reported missing?

Unless they have, and the queen hasn't wanted it to be public knowledge.

Six vans from the estate show up half an hour later, and

a crew of human servants in white uniforms helps load the bodies. The queen must have given up on trying to keep this quiet, unless she plans to glamour them all later. I stand out of the way and watch, picking at the dirt and dried blood covering my arms.

Reid steps up beside me, rolling his shirtsleeves up to his elbows. "They're in different states of decay," he says. "They weren't all buried at the same time."

"You don't think this was one person doing all of this, do you?"

Slowly, he shakes his head. "I was hoping you could help with that."

I glance at him sideways. Surely there is a spell to find out who did this, but I don't know any yet. But they all probably involve getting up close and personal with the bodies again.

"Come on." He nods toward Alexander's car. "Let's head back. We can talk about this later."

I climb in after him. Despite them now loading the last of the bodies, I can't get that image of them laid out in a row out of my head, the water lapping toward their feet.

CHAPTER THIRTEEN

I DON'T KNOW where they take the bodies. Even somewhere as spacious as the estate, there isn't a place with enough room for all of them. The estate does have something similar to a morgue, but bodies never stay there long, and it's not big enough to fit over forty new people.

Surprisingly, the survivor is not in the hospital. Instead, they put her in a guest room. She's asleep when we step inside. It's decently sized, a bit bigger than my room, with dark wooden furniture and red accents. The girl is curled on her side beneath the heavy comforter, her back to us. A human nods as we enter. There's a fresh bite mark on her neck. She quickly presses a bandage to it and slips back into the hall.

I exchange a look with Reid, and he's the first to approach the bed. The girl doesn't stir, but I can tell she's awake by the tension in her shoulders and the spike in her pulse as the door clicks shut.

There's a small table by the window, and Reid takes the

matching chair and sets it beside the girl. I hesitate by the door as he sits and folds his hands in his lap.

"How are you feeling?" he asks.

The girl doesn't respond, not at first. Then she clears her throat and pushes herself into a seated position on the bed. She clutches the covers to her chest as she takes in Reid beside her, then me by the door. "Better now. They gave me some blood."

"Can you tell me your name?" asks Reid.

"Who are you?" the girl shoots back.

A small smile graces his lips, and he inclines his head. "You can call me Reid. And that's my partner, Valerie, by the door."

The girl's eyes shoot to me. "She's a witch?"

"She's nicer than she looks. Promise."

I scowl at him. He doesn't look at me, but the smile on his face grows.

"Naomi," she says quietly.

"Naomi," Reid repeats. "I would say it's nice to meet you, but these are pretty awful circumstances for you. Valerie and I are hoping you can tell us what happened so we can find who did this and make sure it doesn't happen again."

"Did anyone else…?" She looks between the two of us, and my chest constricts at the hope in her eyes. Hope that someone else survived. She probably had people she loved in that pile of bodies.

Reid clears his throat. "I'm afraid not."

Tears fill her eyes, and she looks down at her hands.

God, she looks so young. I guess I should know better. As a vampire, who knows how old she really is if she was

WICKED SOULS

turned? But I doubt there's any age that can withstand that kind of tragedy and be unaffected.

"Do you know who did this?" Reid asks, his voice gentler than I've ever heard it. I'm just thankful he's taking the lead on this one because I'm still frozen where I stand. "Can you tell us what happened?"

She swallows audibly. "My family owns the Kingston Hotel—down off Tillary? We started having some customers disappear a few weeks ago." Her chin wobbles, and she quickly bites down on her lip. "After about a week, then our employees started to go missing. No signs of struggle or anything. We had the human police involved, even some of your Marionettes were looking into it. At first, I'd thought he was just another one who went missing with the rest—" Her voice hitches, and she buries her face in her hands.

Reid reaches out and lays a hand on her back, but that makes her cry harder.

"He's been acting strange for a while, so maybe it was my fault for not saying anything," she continues, voice muffled against her palms.

"Who was it, Naomi?"

She blows out a breath and straightens again. "His name is Marcus Luz. He's my maker. But you have to understand, he *never* would have done this. This isn't who he is. Something is wrong."

Reid meets my eyes across the room, and my breath catches.

Something is wrong.

A vampire draining other vampires. Forty in just a few weeks, if he's been working alone.

Magnolia had suggested I wasn't the only one the wendigos had targeted, but that was all the way back in York. Could it be the same ones? Are there *more*? Is this something else entirely?

"Thank you, Naomi. You've been very helpful."

Reid joins me by the door.

"He's not a bad person," Naomi says, her voice high. "Just, if you find him, I know you'll probably have to kill him, but he's not a bad person."

"I promise you, Naomi, killing him would be the last resort," says Reid. The hallway suddenly feels very quiet as he closes the door behind us.

"Do you think—" I start.

"Yes, I do."

I fill my lungs with air, my fingers itching for a cigarette. "You really think the queen will accept anything but an execution after this?"

Reid runs a hand under his jaw. "We'll just have to find a cure before we find him."

"Reid—"

"Even when he was out of control enough to drain all of those people—people he probably knew—he left her alive."

"You don't think it was an accident?" I ask.

"The bond with a maker is…" He shakes his head. "I don't think he could bring himself to kill her, even if in the moment, he didn't know why."

The bond between us warms as he says it, and I know he's right. Even in the darkest haze, I don't think I would be able to hurt him. At least, I have to believe that. That no matter what, I have at least that much of me left. That certain pieces of everyone remain intact.

"Do you think we should go check out that hotel?" I ask. "I mean, the guy is probably long gone by now, but maybe someone there..." I trail off because maybe there *isn't* anyone left there who would know something.

Maybe he already killed everyone who knew him.

The look on Reid's face tells me he's thinking the same thing, but he nods. "It's a place to start."

THERE ARE flowers on the side of the road. We pass the spot where we found the bodies where a shrine is already growing—pictures and candles and other offerings. A group of people lingers by the rocks, and they scowl at our car as we pass.

"So much for keeping things quiet," I mutter under my breath. The queen is not going to be happy.

"Someone filmed us cleaning up the bodies earlier," Reid says. "It's already all over the internet."

The car pulls up outside the towering hotel, the tallest building around for blocks. As we climb out onto the sidewalk, I'm consumed by the feeling someone is watching...*following*. I hesitate before stepping through the door, scanning the surrounding street. There's no one there. But then why is every hair on my body standing on end?

"Valerie?" Reid stands by the door, his frown lines deepening. I try to shake off the feeling as I follow him inside the vast and empty marble lobby. The only other person in the room is behind the check-in desk. The woman's head is tilted back, watching the TV mounted on the wall. A news reporter stands on the screen, the Brooklyn Bridge behind him.

"At least forty bodies have been recovered, all drained of blood," he says into the microphone. "Authorities suspect other attacks have been to blame for the disappearances on the rise throughout the city. We reached out to the Carrington estate, but no response so far."

Reid clears his throat as we approach the counter. The girl looks up, but her expression remains disinterested.

"Already talked to a few of your guys," she says, turning back to the TV and smacking her gum. A hint of a smile plays on her lips as she watches the broadcast.

She's human. I can smell that much.

"Did you know Marcus Luz?" I ask.

Her eyes flicker from us to the screen again. "Uh, yeah. He works here. Well, kind of. Dating the boss's daughter and all that."

"Have you seen him around lately?" asks Reid.

The girl snorts. "He's here almost every night."

"When's the last time you saw him?" I push, annoyance starting to tighten the muscles in my shoulders.

"I don't know. I had a few days off, so probably the last time I worked. Four days ago? What do you want with Marcus anyway? Is he in some kind of trouble?"

I can't tell if she's playing stupid or really couldn't care less about what's been going on under this very roof. According to Naomi, people have been disappearing left and right around here.

"Do you have a home address or a phone number?" Reid asks.

She sighs as if this is a major inconvenience, but gets up from her chair and heads for a door in the back.

The man on the TV keeps talking as the camera pans the area where the bodies had been earlier today. "Whoever is going on a killing spree through New York seems to be targeting vampires. Motive is unknown, as evidence points to the killer also being a vampire..."

The girl returns and slides a piece of paper across the counter to us. It looks like an old job application. Marcus's name is at the top, along with all of his personal information and a photo from the shoulders up.

"Thanks." Reid folds the paper and slides it into his pocket.

The girl falls back in her chair, attention on the TV, and snorts. "Funny, isn't it?"

"Funny?" Reid asks.

She shrugs and looks at us over her shoulder. "Looks like your kind is finally getting a taste of what it's like at the bottom of the food chain."

CHAPTER FOURTEEN

THE FIRST THING I do when Reid and I make it back to the estate is take off toward the human floor. I hesitate outside Connor's door for what feels like a long time, trying to muster up the courage to knock.

I don't blame him for not responding to me earlier. He was probably stressed about the review. But I was hoping he'd at least tell me how it went and reply to me once it was done. Hours have passed, and still, nothing.

You don't just go from being willing to die for someone to feeling nothing for them overnight.

Adrienne's right. I have to believe that. I have to believe we can make this work.

Taking a deep breath, I raise my fist to knock. I never get the chance to because the next thing I know, the door swings open. Connor looks unsurprised to see me and nods for me to come in. With his new vampire senses, he probably heard me standing out here and got tired of waiting for me.

My gaze locks on the two suitcases spread out on his bed and the duffel bag on the ground. I guess I shouldn't be surprised he'll no longer be on the human floor, but the thought still makes a lump rise to the back of my throat. This room has become as familiar to me as my own. I've spent as much time in it, maybe more. The pillow with the blue case is unofficially *my* pillow. I always get the right side of the bed. When he used to help me study, he'd sit at the little desk chair in the corner while I splayed out on his carpet. One of the drawers in the dresser is filled with clothes I like to sleep in, and there's extra makeup and moisturizer on the top.

My gaze slowly trails back to where he stands at the end of the bed. He picks up a shirt, folds it, and stuffs it into one of the suitcases.

I close the door behind me and lean against it. "Can we…talk?"

"Sure," he says, moving onto the next shirt.

He doesn't look at me. I don't know if it's intentional, or if the clothes he's folding are more interesting to him.

"Do you not feel anything when you look at me anymore?" I blurt out.

Finally, he stops folding and looks up. They're the same wide, blue eyes, but also not the same at all. The depth I used to see there, the emotion, it's gone. I used to *feel* it when he looked at me, like I could read what he was thinking. His eyes smiled even when he didn't.

He studies my face for what feels like a long time, as if it's something vaguely familiar and he's trying to place where he's seen it before. "I'm not trying to hurt you,

Valerie. I still…remember everything. I look at you, and I know you used to be someone important to me."

Used to be.

"I don't know how to explain it," he continues. "It feels like I'm remembering a story someone else told me. Not my own life. It's very detached. Detailed, but detached. And I know that must hurt you. And I do feel…sorry about that."

Slowly, I sink onto the chair beside the door, not trusting my legs to keep holding me up.

"So that's it then?" I whisper. "Twenty years of knowing me, twenty years of being my very best friend, and now you just don't care?" I can't help it. A tear breaks free and runs down my cheek. "A week ago, you loved me and were willing to die for me, and now you can hardly look at me? If this is about the final task—" My breath hitches, and I clutch my chest with one hand. "Connor, I'm *so* sorry. I can't even tell you how sorry I am. But please—"

"That's not it. Valerie, I don't blame you for that." He sits on the edge of the bed and turns his head away, looking more uncomfortable than anything else. "And I still care," he says quietly. "It just feels different now. I wouldn't want anything to happen to you. But I also don't want…"

"Me," I finish for him. "You don't want me anymore." I try to hold it together—for my pride's sake, if nothing else—but my lower lip starts to wobble, and I have to look away.

Maybe filling in the blanks in my mind *had* been better. Hearing him say it out loud is more gutting than any blade could be. All of those hopes I'd been clinging to for the past week deflate in my chest, sinking into the pit of my stomach until I feel like I'm going to be sick.

You guys will figure it out.

It could get better.

I don't think you should give up on him yet, Val. Keep trying. He's gotta still be in there somewhere.

I squeeze my eyes shut until colors burst behind my eyelids.

He doesn't respond, and silence fills the space between us for several moments. He stands again and goes back to folding his clothes. "I requested to be discharged from the estate. Now that I'm not human…well, my position doesn't fit anymore, and I have no interest in being an employed vampire here. They granted the request."

My head snaps up. "You're leaving?"

He yanks the zipper on one of the suitcases closed. "That was always the plan eventually, right?"

"When?"

"Whenever I can get myself set up somewhere else."

My heart aches at the memory of the last time we talked about this. His plans. His savings. He just wanted to feel safe. I suppose now as a vampire, at the least, he has that.

But for him to leave, for him to be gone for good—

"So that's it then?"

"For now, at least," he says. "I think getting some space away from all of this will be good."

Some space away from me, he means.

I know I don't have any right to be angry about this, to be upset. I'm the reason he's in this situation in the first place. *I'm* the reason he's changed. And if a fresh start is what he wants, that's the least of what he deserves.

At least, that's what I'm going to repeat over and over again to myself until I believe it.

"Well, good for you, Connor," I whisper and wipe the tears from my cheeks with the back of my hand. I need to get out of here before I have a full breakdown. Just the thought of not having him in my life—of having to do anything without him—of never getting to hear his laugh again—never feeling his arms around me again—never being able to go to him when I can't go to anyone else—

Suddenly, he's in front of me. He gets down on his knees and looks up at me through his lashes, and for a moment, he looks the way he used to. But that makes the tears come harder. He reaches up and brushes them away with his thumbs, his brow furrowing.

I let out a choked sob and squeeze my eyes closed.

"I think I'll always love you, in some way," he says. "And I'm sorry it can't be in the way you need anymore."

I nod and pull in a shaky breath. "I should go."

He releases my face, but instead of backing away, he leans forward and pulls me against his chest. All of the air rushes from my lungs as his familiar scent surrounds me, now tinged with something new.

It occurs to me this may be the last time I get to touch him like this, to be this close to him. It feels like my heart is cracking right open, and I want to beg him not to go. To stay, just a little while longer. Because I can't imagine a single piece of my life without him, and it's impossible to fathom that he can.

But I say nothing. I cling to his shirt and press my face into his chest, tucking myself into him for as long as he'll let me. And we stay there, him holding me and letting me cry, until I don't have any tears left.

———

THE ROOM IS UNBEARABLY HOT. It weighs down the air so much it's difficult to breathe. My head jerks, lolling against my chest, and I sit up straight. The bright lights overhead pierce my eyes. I try to lift a hand to shield them, but they're bound behind my back. I blink, trying to remember where I am, how I got here. Looking down at myself, I realize I'm tied to a metal chair, a drain beneath my feet.

My blood runs cold.

No.

My head whips back up, taking in the room around me, as my breaths come in short, harsh gasps. I yank against the ropes desperately, thrashing like a wild animal, trying to break free.

I can't be back here. Not again. *Not again.*

I must be dreaming. This can't be real.

The restraints dig into my wrists, stinging and cutting and pulling until blood runs down my fingertips and hot stabs of pain shoot up my arms.

It *feels* real.

Metal creaks as the door opens. Two men step into the room, each holding knives and smiling. I pull harder against the ropes at the sight of them, tears running down my face now. My chest heaves with each breath, but no oxygen reaches my lungs.

No. *No.*

"Please," I whisper.

They either don't hear me or don't care.

Oh God. *Oh God.* I can't go through this again. I can't.

They kneel on each side of me, talking to each other in Russian. The one on my right pushes my hair behind my shoulder, and I flinch. The other chuckles lowly as he skims the blade of his knife up my thigh, not quite breaking the skin, but pressing hard enough that every one of my nerves comes to life. My body trembles, and I squeeze my eyes closed.

This has to be a dream. I have to wake up.

The other one trails his knife along the side of my throat, then slowly brings it down my sternum. The moment it reaches my stomach, my entire body flinches, the memory all too sharp and fresh.

"Please stop," I whimper.

Then, without warning, he plunges the blade into my skin. Not a surface cut this time either. He shoves the blade straight into my abdomen, tearing through flesh and muscle and organs. I cry out as the pain blazes through me, and I choke on it. If this is a dream, why does it feel so real? My eyes fly open—

—to find Reid in the room. He's standing a few feet away, frozen, watching with a horrified expression. His gaze sweeps over every inch of me, his chest heaving with his breath. When he reaches my face, his eyes widen as he realizes I can see him.

The man digs the knife deeper, and I let out a small, choked sound, my head slumping against my chest.

Reid rushes forward and falls to his knees in front of me. Neither of the men flinches, so they must not be able to see him. He grabs my face with both hands.

"Wake. Up."

I whimper as the second man carves a line down my thigh.

Reid's fingers tighten and pull my face closer until our noses brush. His eyes are wide, wild. "Wake up, Valerie," he says. "Wake up."

I let out another choked sob, and he shakes me, his words coming out through his teeth. "*Wake up.*"

I gasp and lurch up in my bed, shivering and covered in sweat. Whipping my head back and forth, I take in the space around me. I can still feel the heat of that room, the bite of the blades, the man's breath as he leaned in close to my ear—

"Shh. Shh. You're okay. You're okay."

I startle as a presence climbs in beside me in the bed. Reid grabs the sides of my face, forcing me to look at him, like he had in the dream. I stare back at him, my breaths still coming in short, shaky gasps.

He studies my face. "You're safe," he whispers. "I've got you."

I can't stop shaking. He pulls me against his chest, his arms wrapping tightly around me, and tucks my head beneath his chin. "It was just a dream. You're okay."

It takes a few minutes for my breathing to calm and my body to stop trembling, but he just holds me there, murmuring in my ear over and over again.

Once I catch my breath, I whisper, "How did you…?"

He shakes his head. "I don't know. At first I was just seeing it…then I was there." He smooths his hand over the back of my head, and I press my face into his chest.

I don't have the space in my mind to try to comprehend

this. It almost feels like that night I'd woken up on his bedroom ceiling, but then I'd been asleep, and he'd been awake. I'd seen his dreams before too, back when I was taking my tests, but I never thought we could go *into* each other's dreams. My head spins. Every time I think I'm starting to understand this bond, something else happens.

"Do you get those a lot?" he asks, voice quieter now. "The nightmares?"

Slowly, I nod. I should probably pull back from him now that I've calmed down, but I don't think I could let go if I tried. My fingers are tightly wound around his shirt, holding myself to him like an anchor. My heart hammers in my chest, and I can still *smell* that room. Feel the bite of the ropes around my wrists. The sting of the blade still echoes on my skin. It had all felt so *real.*

"Is that where they took you?" he whispers.

I nod again, and his body stiffens, the muscles in his arms tightening around me. But then he pulls back enough to frame my face with his hands. Tears stick in my lashes, and my breath comes out shallow and small between us.

"I'm not going to let anything happen to you, okay?" he says, voice firm.

Another tear leaks out, and he presses his thumb to my cheek, trapping it.

"Okay?" he repeats, quieter this time.

I close my eyes, and he brings me back against his chest, his hold even tighter than it was before. I press my face against the side of his neck, focusing on the heat of his skin as I try to force my heart rate to return to normal.

"I know how you feel about glamours," he says after a

moment. "But if you ever wanted me to, I could make you forget, Valerie. I could probably make the nightmares stop."

Truthfully, it's tempting. But making me forget and making it so it didn't happen in the first place aren't the same thing. I don't think having a gap in my memory will solve anything. Because as much as I hate remembering what happened in that room, I don't think that's the reason the nightmares keep coming back.

It's the fact that there has been no trace of the Russians since. No hint as to where they are...or what they want. They could come back at any second, or not at all. And it's the uncertainty that has my shoulders tense constantly, my senses on high alert. There's no way this was the end of it.

Forgetting what they did to me won't protect me from whatever they have planned next.

Slowly, I shake my head.

"Okay." He runs his fingers through my hair and takes a deep breath.

I bring a hand to my face to wipe away the tears, and my fingers are still shaking.

"I can stay," he whispers.

My pride doesn't want to admit how much comfort the thought brings me. I don't know if it's having someone here that makes me feel more at ease, or if it's *him*. Whenever I used to have nightmares, I'd go crawl into Connor's bed. It was the only thing that would calm me down. The only thing that could make me feel better. The thought makes more tears rise to my eyes as I remember our conversation yesterday, and it occurs to me I might never be able to do that again.

My voice breaks as I whisper, "Just until I fall back asleep?"

"I'm here as long as you want." He runs his thumb up and down the back of my neck. The bond heats between us, a steady, comforting warmth. As my own heart starts to slow, I realize his is beating just as hard in his chest beneath my ear. Slowly, my thoughts quiet as his fingers stroke the back of my head over and over, until eventually, my eyes can't keep themselves open any longer, and sleep takes me once again.

CHAPTER FIFTEEN

"DARKMORE," someone hisses behind me. A pencil hits my shoulder and lands on my desk. I slowly turn around, and Daniel grins from the chair behind me. At least it's not just the two of us today. But even with the first years filling the rest of the desks, that still only brings us to a whopping six students.

What? I mouth.

Our teacher—I already can't remember her name—has her legs propped on the table at the front, a trashy romance book in her lap. Judging by the light snoring filling the room, she's as enthralled with this class as the rest of us. Even meeting once a week feels like too much.

But I especially don't want to be here today. Despite over a week having passed, that conversation with Connor is still fresh in my mind.

I haven't run into him since. Not once. And I can't decide if that's a mercy or not. The estate is big, but not that big. Maybe he just hadn't bothered to say goodbye, and he's already gone for good.

But no, Reid would've told me, at the very least. Connor's probably just avoiding me.

Which I guess would make sense because it wasn't just a conversation. It was a breakup. A hint of tension releases in my chest as I think the word—the first time I've allowed myself to since it happened.

Connor and I *broke up*.

For the first time in six years, we're no longer together.

We've never even kind of broken up before. No taking space or taking a break and then getting back together. Nothing ever even close to that.

And now, we're just done.

I suppose after the weeks of uncertainty following my final trial, I should be happy I have an answer now.

I should be.

Daniel leans forward and flashes me his perfectly straight smile. "Let's get out of here."

I snort and start to turn back around, but he reaches forward and pokes me with his pen. "I'm serious. You really think she'll notice?" He nods at our teacher, who may or may not be drooling.

I glance back at the book on the table in front of me. I guess reading the material here and reading it in my room later aren't that different.

In some small act of grace, the nightmares have left me alone since that night with Reid. Probably because my brain is now too preoccupied trying to process this latest shift in my life.

When I'd woken up the next day, Reid was already

gone. For a moment, I felt like I'd imagined the whole thing. But there was no missing the redness and puffiness in my face, which is how I've looked every day since.

Hence the hat and extra concealer.

I suppose I should be grateful Reid has been gone the past week, off with a few other members of the estate to Locklear in Alaska. Although geographically our two regions are pretty distant—a fourteen-hour flight, on a good day—we've had the strongest alliance among the estates for decades. They have a few members from the Carrington estate attend any time they amend their policies. As a show of good faith, or because they actually want their input, who knows?

A run-in with him after he spent the night in my bed would've been awkward, but honestly, I miss having him around. Which is probably pretty stupid, seeing as a little over a month ago, he wasn't even a part of my life.

A month. All of this has happened in just a month. I can't wrap my head around it.

I close the book on my desk.

Daniel appears at my side a moment later and grabs my bag off the ground, looking far too pleased with himself. He holds it open so I can shove my book inside, then we slip out of the room, not bothering to see if the other students are watching us.

We stay silent as we exit the library, but as I turn away from him in the hall, he hooks his arm around my elbow.

"Nope. You are officially stuck with me for the evening."

I sigh. "Daniel—"

His smile falls. "Are you really telling me you don't want to get out of here for a while? It looks like you could use it."

My cheeks warm because I know it's all over my face. What's worse is the pity in his eyes. Everyone knows about Connor at this point. Maybe not exactly what happened, but they've seen him around the estate.

They've seen the two of us obviously not together.

And I don't want the pity. Especially not from Daniel.

I elbow him in the ribs. "Don't go all soft on me now, Abney."

He grins and throws his arm around my shoulders, crushing me against his side. "I gave you, like, two weeks to mope. But that's all you're getting from me."

"What are we doing? Is it illegal?"

He squeezes me again as he steers us toward the doors. "Only a little."

"Daniel, what the hell are we doing here?"

The car drops us off on a corner, and horns blare as we climb out. Daniel starts down the street, not bothering to see if I'm following. I recognize the building on our right immediately—Memphis Tattoos. The open sign glows in the window, and as I pass, I meet the eyes of an older man through the glass. Three red lines are tattooed on his cheekbone, almost like claw marks. He scowls at me, then quickly releases the shades in his hand, covering the window.

This, apparently, is not where we're going, because Daniel is still several yards ahead of me.

"Daniel." I grab his arm.

"Chill, Darkmore. We're here." He turns, leading me to the side of an old apartment building. A cat—or I'm hoping it's a cat—rustles through something near the dumpster at the end of the alley as Daniel jumps and grabs hold of the fire escape. Screeching metal fills the air as he pulls the ladder down.

"Okay, Wes might be down to be your partner in crime for whatever the hell the two of you are always doing, but I am not—"

He nudges me toward the ladder. "Shut up and climb."

I huff but grab the rungs and start pulling myself up. Daniel follows along behind me, instructing me where to go as we scale the side of the building. Someone clearly propped and secured a few of the ladders in places they don't belong. Whatever this is, someone uses it frequently. Luckily, the building is only four floors, so it doesn't take long. Daniel heads up the final ladder first, then reaches a hand down to help me over the edge.

The roof is scattered with mismatched chairs, and a line of potted plants takes up the center. Upon closer inspection, I realize the plants *aren't* taking up all the space. They're surrounding something. Various boxes and supplies sit in the middle—herbs, crystals, chemicals, books. Looks like some kind of meeting ground for witches.

I quirk an eyebrow at Daniel over my shoulder. He grabs a chair and plops into it, leaning his head back to take in the stars overhead. A makeshift mini golf course is set up behind him.

"How the hell did you find this place?" I ask.

Metal clanks behind me before he can respond, and I turn as several other people climb onto the roof, one after the other. My muscles tense, but Daniel swings his head back around and smirks.

"Took you long enough," he says.

There's five of them in total, all of whom I've never seen before. But judging by their scents drifting to me on the breeze, they're all witches.

A beefy guy with curly black hair sets a bag down near the plants. He nods at me as he digs out a bottle of bourbon. "Who's the princess?"

A nearly identical guy squats beside him and pulls a second bottle from the bag. They must be twins, I decide. Or siblings, at the very least.

Daniel snorts. "Dude, that's Valerie Darkmore. She could end you."

"No shit?" The guy grins, looking more like an eager puppy than a threat now as he bounds over to me, holding out his hand. "Emery Davis. Pleased to make your acquaintance."

My eyebrows lift, but I shake his hand.

"Just a lowly skinwalker like your boy Daniel over there," he adds. "Let me introduce you to the crew. That's Jago." He points to his lookalike. "Darius." The beanpole of a guy next to him nods. "That's—"

The little blonde girl steps forward and holds out her hand to me. "Petra. And this is Winnie." The curvy brunette beside her waves.

"You got tired of losing?" Petra calls, looking at Daniel now. "Your boyfriend wasn't much better, so you bring a blood witch?"

"I mean, yeah." Daniel gives her a lazy grin. "Darkmore's totally gonna kick all of your asses, but she's cool."

Jago pours some whiskey in a plastic cup and offers it to me. I take it, eyes shooting to their arms even though I know I won't find the Marionettes markings on them. "Welcome to the party."

Music trickles from a Bluetooth speaker as conversation fills the roof. I sip my drink and wander over to Daniel, still lingering by the golf setup, though now he's sitting on the ground with his back propped against the wall. I sink down beside him, and he smiles, sipping his own drink, but there's a heaviness in his eyes that wasn't there before.

How long has he been coming here and hanging out with these people? How does he know them? What's probably most surprising is how they seem to like him. Most witches outside the Marionettes hate the ones who are in.

The others are crowded over near the edge, having a conversation with someone down on the street.

"Friends of yours?" I say.

"Used to live here before my mom got initiated. Most people didn't want to keep in touch. Figured I'd follow after her, you know?" He juts his chin toward the others. "But they're cool."

"You usually come here with Wes?"

He laughs. "All it took was one night here, and they all like him more than they like me."

"Hate to break it to you, but that's about to happen again." I pull my knees into my chest and gesture to myself.

He bumps his shoulder against mine, and I smile, a little touched he brought me to meet them.

"*So*," he says. "Do we want to talk about the whole thing with your no-longer-human boyfriend, or is that off-limits?"

I slump against the wall. "Ex-boyfriend."

"Ah, shit. I'm sorry. I figured as much, but I was hoping you guys were just fighting or something. You were together for, like, ever."

I take a long sip of my drink.

"Looks like you've got another prospect though," he continues, his voice light. He glances at me sideways. "Too soon?"

I snort. "What are you talking about?"

"Oh, please, Darkmore. You're not blind."

I stare at him.

He widens his eyes and sets his drink on the ground beside him. "You've got to be kidding me. You've seen the way his *royal highness* looks at you."

His royal highness…?

"Pfft." I wave my hand, but my stomach flips a little. "He's my partner. You know how the bond is."

"Uh, yeah. And I like Warren. But I'm not constantly eye-fucking him."

I shove his arm. "You're an idiot. And you have no idea what you're talking about."

"Actually, I think *you* have no idea."

"What do you think, Abney?" calls one of the twins. "You up for a rematch?"

"Dude, we just got here," says Daniel.

"Sounds like an excuse to me," says Winnie.

"He's too afraid to lose," agrees Petra.

My gaze bounces back and forth, trying to keep up. "What are they talking about?"

"You didn't even explain the rules to her?" demands Petra.

"We're just hanging out," says Daniel. "I'm sure Valerie's not interested in your stupid competition."

"A competition of...mini golf?" I ask, looking over at the course.

"Oh no," says Daniel. "Not here. But we have a..." He tilts his head to the side, as if debating the wisdom of his next words. "Tradition around here."

"Anyone who comes up here has to play," agrees one of the twins as he tilts his cup back and finishes the rest of his drink. "It's like an initiation."

I lift an eyebrow. "So why don't you think I want to play?"

"See, she wants to play!" calls Winnie.

"Yeah, Daniel," the twins say simultaneously.

Daniel shakes his head, but he's smiling. "You guys are the worst."

"So, it's settled!" announces Petra.

"Don't worry." The skinny one steps up, his grin so wide he looks like a cartoon, and slaps a hand on my back. "We'll go easy on you."

———————

SOMEONE LETS OUT A LOW *WHOOP!* to our left as all of the bowling pins in their lane clatter together and fall.

"Here we are." Emery slides two pitchers of beer onto our table while the rest of us lace up our rental shoes.

I stand to go find a ball, but Daniel catches my wrist. "Jago and Darius will grab them."

I spread my narrow fingers in front of his face. "Uh, I doubt we'll be the same fit."

His smile grows. "Trust me, that won't be a problem."

"All right, Darkmore." Emery squats in front of me and clamps his hands together. "You guys have me on your team tonight, so you better not let me down."

My eyebrows lift. "You guys take your bowling really seriously, huh?"

"Not just any bowling," Winnie informs me as she takes the seat on my other side, apparently also on our team.

"You have to use your magic for each turn," explains Daniel.

"No human body parts touch the balls," says Emery. "That's the only rule."

Darius and Jago chuckle behind them.

Petra smacks them in the chest. "Oh, grow up!"

"You get bonus points for how creative each turn is too," says Winnie.

"I'll show her how it's done," Jago announces.

Emery leans back in his chair. "He does the same thing every time," he mutters as his brother saunters up to the line of balls.

Jago glances at me over his shoulder and winks, his fingers twisting some kind of rock hanging around his neck. He focuses on a neon yellow ball, and I lean forward, squinting at it. The surrounding air turns blurry for a moment, then the ball shifts, its edges softening like it's no longer solid.

Jago takes a step back, and the ball follows over the

edge like some kind of Slinky, stretching down until it reaches the floor.

I stare, wide-eyed, as Jago flicks his fingers and leisurely heads for the lane, the ball—if it can even be called that anymore—slithering after him. As it reaches the lane, he tightens his hand into a fist, solidifying it back into a ball. With a swing of his arm, it takes off for the pins, knocking them all down in one go.

He turns back to us and does a little bow. His teammates erupt in applause, but Daniel, Emery, and Winnie roll their eyes, clearly not impressed.

He must be an alchemist.

"Lame," says Emery, but he high-fives his twin as he returns to his seat.

Winnie claps as Emery heads for the balls, and Daniel leans toward me, a smirk pulling at one corner of his mouth. "Don't be fooled. Emery also does the same thing every time."

As he says it, Emery's form shifts midstride, and a gray wolf takes his place. The bowlers at the lanes next to us hardly give him a second glance as he guides the ball with his tail. Once it's properly lined up, he turns away, hunches down, and launches it forward with his back paws.

It shoots straight, knocking all but one pin down. He turns and growls.

"Hey! Guys, really?"

I whip my head up as an older man with graying hair and a widening midsection calls down at us from the eating areas. His hands are on his hips, but his expression is less than surprised.

Daniel holds up his palms. "Sorry, Benny!"

Emery shifts back and smooths his hands over his clothes. "I didn't even scratch the floor!"

The man—Benny, apparently—mumbles something under his breath and heads back behind the food counter.

"He's the owner," Daniel explains. "He puts on a good show, but he doesn't actually give a shit what we do."

"You ever get mistaken for a were?" I ask as Emery collapses into the seat next to me, waiting for his ball to return.

He scoffs and brings one hand to his chest. "Low blow, Darkmore. Low blow."

"What?" I ask.

Daniel nudges me with his knee. "Kind of poor form to compare walkers and weres. Macavei never taught you that?"

"Well, she shifts into a cat, so," I deadpan. "I've never met a wolf."

Emery puffs his chest up and lifts his chin. "It's rare."

Daniel snorts. "And you know that, how? You've never met another one?"

"Have *you*?" Emery counters.

"Not in New York," Daniel admits. "But New York isn't the whole world, bro."

Emery beams as he gets up to retrieve his ball. "Isn't it though?"

Petra from the other team goes next, making short work of her turn by summoning enough wind to blow the ball down the lane. An elemental witch then. Though she only manages to knock down eight pins.

"All right, princess." Emery pats my leg. "You're up."

"You want some pointers?" Daniel asks on my other side.

"I think I'm good."

"Yeah, man, back off," says Emery.

The rest of the group quiets as I walk up, straight past the line of balls. This would be a lot easier if the pins were, say, *alive*, but I can make do. I don't want to cause any lasting damage to the place either. Something tells me Benny back there already has his hands full with his usual clientele. I flip the blade out of my ring and dig a line in my palm. As the blood wells in my hand, I close my eyes, trying to imagine the pins' makeup. All I need is for them to be a *little* off balance…

I squeeze my hand into a fist and open my eyes.

The pins tip and fall.

I turn and find them all staring at me.

"That counts, right?" I ask. "I didn't touch the balls."

Emery nods slowly. "You did not touch the balls."

Shouts ring out somewhere near the front, followed by a loud *thud*.

"What now?" Benny mutters, throwing his apron onto one of the metal tables and taking off running toward the door.

I exchange a look with Daniel.

"I don't know about you guys," he says, "but I'm not missing that."

The rest of the group scrambles to their feet, taking off after Benny, Daniel and I taking up the rear. Glass shatters, and someone grunts.

"Get the hell out of here!" a deep voice yells.

"What's the problem?" Benny demands.

I skid to a stop beside Daniel as we reach the front of the bowling alley. A broad-shouldered man is holding a slightly smaller man back, pinning his arms. A teenage boy with unruly dark hair is hunched on all fours on the ground, blood dripping out of the corner of his mouth, his fangs extended.

I suck in a sharp breath and tighten my hands into fists at my sides. The heady scent of his blood hits me like a train. My gums *ache* with the sudden, intense need for it.

"Benny," grits out the man still being held back by his friend. "You really gonna let their kind in here? You've seen the news." He shakes out of the other guy's hold, and my muscles tense. I wait for him to take another swing, but he just spits onto the floor.

"What I don't let in here is fighting," says Benny.

I stumble back a step, the roaring in my ears too loud to make out whatever he says next.

"Valerie?" Someone tugs on my wrist, and I quickly turn away.

My vision tunnels, the edges turning red. I need to find a bathroom or somewhere I can pull myself together. Preferably not surrounded by witches whose blood smells as good as that vampire's.

Voices layer behind me as the argument continues, but I push through the crowd, a painted restrooms sign hanging a few paces away. I let out a breath of relief as I step inside and find it empty, but that relief is short-lived as the door swings open behind me, and Daniel steps inside.

"Hey—"

I hold a hand between us and back up until I hit the far wall. "I need you to stay back."

Daniel shows me his palms like I'm holding him at gunpoint. "What the hell, Val?"

"Daniel, just go," I growl through my teeth. My chest rises and falls rapidly as my mouth begins to water.

How stupid could I be? Here I was going about my everyday life, thinking I was keeping the hunger under control. As if I have *any* control whatsoever in any of this.

Daniel takes another step, and the scent of him catches the air just right. My fangs extend right into my lip, and blood fills my mouth. A low growl sounds in the back of my throat of its own accord.

Daniel goes still.

I stare at him, wide-eyed and unable to move.

He searches my face for a moment, then slowly backs up. At first, I think he's going to run for it, but he calmly turns the lock on the door, then faces me again.

"Okay," he says. "Now tell me what the fuck is going on."

"I mean it, Daniel. Leave."

"Or what?" He waves his hand toward me. "You'll bite me?"

I say nothing, panic mounting in my chest. My eyes flick to the door he's blocking, then around the room. The only window is the one behind me, so small I'm not sure I could fit, and *fuck*, I can hear his heart rate getting faster from here. But when I look at his face, he seems perfectly calm.

"How long?"

I almost laugh. "The vampire thing or the hunger thing?"

His eyebrows rise. "They're different?"

"Well, as far as the hunger goes, it looks like both of us got some souvenirs from attacks on campus."

He leans against the door as understanding washes over his face. "Does anyone else know about this?"

"Reid," I say quietly. "And Monroe."

Voices sound on the other side of the door, and he straightens.

"How much do you need?" he asks.

"Daniel—"

But he's already rolling up his sleeve and walking toward me. "For fuck's sake, Darkmore, just let me be the one to sweep in and save the day for once. I've been the damsel in distress one too many times lately."

I meet his eyes, and he flashes me a crooked smile. The hunger decides for me, and I cross the rest of the distance between us.

"You're going to hold this over me forever, aren't you?" I say as I grab his wrist.

He shrugs. "I think we can call it even for now."

The moment his blood hits my mouth, the hunger lurches forward, desperate to take over. I breathe through my nose, forcing myself to stay present. Forcing myself to see Daniel's face in front of me instead of an artery waiting to be torn open.

Once I think I've had enough to at least get me through the rest of the day, I pull away and put a few feet of distance between us. He stumbles back against the sinks, and at first, I'm worried I took too much. But then I notice the slight haze settling over his eyes—it's the venom.

"You good?" I ask.

His grin widens to fill his face. "Oh, I'm grand, Darkmore."

"Let me at least heal that before anyone sees." I grab his arm again, prick one of my fingers, and let the drop of blood fall onto the cut.

"What does that make you now?" he murmurs. "A halfling—?"

"*Shh*," I hiss.

"What? I mean, it's uncommon, but it's not like it's illegal."

"Reid seems to think me being a blood witch makes it more complicated." I hesitate, staring at the side of Daniel's face. Reid is so going to kill me when he finds out how well I've kept to his *don't tell anyone* advice. But seeing as I can now feel the warmth of Daniel's blood *inside* of me, I think we're already past that. "He didn't turn me. Not really, at least. When we did the blood exchange, it just…happened."

His eyes are wide open now and staring at me. "Well, that's strange."

"You think? Wait, how do you know anything about halflings in the first place?"

He swallows, sobering a bit, and glances back at the door. He bites his lip before responding, as if debating his next words. "Winnie's one."

"Wait, *what*?"

He gives me a hard look. "And she doesn't like people to know."

I hold up my palms, though my mind is now spinning in a million different directions.

"But yeah, her dad's a vamp. He left when we were kids, and she and her mom have always kept that kind of quiet, you know? Didn't want to draw any extra attention, especially since they had no desire for her to join the Marionettes. I mean, you'd think with all of the witch and vamp couples, it would be more common, right? But the kid usually comes out as one or the other. So I get wanting to avoid the spectacle. I'm sure Queen Carrington would take interest in one in her territory…" He trails off and glances back at me, a question in his eyes.

"No, the queen doesn't know. And she's not going to find out."

He nods and stands up straighter. "No one will hear it from me. But how does being a blood witch play into it?"

A shiver runs up my spine, and I wrap my arms around myself. "I don't know for sure." I clear my throat and lower my voice again. "Reid said there were legends about it. That being half blood witch and half vampire was nature's way of preserving the necromancers after they went extinct. Like an evolution. And according to him, that execution was not an accident. So if the vampires saw them as a threat, then they'd probably feel the same way about me."

I don't know why I'm telling this to Daniel all of a sudden, but a weight lifts from my chest the moment I do. I guess a part of me hadn't wanted to talk about it with Kirby or Monroe. I didn't want to give them anything else to worry about on top of everything that's already happened.

"So do you think that's true?" he asks, his voice barely a whisper. "That you can…?"

I fill my lungs with air. "I know it's true."

He stares at me. "That's intense."

I lean against the sink beside him. "Not really how I pictured my initiation panning out, for sure."

"Well, if you wanted me to—and she's totally going to attempt to murder me after I tell her I told you, so I hope you're right about your nifty new powers—but I could ask Winnie if she'd talk to you. About this. I mean, I don't think she knows anyone else who is…you know…either."

For some reason, the thought makes my throat feel tight. We might not be in the exact same boat, but it's probably the closest I'll come to finding someone going through something similar to me. I hadn't considered the possibility of finding another half vampire. Hadn't considered the possibility there would be another one out there. And for her to be this close? The skeptic in me screams this can't be a coincidence, but stronger still is the curiosity. To be able to talk through this with her, even if for just a few minutes, to know if she's experienced all of the same things I have…

"That would be really cool, actually," I whisper.

He nods, and I nod back. We look at each other, then away.

"Right, well." He clears his throat.

"You think they're still fighting out there?"

The last remains of the venom-haze clears. "Honestly? If these attacks around the city continue, I think it's only going to get worse from here."

CHAPTER SIXTEEN

I SPEND the next several days religiously checking my phone. Daniel gave Winnie my number, and every time my phone chimes—a picture from Kirby of her trip, Monroe complaining about one of her professors, or Reid telling me he's flying back in tonight—my neck practically snaps from how quickly I look at it. But it's never her.

I can understand her hesitation. But she has to be at least a fraction as curious about me as I am about her, right?

But I guess if this is something she's been dealing with her entire life, maybe it's old news. Maybe she's mad at Daniel for telling me. Maybe—

My phone chimes.

I leap across the room and snatch it from my bed. A text from an unknown number waits on the screen.

The roof. 4am.

And that's it.

At least, until a few seconds later, when a second message appears.

Come alone.

The words burrow a chill under my skin that stays there for the rest of the night, until finally, the time comes, and I teleport myself into the alley Daniel had taken me to. I could've tried going directly to the roof, but if I somehow missed, even by a little…

Not worth the chance.

I blink, loose gravel cutting into my knees. Drunk voices carry over, and the bar across the street vibrates with music. My nose scrunches at the stench of rotting food coming from the dumpster beside me, and I quickly push myself back to my feet.

The noise from the street grows louder as I approach, but no one pays me any mind as I grab the ladder and start climbing. The metal screeches beneath me, and despite the bustle of the city carrying on once I reach the top, there's something inherently more peaceful about it from up here.

Winnie isn't here yet, so I pace around. Everything looks pretty much the same as the last time I was here. My phone says it's 4:00 a.m. on the dot. I blow the air out of my cheeks and do another lap around the roof, my hands starting to get jittery.

Maybe I should've double-checked with Daniel that was her number. Maybe she changed her mind and isn't going to show.

The metal ladder screeches behind me. Winnie meets my eyes over the edge of the roof and hesitates a moment before climbing the rest of the way up. Unlike the other night with her skinny jeans and trendy top, tonight she's in matching black sweats, the hood drawn up over her head. They fit snugly to her curves, and her brown hair spills out the neckline in thick curls.

"Thanks for meeting me," I say.

She doesn't respond. At first, I think she's ignoring me, but then I realize she's chanting something under her breath, her eyes trained on the moon over our heads. I take a hesitant step back, my heart beating a little faster in my chest, but then she stops abruptly and looks at me with a sheepish smile.

"Sorry. We're alone. Just making sure no one could listen in."

My eyes slowly trail from her to the moon and back again. "You're a lunar witch," I say.

She nods and takes a seat on the brick ledge surrounding the plants in the center of the roof. When I don't move, she gestures for me to join her.

"I don't have a lot of time," she says.

"I'm sorry if this put you in a weird spot." I take a seat a respectful distance away and tuck my hands under my thighs, suddenly desperate for a smoke. "Daniel said you don't like to talk about it."

"Well yeah, with him. But he's an idiot." She grins, and the remaining tension between us dissipates as I return it. "He said you probably had some questions. I don't know how helpful I'll be, but we can give it a go."

I let out a small laugh. "I don't even know where to start. When did you—*how* did you—I mean, did you turn, or—"

"So my mom's a witch. Lunar, obviously. There's not a lot of information out there about halflings, but from what

I've seen over the years, the child is usually one or the other, and they typically take after the mom. My sister, she's a lunar. And that's what my mom had expected with me. Imagine her surprise when I came out a vamp."

"Wait, so you were born with it?"

She presses her hands together between her knees and nods. "Didn't know about my witch side until I was thirteen. One full moon, and suddenly, everything felt different. So you obviously started out all witch?"

"Yeah, until I did the blood exchange with my partner for initiation. He thinks the blood woke that part of me up."

Winnie frowns, and there's something eerily familiar about the scrunch her nose makes with the expression. "Interesting."

"So your dad's a vamp?" I ask.

She shrugs. "As far as I know. I don't remember him at all. He skipped out shortly after I was born."

"Oh." I swallow hard. "I'm sorry."

"Don't be," she says, voice light. "Heard pretty much the same thing about yours, right?"

"Yeah."

"Men suck," she says matter-of-factly. "Pun not intended."

I let out a snort, and drunken laughter echoes on the street beneath us. Winnie turns to glance over the side of the roof, and the wind picks up and scatters her hair into her face.

Her words and what they imply makes me pause. Her vampire side obviously came from her dad, but my dad's a skinwalker. Is that something that could skip a generation or two and get passed down? Where the hell did my vampire gene come from? If it was further up the family tree, it could be on either side of the family. But if it had been on Mom's blood witch side, I guess it wouldn't be surprising if they'd kept it a secret for the same reasons I am.

It's not something I can outright *ask* Mom. Not without her finding out. And telling her would most likely go one of two ways: she'd do everything to help me keep it a secret.

Or she'd be the first to tell the queen.

I shake my head, trying to clear it. "How do you get blood then?"

"My family has always been super generous. My mom and sister each *donate* a bag to me, so to speak, if I'm in a pinch. And there are some...*lesser-known* markets, especially on this side of town. We have a guy. God." She scrunches her nose again. "Makes it sound so sketchy. *I know a guy.*" She rolls her eyes at herself. The amusement in her expression fades as she looks at me. "I imagine that's been challenging for you at the estate. Keeping it secret. Especially with all of those stories about the half blood witches."

"You know about that?"

"Girl, I've been a halfling my whole life. Leaves plenty of time for research."

I blow the air out of my cheeks. "Yeah, well, it hasn't been ideal. I mainly get, well, from my partner."

The corner of her mouth quirks. "You're paired with the prince, right?"

I nod.

"Hmm."

I raise an eyebrow. "Hmm?"

She shrugs innocently. "I've never seen him. Just heard he's really hot."

I snort. "Now you sound like Daniel."

She digs in her eyebrows. "Daniel's got a thing for the prince?"

I laugh. "No—uh—I mean—never mind. Anyway, I know why *I* have to keep it a secret, but why do you? It's not like being half-lunar has the same...reputation."

She tilts her head to the side. "It might not be a death sentence, but it's still...I don't know. My mom didn't want all of that attention on me. When I was younger, she was worried the queen might snag me and pull me into that program the estate has for younger witches that basically funnels them into the Marionettes, just out of curiosity. She's always been paranoid about it."

Metal clashes against metal as someone tosses trash in the dumpster below us, and Winnie rises to her feet. "I should get going." She studies me over her shoulder for another moment. "But I'm around, if you ever need to talk. Feel free to text me."

"Thanks, Winnie," I say. "I appreciate that."

She frowns, then heads for the ladder again. "Just be careful, okay?" And with that, she disappears down the side of the building.

The ruckus from the street below feels twice as loud in her absence as the bar door opens and a drunk group of friends piles onto the street. I should probably get going too, but instead, I ease a cigarette out of my bag and light up, watching as the smoke curls up toward the moon above me.

THE ESTATE IS quiet the following day. I spend the early evening scrolling through the *twenty* videos Kirby sent me while I was asleep, giving me tours of the Thailand estate and surrounding town, her rosy cheeks occasionally popping into frame as she grins and whispers to the camera like we're in on some kind of secret.

Once I roll myself out of bed, my eyes land on the massive folder abandoned on my floor. I have a few weeks before the representatives meeting, but I still feel woefully underprepared.

After I shower and pull myself together, I tuck everything into my backpack and head out toward the garden. A few human servants are milling about on the grounds as I cross the grass, and there's a few people swimming laps in the outdoor pool, but that's it.

I spread a blanket on top of the hill that looks down at the estate, then dig my study materials and snacks from the bag. Maybe I've been having such a hard time trying to focus in my room. The fresh air could help.

Twenty minutes of staring at the books later, it quickly becomes apparent that was not the issue. Groaning, I lie back, willing the earth to swallow me whole. When that doesn't happen, I prop the open book on my face instead. Maybe my brain will absorb the information through osmosis.

I think deep down, I know this isn't really about the meeting. It's not some kind of written exam or secret test. I've passed initiation. The trials are done. But right now, with so many things happening around me that I have no control over, here's this one thing I do.

And I can't even manage to remember the damn names.

Footsteps crunch through the leaves, and my muscles tense for a moment before that familiar heat passes through the bond. His presence settles in beside me, but I don't look up. I wonder when their flight got in, because up until now, the feeling through the bond hasn't led me to believe he was close by.

"Sorry to interrupt your meditation," he says.

"I'm not meditating," I mumble, my voice muffled by the book. "I'm waiting to die."

"Ah. Much more practical."

Papers rustle beside me, and I slide my head out enough to see Reid pick up the stack of papers and shuffle through it. He looks strikingly...*casual* today. Dark jeans, black T-shirt, and his hair is standing up like he ran his hands through it a million times.

"You writing a novel?" he muses.

I scowl, then drop the book back over my face. "You know, this is *your* fault. The only reason I have to be in that stupid meeting in the first place is because of you."

"All right, then let me help."

"You can't. I'm doomed."

He shuffles the papers some more. "Come on." When I still don't move, he reaches over and pries the book from my face.

"It was a lot more peaceful when you were gone," I mutter, but shove myself into a seated position beside him.

He points to the papers on the ground in front of us, now separated into two piles. "This one," he says, picking up the larger of the two, "you can forget about. You don't need it. I don't know why they gave you all of this information to begin with. No offense, but you probably won't even talk in this meeting. The hard part is, we won't know *which* representatives will be there until pretty last minute, but it'll be good for you to learn all of their names eventually anyway." He leans forward to grab the other stack of papers, his hair falling into his eyes as he flips through it again. "A lot of this meeting is a formality, but they *will* probably broach a few new topics that need to be voted on. Trade agreements. Funding for the Marionettes academies. Border security."

His next words die on his lips at whatever he sees on my face. He gives me a small smile. "One thing at a time. Like I said, you'll probably just sit there. I'd focus on the names first."

He hands me the stack of papers, and I nod, staring at the one on top.

After a moment, he asks, "How are you holding up?"

"Fine," I say a little too quickly. "How was your trip?"

He snorts. "About as interesting as your studying, I imagine."

I glance up, but he's not looking at me anymore. His arms are propped on his knees, his gaze trained somewhere on the grounds.

"I talked to a few people while I was gone, and they pointed me toward a specialist from Auclair. He works with a lot of other creatures, but he specializes in wendigos."

My eyes snap to his face.

"Of course," he sighs, "he's been on some expedition, and they don't know exactly where he's at right now. They think somewhere in Northern Canada, but they can't get ahold of him. He's due back to Auclair in a few weeks though, so I'm hoping I can talk to him then."

Weeks. "Oh."

"I know it's not—I just thought you should know."

"No, thank you for telling me," I say. "It's…something, right?"

The breeze picks up around us, and he grabs the papers before they can fly off, a line forming in his forehead as he looks at his hands. "How are things with your mom?"

A jolt goes through me at the sudden change in subject, but the surprise quickly sours in the pit of my stomach. "I haven't seen her since the trial. Why?"

He frowns and shakes his head. "I ran into her on my way over here. She asked about you."

My spine straightens. "Asking what, exactly?"

"Just how you were doing." His face twists like he's debating his next words. "She seemed to…mean it."

I swallow hard against the tightness in the back of my throat. I don't care if she's asking about me. I don't even care if she actually *does* care all of a sudden. It's a little too late for that. "I have no desire to talk to her."

"I don't blame you."

Another beat of silence passes between us. Sighing, I lie back down on the blanket, tracing the lines of stars with my eyes. A moment later, Reid lies next to me, his shoulder barely brushing mine, and the woodsy trace of his after-shave floods my senses. My eyes close and my heart rate slows at the smell of it. It's calming, for some reason.

"I can go, if you wanted to be alone," he says.

"No," I respond, almost too quickly. "It's—it's okay. I just wanted some fresh air."

"You want me to quiz you?"

I groan. "Yeah. Just let me wallow in self-pity for a little bit longer first, okay?"

He chuckles, and when he speaks again, his voice comes out so low it's barely audible. "We can lie here as long as you want to."

CHAPTER SEVENTEEN

THE FOLLOWING weeks pass in a blur of classes with Daniel, studying with Reid, and doing extra wendigo-related research every spare moment. And no matter how many FaceTimes or texts I get from Kirby and Monroe, I feel their absence more and more every day. I don't know if we've ever been apart for this long since we became friends. Some of the other students hanging around the estate this summer have been living it up, heading to different bars in the city every other night, but with everything else going on, the idea of going out isn't even appealing anymore.

I slam my face into the open book in front of me and let out a groan. Someone at a table nearby hushes me, but at this point, I think I'd prefer getting kicked out of the library. The meeting with the visiting estates' representatives is coming up, and despite the flashcards Reid helped me make, I still keep getting half the names mixed up. I've been officially paired with him for a few months, and they're already going to replace me for being utterly incompetent.

In addition to the names, I've been trying to familiarize myself with the list of topics for the meeting. But all they gave me on these sheets are brief bullet points, and I don't know what half of them mean, leaving me to fall into a two-hour pit of research on my laptop each time.

There are a couple of different agreements among the estates—the largest being the alliance. All of the other estates get to keep their royal families and maintain control over their individual regions as long as they honor the peace treaty and acknowledge the ruler of the Carrington estate as the ultimate authority. But representatives from the different estates all come together to vote on new policies when there's enough support for them.

Seeing as Queen Carrington's ties outside of the regions and her armies are supposed to provide protection for all of the estates in the alliance, and there have been more breaches to the borders than ever, it seems a lot of people are unhappy.

It's hard enough to wrap my head around all of the different politics from estate to estate, let alone all of the different agreements Queen Carrington has with groups outside of the region—pack masters, tribes—but it's clear no one else has anywhere near the number of connections she does, something she's used as leverage for decades.

"How's it going down there?"

I jerk upright in my seat. Quinn is standing beside my table, a pile of books tucked against her chest and a small smirk resting on her lips.

"Catastrophic," I say.

She nods, turning her head sideways to see the book. "Politics were never my strong suit either. I *did*, unfortunately, pick up quite a bit of the whole foreign affairs thing when I was helping Reid learn." She slides into the seat beside me and sets her books on the table. "Want some help?"

"Oh." I wave a hand in front of my face. I must have looked really pathetic for her to take pity on me like this. "It's okay. It's this meeting coming up. I'm going to look like an idiot."

"You have a study guide?" she pushes.

I slide it out of my notebook and hand it to her.

Quinn leans forward again, reaching for my textbook. Her red hair falls over her shoulder, and a wave of her scent hits me—her shampoo, sweat…blood.

I inhale a sharp breath and lock my jaw. She takes the book in her hands and looks at me again. I quickly rifle through my backpack and pull out my water bottle. I've been adding Magnolia's herbs at the start of every day, just in case it hits me out of nowhere like at the bowling alley again.

I chug the water, wincing at the weird smell of the herbs and the aftertaste they leave behind. As I set the bottle back on the table, I catch Quinn watching me out of the side of her eye.

"You have any luck with that wendigo research you were doing the other day?" she asks, voice light, and flips the page.

I meet her eyes. Did Reid tell her?

She nods at my water bottle. "I can smell them from here." I frown, but before I can respond, she continues, "I only ask because if not, I actually think I may know someone who can help. She's down in the city. No pressure, but it couldn't hurt, right? I could take you, if you wanted?"

"I—" I shake my head. "Why are you being so nice to me?"

"Why wouldn't I be?" The smile she gives me is small and confused, as if any other alternative is simply unthinkable. Nice is just her default setting. Maybe I'm jaded, my suspicion fed over the years by every time my mother used kindness to lure me in when she had an ulterior motive.

Most people don't think like she does, I remind myself, and force myself to return Quinn's smile. The truth is, I'm drowning and in no position to refuse help, no matter where it comes from. "Well," I say, "to answer your question, I've found absolutely nothing helpful. So if you think you have something that can help, I'm all ears."

She glances down at her watch, then at the library around us. Aside from a few other students at the nearby tables, it's empty.

"Grab your bag," she says.

"I—what? Right now?"

She raises an eyebrow, already standing up again.

"Okay then." I shove my things back in my bag and hurry after her.

———

COLUMBIA UNIVERSITY's campus is bustling with students when we arrive. The streetlamps reflect off the wet pavement, but it's the building in front of us I can't tear my eyes away from. It's enormous, the front covered with

210

rectangular windows full of warm, golden light that makes the entire structure look like it's glowing from within. The lawns are all perfectly mown and sectioned off in neat squares between the paths, everything exactly where it's supposed to be. A group of girls laughs as they pass us, their ponytails bouncing and field hockey sticks propped on their shoulders.

I let myself wonder for a moment what it would have been like to go to a normal college like this, to study things other than magic and foreign vampire affairs. What other classes are even out there? Could I have majored in music? Science? I could've stayed on the night timetable if I wanted to, since the college offers schedules for both to accommodate its human and vampire students.

I squash that line of thinking before it can get any further. It's useless to daydream about. That kind of life was never meant for me.

Heat creeps up the back of my neck, like I can *feel* someone's eyes on me. I run my hand over my skin, but when I look over my shoulder, no one seems to be paying attention to us. They're all going about their business.

This paranoia is getting out of hand.

Maybe it's another byproduct of the psychosis.

"I think her office is this way," says Quinn, pulling my attention back to her as she leads me through the crowd.

"How do you know her?" I ask, neck still craned back, taking in the campus. *Campus* being a generous term since it's smack in the middle of the city. It somehow still feels like its own little world. It's warm enough tonight that students are lounged out on the lawn and the steps leading up to the buildings. I follow Quinn as she veers right, thankful she at least knows where she's going. Compared to the size of the academy, this place feels like it could swallow me whole.

We come to another building, barely distinguishable from the ones around it, and step inside. It's quiet in here, and the plush chairs in the lobby are empty.

"I used to watch her kids after I was dismissed from the estate, actually. They're probably about your age now," says Quinn. "Here we are."

We wind through the hallways and come to an office near the back of the building, the sign beside the door reading Dr. Kapoor, Astronomy. When Quinn knocks on the door, another woman opens it almost immediately.

She's younger than I'd been expecting, probably not much older than Quinn, though the years don't show themselves in her dark skin. The graying hair is the only give-away. She nods for us to come inside, and I quietly close the door behind us.

"Sorry to call you so last minute like this," says Quinn.

"Oh, it's no problem at all." Dr. Kapoor turns, shuffling papers and files on her desk. There's a mountain of them, so many I can't see the surface beneath. "I'm Dr. Kapoor." She turns and offers her hand to me. "But you can call me Ela."

"Valerie." I shake it, momentarily thrown by how firm her grip is.

"Oh," she says the moment our skin touches, then looks to Quinn, who nods.

"Oh?" I ask.

"We can't do this here," she continues, turning her back again to rifle through a cabinet behind her desk. "The moon isn't full, but we'll have to make do."

The moon? I look a little harder at her and take a deep breath through my nose. Definitely a witch. Probably a lunar then.

I glance at Quinn out of the corner of my eye. Why would she think a lunar witch could help me?

"Are you familiar with Morningside Park?" asks Ela.

"The waterfall?" offers Quinn.

"Good." Ela nods, still not looking at us as she pulls out a tote bag and starts stuffing crystals inside. "I'll meet you there." She pauses, straightens, then turns her gaze on me. "And make sure you aren't followed."

MAKE sure you aren't followed.

The words fill my chest with ice. The last few days, constantly feeling watched, followed, I'd thought it was all in my head. But if it isn't, if there really is something to be worried about, who...or what...has been following me?

As Quinn and I walk to the park, every hair on the back of my neck stands on end, my shoulders tense. Other people pass on the street, paying us no mind. I follow Quinn, who clearly knows where she's going. The park is less crowded than the street, though there's still a few joggers clogging the paths.

Lush, green trees line the sidewalk as we reach the waterfall, which is nearly covered by the surrounding brush. The darkness makes the water of the pond look black. A few benches sit beneath a lamp, and Quinn sits, letting out a long, slow breath.

I sit next to her, listening to the bugs and birds around

us, still not quite able to shake that feeling of being watched. When I look around though, we're the only two people here. I can't smell anyone nearby either.

"Thank you for doing this," I say.

"Of course," she says. "You're important to Reid, so you're important to me."

Coming from anyone else, I'd probably roll my eyes. Maybe even not believe her. But if Reid trusts her, that's all I need to know. And there's something about Quinn that exudes motherly energy despite having no kids of her own—so strikingly different from the woman I call my mother.

I clear my throat. "So, she's a lunar witch?"

She nods and rubs a spot under her jaw. "Her practices are probably a bit…unconventional, by your standards."

Before I can ask what she means by *unconventional*, footsteps sound down the path, and Dr. Kapoor steps into the light, tote bag in hand, a hat now pulled down low. She heads straight for a patch of moonlight by the water, I guess assuming Quinn and I will follow.

A woman of few words, apparently.

"I'll need your hand," she says.

"What are you going to do?" I ask.

"I'm going to read you," she says simply, then waves her hand for me to follow. I glance at Quinn out of the corner of my eye, and she gives me an encouraging nod.

I step into the circle of crystals Dr. Kapoor laid on the ground and offer my hand. She stabs a small pin into my palm, and a bead of blood rushes to the surface. I let out a surprised hiss through my teeth—since when do lunar witches use blood?—and watch as she makes an identical cut in her own hand, then grabs mine, smearing our blood together.

A rush of energy buzzes through me at the contact, and I momentarily lose my breath.

Dr. Kapoor tilts her head back, letting the moonlight fall on her face, and closes her eyes.

"You were marked by the wendigo weeks ago," she murmurs under her breath, "and have been suffering the psychosis. The herbs you've been taking are keeping it at bay, for now."

I hold my breath, wondering if she's somehow *seeing* this, or if Quinn relayed it to her on the phone earlier.

"Darkness still follows you. Lots and lots of darkness."

A chill runs down my spine.

"And you're running out of time. The more you use the herbs, the less effective they will become. If you do not find the one who can reverse this before it is too late, then the darkness will find you."

"The one who can reverse this…?"

"*Shh.*" Her hand tightens around mine, her nails digging into my skin, but she keeps her eyes closed. "They've been gathering. Many. Waiting. You will see them soon."

She drops my hand abruptly and takes a step away from me, out of the circle. She swallows hard. "I'm afraid there's nothing I can do."

"Ela—" Quinn starts, stepping up beside me.

"I'm sorry." She looks like she means it too. "You must find James Westcott," she says, quieter now. "At this point, that is your only hope."

"Do you know where I can find him?" I demand, trying

not to let my irritation show in my voice, but it bleeds through just the same. Everyone keeps spouting the same warning, but no one seems to be able to offer anything *helpful*.

A branch snaps behind us.

A light breeze rustles through the trees, but the surrounding paths are empty.

"What is—" Quinn starts, but I hold up a hand to quiet her as I sniff the air.

My stomach roils as a rotten stench reaches me, and I motion for Quinn to get behind me. Fear makes her heart beat faster in her chest, the noise distracting. I lick my lips, fighting back the ache in my gums.

Not right now. I can't afford to think about that.

Quietly, Dr. Kapoor steps up beside me, gaze locked on the trees in front of us.

Another branch snaps, then another, drawing closer.

"Quinn, I need you to run back to the street," I say under my breath.

"What? Valerie, I'm not—"

The vampire springs out of the darkness, crashing directly into me. We both fall, and I land hard on my back, his weight pinning me to the ground. Blood drips from his chin onto my chest as he snaps his teeth at me over and over. I hold him back by the shoulders as Quinn cries out somewhere behind him.

The man growls, his blue eyes unfocused.

Marcus.

He's barely recognizable from the hotel's picture in his file—his skin paler, his face thinner—but it's him.

Dr. Kapoor chants something I don't understand. I'm

not even sure what language that is. Something metallic catches the light above us.

"Don't hurt him!" I call before she can bring the blade down.

Marcus snaps his teeth at me again, and I dig my nails into his shoulders. "Look at me," I say through my teeth. "You can fight this. You don't have to do this."

He lunges for my throat again, and I hook my legs around him, spinning us so I'm now pinning him to the ground.

"Marcus!" I shout.

His nails dig into my arms, drawing blood. I let the magic coat my skin, then imagine his blood turning to stone in his veins. He stops fighting me. I hesitate for another moment before standing, making sure he can't move.

"You know him?" Quinn asks, voice small.

I glance from her to Dr. Kapoor, still standing there with the knife. I swipe the blood off my face with the back of my hand. "Not really. He's the one who killed those vamps down by the Brooklyn Bridge. He and I have a similar...affliction."

Her eyes widen in understanding.

"Get my bag," I say.

Quinn snatches it off the ground and hands it to me, and I dump the contents on the ground, sifting through until I find my water bottle. Marcus hisses as I approach, his mouth apparently still working. I grab his chin with one hand, and he tries to bite it. I yank it back.

"Fucking hell, Marcus. I'm trying to help you. Can someone hold his head?"

Quinn squats above him and grabs each side of his

skull, holding him in place. Not bothering to try to open his mouth this time, I pour the water bottle over his face, hoping at least some herbs make it in his mouth.

He lets out an inhuman screech as it hits his face, and I take a step back, waiting, but I don't release the magic holding him. Quinn comes to stand beside me again, one hand covering her mouth. Marcus continues to snap his teeth.

"It didn't work," I whisper.

"Maybe he's already too far gone," says Quinn.

I dig my teeth into my lip. I have no idea what to do. I don't want to kill him. All I can picture is Naomi's face as she insisted he was a good person. But I can't very well bring a vampire intent on killing every vampire in his path to an estate *full* of them.

"I might have an idea," says Dr. Kapoor. She disappears back into the shadows by the water without another word.

I look to Quinn. She shrugs, eyes still locked on Marcus's twitching form on the ground. "How long has he been like this?"

"I don't know. At least as long as me, I think."

"Hopefully, we're about to find out." Dr. Kapoor returns, crystals in hand, and starts arranging them around Marcus. "If we can see back to what happened to him," she explains, "maybe that'll give you some more information to work with on James Westcott. At least, more information than we have now." She finishes laying the crystals and crouches beside him. "Can you keep him still?"

I nod, and she slices open her palm.

Marcus growls as the scent fills the air. His resistance

yanks me forward a step, but I keep my hold. Sweat breaks out across my forehead, and I clench my jaw as Dr. Kapoor grabs Marcus's hand, her blood smearing across his skin. A small gasp escapes her lips, and her eyes fall shut, flitting around beneath the lids.

"It's...raining...not far from here. He's alone. He's walking across a street. He doesn't seem concerned."

Marcus lets out a small whimper from the ground as Dr. Kapoor tightens her hand.

"A man in a window," she mumbles. "Shaved head. Red tattoo beneath his eye, three lines. Marcus goes inside." Dr. Kapoor breathes in sharply, then drops Marcus's hand and climbs to her feet. "That's where it happened. In that store." She closes her eyes and shakes her head, like she's struggling to see whatever's in her mind. "Black chairs everywhere. A dentist office, maybe? A barber? A—"

"It's a tattoo shop," I say quietly.

Dr. Kapoor's eyes fly open and lock with mine. "You know it?"

"I think I saw the man you described. At Memphis Tattoos. It's where all of the Marionettes go." I glance back at Marcus. He's still awake and watching us, but he seems to have given up fighting me for the time being. "But he isn't a Marionette," I add.

Dr. Kapoor's brow furrows.

"Did you see anything else?" Quinn asks.

Dr. Kapoor rubs her forehead, her face twisted in a grimace now. "I'm sorry." She shakes her head. "This is— this is *dark* energy."

"Do you think this man, the one you saw, might know something?" Quinn suggests.

Dr. Kapoor abruptly drops her hand and takes a step away from me, the color draining from her face.

"What else did you see?" I demand.

She swallows hard as she grabs her bag from the ground, abandoning the crystals, and backtracks in the direction she'd come. "I'm afraid there's nothing I can do."

"Ela," Quinn calls after her, but she's already gone.

Marcus squirms on the ground, growing restless again. He bares his fangs and lets out a low snarl.

"What now?" asks Quinn.

I meet her gaze over Marcus's wriggling form. "I think we should call Reid."

I DON'T KNOW how long it'll take Reid to find us, but my muscles are already shaking, and I'm covered in a fine layer of sweat from using my magic for such an extended period of time. I don't think I'll be able to hold Marcus for much longer. He's still on the ground on his back, growling and twitching, but he seems to calm down the longer he lies there. Instead of focusing on keeping him in place, I close my eyes, visualizing the amount of oxygen in his blood pumping to his brain. I don't want to kill him, but if I could make him pass out...

"Is he supposed to look dead like that?" Quinn asks beside me.

Marcus is now limp against the pavement, but his chest rises with his breath.

"He's fine," I breathe, then promptly collapse onto the bench beside the path and pull a cigarette out of my bag.

"If he starts moving again, that's when we'll have a problem." I tuck my cigarette between my lips and let my eyes fall shut as the smoke fills my lungs, trying not to think about the fact that I'm already hungry despite taking the herbs earlier today. "You can head home. I'll wait for Reid."

"I'm fine here." Quinn slides onto the bench beside me.

I blow out a cloud of smoke and offer her a cigarette. To my surprise, she takes it.

"So, this James Westcott person we need to find," she says around the cigarette in her mouth as I lean over and light it for her. "I'm guessing Reid is already looking for him. Have there been any leads?"

I smile a little. *We.* As if getting involved in this is a no-brainer for her despite the fact that her friend practically just ran away screaming.

"I spoke to another witch down in York. Apparently he's gone through a million and one identities, so who knows what name he's going by now? I don't even know what he looks like."

"That certainly makes things more difficult," she murmurs.

"With all of the attacks in the city, though, I can't help but think that means he's here, you know? I mean, they were happening in York too, but nothing as bad as here. So he must be nearby, right?"

"That would make the most sense," she agrees. "Unless he's not working alone. That boy at your school who was attacked, he's not experiencing the same things you are?"

"Daniel? No, not that I know of, at least. But he never came into contact with the wendigos, just a vampire who did. It seems like, I don't know, like maybe the wendigos aren't the point, you know? They're more like a tool. Someone—James Westcott presumably—wants to take out vampires. Or witches. Or witches who help vampires, hence the focus on the Marionettes. So he uses the wendigos to make other vampires and witches go mad and do the killing for him."

She stares at me.

"So whoever this James Westcott person is," I continue, "he must have a grudge for some reason. I'm not sure how helpful that is. Plenty of people in this city don't like how things work…"

Blood in my ears roars, drowning out my train of thought as something else occurs to me. There had been a piece of this that didn't make any sense—the humans. Madison and her family. Ryan. Why would humans be connected to something like this?

Unless they also wanted things to change.

Unless they were *working* with James Westcott.

A branch snaps, and my eyes dart to Marcus, but it doesn't look like he's moved. I strain my ear, listening. Very faintly, footsteps crunch along the path. I stand, gesturing for Quinn to stay put as the person draws closer. The bond in my stomach warms a moment later, and my shoulders relax.

Reid appears around the bend in the path. His eyes find me first as he steps into the circle of light from the lamp, taking in the blood splattered across the front of my clothes.

"It's not mine," I say.

He nods, then walks over to Quinn.

"We're both fine," she says. "But he…" She trails off, looking at Marcus on the ground.

"I didn't know what to do," I admit.

"I'm glad you called." He pulls something out of his pocket as he bends down beside Marcus's body. "I assume this is your doing?" he asks without looking at me.

"I just…put him to sleep for a bit."

Reid nods, then plunges a syringe into the side of Marcus's neck. "A sedative," he explains as he stands. "Just to make sure we don't have any surprises."

"You're going to bring him back to the estate?" I ask.

"He'll have to go down in the cells for now, but I don't have a better solution. Do you?"

I shake my head.

"Alexander has the car." He nods the way he'd come, but hesitates, probably wondering what we were doing out here in the first place. Something flickers between the bond, the briefest flash of warmth, before disappearing again.

"You can wipe that look off your face," says Quinn. "We weren't talking about you."

Reid blinks. "I—"

"Though if I wanted to tell Valerie embarrassing stories of you, there's no shortage of them," she continues. "Just something to keep in mind."

I press my lips together to keep my laugh in.

Reid grumbles something under his breath and wedges his hands under Marcus's shoulders.

"I can grab his feet," I offer.

We meet each other's eyes over Marcus's body as we head back for the street, and Reid scowls. "Stop laughing."

I grin. "I like her."

CHAPTER EIGHTEEN

REID IS UNFLINCHING as we recount Dr. Kapoor's observations on the drive back, his expression entirely unreadable. Even with the bond, nothing more than the faint static of his presence comes through. We drop Quinn off at the human quarters first.

"I'm sorry Ela couldn't be more help," she says as she climbs out.

"Oh, no, it was very helpful. Thank you, Quinn," I say, meaning it. She gives me a warm smile before closing the door.

I expect the car to circle to the back to take Marcus's body—currently in the trunk—down to the cells next, but Alexander pulls up to the front of the estate instead.

"Alexander and I will take care of it," Reid says. "You should go rest."

"I can help—"

"Valerie," he cuts me off. "You look like you're about to pass out. Just go to bed."

I rub my hand across my eyes, the exhaustion more noticeable now that the adrenaline's worn off. Keeping Marcus down for such an extended period of time took more out of me than I'd expected.

"And what Dr. Kapoor saw with the tattoo shop?" I say. "What do you think?"

Sighing, he glances out the window. "It's nearly sunrise. We'll go check it out tomorrow."

Nodding, I reach for the door.

"And one more thing," Reid says. "I found a place for Connor in the city. Just a small apartment. I'm helping him move in, probably sometime next week. I understand if you don't want to be there, but...I thought you should know."

I stare at my reflection in the car window, my hand frozen on the handle. His words hit me like a punch to the gut. When Connor said he wanted to move out, I'd thought there would be more time first. But so soon? I guess a part of me had been holding on to hope this new version of him might still wear off. That if I just waited it out...just a little bit longer...

"That's good." I nod again. "I'm glad...he has you to help him." Clenching my jaw against the rising feeling of tears in the back of my throat, I open the door and step out.

This isn't a surprise. I'd known this was coming.

The window starts to roll down behind me, but I hurry inside before Reid can say anything.

Reid's not at the estate when I wake up the next day. I know before I even check my phone. The bond feels hollow, like it's stretched thin by how much distance is between us. But sure enough, when I check my texts, I have a message waiting from him, short and to the point, like he always is. *Meet me at Memphis Tattoos at 9.* I frown at the phone for a few moments before pulling myself out of bed. I guess it's none of my business what he's doing this early in the evening. But I can't help but feel like he doesn't want me to know. The bond isn't completely closed off, but it's certainly not letting anything through.

I spend twice as long in the shower as usual, trying to scrub the dirt and blood from the incident with Marcus off my skin. It's dried and stuck in every little crevice now. I guess that's what I get for immediately falling into bed when I got back.

A shiver runs down my spine at the thought of Marcus. His snapping teeth, no recognition in his eyes as I said his name. The way the herbs hadn't worked.

How long until that's me?

The more you use the herbs, the less effective they will become.

That's what Dr. Kapoor had said. But which is worse, taking them too much until they can't help me anymore, or cutting back and risking going off the rails again?

I shut off the water and climb out, not even looking at my clothes as I throw them on. I still have a little time before I need to head into the city, so I crouch over my laptop, my eyes darting to the water bottle full of herbs.

I grab it and shove it under my desk.

The Memphis Tattoos website is flashy, modern. Pictures and text glide onto the screen, all set against a matte black backdrop. It's mostly examples of tattoos they've done. I scroll to the artist tab, and tiny pictures of each of the artists appear on the left-hand side, followed by their contact info and links to their portfolios.

I recognize the guy who did our Marionettes' tattoos and a few others who had been there that day. I keep scrolling until I reach the bottom of the page, then sit back in my chair, frowning. No sign of the bald guy with the face tattoo. So he's not an artist there. I click through the rest of the pages on the website, but there are no other pictures of people. What if he doesn't even work there?

The website says they don't open until 2:00 a.m. I guess Reid wants to get there before they open so we don't have to deal with customers. How he's sure anyone will be there this early, I have no idea.

Still, I grab one of the estate's cars and head for the city, staring out the window as the driver hums along to the rock song on the radio. I stretch my neck, trying to ignore the hunger already starting to build. It's not bad yet. I'll be fine.

The blinds are drawn when we pull up outside of the shop, the open sign unlit. I hesitate before climbing out of the car, ducking my head to see the full building through the window. Car horns blare around us.

Reid's presence in the bond grows stronger as I approach the building, so he must be inside. I test the handle, and it gives way easily.

The lobby is empty and dark, and I cringe at the sound the door makes as it closes behind me. The scent of ink and antiseptic hangs heavily in the air, and a trace of light peeks from beyond the front desk and curtains sectioning off workstations. I venture past the leather couches and coffee tables, and a figure steps out at the back of the room.

His face is hidden in the shadows, so all I can make out is his towering form and the wide set of his shoulders.

And the gun he pulls from his hip and points at me.

I freeze in my tracks as a second man appears behind him.

"She's with me. She's with me," calls Reid's voice.

I dig my nails into my palms until I create eight bloody crescents, ready to use the magic now buzzing against my skin. Finally, he lowers the gun.

"This is my partner," Reid explains. "Valerie."

The man says nothing, just turns and disappears behind the curtain. I don't recognize him from the last time I was here, and he's not the man with the face tattoos. Reid nods for me to join them.

They're in one of the sections in the back—the same one I'd been tattooed in—huddled around the padded leather table. The man I don't know sinks into a rolling chair in the corner. He has a thick gray beard and a matching full head of hair, and nearly every inch of his body is covered in tattoos—his neck, up the sides of his face, the backs of his hands, his fingers. He looks me up and down, then grunts.

I'm left to assume this is a noise of approval.

"This is Vince," Reid says, gesturing to the man.

Vince still says nothing.

My eyes drift from Reid to Vince. The second man's silence is unnerving. I'm not sure if I should address him directly or if Reid simply speaks for him.

"Well?" I prompt.

Vince grunts again. "She is impatient."

"We're looking for a man who was seen in your shop," Reid says.

"Bald. Red tattoo on his face—three lines," I add.

Vince looks between the two of us, his expression unreadable. "Why?"

"That's not really your concern," says Reid. "Does he work here?"

Vince holds his gaze for several moments before saying, "No."

"But you know who we're talking about?" I push.

Another pause. "Yes."

I scowl at his short responses, and he smirks. He's enjoying this.

Almost too fast for me to see, Reid is in front of him, hands braced on the chair's arms, and leans forward until their faces are inches apart. The man goes rigid.

"This will be a lot easier if you give us more than one-word answers." His voice comes out low, smooth. A clear threat lurks beneath the surface, and it raises the hairs on the backs of my arms. I don't think I've *ever* heard him sound that way.

Fear rolls off the man in waves, thick enough I can smell it. But he sits up straighter and meets Reid's eyes. "Then stop asking yes or no questions."

Reid bares his fangs. "My patience is wearing thin. Give us a name."

I stand frozen, hoping the man will just give us what we want because for once, I honestly don't know what Reid will do if he doesn't.

When Vince doesn't reply, Reid moves again. The chair

229

flies across the room, hitting the ground with a loud crack. Reid holds Vince up by the throat, then slams him against the wall. I stumble back a step in shock, trying to feel out what the hell is going on with Reid through the bond, but I can't feel him at all.

But he must have a reason—he always does—so I school my expression into one of indifference, trying to follow his lead.

Vince is easily as big as Reid, but Reid makes it look like the man weighs nothing. The older man gasps, his feet dangling above the ground, as Reid leans in close and says something I don't catch in the man's ear.

"You're looking for Terrence McCullough," Vince gasps, his face red. "His name is Terrence McCullough."

Reid lowers his feet to the ground but doesn't let go of his throat.

"Where can we find him?" I press.

"I—I don't know."

He opens his mouth to say something else, but then the front door creaks open, and several sets of footsteps enter the shop. There's a distinct shift in the room, a sort of vibration in the air.

Reid releases Vince and inhales deeply through his nose. I sniff, trying to catch whatever his senses are picking up. There's a musky scent, but I'm not sure what it means. A muscle above Reid's jaw ticks, but then he looks at me, and a line forms between his brow. Something like…concern.

"Go," Reid tells Vince without looking at him.

He's letting him *go*? But we haven't—

Reid gives a slight shake of his head as Vince hurries to

the front of the shop. Reid grabs my wrist and wordlessly pulls me toward a metal door in the back. It's not until we're in the alley behind the shop that I pull away.

"What was that? You're just letting him go?" I ask. "He knew something."

Reid's gaze lingers a moment too long on the shop behind us. "Weres."

It takes a moment for the pieces to click in my brain. "As in—"

Reid silences me with a look. "We have a name, and now we're leaving."

He walks toward the street, but I hesitate. Judging by the footsteps, there are at least four werewolves in there, if not more. If the queen knew a pack had broken the law and crossed into the region, she'd have them put down, or worse. So why would they risk it by being so blatantly out in public, especially this close to the estate? This side of the city is crawling with vampires and witches who are loyal to her.

And why is Reid, of all people, just looking the other way?

"Valerie," says Reid, his voice firm, but it's the tension in the bond that makes me follow.

Another silence wraps around us on the drive back to the estate, and I try to tease out through the bond which kind it is, but nothing is transferring over to me, and it seems like he wants it that way.

In the quiet of the car, the hunger hums louder in the back of my mind, demanding my attention. I wonder what Marcus made of all of this when it first started happening to him. Did he understand what was going on? How long until he turned into the version of himself I saw in the park?

How long until he killed the first person he knew?

I shake my head, trying to clear it.

"So." I clear my throat. "Marcus…"

Reid continues watching the city pass through the window. "I don't think anyone will notice another body in the cells, at least not for a while. He's…agitated."

"I tried to give him some of my herbs in the park," I say. "It didn't help him though. Quinn thought maybe it was too late. He was too far gone or something. Do you think she's right? That there's a point all of the other people like me might reach, when it'll be too late to help them, and they can't come back?"

Finally, he turns to me. His eyes sweep my face, a heaviness behind them that wasn't there before. Then it hits me. He's worried. About me. About not being able to stop this. He's been the picture of calm so far, but the doubt is starting to bleed through. That there very well might not be a way out of this for me. He turns back to the window. "One thing at a time, Darkmore."

"He could've given you a fake name," I say.

"He didn't."

"How do you know that?"

"I'll take care of it—"

"Would you stop saying that?" I say louder than I'd been intending, but the frustration that's been building in the background for a while now mounts inside of me.

He turns around again. "Saying what?"

"That you'll *take care of it*, and then disappearing off doing God knows what and not telling me anything, then expecting me to sit around and wait for a solution. This is happening to *me*."

"You think I don't know that?" he snaps. "You think I can't *feel* it?" He presses his hand to his chest. "Every few hours, I feel it start to build again. I see it in your face."

I blink at the intensity of his voice. "Then—then why are you shutting me out?"

"Because I have no fucking idea what to do! And I—" He runs his hand over his eyes and sighs. Then, quieter, he says, "And I don't want to say that to you. I don't want to look you in the eye and tell you that I can't help you."

My next words die in my throat as he lowers his hand.

"Reid," I whisper. "I'm not expecting you to fix this for me."

"I know you're not." He swallows hard. "But I want to."

I look away, clenching my jaw against the burning in the backs of my eyes. I don't respond. I don't know how to. What comes next if this name turns out to be a dead end? If the hunger keeps getting worse? If I start looking more and more like Marcus? Will they have to put me in a cell?

Or worse?

Warm fingers brush the back of my hand, then slide around and lace through mine. I don't look up. I just hold on as tightly as I can as we sit in silence for the rest of the drive.

CHAPTER NINETEEN

By the time we make it back to the estate, I've chewed so hard on my lip that my mouth fills with the taste of my own blood. Which, of course, just reminds me of how badly I need to feed. So clearly cutting back on the herbs was a stupid choice.

I can feel Reid's gaze on me as we step into the estate, probably feeling some of the hunger through the bond, but I don't look at him.

"Oh! There you are, Your Highness." A plump, dark-haired servant freezes in the foyer and gives a quick curtsy. "The queen has called a meeting in her office." Her eyes dart from him to me. "You're welcome to attend as well, of course, Miss Darkmore."

"What's this about?" he asks.

Her face burns bright red. "I—I'm not sure, Your Highness. I was only sent to escort you."

Reid's eyes cut to mine. *Go upstairs and feed.*

I startle a little at the presence of his voice in my head. *I'm—I'm fine—*

No, you're not. He gives the servant a tight-lipped smile. *It's okay. Go take care of it. I'll fill you in on whatever this is about later.*

I can't even pretend to argue. There's no telling how long that meeting will last, and in a room full of people who definitely can't find out about any of this—not worth the risk. He says something else to the servant, but I can't make out the words as I turn for the stairs, my pulse thundering in my ears.

Not for the first time, a sinking, stinging heat washes over me as I slip into my room and close the door behind me. I immediately pull out a blood bag and tear it open with my teeth. I don't stop drinking until the bag is empty, then stand there in the middle of my room, waiting as my vision clears and the monster of hunger stops growling inside of me. I let out a slow breath and close my eyes.

People hear the word *addict* and think of dingy alleyways and needles in skin. Calla had been perfect. The first golden Darkmore child before the title was passed on to me. Perfect grades, perfect smile, perfect reputation. Everyone had liked her. Everyone.

Until, one day, they didn't. At least, not enough to look past what happened.

I've spent the last two years of my life terrified of turning out like her. By the end, she'd been shaky and skinny and irritable. Barely recognizable as the girl I'd grown up with.

Slowly, I sink down until I'm sitting on the floor and stare at the bag in my hands. Maybe this is what I deserve.

Even if I hadn't wanted to admit it to myself, despite logically knowing it hadn't been her fault, that there was nothing she'd done wrong, a part of me had judged her. For giving in to it. For not fighting back harder.

For leaving us.

A drop of blood leaks out of the bag and onto my thumb. I stare as it drips down my skin. It might not be venom, but somehow, I've still ended up exactly where I'd been running from.

THREE HOURS of internet research later, and I don't know any more about Terrence McCullough than I did before... except there are many, many Terrence McCulloughs in New York, and none of them look like the one I need to find.

It quickly became apparent the meeting was not going to be a short one when I didn't hear from Reid, so at least the research kept my hands busy.

I try to feel out what's going on through the bond. There's tension, but I can't figure out what it means. They could be talking about anything. The upcoming representatives meeting, the Russians still being unaccounted for, or worse. The queen could be asking for more updates on our investigation into the bodies found in that field or Candace. The chaos of the estate as everyone has been getting ready for the other representatives might be a blessing in disguise.

Not that it'll matter in a week or two if I can't find anything about Terrance McCullough. By then, I'll probably start snapping at people like Marcus, and it won't be too difficult to connect the dots.

When my eyes burn from staring at my laptop screen for too long, I head for the gardens out back, just to walk around. Get some fresh air. Burn off this anxious energy. Somehow come up with a brilliant solution.

The humidity weighs heavily in the air. It's suffocating. No matter how much air I try to pull into my lungs, it isn't satisfying. Up until now, I've been calm. As calm as can be expected, at least. But seeing the panic in Reid's eyes today —raw, true panic—shook something inside of me.

With the rate the hunger's been progressing, I probably don't have a lot of time.

"Valerie?"

A hand brushes my shoulder, and I realize I'm still standing at the entrance to the gardens. A lawn mower groans in the distance, and I turn to find Daniel watching me.

"You've been standing here for a while." He gestures to the library windows. He must have seen me from up there. "Are you okay?"

I could lie to him, I suppose. But considering he's already let me drink his blood in a bowling alley bathroom, I think we're past that point.

He glances around us, but we're alone. "Do you need…?"

"No, no, it's not that. I—"

Daniel stares at me, waiting for me to continue. His heart beats steadily in his chest, pumping warm blood through his body. Blood I already know the taste of. My gaze trails down to his throat, the skin exposed above the collar of his shirt. And suddenly, I know what I need to do.

I blink, forcing myself to look away.

I will not be like Marcus and take everyone I know down with me. And if I have any say in it, I'm not going down like this at all.

I meet Daniel's eyes again, who now looks confused more than anything else.

"I have a proposition for you," I say.

If Daniel were any other kind of witch, I never would've involved him. But seeing as he's one of the only skinwalkers I know—and Monroe is all the way up in York—I have limited options and limited time.

After filling up on so much of Reid's blood I'm buzzing with it, I teleport the two of us into the city. It takes a lot more energy than teleporting just myself, but I don't trust any of the estate's drivers enough. And I want to be able to get in and out quickly, though I suppose Daniel is probably more than capable of getting himself home.

People stream past on the sidewalks as we teleport into the alley a few stores over. Daniel steadies himself against the brick wall, looking a little green. I glance around the corner as he gets his bearings again, eyes finding the tattoo shop. The blinds are still shut, the closed sign hanging in the window.

"You know what to do?" I ask.

Instead of responding, Daniel shifts, and a raven takes his place. He beats his wings a few times, and a gust of

wind catches my hair, then he flies up and over the buildings beside us. I crane my neck back, trying to keep track of
him while also staying hidden in the shadows of the alley,
but it's no use. I can't see anything from here.

I visualize the bond stretching between me and Reid as
I wait, then mentally lock it behind the thickest metal walls
I can imagine.

Hopefully, it'll be enough.

The wind in the alley picks up again, and Daniel
swoops back down, shifting as he goes, and lands gracefully
on his feet. He grins as he straightens, as if he's performed
an impressive trick.

"Two guys inside, that I could tell," he says. "Big older
guy with a beard, and a bald guy—"

"With a red face tattoo?" I demand.

Daniel furrows his brow. "How'd you know?"

I gnaw on the inside of my cheek. He's *here*. Maybe I
should try to get ahold of Reid. And yet, the shop is
opening in less than an hour. Odds are, he's not going to
stick around for long. I won't lose this chance. I can't.

"They were in the front of the shop," he adds. "You
should be able to slip in the back."

"Stay here," I tell Daniel, then walk toward the opposite
side of the alley to circle to the back door.

"I don't think you should go in there alone," he says.

"Stay here," I repeat. "Keep watch, okay? Text me if
you see anything weird or if anyone else is coming."

Daniel looks like he wants to protest some more, his
eyes darting from the street to me.

"You really think I can't handle myself, Abney?"

"I'm giving you five minutes in there alone," he decides.

"That's it. If you're not back out here, I'm coming in after you."

"Daniel—"

"Take it or leave it." He glances at his watch. "Starting now."

I roll my eyes, but head for the end of the alley at a jog. "Fuck you, Abney."

He flashes me a grin before I slip around the corner. "Love you too!"

I find the back door easily, the same one Reid and I exited through a few hours before. Unsurprisingly, it's locked. The tang of burning metal fills the air as I slice the knife in my ring along my palm and visualize the lock melting down. I could have just unlocked it, but it might be best to leave a clear path if things go south and Daniel needs to come in.

My throat tightens at the thought, but I steel myself.

There are only two men in there. And I'm a Darkmore. I am more than capable of taking care of myself.

Slowly, I crack the door open and slip inside. The over-head lights are off, shrouding the entire back of the shop in shadow. The neon signs in the lobby cast the rest of the space in a red haze. Low voices talk quickly. It sounds like they're coming from the front, like Daniel said.

I inch forward, keeping myself hidden behind the curtains that section off the different tattoo stations. My heart beats faster in my chest, hammering against my ribs until I feel the reverberations all throughout my body.

"How long does he expect this to go on with these conditions?"

I hold my breath and take another step. I need to take

them by surprise and have one of them knocked out before they realize what's happening. Taking both of them on at once wouldn't be impossible, but it's a chance I'd rather not take.

"You can't keep showing up here," says a different voice, one I recognize. Vince. "People are asking questions."

"Who?" demands the deeper voice. "Who is asking questions?"

There's one station between us now. I flip the blade out of my ring and freeze when it makes a small *click*. I hold my breath, every muscle in my body tense.

Vince sighs. "You've caught the attention of the prince from the Carrington estate."

The other man lets out a low, derisive sound in the back of his throat. "So we'll kill him a little sooner than expected."

My blood heats, and my hands clench into fists at my sides. Before I can hear whatever Vince says next, I carve a line in the back of my arm, long and deep. My skin burns as the magic surges through my blood. I close my eyes, seeking out the two heartbeats at the front of the store.

Vince's is a bit weaker, slower.

We'll start with him.

I squeeze my fist tighter until my nails bite into my palm, then his heart starts to slow.

"Vince? Vince?"

Something thuds, then glass shatters across the floor. There's a second, louder thud as his body hits the ground.

He's not dead. But he won't be getting back up any time soon.

"Vince!"

I step around the corner, skin still on fire. Terrence is bent over Vince on the floor, his back to me. A vase lies on its side by Vince's feet, the desk chair turned over. He must have knocked into them on his way down. My shoes crunch in the broken glass with each step.

Good. I want him to hear me coming.

Terrence stiffens and whips around. His brow furrows as he looks from my face to the blood dripping down my arm. He crouches and bares his teeth, a low growl ripping from his throat. I clench my hand into a fist, still slick with blood, right before he can pounce, and he freezes in place. It takes him a moment to understand what's happening, then his eyes narrow.

"Witch," he spits.

"Werewolf," I reply calmly, though my heart is anything but calm. "Here's how this is going to work. You answer my questions—and I'll know if you're lying—and you get to walk out of here."

"Or, you can't hold me like this forever, and the moment you let go, I rip out that pretty little throat of yours."

I hold his gaze and tighten my fist, imagining my hand is inside of his chest, my fingers clenching directly around his heart. Red creeps up his neck, and he gasps.

"I wouldn't underestimate me."

I squeeze harder until he lets out a choked sound, then release my fist. He pants, hatred shining in his eyes as he looks up at me.

"Now, let's try this again," I say. "What do you know about James Westcott?"

The smallest hint of a smile curls his lips. "You have no idea what you've just walked into."

The low, amused quality of his voice sends a shiver down my spine, but I don't let it show on my face.

"You know who he is," I say. It isn't a question, and he doesn't answer. "Is he in the city?"

When he doesn't respond again, I squeeze his heart.

"I *don't know*," he grits out.

I don't loosen my hold. "I don't believe you. A vampire was seen walking into this shop, and *you* were seen here. His name is Marcus Luz. Any idea what happened to him?"

Slowly, he smiles up at me, crinkling the red lines tattooed on his face. "We both know you're not going to kill me. If you did, you wouldn't get any of the answers you're looking for."

I hold his stare, and a haughty sort of smirk settles on his face, like *he's* the cat playing with a mouse. He sees a little girl standing in front of him. A girl with magic, sure, but a physically small, easy to overpower girl all the same.

But he doesn't see the red-hot rage lurking beneath the surface as I think about Marcus rotting down in a cell. As I think of the bodies I had to burn in that field, the power-lessness that comes with having no control over yourself in those moments. And here's a man who probably had a hand in what happened to me, and who knows however many other people. In my eyes, he's just as responsible. In my eyes, he's just as much to blame.

And he deserves everything he's about to get.

Silently, I grab the overturned desk chair off the floor, pull it up a few feet away, and take a seat in front of him.

"Are you familiar with blood witches, Terrence?" I ask. "Can I call you Terrence?"

He says nothing.

"You see, blood witches are pretty different from other kinds of witches. Even more different than people realize. And we like to keep it that way. We like that people don't know everything we're capable of." I flip the blade out of my ring and slowly run my finger along the blade. "Would you like to see all of the things I can do, Terrence?"

His scent changes. That musky tint from before is still prevalent—the scent of werewolves, apparently. But the sharp tang of his fear is unmistakable, even if none of it shows on his face.

"I'm not afraid of a little girl," he says, then spits. It lands near my feet, not quite touching my shoes. His body trembles, and I loosen my hold, just enough for him to think he's gaining ground. Just enough for him to think he stands a chance.

"No." I smile at him. "But you will be."

A hint of uncertainty creeps into his brow.

I rise from the chair and calmly walk over to one of the tattoo stations. "What's interesting about blood witches," I say as I rifle through the drawers, "is we can just as easily use someone else's blood as our own." I pull out a long, thin needle and spin it around in my hands. "And we're very familiar with the human body, as you can imagine. How it works. Where things are. Where it would hurt the most. Exactly what a person could endure without dying."

He swallows as I step back in front of him and hold the needle between us.

"I realize I may have been too hard on you before," I

say. "So, let's start over with an easy question. Are you working with James Westcott? Yes or no."

He considers the needle in my hands.

Then, slowly, he nods.

I beam at him. "Very good. Now, look, Terrence. You and I could do this all day. But you're not the one I want. So all you have to do is give me something useful, then you can be on your way. All I want to know is where I can find James Westcott."

"You know," he says casually. "I'm surprised you're so coherent right now. You were one of the first targets. You should be foaming at the mouth like the rest of them."

My eyes snap to his, my jaw clenching.

"How many people have you killed so far?" he whispers.

I jam the needle into the side of his neck, right through the carotid artery.

His eyes go wide as I leave the needle there and step back. Blood seeps down his throat.

"If I pull that out," I say, my voice light, "you'll choke to death on your own blood. Shh." I smile as he tries to open his mouth. "You probably won't want to talk right now. But lucky for you, I can also heal that artery I just cut so you don't die. But without me, well, I don't think you'll last very long. Less than fifteen seconds if I take it out. Probably not much more, even if I leave it in. Decide quickly. Are you going to be helpful?"

I yank the needle back out before he has the chance to respond. Blood flies from his mouth, and he makes desperate choking sounds.

Then just as quickly, I let the artery stitch itself back together.

He lolls against the invisible hold I have on him, eyes half-open, as I fall back into my chair. I glance down at the mess of blood on the floor and frown as I realize I got it all over my shoes.

"You probably won't survive another one of those, not with how much blood you just lost. So, can you tell me where James Westcott is or not?"

He wheezes as he tries to clear his throat. "I don't know where he is."

I rise back to my feet.

"But no one does," he adds quickly.

I twirl the needle between my fingers, slick with his blood. This was my only lead. My only hope. He has to know something. He *has* to. I force my face to remain neutral, though if I can smell the fear coming off him, I'm willing to bet he can smell the desperation on me. "Then you're not useful to me."

I tighten my fist, making the pressure increase around his heart again. He chokes and gasps, the veins standing out in his neck.

"Wait—I—wait."

I release him and raise a single eyebrow.

"I have an address. I don't know if he's there. But it's where he had me meet him."

"When was the last time he was there?" I ask.

"Two days ago."

I narrow my eyes, listening to the rhythm of his heart in his chest. He could be lying, but it doesn't sound like it. I grab a pen and pad of paper from the desk, then release my hold on his hand. "Write it."

His eyes dart from me to the pen. I know he's probably thinking of ways he could take me out with just his hand. I dare him to try it. He takes the pen and quickly scribbles on the notebook in my hand, the words barely legible.

I shove the paper in my pocket when he's done, my shoes crunching in the broken glass as I take a step away. I can't leave him here like this. He knows who I am. He knows who Reid is. He'll come after us, probably with other wolves.

The hinges on the back door squeak, and my head snaps up. Soft footsteps draw closer, then Daniel's face appears. I sigh, my shoulders relaxing.

"You should've stayed outside," I say.

His gaze lands on Terrence behind me, then Vince behind him. He stiffens, but just asks, "Did you get what you came here for?"

I nod, then glance at Terrence over my shoulder. "If you're lying to me, I *will* find you again."

He glares at me, but slightly inclines his head. "I swear on my pack and the moon."

Daniel's eyes widen.

I nudge him back toward the door. "Go."

"If you got what you needed—"

"*Go*, Daniel."

He looks from me to Terrence one more time, but then he does as I say and slips out the back door.

"You said I was a target," I say once he's gone. "Who's next?"

Terrence shakes his head. "You can't stop it. You can't save them."

"Who is next?" I repeat.

He raises his chin. "You might as well get on with it. I have nothing else to tell you."

The smart thing would be to kill him now. It's what my mother would do. It's what *he* would do if the roles were reversed. And it would be all too easy to stop his heart or cut his throat again. All it would take is closing my fist.

But that's exactly what they want, isn't it? To turn me into a killer. The very thing I'm running from, I'm standing knee-deep in now.

But being the bigger person doesn't keep you alive.

I step closer until there's barely any distance left between us. He stares me down, waiting. But instead, I carve a small symbol into his shoulder with the needle—a star made of squares with eight points—and mutter the incantation under my breath, hoping I'm remembering it right. It's not something I've done before or something I ever thought I'd do. But I remember the page in a book of my mother's vividly. The one I used to steal when I was young and read beneath the covers in my bed, memorizing spells and potions as best I could.

When I'm done speaking, the lines in his skin glow orange, like embers burn beneath the surface.

He lets out a small hiss as I take a step back.

"What is this?" he asks through his teeth.

"You've been marked," I say simply, then turn for the door.

DANIEL DOESN'T SAY anything as I teleport us back, but I can feel him watching me.

We head up to the front of the estate in silence, and it's not until we've climbed two flights of stairs that I finally sigh and say, "I didn't kill him, if that's what you're wondering."

He nods slowly.

"What?" I snap. The earlier anger and desperation still buzzes along my skin, and I can't quite shake it off.

He shrugs, a corner of his mouth lifting. "Guess I'm glad I'm not on your bad side."

"*Darkmore.*"

My head whips up as Reid pounds down the stairs, murder in his eyes.

Shit.

Clearly, I hadn't cut off the bond as well as I'd thought. Now it *burns* between us, loud and pulsing. He's not just angry.

He's livid.

I glance at Daniel sideways. "You should probably go. You're not going to want to see this."

Daniel glances between the two of us, then quickly hurries down the hall. I brace myself as Reid reaches me. He grabs my arm and yanks me back up the stairs after him. I open my mouth to speak, but he shoots me a glare over his shoulder, silencing me. His gaze is alert as we head toward his room, eyes sweeping the halls, but other than a few human servants bustling about, we're alone.

The second we cross the threshold into his room, I yank out of his grasp. "Let go of me."

"What the *fuck* were you thinking?" he demands, his voice so low it sends a shiver up my spine. "You went back there alone?"

"They had answers I needed—"

"Did you leave them alive?"

I stumble back a step. "I—yes."

He shakes his head and rubs his eyes. "You have no idea what you've just done."

"I just got a lead," I say, pulling the paper with the address out of my pocket, anger sparking in my chest. He can be mad at me all he wants, but if it were up to him, this opportunity would've slipped right through our fingers. No doubt Vince was telling Terrence all about me and Reid asking about him earlier, then he probably would've disappeared along with any chance of finding James Westcott before it's too late. "*That's* what I did. This was the only one we had, and if I didn't—"

"You could have been killed!" he shouts.

I sputter, thrown by the sheer volume of his voice. "I—I can take care of myself—"

He walks forward, closing the distance between us. My back hits the wall, and I have to crane my neck to look up at him. I can *feel* the anger rolling off of him, and a hint of uncertainty creeps in. "Against an entire pack of wolves? No, Valerie, you can't. You're lucky they weren't still there. You'd be dead—"

"I already am!" My voice cracks. "Don't you get that? If I can't find something to fix this, and soon, I might as well already be dead."

He swallows hard before he drops his gaze. He rips the paper from my hand and glances at it. "What is this?"

"The last address James Westcott was at—"

"So they claim."

"*Which*," I continue, "he probably won't be at for much longer, if he's even still there. So we have to go now—"

"Absolutely not."

"*Reid*—"

He crumples the paper in his fist and leans in until our noses are inches apart. "This address could be anything. A trap at the worst, and a pointless trip at best." His eyes sweep my face, and he takes a deep breath before continuing, his voice quieter. "You're desperate right now, which clouds your judgment."

"Then what would you have me do? Nothing?" My throat closes up, making my voice break around the word, and I drop my gaze.

"Valerie."

I don't look at him because now tears are burning in my eyes at the utter hopelessness of the situation. I desperately try to cling to my anger, but it's already long gone. Because what if that is a fake address? What if it's already too late?

"Valerie." Reid takes my chin between his fingers and forces my gaze up. He sighs. "I'll send some people to scout it out. Today. And if it looks clear, you and I will go check it out. Together. You do *not* go without me, do you understand?" He tightens his fingers when I don't respond.

"Okay," I breathe.

He hesitates another moment before dropping his hand. He takes a step back, his jaw still locked. "Don't do anything else stupid," he says, then turns to leave.

"Are you going to tell me what happened in that meeting?" I ask.

He stops a pace from the door, his back still to me. The

bond kind of...*deflates* between us. "There was an attack on one of the other estates."

My stomach plummets, thinking of all of my classmates off for their summer classes. Kirby. "Which estate? What kind of attack? What—?"

"Auclair in Canada," he says. "We've gotten conflicting reports, and we haven't been able to get ahold of them. They're dispatching a team today to go check things out." He faces me again, his lips pressed together in a hard line.

"What is it?"

He nods his head to the side. "Most of the reports have mentioned wendigos."

We stare at each other.

"What do you think that means?" I finally whisper.

"Well." He scrubs a hand against his face. "The good news is, all of the estates have bunkers. They're coated in several layers of protections—spells, elements. If they got down there in time, nothing should've been able to get past the seal. My mother thinks we might not be able to get ahold of them right now because they're still down there. We should know more in a few days."

"And this isn't like the attacks around the city...?"

He shakes his head. "From what we've heard, they were surrounded." He clears his throat and crosses his arms over his chest. "Anyway. Like I said, they're sending reinforcements and trying to get to the bottom of this. Meanwhile, we're increasing the security around here. If I hear anything else, I'll let you know."

Neither of us says anything for what feels like a long time.

"I'm sorry for going back there." I sigh. "I mean, I'm not sorry I did it. But I'm sorry I didn't tell you about it."

"I shouldn't have expected anything less from you." When I look up, he's smiling and shaking his head. "At this point, the day you stop giving me hell is when I'll be concerned."

CHAPTER TWENTY

THE NIGHT COMES AND GOES, and my anxiety grows with each passing minute our window of opportunity could be closing. True to his word though, Reid sent a team to check out the address. It takes everything in me not to text him a million times for updates. I know, logically, if he has any news, he'll tell me. But I also can't help but feel utterly powerless sitting here and doing nothing.

And on top of everything else, Connor left today. He and Reid headed out hours ago to settle him into his new place in the city. The idea of him leaving now, especially after the news about Auclair yesterday, has every nerve in my body on edge. But then again, if they're targeting the estates, maybe he's safer away from here.

Half of me had wanted to go with them, to be a part of this new phase in his life. See his new home. Maybe try to build a different kind of relationship with him, even if it can't be like what we had before.

But the other half of me knows I won't be able to

handle it. Even worse, he probably doesn't want me there. I think being around me just makes him uncomfortable.

I didn't ask where in the city Connor's new apartment is. It might be better if I don't know. I'll be less tempted to go see him because then I'd have to ask Reid where to go first. If Connor wants a clean break, I'm going to give it to him. It's the least I can do after all he's done for me.

Even if it kills me.

There's a running trail around the grounds of the estate. It starts behind the garden and circles through the trees and open space. It's only about a two-mile loop before you end up back at the estate's entrance, but it's better than being around people at the indoor gym.

Monroe and I used to jog it sometimes when we were off from school. Well, she'd convince me to come run with her, and I'd complain the entire time.

My gaze drifts to the empty space beside me as I find an easy rhythm and pump my arms at my sides. I try to imagine what she would say if she were here. What random, usually cheesy joke she'd spew out. I could call her, but the idea is exhausting.

So, instead, I run.

It's warm tonight. Warm enough that I immediately start to sweat. The trail here is flatter than the one at the academy, fewer bends and hills. Everything physical also seems to be easier these days with my new vampire half. My brain gets stuck on the word *new*. Reid thinks this part has always been inside of me, dormant, just like with Winnie. It sounded like she came into her powers around puberty, the same time most witches do. So then if I've had this part of me all along, why hadn't it showed up on its own like Winnie's did? Why did I need vampire blood to do it?

Yet another question I can't answer. It feels like that's all I have these days.

My throat starts to burn about halfway through the run despite downing one of Reid's bags before I left. I grit my teeth and run harder, hoping it'll blot out all of the panicked thoughts arising. It's starting to feel like a never-ending chase, trying to keep the hunger at bay. Just when I finally get myself out of its reach, it sneaks back out of the brush, ready to pounce.

When I circle to the front of the estate, I pause on the lawn, hands braced on my knees as I catch my breath. Sweat drips down my nose, but my mind isn't as clear as I'd hoped it would be. Monroe always pushes me so hard I can barely remember my name by the time we're done.

An overwhelming wave of grief crashes into me so hard I nearly topple over. My breath catches in my throat, and my chest *aches*. I straighten, breathing hard.

Monroe's only been gone for a few days. And it's not like I couldn't go see her—

It's Reid, I realize. It's coming from him, pumping black smoke into me through the bond like some sort of ventila-tor. It creates a fog in my mind so thick I barely see what's in front of me. The emotions layer and tangle together in my chest, but the loudest are grief…and anger.

I don't know how to tug on the bond the way he does with me sometimes, but I close my eyes and focus on it, trying to wade through the sea of feelings pouring out of him to get a sense of where he is.

My feet start moving before I realize it, and I'm heading

through the estate's foyer, the AC hitting me in the face as I step through the door. Is he back already?

A human servant polishing the décor glances up at me, but I turn and head for the stairs, not entirely sure where I'm going, but also knowing I'll get where I need to be.

My stomach sinks with each step. I've never felt this from Reid before—not just this emotion, but this kind of intensity. Sometimes his feelings will seep through, but he's usually quick to rein them back in, giving me flashes and glimpses. This feels…out of control.

My legs carry me up past the witches' floor, past the humans', and to the opposite side of the estate toward the vampire accommodations. He must be in his room. I hesitate once I reach his door, bracing myself for whatever I'm going to find inside.

Oh God, what if it's Connor?

What if his scouts had bad news?

What if he's hurt?

But when I push the door open, it's quiet. At first, I think I got it wrong and he's not here at all, but then I see it.

Shattered glass and ceramics line the floor. A broken lamp lies on its side next to the bed, and the chair in the corner is flipped onto its back. There's a fist-shaped break in the mirror on the wall with cracks fissuring out around it like a spiderweb. Fresh blood still drips from the shards and onto the wooden dresser beneath it.

Reid stands on the opposite side of the room, facing the window with his back to me. I know he's heard me come in, but he doesn't turn, and he doesn't say anything.

But he also doesn't tell me to leave.

Slowly, I close the door behind me and venture inside.

My first instinct is to ask *Are you okay?* but I swallow it down. Every muscle in his back is hard, his hands balled into fists. When I make it to his side, his jaw is flexed, his gaze trained out the window. Despite the anger hardening every line of his face, it looks like he may have been...crying.

"Reid?" I breathe.

He inhales through his nose and blinks slowly but doesn't respond.

"Reid," I repeat, louder this time. "What happened?"

A long beat of silence passes between us, to the point where I don't think he'll respond at all. But then, finally, in a voice that barely sounds like his, he says, "Quinn."

The pain reverberating through her name makes my stomach drop. Of all the things I'd thought he'd say, that hadn't even been a consideration. I open and close my mouth a few times before squeezing out, "What about her?"

He clears his throat and crosses his arms over his chest, never once looking away from the window. His knuckles are split and bleeding. "She's dead. They just found her body on the grounds," he says, voice flat. "In the same state as the other attacks."

No trace of emotion seeps through his face, and the bond between us feels cold.

She's dead.

But Quinn can't be. I just saw her a few days ago. She was just here. She was...she was...

"That, of course, makes no sense," he adds, his voice tight with barely contained rage. "Because she's—" His voice breaks, and he drops his gaze to the floor. "She *was* human." He shakes his head slowly back and forth. "She has no family left. No one in the city. Sebastian has been missing since she was found. There's no one to claim her. I never should have brought her back here. Now her body is down in the morgue, and I don't know what they'll do with her... I don't know who killed her, but whoever did, they purposefully botched the cover-up. They *wanted* me to know." His voice shakes around the last words, and he turns away, his shoes crunching against the glass on the floor.

I let out a breath, and it feels too loud in the silence between us. I fumble for words, for *anything*.

But nothing will make this better. I remember that moment after finding out about Calla all too well. There was nothing anyone could've said or done. I was floating and drowning at the same time, far enough underwater that no one could reach me.

From the moment I found out to the moment we watched that casket lower into the ground, I was suspended in a weird in-between place. Existing, but just barely. The funeral, finally, snapped me out of it. At least a little.

And now he won't even have that—a burial. A place to visit her. A chance to say goodbye.

"Reid."

He sits on the edge of his bed, his gaze on his hands in his lap.

"You said there's no one to claim her."

He nods.

"Can you? Are there any rules against that?"

Slowly, he shakes his head. "There aren't any rules against it."

I pace over and sit beside him. "I know it doesn't make it better," I whisper. "But I could—if you wanted to—we could go claim her. Spread her ashes somewhere she liked. So you can say goodbye, at the very least." I raise my head to find him staring at me. "Only if you want to," I add. "I just thought—"

"Yes," he whispers. "I want to."

I let out a long exhale and face forward again. I hesitate only a second before reaching over and laying my hand on his. "Okay," I murmur.

He tightens his fingers around mine. "Okay."

I WAS wrong about the morgue. I don't know why I'd always assumed it was in the underground levels of the estate, but Reid leads me to a building out back. It immediately becomes apparent which one it is because there's a line of body bags leading up to the door lying in the grass. Are these all of the bodies we found down by the bridge?

Reid sucks in a sharp breath but keeps moving forward. My gaze lingers on the bags as we pass them. Hopefully they have some kind of system and we're not going to have to search through them all to find Quinn.

"Your Highness!" a squat, balding man calls as we open the door. He stands behind a metal table with a black apron draped across his chest and some kind of metal instrument in his hand. I pointedly don't look at the body lying on the table in front of him. "What can I do for you? If you're here to start investigating with the bodies...I haven't finished cataloging them yet, but I can give you the ones I've finished with."

I glance at Reid, but he's frozen.

"We're here to claim the human body that was found today," I say.

The man's eyes cut to me, apparently noticing me for the first time, then sighs and pulls off his gloves. "Follow me." He turns and heads for the hallway before waiting to see if we're behind him.

I start to follow, but Reid still hasn't moved from the doorway. His mouth is tight, but everything he's feeling is right behind his eyes.

"Reid."

"I just need a moment," he says.

"Okay."

I debate walking back over to his side, but he looks like a wild animal, and any movements or sounds might spook him. So I stand there and wait. No amount of time is going to prepare him to see her. We don't even know how bad of a shape she's in. Is she torn apart like Ryan was? Or drained of blood like the vampires around us? Maybe this was a bad idea. Maybe I should've left well enough alone. My throat tightens at the thought, but I clench my jaw, forcing any tears away. The last thing Reid needs right now is *me* falling apart.

"Okay." He nods, seemingly to himself, then steps up beside me again.

We're both quiet as we follow the wide hall, lined on both sides by metal drawers with dozens upon dozens of bodies inside. The man waits for us at the end of the wall, hand poised to open the drawer.

"We can take it from here," I tell him.

He scowls, but nods and steps away, his heavy footsteps following him back down the hall.

Once he's gone, I fish the urn I'd brought out of my bag. "You don't have to watch this part."

"I want to be here," he says immediately. "I don't want her to—she deserves to have someone here."

"Okay." I swallow hard and pull up a table to set the urn beside the drawer. Usually when we do this, we're not so concerned with how messy it might be. But if I can control a bit of the cold air coming in from the AC, I should be able to guide the ashes into the urn. I glance at Reid one last time before pulling the drawer open.

It slides easily, the barest *ting* of metal on metal.

Reid sucks in a sharp breath, and I wait as he takes a step closer and lays a hand on the top of her head. Her skin is pale, a single puncture wound standing out against her throat. He smooths her hair down, his expression unreadable as he looks at her.

My chest tightens as he leans down and murmurs something too low for me to hear. Despite my best efforts, the backs of my eyes burn. The time I'd spent with her was nowhere near what Reid had, but she'd been nothing but kind to me. It could never compare to the grief of knowing her a lifetime, but missing the opportunity to get to know her feels cruel in its own way.

He squeezes her hand, then straightens and takes a few steps away. "Go ahead," he says roughly.

My hand shakes as I slice open my palm, trail the blood around her, then smear it on my chest. "I'm sorry," I whisper before starting the incantation.

The air around me warms. I imagine my blood coursing through her veins, breaking down her body through each stage of decomposition. Heat burns against my skin as the spell rapidly wears her down to bones, then ash. When the heat starts to fade, I open the urn, and the air helps me sweep the ashes inside.

I can feel Reid watching me, but he doesn't say anything. I close the urn and nod toward the back door. "You ready?"

His eyes sweep over my face, and he nods.

***

REID DOESN'T SAY anything once we leave the morgue, so I let him lead the way. It's a little windy tonight, and probably cold, but it doesn't seem to affect me as much as it did before.

There's an arched walkway behind the gardens that leads to a large gazebo with a small pond situated behind it. Vines and flowers frame us as we walk, and Reid holds the urn tightly to his chest.

This side of the estate is noticeably deserted—no gardeners, servants, or other residents of the estate around —though I can vaguely hear voices coming from the other end by the pool.

Reid stops at the edge of the water behind the gazebo.

"She used to bring me here when I was a kid," he says as I step up beside him. A single corner of his mouth lifts. "She'd read to me, and if I wasn't paying attention, she'd toss me in the water over here." His gaze trails down to the urn, and his smile falls. "I think she'd like to be put to rest out here."

"I can take it," I offer. I hold it out for him once he hands it over, and he takes a fistful of the ashes. I follow suit, and we open our palms at the same time, letting the breeze scatter them among the water. Neither of us speaks. We just repeat this over and over until the urn is empty.

When we're done, Reid puts his hands in his pockets and looks out at the water.

"Do you want to say a few words?" I murmur. "Or I can?"

He doesn't respond at first, and a muscle in his jaw flexes. "She was more of a mother to me than my own ever was," he says quietly. "She was kind and understanding. And any good qualities that I may have undoubtedly came from her. She saved my life because I don't even want to think of who I would have become if I'd never known her. She deserved more than this."

A tear trickles down my cheek, and I quickly swipe it away before he can see. When it's clear he's not going to say anything else, I take a deep breath, caught between not wanting to overstep, but also, everyone deserves to have nice things said about them when they die, official funeral or not.

"I wish I'd had the opportunity to get to know her more," I whisper. "From the few interactions I had with her, she was nothing but welcoming and warm. And if she can make a total stranger feel at home, I can only imagine the kind of impact she had on the people in her life."

The wind rustles the trees around us, and we lapse back into silence. It stirs a memory in me that I try not to think about often. Standing just like this, over a freshly dug grave, watching my sister get lowered into the ground. Connor had been standing beside me, his hand in mine the only thing keeping me up.

I glance at Reid, at the hurt so plainly showing on his face now. He's not even trying to hide it anymore. Impulsively, I reach over and take his hand. He lets out a shuddering breath and tightens his fingers around mine.

"Are you okay?" I ask.

He sniffs and nods. "Yeah, I'm fine."

We stand there for another beat, watching the water move along.

"When my sister died," I say, staring straight ahead, "everyone was always asking me that question. If I was okay. And I told them I was. I didn't want anyone around. I pushed them away and said I wanted to be alone. But I think all I really wanted was for someone to realize I wasn't okay. To care enough to notice, so just…" My face burns under the weight of his gaze, but I focus on the gentle ripples on the surface of the pond. "It's okay. If you're not actually okay."

After a moment, we meet each other's eyes, and a hint of the tension in his expression eases.

"Thank you, Valerie. For doing this."

In response, I wrap my other hand around his arm and lean my head against his shoulder. His chest rises and falls with his breath, and we stand like that long after the ashes disappear.

CHAPTER TWENTY-ONE

Days pass, and there's no sign of Reid, not through the bond or around the estate. The day Quinn was found, he texted me to let me know what his scouts reported back. The address—a warehouse—had at least two dozen people coming and going, but it didn't look like they were clearing out. With that many unknown people inside, we agreed not to go until we had a plan.

Well, I'd agreed when I'd thought that meant we would then *come up with a plan.* But now Reid's disappeared off the face of the earth, and with the summer courses in full swing, my days have become a blur of religiously taking Magnolia's herbs so I don't accidentally kill someone, forcing myself not to panic about the increasing frequency of needing the herbs, and trying to memorize everything for the upcoming representatives meeting.

Summer always used to be a welcome break from the academy, a few months of freedom and fun. This year, it feels like I'm wading in the middle of an ocean, trying not to drown.

I tap my pen against the book in my lap. Various family trees are scattered on the bed in front of me, color coded by region. I sigh inwardly, sifting through the pages again. My phone buzzes somewhere in the blankets, and I toss my pen onto my pile of failure.

I jab the speaker button. "Hello?"

"That's all I get? *Hello?* I've been gone like a month and I'm already demoted to a stranger?"

I roll my eyes and smirk as Monroe huffs on the other end. "Please accept my apologies," I say. "What would be the proper way to address you?"

"Maybe just tears of relief to hear from me since you've missed me so much."

"You can't see me. You don't know that I'm *not* crying."

"Touché."

I get up from my bed and cross over to the window above my desk. I peer out at the front lawns of the estate, at the guards pacing back and forth at their posts. There seems to be more out there than usual.

"I'm calling with bad news," says Monroe. "Or good news, depending on how you look at it."

I frown, scoop the phone off the bed, and start pacing the length of the room to get the blood flowing in my legs again. "What is it?"

"Well, the attacks in York have been getting worse. A dozen dead vamps, by the sounds of it. At least, that's the rumor. They're not telling us anything. Also a few dead witches from town, and they've taken at least three undocumented new vamps into custody. Just as fucked up as that one who attacked Daniel. Anyway, they're shutting down the academy. All of the summer classes are canceled until further notice."

I stop in the middle of the room. "Oh my God."

"I know. Are things as bad over there?"

An involuntary shiver works its way down my back as an image of the bodies on the shore rises up in my mind— so many and so close together it was difficult to tell which limb belonged to whom. And that, presumably, was the work of one vampire—Marcus. How many more sites like that are there around the city that we haven't found yet? Not to mention whatever happened at Auclair. "You have no idea," I mutter. "Does that mean you're coming home?"

"I guess. No reason to stay. Definitely don't want to be stuck in York if I don't have to be. I'm gonna grab the first train next week."

My phone buzzes, and I pull it away from my ear to glance at the screen. A text from Adrienne appears.

Are you home/do you have some free time? I'm in the library and could use some help.

"Hellooooooo."

"Sorry, Roe. Can I call you later? I've gotta help Adrienne with something."

"You two are actually talking? A miracle. Hell yeah. I'll see you when I get back!"

After we hang up, I send a quick text to Adrienne to let her know I'll be right there. Her response is almost immediate.

I forgot one of my books in Mom's room—can you grab it? It should be right on that front table.

I groan internally but tell her I will. Maybe I'll get lucky and my mother won't be in there. After steeling myself for several moments, I head next door. I strain my ear, trying to determine if she's home, but it seems quiet. I nudge the door open and poke my head inside.

A fire burns in the hearth—odd, considering how hot it is today—but no sign of my mother. I spot Adrienne's book a moment later and step all the way into the room to reach for it.

Which is precisely the moment my mother decides to step around the corner. She doesn't see me at first, too preoccupied grinding something in the small black bowl in her hands. The scent of it hits me a moment later, and I go very, very still.

She glances up and rears back as if startled. "Valerie! I didn't hear you come in."

I could explain about the book, but I don't. I stare at her, my chest on fire, though my heart no longer feels like it's in there. Everything inside of me has bottomed out. I look from the bowl in her hands to her face.

"What are you doing?" I ask. Surprisingly, my voice comes out steady, calm.

"Oh." She shrugs and sets the bowl on the mantel. "Just experimenting. The queen has nearly every Marionette on this case with the dead vampires, so we're all trying to come up with something."

It would be a perfectly reasonable excuse. It would certainly make sense, given the circumstances. It would be believable.

If only I couldn't smell it.

The Vexillium isn't even what gives it away. It's the perfect mixture that nearly covers the Vexillium's earthy scent. The same mixture I'd smelled in my perfume bottle day after day.

"Well?" she asks, a hint of impatience bleeding into her tone now. "Did you need something?"

I should turn around and not say anything, file away this information for later. It would be the smart thing to do.

It would be what she would do.

Instead, I swallow hard and narrow my eyes. The entire room blurs around me, and my pulse thuds in my ears. My voice comes out barely above a whisper. "You poisoned me."

"What a ridiculous thing to say." She picks up the bowl again. But she doesn't deny it, and she doesn't seem surprised by the words.

A scorching wave of rage roars through me. "You *poisoned* me," I repeat, louder this time, and take a step toward her. "For months."

"Honestly, Valerie, I have no idea what you're talking about."

Every time I'd gone to bed huddled in every sweatshirt I could find because I couldn't get warm, every time I'd fainted from doing basic tasks, every night I'd lie awake terrified of whatever tasks they'd have me do, that I wouldn't be able to manage without my magic, the painful cuts and bruises and injuries that suddenly couldn't heal—it was all because of her.

And she'd known. She'd seen me that day with the cut in my arm. She'd known what it was doing to me.

And she didn't *care*.

She probably saw the pain on my face and felt…satisfied.

"Stop lying." Crossing the rest of the distance between us, I grab the bowl from her hands before she can react and throw it to the ground, finding no satisfaction at all as it shatters.

I can see it in her eyes when she looks at me. I think maybe I always have and didn't want to admit it. Even when it's not at the forefront, it's always there, lurking beneath the surface. Plain, unadulterated hatred. I harden my jaw to keep my voice from breaking. "I just want to know why."

Her nostrils flare as she looks from me to the mess on the floor, seemingly more concerned with the broken bowl than what I'm saying to her. "You need to calm down," she says through her teeth.

"I've put up with your shit for years, Mother, but this was too far—"

"Mind the way you speak to me."

"To what end?" I shriek, the rage overflowing in my chest. "What was the *point*? Or was there even a point? Maybe you just enjoy watching me suffer."

"I *said*, mind the way you speak to me."

"How can you look yourself in the eye and call yourself a mother—"

A sudden gust of air tears through the room and shoves me. I stumble back a step, and she hits me with another wave, over and over again until my back is against the wall. I hit it hard enough that it knocks the wind from my lungs. I try to take a step forward, but the air holds me in place like an invisible wall. She slowly prowls toward me, her high heels clicking against the floor as she walks, until she comes to stand just inches away. Her nose nearly brushes mine as she leans forward.

"How dare you accuse me," she snarls. "After everything I've done for you."

A montage of slaps and cuts and belittling words cycles through my head. I try to think of a nice, touching moment between us. Any warmth or kindness that wasn't a ruse. But nothing comes to mind. "What is it that you think you've done for me?" I spit.

She slaps me, and my head whips to the side. The taste of blood fills my mouth. I try to fight the invisible wall, but she tightens it around me until it becomes difficult to breathe.

She seizes my chin between her nails, the razors lining the edges digging into my skin, and forces me to look at her. Slowly, she shakes her head as her eyes flit up and down my face.

"You were always the weakest one," she whispers. "The softest. You would be *nowhere* without me. You barely deserve to hold the name Darkmore as it is."

I try to pull out of her grasp, but that only makes more blood run down my chin. The wound burns. She must still have Vexillium on her fingers.

"If I'm already so *weak*," I say, "then why did you feel the need to weaken me?"

"You have no idea what you're talking about. I'm the reason you're *alive*." Her hot breath washes over my cheek as she yanks my head to the side and leans down, letting her lips brush my ear. The low tremor of her voice raises the hairs on the back of my neck. "Honestly, I don't know why I wasted my time. It should have been you."

She drops my chin and turns away, my blood dripping from her nails onto the floor. Ice-cold shock holds me in place more than her wall at this point. She doesn't elaborate, and she doesn't need to.

It should have been you.

"Get out of my sight," she mutters. Before I have the chance to move, she uses the air to shove me. I hit the ground on my knees as she yanks the door open. With one last gust of air, she throws my body into the hallway, and I roll until I slam into the opposite wall.

I hit the ground, breathing hard, my face still bleeding. I stare at the door for a few more moments before my body starts to shake. Wiping the blood dripping from my face with the back of my hand, I climb to my hands and knees. My chin wobbles, and I clench my teeth against it, but that's not enough. The burning builds in the back of my eyes as I look from the door she'd slammed to mine beside it. I can't go in there. She'll hear everything, and that will probably bring her more satisfaction than anything else.

My feet move for the stairs, but I freeze as I turn for the human floor—a habit, but one that's no longer available to me. I can't go to Connor. Monroe and Kirby are both still gone too.

My breathing quickens as I look up and down the stairs.

I have nowhere to go.

I don't know how long I stand there, frozen in place. But then I hear footsteps on the stairs below me, and a small shockwave travels through my body, urging my feet onward.

At first, I don't know where they're taking me. Anywhere but here. Anywhere no one will see me like this.

But as I draw closer, I realize where I'm heading. Thankfully, as I reach Reid's door, I can tell through the bond he's not inside. Maybe he's in another meeting or something. Either way, I just need a few minutes to pull myself together, and then I'll be gone before he gets back.

I slip into the room, finally able to take what seems like my first breath as the door closes behind me. I stay there with my back planted against the wall, staring blankly ahead, my vision focusing and unfocusing. A hot tear rolls down my cheek, and I angrily swipe it away.

I want to be unaffected. I want to be as cold as the way she looked at me. But I guess she was right about one thing. I've never been able to be anything like her. No biting comment she's made, no slap or hit or cut she's ever inflicted has left me unaffected. I just learned over the years how to hold it inside until I could get away so she couldn't see it. So she couldn't see the tears. She couldn't see the pain. She couldn't see anything but the cold shell of a person she'd been trying to make me into.

But I guess if today is any indication, despite all of my efforts, she still saw right through it.

I sink to the floor and pull my knees against my chest. The blood is still sticky against my chin as I rest it on my legs.

It should have been you.

It shouldn't bother me. Not this much, at least. She's said worse. She's *done* worse.

Or maybe she hasn't.

It should have been you.

Calla's face rises up in my mind. Her easy smile. Her

contagious laugh. She'd always been the favorite—that's nothing new.

I press my forehead against my knees and squeeze my eyes shut as far as they can go, willing the image to fade away.

Maybe it *should've* been me.

I don't know how long I sit there. Despite the emotions that had been threatening to boil over in the hallway, now that I'm alone in the quiet, I can't seem to muster any kind of feelings at all. I'm just…tired.

The shock ebbs away, and my mind combs through the rest of her words. *I'm the reason you're alive.* What does that even mean?

Movement on my left sends my heart into my throat, and my head jerks up. Reid sinks onto the ground beside me, arms braced on his knees.

God, I hadn't heard him come in.

I wait for him to ask, but he doesn't say anything. I exhale my relief and put my forehead back down on my knees.

"Sorry for breaking into your room," I murmur against my legs. "I just…I didn't have anywhere else to go."

Still, he says nothing, but I know he's looking at me. I can feel his gaze on the back of my neck like the heat of the sun. I pull in as deep of a breath as I can and slowly sit back up. The dried tears feel hard against my face.

"My mother," I explain, and my voice comes out flat, emotionless, "wishes I was dead. Which isn't a surprise, really. I think I've always known it. But I guess I didn't think she would ever say it to my face." I dig my nails into my legs to fight back the lump rising in my throat. "She wishes it had been me instead of Calliope," I whisper. "That's what she said. After calling me weak and a disgrace to the Darkmore name."

Reid shifts his weight beside me, bringing him close enough that his shoulder rests against mine.

A tear rolls down my cheek despite myself. I swipe it away with the back of my hand, annoyed. "I'm fine."

"Okay," Reid says quietly.

Another tear slips out, and I grit my teeth. "I'm fine."

"Okay."

My chest starts to tremble. "I'm fine."

Reid's arm wraps around my shoulders and pulls me against his side. I let out a shuddering breath as more tears escape down my cheeks. He rests his chin on the top of my head and wraps his other hand around my knee. "Okay," he breathes into my hair.

I shake my head over and over as I cover my face with my hands. "I know it's stupid," I say.

"It's not stupid."

"I've just—I've spent my whole life trying to make her happy, you know? And it's never been enough. I can't believe it's taken me this long to realize it's never going to be enough."

His thumb runs up and down my shoulder. "It's enough, Valerie," he whispers. "It's enough."

He takes my face in his hand—the touch strikingly different than when my mother had done it minutes before —and forces me to look at him. His face is smooth, calm. Tears stick in my lashes as I blink.

"You and I are going to think on what she said to you

for five more seconds, but that's all. Because that's all the time it deserves, do you understand?"

The calmness in his expression somehow sinks into me, forcing my muscles to relax. Slowly, I nod.

"Okay." His eyes sweep my face, and his thumb trails under my jaw. "Five, four."

His eyes hold mine, something burning beneath the surface.

"Three."

My chest rises and falls as my breath hitches.

"Two."

He hesitates a moment more, his hand tightening on my chin, before whispering, "One."

He doesn't release me, not at first, and our eyes stay locked like that. I should probably be embarrassed—God, he's seen me break down twice now in just a few days—but the relief is so much stronger. The only person who ever really knew the extent of things between me and my mother was Connor. Kirby and Monroe have always known things were bad, but not like this, and I never wanted them to know. I never wanted to see the pity in their eyes.

But now, as Reid looks at me, there's no pity, just understanding. An understanding I didn't even see with Connor. There's a reason my mother and the queen make such a good pair. Growing up with her couldn't have been any easier.

His gaze trails down to my mouth, and I stop breathing. My stomach clenches—no, the bond does, going taut between us.

But neither of us moves.

The wounds from Connor still feel fresh in my chest,

and it almost feels like a betrayal to him, as if the human version of him, *my* version of him, is separate and still here somehow.

But he's not. And he probably won't ever be *my* version again. This version couldn't care less about what I do. The utter helplessness of that thought is deep enough to drown in.

Reid's eyes flick to mine, a question in them. I stare back, wishing I had an answer. Wishing everything weren't so complicated. Wishing I could stop thinking about it all for just a second.

But then also, very quietly, in the back of my mind, there's this awareness that I've never kissed anyone but Connor. Never done anything with anyone but him. Never wanted to.

But when Reid looks at me like this—like he's looking directly into me and seeing everything there is inside of me —something twists and sparks in the pit of my stomach. And in all of the years I was with Connor, somehow, I never felt this. And that scares me more than anything else.

I'm the first to look away, and I pull back, forcing him to drop his hand. "I should go."

A single corner of Reid's mouth turns up, and before I can react, he throws his arm back around me and hauls me against his side. I let out a breathy laugh as he tightens both arms until I'm pinned against his chest.

"Reid—"

He rests his chin on the top of my head again, and I can hear the smile in his voice as he says, "Shut up."

"Reid," I try again.

"We both know you're not going anywhere," he says.

"So just shut up and sit here with me." When I don't respond, he adds, "Okay?"

I let myself relax against him, allowing myself to acknowledge how warm he is. How nice it feels to be held. How much I really *don't* want to move.

"Okay," I whisper.

"You know." He runs his hand up and down my back. "When the two of us got paired, I thought I was going to hate you."

I let out a startled laugh. "Oh?"

He nods. "I figured I was getting a mini Rosemarie Darkmore, and I didn't know what the hell I was going to do with you. Well, I still don't know what the hell to do with you. But I could tell—even before we met, even just seeing you in the throne room that day—I could tell I was wrong. And then with our first task, I knew immediately you were nothing like her. You were *funny*. And smart. And kind to humans when you had no reason to be."

He pulls back again to look down at me, a furrow between his brows. "Valerie, you had every opportunity to turn out just like her. You had every reason to be cold and cruel. And you're not. But just because *she* sees it as a failure, don't you dare for a second let her make you think having decency is a weakness."

I wipe the remaining tears from my cheeks. His gaze trails to my chin, and his expression darkens. Slowly, his fingers glide down my jaw and tilt my head.

"Does it still hurt?" he murmurs.

"No." It feels healed now, so he's probably seeing the leftover dried blood.

He pushes himself to his feet and offers me his hand. I

take it, avoiding his eyes. Now that I've calmed down, my defenses are rising back up. A blush creeps up the back of my neck, and I cross my arms over my chest. "I'm guessing you don't have any news about the warehouse?"

"I have some scouts monitoring it for me. They've been trailing and identifying as many of the people involved as they can."

"And no sign of James Westcott?"

He shakes his head. "A lot of wolves though. Which we might be able to use to our advantage."

"Why would that be an advantage?"

"The punishment for crossing the boundary is execution," he explains. "I might be able to negotiate with them. Or at the very least, it would only take one weak link willing to trade information for their life."

"You really think they won't just kill you if you walk in there?"

He nods his head to the side, acknowledging this. "For now, the scouts are under the impression they're investigating the border trespasses for the queen. But if I bring in a team for backup and they overhear me asking questions, that cover story won't last for long."

And then they'll all know about *me*, is what he doesn't say.

"So we'll go alone," I say.

He meets my eyes, not looking pleased, but also not disagreeing. "If there are no developments by tomorrow night, we'll go."

I put a little more distance between us and wipe at my face again. "I should get going." I let my eyes rise to his, and my muscles relax at the calm expression staring back at me, no pity or concern. Like it never happened. Not knowing what else to say, I head for the door, but pause before stepping out into the hall. I feel like I should have something more significant to say, but I settle on, "Thanks, Reid."

He smiles—a soft, small tilt of his lips—then I close the door between us.

I DON'T LET myself look at my mother's door as I slip back into my room and try to convince myself it doesn't make a difference whether she's on the other side of that wall or not.

I need a room change. Anything to get more space between us. Bracing myself, I bend down to inspect my reflection in the mirror. Mascara is smeared everywhere, and there's still dried blood along my jaw, but I'd been expecting worse. I scrub at the remaining streaks on my face.

It should've been you.

I press harder, digging my fingers in.

You were always the weakest one.

My skin flushes red the harder I scrub at it, but I still can't get all the makeup off.

A knock on the door startles me out of my trance. It comes again—three swift knocks.

My mother would never be so patient.

I open the door to find Adrienne standing in the hall, a stack of books under her arms. Her face is perfectly blank as she takes in the room behind me.

"Oh God," I whisper.

"Why even tell me you were coming if you were just going to blow me off?"

"Adrienne—"

"I sat there waiting for you for over an hour."

"Adrienne, I'm sorry."

"Just forget it." She turns, and it's the lack of anger in her expression that cuts the deepest.

"Adrienne." I grab her arm before she can leave, suddenly feeling like I'm going to cry again. "I was on my way, I swear. I went to get your book, then Mom and I had it out with each other, and I just got kind of—and it completely slipped my mind. I really am sorry."

"Whatever." She swallows hard and shifts the books in her arms. "It was probably my fault for actually believing you'd come through on something."

I shake my head, but I can't think of anything else to say to make this better. "Adrienne—"

She turns and walks away before I have the chance.

CHAPTER TWENTY-TWO

THE ROOM IS full of the faces I've failed to memorize in my study sessions the past few months. Luckily, I can at least go off their different styles of dress to try to figure who is who. The chair at the head of the table is left open for the queen, but Reid takes the spot on the right, and I get the one beside him.

One of the princes from Norway is across from me— Harry, I think it is—with Avery beside him. He's in a decorated black suit with a thick red sash across the front, not unlike what Reid's wearing. The Marionettes' uniform varies by region, but none stray too far from our version. The all-black gear hugs Avery's figure, covering her from her throat to her ankles, though it's sleeveless to show off the red mark of her station.

A single representative from each region fills the rest of the spots, along with their corresponding partners. Members from the estates in China, Russia, and Brazil are all noticeably absent.

And, of course, none of the representatives I'd assumed would be here are. No one with that high of station is, aside from Reid. He did say this was an annual thing, so maybe it's more of a formality than anything else. It can't be that important if the best the Canadian estate could offer is their youngest heir—one of *sixteen* children—who will never get anywhere near their throne.

Avery meets my eyes across the table, and I can't help but notice how strikingly different she looks from the last time I saw her. Her blond hair is slicked back in a high ponytail, and dark kohl lines her eyes. Her face looks fuller, her skin tan. She pops her eyebrows and gives me a small smirk.

Everyone at the table rises as the door at the back of the room opens. My muscles seize, freezing me to the spot, as the queen strides inside in a long, golden gown, her crown proudly sitting on top of her curls. She spares no one a glance as she makes her way to the head of the table, focusing instead on the vast window on the far wall that overlooks the front grounds of the estate.

It's the person who follows her, however, that makes my lungs forget how to breathe.

I will myself to look unaffected as my mother joins the room and takes her seat beside the queen, just feet away from me. But I may as well be anyone else, anyone equally as insignificant to her, because she doesn't acknowledge my presence.

A shiver runs through the bond, like the barest brush of fingertips on skin.

I focus on the queen instead.

"We have a number of matters to discuss," she says.

"We were led to believe *all* representatives would be in attendance today," cuts in a squat man at the opposite end of the table. Hints of a French accent pull at his *r*'s. Definitely from Auclair. I remember his picture. Gabriel. Or was that the brother slightly older than him? Aaron, maybe?

I meet Reid's eyes for a brief moment. To anyone else, he probably looks indifferent, but I can see the clear twinkle of amusement in his eye as he watches my frustration play out on my face.

Aaron Auclair, he says in my head.

Aha, so I was right.

The queen's face twists at the interruption.

"How are we to vote without them present?" adds a petite brunette woman.

"All estates interested in continued participation in the alliance have a representative present," says Reid. I turn to look at him, at the obvious tightness in his voice.

The table goes quiet for a moment.

"So it's official," says the woman beside me. "They've rejected the alliance."

A muscle ticks above the queen's eye. "Yes."

Nearly everyone at the table starts talking at once. Their voices flood my senses until my ears ring. My head swivels back and forth, trying to follow and not let my confusion show on my face, but the outrage in the air is palpable, suffocating.

Reject the alliance altogether? It's the only peace treaty among all of the estates that's withstood the centuries. From what I've read, though terms with Russia, China, and Brazil have been going back and forth for years, it seemed like the queen was pretty confident she'd be able to bring them back.

For any one of the estates to outright refuse…well, it would be the first time since the alliance was created.

My mother's mouth moves the way she does when she shouts, and she slams a fist on the table.

"There have been an increasing number of breaches at the border. Not just here, but in *all* of our regions," says Prince Harry across from me.

"Not to mention the growing number of attacks on the estates themselves," adds the woman beside me.

Growing number? Exactly how many has there been?

I try to meet Reid's eyes, but he's not looking at me.

I'll explain later, he says in my head.

"We've had no less than ten missing vampires reported each day for weeks," a faceless voice chimes in farther down. "Is there a plan in place? It's only been getting worse."

"I don't think we should be discussing any other issues until these attacks are resolved," adds another deep voice at the other end of the table. "This is much more urgent."

"Or you're just trying to avoid some of the topics on the agenda," mutters the thin woman beside him.

He whips toward her, nostrils flaring. "Do you really think discussing *budgets* is a better use of our time right now?"

"I think we should discuss any of the matters that receive enough support to warrant it," she says, her nose rising into the air.

A fist pounds on the table, cutting off the man's response. "I move to vote on the ban for turning protocols."

The table falls silent, and I crane my neck, trying to get a look at the man speaking. *Ban for turning protocols?* His head towers over everyone else, and his pale hair is cropped close to his scalp. Icy blue eyes sweep the table, narrowed and sharp. Definitely an Olofsson.

"I second the motion," says the man beside him, his opposite in every way. Strikingly dark skin and eyes, and probably half the first man's height.

Reid's expression is carefully blank. His mother, on the other hand, presses her lips together in a firm line, a muscle in her jaw ticking. A long silence fills the room, but no one else speaks, all eyes on the queen. She's required to have the vote now.

"Those in favor of the ban?" she says tightly.

The two men who'd suggested the vote are the only *aye*s in the room.

"We have more pressing matters to discuss than this," scoffs the woman beside me.

"By all means." The blond man shoves his chair back, stands, and straightens his suit jacket. "Continue to discuss. But you can consider Olofsson officially out of the alliance."

The shorter man stands too, bowing his head. "Jógvan as well."

The queen stands, her face flushed.

But both men turn and leave the room before she has the chance to speak.

I SIT QUIETLY through the rest of the meeting, but once we're out in the hall, I grab Reid's sleeve.

He puts his hand over mine, not looking at me. "Not here."

The mood is much heavier than when we started, and the other representatives either linger behind or silently disappear back to their guest rooms. I slip out of the room the first moment I can, wanting to put as much distance between me and my mother as possible. It's not until we're back in Reid's room that I feel like I can breathe again.

"I don't understand what just happened. Those guys who walked out…"

He closes the door behind us and leans against it, sighing. "This has been an ongoing point of contention. It's a more progressive belief system—purist, some would say. They don't believe in turning vampires. Some find it unnatural, since we can't do it without the help of a witch. And even then, as you've seen, turned vampires are different than ones who are born. Some believe we should outlaw it completely, especially as the number of turned vampires continues to rise. They outnumber born vampires at least two to one at this point."

"I—why have I never heard about this before?"

"It's not a popular opinion, and certainly not in this territory. But some believe…strongly in it."

"And you?" I ask, my voice quiet. "What do you believe?"

"Truthfully? I think they make some decent points. I think there's merit to what they're saying, but they're losing the chance of getting anyone else's vote at that table with how extreme they made the terms of that ban. They don't just want to stop people from turning *new* vampires. They want to limit the lifespan of currently turned vampires, place more restrictions on them. They even want to place restrictions on how long a born vampire can use a witch to freeze their aging. Both the queen at Suksai and my mother have held their positions longer than anyone else in our history. A lot of people question whether a single person should be able to rule indefinitely. But plenty of people in that room have turned vampires they care about. Queen Suksai herself was turned over a century ago. They think she's going to let her representatives vote in favor of shortening her life? Of course they're not going to go for that."

"But leaving the alliance altogether over this—"

"They may have made it seem like this was the sole reason today, but…" He trails off. "The queen likes to believe our alliances are stronger than they are. Things have been unstable long before now. If they were willing to walk out today, my guess is they've been preparing to do so for a while."

I slowly sink into the chair by the window, my head spinning. Even if I hadn't been completely failing my attempts to memorize everything in my foreign affairs class, I still wouldn't have been prepared enough to be in that room.

"And the attacks? In the other regions? Have they been…?"

He nods. "Similar to what we've seen here. And similar timeframes. From what I understand, we've still had the most."

"They said other estates have been attacked. Did they mean wendigos?"

"Auclair and Queirós, from what I've heard. Auclair, at least, seems to have gotten things under control."

"I don't understand what all of this means," I admit.

He sets his jaw off to the side. "I don't think any of us do."

CHAPTER TWENTY-THREE

MONROE STUMBLES OUT of the black car parked in front of the estate and throws her arms around my neck. I hug her back, the strength of her arms nearly cutting off my breathing. When she pulls away, I notice the red splotches covering her face, like she's been crying.

A few human servants pop the trunk and carry her bags inside as I help her with the two duffel bags in the back seat.

"Have you heard from Kirby?" she asks.

"Not in a little while. Why?"

She sniffles and throws the bag over her shoulder. "I haven't been able to get ahold of her in a few days, and I keep hearing all of this stuff about attacks happening around the other estates too. I'm overreacting, right? I'm being stupid."

I put my hand on her back as we trek toward the estate, my stomach twisting. It sounds like she's just referring to the rabid vampire attacks. I don't think telling her about the wendigos outright attacking other estates is going to help.

"I'm sure she's fine," I say. "I haven't heard anything bad about Suksai. Maybe they're out traveling around or something and she doesn't have phone service."

"Right," says Monroe, her voice tight.

"Roe." I grab her shoulders and force her to look at me. "Let's not worry unless we have to, all right? Someone around here must know the schedules for the summer programs. Let's see if we can find out where she is, okay?"

Relief softens the muscles in her face, then her lips quirk to one side. "It truly is desperate times if Valerie Darkmore has turned into the voice of reason in the group."

"You know what? I'll let you have that jab. Only because of your *fragile* emotional state. But it's the only one you're going to get."

"There she is! Roe Money!"

I turn as Nathan comes barreling down the stairs in sweaty black workout clothing. I stumble to the side as he scoops Monroe up and spins her in a circle.

I raise my eyebrows and meet her gaze over his shoulder. *Roe Money?* I mouth.

She rolls her eyes, but she's smiling as he sets her down.

"Oh, Nate, you remember my friend, Valerie?"

Nate?

I try to keep the utter shock off my face as he turns his blinding grin on me and shakes the hair out of his face. "Our very own prodigy blood witch, how could I forget?" He claps Monroe on the back. "Good to have you back, kid. Heard about the academy shutting down. Bummer."

She shrugs. "Guess you'll have to entertain me."

"Looks like the old man wants me to stick around after all, so I can do that."

The human servants nod at us as they pass and head up the stairs with Monroe's bags.

"You hear about the big representatives' meeting?" Nathan continues. "Oh shit." He turns to me. "You were there, weren't you? I heard it was dramatic as *fuck*."

"That's definitely one word for it," I mumble.

"Heard the Swedes dipped." He throws an arm over Monroe's shoulders with the kind of familiarity I'd expect from Kirby. "They've always been a bunch of buzzkills. Speaking of buzz though, we're having a party up in Percy's room tonight. Can I count you ladies in?"

I feel a tug on the bond before I see him. Reid walks toward us from the far end of the hallway. He rolls up his sleeves and gives a swift nod to a few servants as he passes, then raises his head as he reaches us in the foyer. He flashes Monroe and Nathan a tightlipped smile, but his eyes find me.

The scouts said the coast is clear, but I'm not sure for how long.

I startle a little at the presence of his voice in my head, but nod.

Okay. Right now?

Monroe's gaze flits between the two of us, and her lips part. "You two are totally talking to each other in your heads right now, aren't you?" She smacks Nathan on the chest. "How come we can't do that?"

I squeeze Monroe's shoulder. "I'll catch up with you later, okay?"

"Wait, where are you two going? Wherever it is, can I

come with?" She pushes out her lower lip. "I feel like I haven't seen you in forever, and I have nothing to do here alone."

"I'd be down for an outing," Nathan adds. "Especially if it includes party favors."

"We're not going to get drugs," Reid says flatly.

Nathan shrugs, unperturbed. "Disappointing, but not a deal breaker."

Reid glowers at me. *Valerie…*

It might be helpful. I shrug. *Monroe's a skinwalker. Maybe she could shift and check the place out before we head in.*

Reid raises a single eyebrow. *And the frat boy?*

Well, they're bonded, so at least he could let us know if she's okay while she's in there.

This isn't a joke.

I glare at him. *You think I, of all people, don't know that?*

Monroe sighs. "You're doing it again, aren't you?"

Reid holds my gaze for another moment, the corners of his eyes tightening.

Fine, but we're leaving now.

RAIN DRUMS against the roof of the car as we wind our way through the city. I sit squished in middle seat in the back, Nathan and Monroe on each side. They chat around me, catching up like old friends.

I had no idea they'd gotten close. Or…friendly. Maybe I'd been paranoid about the whole Avery thing. Sticking my nose in places it doesn't belong. Especially considering I don't even know what happened between them. And I trust

Monroe's judgment. If she's happy being paired with him, I guess that's all that matters.

Reid sits silently in the front seat, staring straight ahead, and his tension bleeds through the bond.

I meet his eyes in the rearview mirror.

If anything goes wrong, I want you to teleport the two of them back to the estate, he says in my head.

I narrow my eyes at him. *I'm not leaving you behind.*

They won't kill me unless they want even more problems with my mother.

That doesn't make me feel any better.

When we pull around the back of the warehouse, there are no other cars in sight. There's a large garage door propped open with a cinderblock and a metal door beside it. I strain my ear, trying to hear if anyone's inside, but it doesn't seem like it.

My stomach knots. What if we're already too late?

"You ready for this?" Nathan asks Monroe.

She shoots him a sly grin and unbuckles her seat belt. Wordlessly, she throws the car door open and shifts before she makes it all the way outside. Her small black cat form glances at us over its shoulder, then trots toward the building, tail held high in the air.

"You'll be able to tell us if anything goes wrong?" I say.

Nathan nods, but he still has that easy smile on his face. Like he's not too concerned. Reid meets my eyes in the rearview mirror again, the same tension I'm feeling showing in the lines of his face. We all watch as Monroe squeezes in under the garage door and disappears into the dark.

"If she's not out in five minutes, I'm going in after her," I say.

Reid nods his agreement. He sits stiffly in his seat, his eyes scanning through the windshield, probably making sure no one else arrives and surprises us.

"What are you expecting to find in there?" Nathan asks.

Reid and I exchange a look.

"Is this about all the attacks lately?"

I lift a single eyebrow. So Monroe's frat boy is a little more observant than I'd given him credit for.

"That's what we're hoping to find out," says Reid. "If there's anyone still here."

Before any of us can respond, Monroe's cat form reappears through the garage, but she doesn't come back to the car. She sits down in front of the door and cocks her head to the side.

"I guess that means it's safe to go in," I murmur.

The silence is twice as thick once we climb out. If I still felt cold the way I used to, I imagine the hairs on my arms would be standing on end.

The gravel crunches under our feet as we head toward the warehouse, and Monroe slips back inside without waiting for us. Nathan bends down and lifts the garage door, seemingly with ease. It groans and creaks as it moves. Every muscle in my body tenses as I look around, but we're still alone.

He holds the door open and nods for us to step inside. "After you."

The floor is littered with debris, and there's a hole in the ceiling where the smallest trace of moonlight trickles in, leaving a spotlight on the floor. Graffiti lines the walls, and our footsteps echo in the darkness. I can't see Monroe, but I can hear her little paws tapping against the ground as she explores some more.

I inhale deeply, trying to catch the scent of anyone or anything. It just smells like dust and mold. And maybe cleaning supplies.

Reid ventures farther into the room, starting at the walls and slowly making his way toward the center. A hallway branches off on our right, and Nathan heads that way. Whatever I'd been expecting to find in here, it wasn't this.

I meet Reid in the center of the room.

"I thought your scouts said there were lots of people coming and going."

Reid nods.

"And they didn't mention anything about them clearing out?"

He frowns and shakes his head.

"Then where did they all go?" I ask. "You think there's a basement or something they could be set up in?"

He tilts his head back. "Do you smell that?"

"Smell what?"

"The bleach."

I nod.

"If this place was as abandoned as it looks, why would someone be cleaning in here?" he murmurs.

"You think the bodies were here first?" I glance around the empty room again, my heart weighing heavily in my chest. There must be something here that could help. If they'd left for good, surely Reid's scouts would have said something, right? There's no way his scouts would've missed that. Unless…they *had* seen it. And hadn't told Reid on purpose. "There was a spell Quinn's professor friend did when we ran into Marcus," I say slowly. "It tracked where he'd been, what had happened to him. I might be able to do something similar with the building, see what happened here."

Reid looks around us and frowns. "Where'd Nathan go?"

Soft footsteps sound down the hallway. We hurry after him, the tang of bleach hanging in the air growing stronger with each step.

It happens in a split second. The space between blinks. I smell it first, the distinct hint of wood. And then the air moves around me. My brain doesn't have time to catch up before my instincts kick in. Nathan lets out a high-pitched yelp up ahead, and I jump in front of Reid and shove him to the side.

The impact comes next.

It hits the back of my tricep and shoots all the way through my arm. Blood roars in my ears, and I pitch forward at the waist, gasping as it knocks the wind clear from my lungs.

"Nathan!" Monroe's voice calls up ahead, but I can barely hear it.

My vision slants and blurs. Reid's face appears in front of mine, his hands grabbing my cheeks.

"Valerie."

I look from him to my arm, where a wooden arrow is sticking straight through it. "Fuck," I groan.

We'd thought we've been so careful scouting this place out, coming in tonight. Whoever had been here clearly saw the scouts, and they've been expecting us, enough to booby-trap the place. Given the materials of the arrows, they were expecting the vampire variety of visitors. Maybe this was Terrence's plan all along when he gave me the address. I should've listened to Reid. Of course this was a bad idea.

Reid disappears for a moment. "It's clear," he calls out. "No one else is here. They just had a couple of traps set up. I didn't see any more."

My entire body trembles, and cold sweat breaks out along my skin. It hadn't really occurred to me how much this would hurt now with my half vampire side.

Reid steadies a hand on my arm, and the movement jostles the arrow. A wave of pain rolls over me so hard it nearly knocks me off my feet. My other shoulder slumps against his chest, and he holds me up by the waist.

"Just pull it out," I say through my teeth.

"What the hell were you thinking?" he growls.

"It was going to...hit you...in the chest," I manage to grit out. The wound burns, like something is leeching out of the wood and into my blood. A small moan escapes my lips despite myself, and I lock my teeth together.

Reid's hand comes up to the side of my face. "You saved my life."

I try to laugh, but it comes out as a pained, shaky breath. "That's my job."

He tightens one arm around my back, holding me to him as he braces his other on the head of the arrow. "I'm going to break off the end first. You may want to hold on to me."

I do as he says, burying my face against his chest and fisting my hand in his shirt.

He breaks off the front of the arrow, and I gasp.

"Okay, okay. Almost done," he breathes.

My entire arm pulses around the arrow.

"Reid," I whimper.

"You want me to give you a warning?"

"Just pull it—"

He yanks the arrow free, and my knees buckle. He catches me around the waist, but my arm still feels like dead weight. I collapse against him, unable to do anything but desperately try to draw breath.

"Nathan?" I gasp. "Is he—?"

"It hit him in the leg. He should be all right."

I pull my arm against my chest and let out a low groan. Blood seeps from the wound. It's healing, but slowly. "They knew we were coming."

He nods. "We should get out of here in case they have anything else in store. Can you walk?"

I try to push off his chest, but my balance falters, and he has to reach out and catch me again.

"It's all right," he murmurs. "I've got you."

"Roe?" I call, my voice cracking.

"We're okay!" she yells back. "We'll meet you at the car."

Reid bends down as if to pick me up, and I start to pull away.

"You are *not*—"

"Valerie, I mean this in the kindest way possible." He scoops my legs out from under me and hoists me into his arms. "But just for once, shut the fuck up."

CHAPTER TWENTY-FOUR

THE THROBBING LINGERS long after we leave the warehouse. Reid gives me his blood, which helps the wound heal, but the pain has seeped into my bones, filling me with a full-body ache.

The estate is flooded with activity when we pull up out front. Dozens of cars litter the drive, and people bustle back and forth. All of the outdoor lights are on, their harsh beams cutting through the dark, and there's at least double the amount of security out here as usual.

The moment our car comes to a stop, several of the estate's guards swarm the vehicle. They peer through the windows and start talking into the headsets in their ears. Nathan opens his door first, and they practically rip him out of the car. We follow suit, and they usher us toward the building, all speaking over each other so I can't understand what any of them are saying.

The mayhem doesn't stop once we get inside, where people are scrambling through the halls.

"What's going on?" I try to ask a servant passing by, but he continues up the stairs, running.

"Where have you been?" My mother's voice cuts through the chaos as she stomps toward us.

I open my mouth to respond, but she doesn't seem that interested in what I have to say. She shoves me down the hall, then looks back at my companions, irritated they didn't immediately follow.

"You too, Your Highness." Her voice shakes around *Your Highness* as if being pleasant is causing her physical pain. She juts her chin at Monroe and Nathan. "Them too."

Red lights flash overhead, along with an emergency siren.

Are we having some kind of drill?

She keeps walking until we reach the throne room. The moment we're inside, she turns and heads back into the hall. I call after her, but Monroe grabs the inside of my elbow and nods toward something behind me.

The circle of glass where the queen likes to display her blood in the center of the floor is missing. It's propped open like a door, revealing metal stairs heading straight into the earth. I glance at Reid, but he doesn't look surprised. A harsh line slices through the middle of his brow.

"What is it?" I ask.

"There's a bunker down there," he explains. "It's only supposed to be used in cases of extreme emergencies."

All of the estates have bunkers. That's what he'd said about the attacks happening at the other estates.

Oh God.

The door opens again behind us, and my mother shoves in another group of vampires who I recognize from around the estate. They glance at us, but then head straight for the bunker.

"Hey," calls Monroe. "Do you know what's going on?"

The one at the back of the group, a tall, blonde woman, glances at us over her shoulder. "We're on lockdown," she says. "We're surrounded."

"Surrounded?" I echo. We'd *just* pulled into the estate. Other than the crazy amount of security out front, nothing had seemed particularly off about the grounds. Certainly no one surrounding it. "By who?"

"More like *what*," says the man beside her.

She meets my eyes just before her head disappears below the floor. "Wendigos."

A GROUP of three men in black Marionettes uniforms awaits us at the bottom of the ladder, which ends at a forked path with three branches—two hallways and another ladder that leads farther down. The broad-shouldered one in the middle takes one glance at our group, then grunts something to the taller man on his left.

"Group one," says the taller one. He juts his chin to the left—the next ladder.

Reid heads down first, and I grit my teeth, steeling myself. The wound in my arm is still burning from the first climb down. Metal walls surround us, lit by some kind of magic-fueled lights along the ceilings. We all climb down the second ladder, silent save for our labored breaths. The tunnel is at least a foot wider than my shoulders, but it still feels like too tight of a fit.

"Good thing no one's claustrophobic, right?" Nathan calls, voice still cheery.

"How many levels are there down here?" I ask.

"At least a dozen, as far as I know," says Reid.

"Please tell me we're not climbing down twelve of these," calls Monroe.

Another group of Marionettes is at the bottom of this ladder, this time three women and one man. The metal walls give way to what looks like white stone, almost mirroring the architecture of the estate aboveground.

"Group one, I presume," says one of the women, sounding bored. She nods toward the hallway on her left, this one with a much wider mouth. "You can head in there to await further instructions, but your accommodations will be one more level down."

"Accommodations?" mutters Monroe. "How long exactly are we supposed to stay down here?"

The woman waves us on. Nathan and Monroe take the lead. The hall stretches on, and it's not until we're nearly to the end that Monroe's words truly sink in. The hall feeds into a kitchen and dining area with various halls branching out from there. The counter is sectioned off with the boxes they use for human rations up in the estate, though here it seems to be divided by human food for the witches and blood bags for the vampires.

"Move along! Move along!" Two of the Marionettes from before come up behind us, heading for the kitchen. "We're set for a debrief here soon, and you were the last ones for this group."

Thirty or so people are already in the room when we step inside. The kitchen itself is nestled in the corner, the rest of the rectangular space eaten up by metal picnic tables. It's mostly royal vampires and their Marionettes in attendance, though the queen and my mother are noticeably absent.

The representatives from the other regions are spread out among the rest, putting as much distance between them and everyone else as possible. The two who'd walked out of the meeting, however, are nowhere to be found.

I grab Monroe's arm, my heart beating faster in my chest. "Do you see Adrienne anywhere?"

She rises onto her tiptoes, trying to see around the room.

Reid's hand tightens around my arm, and he pulls me back against his chest as he juts his chin to the far corner. I lean against him, trying to see through the other bodies, and sure enough, Adrienne is sitting at the far table a few seats away from Daniel. My shoulders relax, and I let out a breath.

"I'm sure you all have a lot of questions." A redheaded Marionette props herself up on the kitchen counter— Marjorie, I think her name is. She was in Calla's year. In fact, all of the Marionettes we've seen since coming down that first ladder have been pretty young. They must have needed the more experienced members for something else.

"There's no need for panic. This was a precaution. We've detected several disturbances in our borders over the past few weeks, and we've decided to sequester all important personnel down here while we send out a team to deal with the matter. Hopefully, they'll wrap it up sooner rather than later. The moment we have more information, you all will be the first to know. Any questions?"

Disturbances in our borders? That definitely doesn't line up with what the others had said about being surrounded. At this point, I'm not sure either of those are true. Whatever's really going on, they don't want everyone to know.

The room erupts with noise as everyone starts talking all at once.

"What kind of disturbances?"

"Where is everyone else staying?"

"What about the attacks happening all over the city? I heard they brought in fifty bodies the other day."

Marjorie holds up her hands and sighs. "I don't know much more than you do. And I'm not going to sit here and spread more rumors. I'm sure there's enough of them floating around anyway."

"What about food?"

"And clothes?"

"And—"

Marjorie climbs to her feet on top of the counter, now towering over everyone. "Enough! We have rations here for everyone, enough to last much longer than we'll need. You'll be shown to your accommodations shortly, where you'll find everything else you need. If you are missing something, feel free to ask any of the servants who will be joining us down here momentarily after they're finished with their debriefing. I think it goes without saying, *no feeding on the humans* while we're down here. We have more than enough blood bags to go around."

A rumble of disapproval circles through the vampire crowd, and my muscles tense.

Footsteps pound down the hall, and another Marionette, a short, dark-skinned man, appears. He swallows hard, catching his breath, then nods at Marjorie. "We're ready for them whenever you are."

"All right." She claps her hands together and jumps down from the counter. "If you want to follow us, let's show you to your new home for the time being."

"You know I'm not one to complain, but you'd think given the size of this place down here, they could've at least given us a *little* privacy, you know?" Monroe says out of the corner of her mouth.

We stand as a group in the doorway of the *accommodations room*.

Room. Not rooms.

It's a large space with a half wall down the middle. Beds sit in neat rows with only a few feet separating them.

At least they're not bunk beds.

There's a door in the back of the room that leads to the bathrooms, but other than that, Monroe's right, there is no privacy.

Which I probably wouldn't have cared about nearly as much if I didn't need to find a way to consume blood in private to prevent killing everyone in here.

"You'll find changes of clothes, toothbrushes, all of that kind of stuff, in here." The man points to the small trunks at the foot of each of the beds. "The rest of the amenities you can find through the kitchen on the floor above us…"

His voice fades away as my vision snags on the red salt embedded in the wall. Just a few inches above the floor, but it lines the entire room. I glance into the hall to see if it's everywhere, but it's just in here.

"What's with the red salt?" I ask.

All heads turn in my direction, and I realize I cut off whatever he'd been saying.

He bristles but inclines his head. "This room also acts as a safe room. Should the urgency of the situation escalate and we need to further protect ourselves, we would lock down in this room." He holds eye contact with me for a moment more before turning away and continuing on with his spiel.

My forehead wrinkles at the explanation. The only thing red salt would protect from is magic, as if other witches would be the threat.

"And, of course, for your own protection, these doors will be sealed and locked during the day while everyone is sleeping."

He somehow makes *for your own protection* sound like a threat. The thought of being locked in here if the hunger gets too bad, surrounded by dozens of appetizing heart-beats, makes my throat tighten.

How long are we going to be down here?

I suck in a sharp breath. I can feel Reid looking at me out of the corner of my eye, but keep facing forward until the Marionettes are finished with their little tour and head back into the hall. Some royals hurry after them, probably to complain about the accommodations, but everyone else quickly spreads out, claiming spaces and beds.

Reid steps in front of me, his gaze sweeping over my face.

"I don't have my herbs down here," I say quietly.

And I doubt my specific needs are going to be met with those rations they have spread out in the kitchen.

Realization is quick to dawn in his eyes.

I'm a ticking time bomb.

I'm a ticking time bomb trapped however many feet underground with all the vampires and witches I could possibly want ripe for the picking. The blood Reid gave me earlier may have helped heal my arm, but it did little more than that. And I forgot to take my herbs this morning.

Who knows how long we'll be stuck down here?

And the back of my throat is already burning.

"Okay." Reid glances around us, then crosses his arms over his chest and lowers his voice. "On a scale of one to ten, how hungry are you right now?"

Slowly, I meet his eyes. "Reid, I just fed, and I'm already at a five."

A muscle ticks in his jaw, but it's the only crack in his calm demeanor. "Okay," he repeats. "I'll take care of it."

"Reid—"

"I'll take care of it," he says, voice firm this time.

Monroe waves at us from across the room as she stakes out some beds next to each other. I force a smile and wave back.

"Can you make it until everyone goes to sleep?" he asks under his breath.

Now that my attention is resting on it, the hunger pulses

beneath my gums, growing stronger with each passing minute. Lights out won't be until hours from now. Who knows how bad it will be by then? I can't afford to black out and wake up surrounded by bodies, not down here. And not with people around me who I care about.

"Valerie?" Reid's hand brushes my back.

I turn my forced smile on him and nod. "Yeah, of course. I'll be fine."

CHAPTER TWENTY-FIVE

THE HOURS DRAG ON, and for a while, it feels like sunrise will never come. By the time everyone collects their rations, explores the different tunnels, and claims spots to sleep, my hunger has jumped from a five to an eight. I shove down a serving of the human food, hoping it'll make the other kind of hunger calm down, but I may as well have been eating air.

Monroe, Nathan, Reid, and I take four beds beside each other near the back corner, but even once the lights are off and snores start to fill the air, I can't sleep. I can't do much of anything but stare at the ceiling, count my breaths, and desperately try not to lean over and rip out my best friend's throat while she sleeps.

I can hear every heartbeat in this room, the blood rushing through veins, the scent of sweat on skin. I can imagine how my entire body would relax, how warm it would feel in my mouth, how—

Footsteps prick my hearing, and every muscle in my

body tenses. My heart rate picks up, blotting out the rest of the room so I can hear nothing but the roar of blood in my ears. I force down a deep breath. Monroe in the bed next to me continues to snore, and the sound of dozens of other slow, even heartbeats makes its way back to me.

The covers rustle, then someone slides into my bed. I gasp, my breath catching in my throat. A hand cups the side of my head, and Reid's scent hits me a moment later. His head squeezes in on the pillow, his nose an inch from mine.

"Sorry," he whispers. "I didn't mean to scare you."

When he exhales, his breath washes over my cheek. I close my eyes for a moment as I wait for my heart to calm.

"Are you all right?" he asks.

I swallow hard, then slowly shake my head.

He pulls the blankets up around our shoulders, shielding us from view, then pulls the collar of his shirt aside, revealing more of his neck.

"Go ahead," he murmurs.

His pulse thuds against the hollow of his throat, and I'm momentarily mesmerized. My mouth waters, and my entire body trembles with how badly I need it. I inch closer to him on the bed. He tilts his head, giving me better access, but I pause, licking my lips.

"Reid," I whisper.

A question knits his brow.

"I'm...*starving*."

His eyes flicker over my face, then he nods his under-standing. "Take as much as you need. I'll be all right."

"No, I—"

His hand finds the side of my head again. "I'll stop you if I have to."

I can't even pretend to hesitate. He must feel how bad it is through the bond too. Given the hunger is beating inside of me like a frantic drum, it's a miracle I haven't already jumped on him.

Tucking my face against his neck, I breathe him in. The smell of his skin wraps around me, but stronger still is what waits underneath. My teeth sink into his neck easily, and his blood floods my mouth.

He lets out a harsh breath near my ear, but I hear it as if from a distance. My eyes roll back in my head. I clamp a hand around the back of his collar, pulling myself closer, wrapping my body around his. He keeps a hand steady on the back of my head, but the more I drink, the more it all fades away—the touch, the smells. I drink and drink, the hunger still screaming for more inside of me. It's burning and blistering like fire inside of my veins, and it *needs more.*

"Valerie."

I sink my teeth in deeper and tighten my hands around him, holding him down. The blood is so warm as it hits the back of my throat, the relief as it floods through me so sweet—

"*Valerie.*"

He grabs me by the throat, then I'm on my back on the bed. All of the air leaves my lungs, and I grit my teeth. Every instinct in my body screams for me to fight back, to flip him over, tear open his throat, and drain every last drop of blood he has left. His face is a blur above me, his features barely distinguishable. All I can see is the blood as it drips from his neck and lands on my chest.

"It's okay," he murmurs. "Sometimes it takes a minute to get out of it. It's okay."

I clamp a hand around his wrist, my nails digging in. My chest heaves as the redness in my vision slowly starts to fade. He leans in close, his face right in front of mine, hand still tight around my neck. His eyes are the first thing to come back into focus, blue and calm. They flit over my face as my breathing starts to slow, and my eyes widen at the mess of blood at his throat.

"Look at me," he whispers. "It's okay."

His blood courses through me hot and strong, satiating the hunger, but also doing something...*else*. The bond warms between us, and my stomach clenches as his gaze falls back to my mouth. We're close enough that I feel every breath he exhales against my skin and the heat of his body pressing against mine.

It occurs to me his hand is still around my throat. He seems to realize it the same moment I do because he loosens his grip.

But he doesn't let go.

Slowly, his thumb traces my mouth. His eyes hold mine as he runs it along the blood lingering on my bottom lip. My breath catches in my throat, but I don't move. Fire spreads across my skin, fed by the way his breathing seems as uneven as mine is. The air between us shifts, *burns*.

I drift closer, until there's no space left between us at all. Our noses brush, our lips a whisper apart, and my eyes flutter shut.

"Valerie," he breathes, his voice ragged.

I'm the one to close the rest of the distance between us,

but the moment our lips touch, his hand seizes the back of my head, his grip unyielding as his mouth crashes against mine. He folds around me, pinning me against his chest. Every nerve in my body lights up as his lips move against mine, hard and sure and desperate. I sigh, and his tongue sweeps in.

The bond pulls taut between us as I fist my hands in his hair, pulling myself closer, suddenly as desperate for this as I had been for his blood. I melt into it, and he kisses me harder, deeper, like he's breathing me in.

He pulls back enough for his lips to trail to my jaw, my throat. Everywhere he touches burns as his hands explore down my ribs, my waist, my hips. When he reaches my thigh, he yanks it up and pulls it around him. He rolls partially on top of me, his weight pressing me into the mattress.

I can feel how hard he is through his pants and *fuck*. My head spins, and I arch against him, not sure what I need more, to feel more of him or for him to touch more of me. I skim my hands up his chest and around his neck, my fingers tightening around his hair. I moan into his mouth as his hips press into mine.

"Valerie," he breathes, his voice low and raw.

We stop kissing, and he hovers over me. Our surroundings slowly trickle back in, and I realize where we are—that we are most definitely not alone right now.

I look up at him, breathless, and he stares back at me like he's never seen me before. My body, however, does not seem to understand the situation, because it's still arched up against him, my fingers knotted in his hair.

But then he pulls away and rolls onto his back, and my

body suddenly feels cold. The bond is still strung so tight it's like an invisible force pulling me toward him.

The snoring beside us continues on, and the only elevated heart rates I can hear are ours. At least we hadn't woken anyone up.

But when I turn my head toward Reid, he's already looking at me with a blazing look in his eyes that makes everything in me go still. He moves onto his side so his mouth is right beside my ear when he murmurs, "Roll over."

Nothing in his expression or voice invites any kind of discussion, so I shift away. One of his arms wraps around my waist and pulls me against him, while the other winds under the pillow and across my chest. My breathing quickens as his lips brush my ear again.

"Bend this leg."

He nudges my top leg, and I bring my knee up. His body urges me forward, rolling my hips.

"Valerie," he rasps. "Tell me if you want me to stop."

I say nothing, and his hand tightens on my chest, working my nipple through my shirt with his thumb. *Oh God.* The touch is light, barely even there, but chills ripple down every inch of my skin. His fingers pinch and tease, faster, harder.

When his other hand finds the waistband of my shorts, the anticipation builds to an almost excruciating degree. His fingers slide along my underwear, slowly, lazily, like he has all the time in the world. I squeeze my eyes shut, focusing on the way his heart is pounding, his breathing rough in my ear. I press myself back harder against him, needing more, needing...needing...

Maybe this is a bad idea, maybe we shouldn't—

All thinking disintegrates as his hand slides beneath the thin fabric, and he trails his fingers between my thighs. His breath hitches beside my ear, his swallow audible. He continues his small, coaxing movements at first, but his touch quickly shifts from exploring to claiming as he feels me relax against him. He falls into a rhythm, and his teeth graze the delicate skin between my neck and shoulder. It's intoxicating, the heat of his skin, the rise and fall of his chest against my back. The sure, slow circles of his fingers. I let out a small whimper despite myself.

He pulls me harder against his chest, his lips brushing my ear as he murmurs, "Can you keep quiet for me?"

I manage a nod.

His fingers move a little faster, and I rock my hips against his hand, a moan building in my chest. It quickly becomes apparent I am in no position to make that kind of promise. He realizes it too, because his hand clamps over my mouth.

My head falls back against his shoulder, my breaths turning into pants. He nudges me forward as his fingers dip inside of me, pushing me further onto my stomach.

"Put your face in the pillow," he orders.

I comply, letting the fabric muffle the desperate little sounds coming from my throat. The hard length of him presses harder against my back as he leans over, his body caging me in, his lips trailing behind my ear. The heat that builds inside of me is maddening, devastating, and I moan against the pillow. The only thing keeping me still is his weight on top of me.

I tilt my head to the side and gulp in a breath. "Reid," I breathe.

He seizes my jaw, pulling me toward him to crush my mouth against his. I twist my arm around to reach for him, impatient to feel him in my hand, but he grabs my wrist and pins our hands together against the pillow.

"If you touch me right now," he grits out. "We're going to wake up every person in here."

Impossibly, my blood heats even more. We pause and listen for signs of people awake in the room, but it's quiet.

I look behind his head, an idea forming. A desperate, heedless idea, but with his body still tangled around me, I can't think about anything else. Nothing exists but his skin, his breath, his lips. Now that I've let myself want this, I don't know how to turn it back off.

Reid follows my gaze. "Bathroom?"

"I—I could spell it to make it soundproof."

His eyes darken, looking nearly black in the dim light. Abruptly, he unwraps himself from me. "Get up."

My feet make no noise against the floor as I cross the room. In a blink of an eye, he has the door shut, locked, and me pinned against it. He hovers close as he whispers, "Did you…?"

The drop of blood from the spell is still warm in my palm, and I barely manage a nod before his lips are on mine. His hands slide into my hair and tilt my head back as his tongue delves into my mouth. My eyes flutter closed as he spins us around and presses me against the sink. Any hesitation that had been in his movements are gone now. His tongue traces along mine, hot and commanding, and my hands find the bare skin beneath the hem of his shirt.

A wave of desire crashes into me so viciously it steals my breath. I can't tell if it's all mine or if I'm feeling a combination of my own pleasure and Reid's. The bond pulses between us like a heartbeat, and I can't pick out which emotions are mine and which are his.

His hands follow the curves of my body, trailing down my shoulders, my waist, my hips, then grip my ass and haul me into his arms. He sets me on the edge of the sink and settles between my legs. Our bodies are already pressed together, but I wrap my arms around his neck, trying to get closer.

"Tell me if you want me to stop," he whispers.

His breath raises the hairs on my neck, and a shiver travels down my spine. When I don't respond, his hand skates over my hip to my inner thigh. His lips brush mine, but he doesn't kiss me. He searches my eyes as his fingers slide beneath my shorts, waiting—watching for my reaction, or permission, I'm not sure. I stare back, and he pushes the fabric of my underwear aside.

I let out a surprised gasp at the jolt that goes through me, but he just keeps moving his hand lower. My eyes flutter shut as he dips a finger inside me, then drags it back up to my clit. My breath catches as he leans in, his lips exploring the skin beneath my jaw.

His other hand pushes the hair away from my face before tightening his fist around it. "How do you expect me to have any self-control when you're already this wet?"

"Then take your pants off," I gasp.

There's fire in his eyes as he pulls back, but a slight smile curls his lips as he leans in to kiss me. "Not yet," he says against my mouth. "I want to watch you come first."

He goes back to sucking on my neck, his fingers moving faster, harder, and I press my lips together as a moan crests inside of me. His mouth works lower, his teeth and tongue grazing my breast through my shirt. But his words make me pause.

I lick my lips. "I—"

He pulls back, his fingers stilling. "What's wrong?"

"Nothing. I just—I might not be able to." My face burns under his stare, but I don't lower my gaze. "I've never…with…"

Understanding lights his eyes, and he lets out a single, low laugh as he presses his forehead to mine. "Why don't you let me worry about that? Put your hands on the counter."

My brow furrows, but I lean back and do as he says.

"That's perfect. Just like that." The low quality of his voice makes my stomach flip. I bite my lip as he hooks his hands beneath the waistband of my shorts and tugs.

Instead of coming to stand before me again, he gets down on his knees. And for a moment, he just looks up at me, his eyes searching my face before traveling down the rest of my body, like he's trying to commit every detail to memory. But then he grabs my thighs in each hand, right above my knees, and spreads my legs around him. I barely have time to catch my breath before he dips his head, and his tongue runs along the length of me.

But just as quickly as he'd started, he pulls back, his lips tracing the inside of my thigh instead. I squirm against the sink, and his hands tighten, holding me in place.

"Do you have any…" He presses his lips to the inside of

my knee. "Idea..." Again, a few inches higher. "How fucking *good*..." Again, halfway up my thigh. "You taste?"

With his last word, he dives back between my legs, his arms holding me down by the hips. My head falls back, and I brace one hand behind me to keep upright, the other fisting in his hair.

Good fucking God.

"Reid," I moan as he plunges two fingers inside of me. My hips rock against him of their own accord as heat builds in my stomach, the soles of my feet, my spine...

I release his hair and bite down on my fist, trying to muffle the desperate noises.

He stands abruptly, his fingers still inside of me, but unmoving now. I let out a soft noise of protest, and I blink like I'm coming out of a haze. His face stops an inch from mine.

"Wh-why'd you stop?" I gasp.

"Don't you fucking dare." He grabs the hand I'd been holding to my mouth and pins it to the counter beside me. "They can't hear you out there, but I want to hear every sound you make. You understand?"

My heart stops, and fire burns through my veins at the intensity in his words. The intensity rolling off every move he makes. I've never seen him like this. All I can do is nod. He holds my gaze as his fingers start to move inside of me again. But there's something about his expression that softens as he watches me. A tenderness there I hadn't noticed before, and it makes my chest ache.

A small, traitorous thought rises in the back of my mind. I don't even want to acknowledge it, but it's there.

I never felt anything like this with Connor.

We watch each other as my breaths quicken, and my hands grip his shoulders. He leans in like he's going to kiss me, but then pauses with his lips barely grazing mine.

Even as I come undone and the moans coming out of my throat become breathy and desperate, I don't break his gaze. He crushes his lips against mine as the last of it ebbs away. I don't have time to recover before his hands slide under my thighs and hoist me off the sink. I wrap my legs around his waist as he pins me against the opposite wall.

"Do you want me to be gentle?" he breathes.

I hesitate only a second before shaking my head.

His mouth curls into a smile against mine. "Good."

It occurs to me then he's still fully clothed, and I tug at the hem of his shirt. He sets my feet back on the ground, then yanks the shirt over his head. Lean muscle covers every inch of him, and my mouth goes dry at the sight— the hard planes of his chest, the V of his hips that disappears into his pants. He grabs my wrists and pulls them over my head so he can pull my shirt off next.

It's dark in the bathroom with the lights off, but if I can see him this clearly with my half vampire vision, I'm sure he can see every detail of me. I'd never really felt self-conscious about my body with Connor before, but now with Reid standing here looking like *that*, I can't help but shift uncomfortably under the weight of his gaze, feeling exposed as it travels the length of me.

He takes my chin between his thumb and forefinger and tilts my face up to his, the touch strikingly gentle. For a moment, all of the intensity behind his eyes is gone. "You're the most beautiful thing I've ever seen."

This time when he kisses me, it's slow, and it melts away

the rest of my apprehension. My fingers trail down his sides, and his muscles tense beneath my touch. He deepens the kiss, his lips hard and devouring as his hands tangle in my hair. They don't break from mine, not even as he kicks off his pants and my back presses against the cold tiles of the wall. His presence is commanding and all-consuming as his body crowds in around me, and he hooks a single arm beneath my knee and pulls it up.

I brace my weight against the wall, and my heart pounds dangerously in my chest, my breathing already rapid.

He leans down and kisses the side of my neck. His lips brush my ear as he murmurs, "Are you sure?"

I nod, a low hum sounding in the back of my throat. He slides two fingers back inside of me, and I shudder, but then all too quickly, he pulls them out again. I dig my nails into his shoulders as he slowly slides his length along the wetness between my thighs. I whimper, then he starts to push inside. The wind knocks clear out of my lungs as he tightens his grip on my thigh.

He stills and meets my eyes. "You doing okay?"

I nod, not sure if I can manage words right now. He holds my gaze as he pushes the rest of the way in, my inner walls desperately trying to stretch around him. He pauses again, letting me get used to the feel of him, and kisses me. His teeth dig into my lip as he slowly starts to move.

I moan as he speeds up and grips the back of my head, holding me inches away from his face as he finds a steady pace. His eyes flick from my eyes to my mouth. "I'm not hurting you, am I?"

I shake my head, both hands wrapping around his neck and pulling myself closer.

"Use your words, love."

"No, Reid," I gasp. "It feels good."

He pounds into me, harder this time, and I let out a small, inhuman noise as I tip my head back, surrendering to him completely. I ache and contract around him until everything melds together, and I can't tell the difference between us at all. All I know is I need him closer, deeper. I need his skin and his voice and the way he's looking at me right now—like a man lost at sea finally seeing the first promise of land.

I haven't wanted to let myself think it. Haven't dared. But I just need him.

"Fuck," he breathes, then his lips are beside my ear again, a smile in his voice. "Like that?"

My entire body pulses, my stomach coiling tight. More small, desperate noises come out of my throat with each thrust of his hips. "Yes," I pant. "Oh God, Reid, please don't stop."

"Say it again," he says, his voice suddenly hard.

"Wh-what?"

He grabs my jaw, forcing me to look at him. "Say my name again."

A small smile rises to my lips as I pull myself closer. "You like that, do you?"

His eyes narrow a fraction, his fingers digging into my hips as he eases out painstakingly slow, then thrusts himself back in faster, harder. "You like toying with me."

I bite my lip, lifting my hips up to meet him each time. "Maybe." I trail my lips down his jaw, his throat, and end right below his ear. My forehead falls against his shoulder, our ragged breathing and the sound of our bodies coming together filling the small space. "Fuck, Reid."

He digs his hands into the backs of my thighs and yanks me into his arms. I gasp and quickly lock my legs around his waist as he slams my back to the wall, driving in so hard I can barely catch my breath.

"*Oh.*" I tighten around him and hold on to his shoulders, my face falling against the side of his neck. I close my eyes, trying to remember how to breathe, trying to remember how to *think*. Despite how composed he looks on the outside, his breathing is as strained as mine is now, his muscles tense beneath my hands. "Reid. *Reid*, I'm—" I breathe, my brain unable to form any other words right now.

"I know."

Just when I think I can't survive another second of this without coming over the edge, he slows and pulls us away from the wall. I lift my head from his shoulder, my vision hazy as I meet his eyes. "What—?"

His face is hard, and he gives me no warning before laying me onto the floor on my back and slamming back into me. I cry out as he braces his forearms around my head and hovers inches above me. He holds my gaze, and the look in his eyes alone threatens to undo me, but then he slows and glances around us.

"Reid?"

He sits up to grab a towel off the rack. He pauses, kneeling before me and taking me in. Hands sliding under my thighs, he bends between my legs and holds my gaze as he slowly slides his tongue back inside of me then drags it up to my clit. A full-body shudder rolls through me.

"Reid," I rasp.

He leans down, his breath ghosting across my lips as he says, "Lift your hips for me."

I do as he says, and he slides the towel underneath my tailbone, a half smile on his face now. "And hold on to me."

I wrap my hands around his neck, holding on to the back of his head as he guides himself back in. A small furrow forms between his eyebrows, and he opens his mouth like he wants to say something. In the end, he leans down, kisses the side of my neck, and leaves his head resting against my shoulder.

"God, you feel so good," he says.

I moan as we fall into a rhythm. My nails dig into his back, probably deep enough to draw blood, and I can feel his heart pounding in his chest as his body presses down, the sweat on his skin mingling with mine.

"Fuck," I breathe.

"Valerie," he whispers, his voice low and raw. I whimper at the sound of it, and he moves faster, his arms sliding beneath my back and holding me to his chest. I tighten my legs around his waist, leaving no space left between us, desperately grinding against him. "You gonna come for me again?"

"Yes," I gasp, my body already tensing up.

He holds me tighter, his lips brushing my ear as he breathes, "That's my girl. Just like that."

"Oh God. Reid. *Yes.*" I fist my hand in the back of his hair, and his muscles tremble around me. We come over the edge at the same time, and I bury my face in his shoulder as I cry out.

He slows, his lips trailing kisses over my neck, my jaw, my face, as he finally stills above me. He stays there long after it's over, our chests heaving together.

I close my eyes, still waiting for my heart to slow. He braces himself on his forearms, and I reach up to push the hair back from his eyes. He smiles, just the softest curl of his lips on the one side, before leaning down to kiss me slowly, gently. Time seems to slow, and everything else fades until he finally pulls away and rolls onto his back beside me.

"Fuck." I let out a shaky breath. "My ears are ringing."

He turns, a wolfish grin on his face now. "Yeah?"

I laugh and nod. He cups the side of my face with his hand, his thumb tracing lightly over my cheek. Despite everything we just did, my face burns beneath his stare as he pulls himself closer and brushes his nose against mine.

"We should probably get back out there before someone catches us, huh?" he murmurs.

I nod, but neither of us moves.

"It's taking every ounce of my self-control not to convince you to stay in here," he says.

I raise an eyebrow. "Don't you ever get tired?"

That damn grin returns.

I laugh again, and he tightens his grip on my face, tilting it up to look at him, his expression softer. "It's good to hear you laugh."

I glance at the door like I'm worried about someone else waking up, but really, I need to break the eye contact. "Can you grab my shorts?" I nod toward the sink.

He gets up, and I quickly clean myself off with the

towel under me and collect the rest of my clothes from the ground. He hands me the underwear first, but instead of his eyes lingering on my body as I slip everything back on, the heat of his gaze burns against my face.

"I'll go out first, just in case," I say as I finish pulling my clothes into place.

His eyes linger on me as he nods, then I slip out the door and head for my bunk.

It takes a few moments for my heart to stop pounding in my ears as I slide beneath the covers. I wait, listening to the breathing and heartbeats of everyone else in the room, but it seems like we're still the only two awake.

Small miracles.

It's not until I'm lying alone in bed that reality filters back in.

My head spins. What just happened? *What just happened?*

The bathroom door clicks shut across the room, but if Reid is heading back to his bed, I can't hear his footsteps. That was so impulsive, and probably stupid, and…

Something lifts the covers off me, and I jerk my head up. Reid slides into the bed as if it's the most normal thing in the world. He meets my eyes before pulling me in against his chest, his arms around me and his hand cradling the back of my head.

Any of the spiraling thoughts that had been building a second ago disappear. I relax against him as he slides a leg through mine, and I wrap an arm around his waist. For a moment, that same feeling I'd had in the bathroom returns, and the rest of the world goes quiet.

Safe, I realize. That's what I feel.

A lump rises to the back of my throat, and I press my

lips together. Whether he senses it through the bond or the tension in my body, I'm not sure, but Reid pulls back.

"What is it?"

I give him a small smile and shake my head, but he isn't buying it.

"You'll have sex with me," he says quietly, "but you won't talk to me?"

"It's nothing bad. I just—I feel safe with you. And I hadn't realized that it had been so long since I've felt that."

He stares at me for a second, his expression unreadable, before pressing his lips to my forehead and pulling me back against his chest. His fingers weave into my hair. Several moments pass, then his arms tighten around me, and he whispers, "I'm not going to let anything happen to you, Valerie. I promise."

I knot my fingers around his shirt, my eyes already too heavy to keep open, and fall asleep counting his breaths as his fingers trace up and down my spine.

CHAPTER TWENTY-SIX

"VALERIE."

I stir, my brain still half in a dream state. Every part of my body feels heavy, and my bed is so *warm* right now. I nuzzle further into my pillow. Five more minutes. I just need five more minutes.

"*Valerie.*"

Sighing, I squint a single eye open. The room is still dark, but Monroe is sitting up in the bed beside me. She stares at me with wide eyes.

I frown and blink both eyes open—and my vision focuses on the hands on the pillow in front of me. One is mine, obviously, but the one on top—the one with perfectly long, strong fingers that are currently laced through mine —is *not*.

The weight of his chest against my back filters in next. He breathes evenly against me, each exhale hitting my neck.

I look back to Monroe, now with equally wide eyes.

Gently, I lift Reid's arm to lay it back at his side. I'm nearly there when he sucks in a sharp breath and his head twitches. He lets out a low groan. His gaze falls on me first, and a sleepy smile appears, his eyes still half-closed.

He notices Monroe staring at us a moment later and bolts upright. He looks from her to me and back again and scratches the back of his head.

"I'm…going to get some water," he says.

Monroe keeps her gaze focused on me as he rolls out of bed and heads for the hall. When I still don't say anything, she arches a single eyebrow. I gesture for her to come closer, and she climbs out of her bed and joins me in mine.

"I don't have those herbs down here," I explain in a whisper. "And those *rations* aren't exactly doing it for me."

"You were *feeding* from him last night?"

"Shh!"

"Right. Right." She holds up her palms in a placating gesture, but that damn eyebrow is still sky high. "I don't know much about feeders, but I didn't realize they were that…*friendly*."

I shove her shoulder and hope she doesn't notice the blush creeping up my cheeks. "Oh, shut up." I nod toward Nathan. He's splayed out on his back and taking up every inch of the narrow bed. "You two seem pretty *friendly* yourselves."

She rolls her eyes. "Not the same thing. At all."

"Isn't it?"

"No," she says, voice suddenly serious, and something flits behind her eyes. Something wistful.

Kirby, I realize. Of course it's not the same with her and Nathan. She has Kirby.

"Still no word from Kirbs?" I ask.

A flush creeps up her cheeks, and she snaps her eyes to my face, probably wondering why the conversation at hand would make me think of her.

"I saw you guys at the Blood Lounge the night before she left," I admit.

The blush intensifies. "Val—I—we were going to tell you."

"Roe." I squeeze her shoulder. "It's okay. I'm not mad. We can…you can tell me about it whenever you're ready. I don't want you to feel like you have to."

"It's just…new," she explains. "We were just trying to figure it out before complicating the group, you know?"

"Yeah, I get it. And not that you need my blessing, but if that's what makes both of you happy, you know I'm all on board, right?"

She leans forward and throws her arms around my shoulders, crushing me to her. I let out a surprised breath but wrap my arms around her waist and squeeze.

"And if it gets bad or anything down here—you know, if we end up here for a while—just—ugh. What I'm saying is, if you need someone else to feed on in a pinch, I'm all yours."

I pull back, grinning. "Are you *propositioning* me?"

"Oh, please." She stands up, stretches her arms overhead, and winks. "If I was, you'd know."

The overhead lights flicker on, filling the room, and a chorus of groans sounds somewhere on the opposite side. I catch sight of Adrienne across the room as she sits up in her bed and rubs the sleep from her face. The moment she notices me, the lines around her mouth harden, and she looks away.

Monroe clears her throat and nods toward the door behind me as Reid steps back inside, a cup in each hand. His shirt is wrinkled, his hair messier than I've ever seen it. It takes me a moment to realize it's probably because of *me*. I can still remember the feel of it between my fingers. Monroe pretends to be busy making her bed as he reaches us and offers me the second cup.

"Thanks," I say, not quite able to meet his eyes as I take a small sip. Now that I've started thinking about last night, I can't turn it off—his skin against my lips, his blood in my mouth, his voice in my ear, his body pressing down on me, his fingers—

"Can I talk to you for a second?" he asks.

My eyes shoot to his face, but his expression gives nothing away.

"Yeah. Sure."

He gives Monroe a tight-lipped smile, then gestures for me to follow him back toward the hall. No one pays us any attention as we step out of the room, but the moment we're alone, the tension in my body doubles. I sip the water, trying to appear unfazed as he glances around us, then leans a shoulder against the wall and meets my eyes.

"Look, Valerie." His gaze falls to the cup in his hands as he twists it around.

I brace myself for whatever he's going to say next, heat crawling up the back of my neck.

"I just don't want anything to be weird between us," he continues. "Or for anything to change. And I…" He sighs. "I know there's been a lot going on, even before all of this."

He gestures around us—to the bunker, presumably. "So, anyway, I would understand, if that's what last night was. If it was just the situation and everything."

The bond is quiet between us. My hand tightens around the cup, but I fight to keep my voice perfectly even as I ask, "Is that what that was for you?"

His eyes snap back to my face, searching it. A long beat of silence stretches between us, until finally, he says, very quietly, "No. That's not what that was for me."

"Okay," I say. The heat spreads down my neck, engulfing the rest of my body. The intensity of his gaze pins me to the spot, but I don't look away. "Me neither."

A hint of tension leaves the set of his shoulders, and a flicker of awareness passes through the bond—not a feeling exactly, just something like contact. Like the warmth of skin against skin.

"Okay," he says, his lips pulling up at the corners as he takes a step closer.

"Okay," I whisper, a smile threatening on my own lips.

He stops inches away, presses his fingers under my chin, and tilts my head up to look at him. A full grin has taken over his face now. "Okay."

Nathan gags with blood still on his lips. He sets the bag on the table and shakes his head a few times. "Stale."

"It's exactly the same blood you usually drink," Monroe deadpans. "They literally just brought the blood bags down from upstairs."

"But they usually warm it up for me," he points out.

She rolls her eyes, but she's smiling.

Reid, on the other hand, has already emptied two bags. I wince a little. I must have taken more from him last night than I'd realized. And to be honest, I could already use some more.

The rest of the kitchen bustles around us as more people trickle in, yawning and rubbing their eyes. I frown, glancing around. The Marionettes who'd gotten us settled yesterday are nowhere to be found. In fact, the only witches I've seen since we got up today are my age or younger.

"So, do you think they're keeping your mom somewhere separate or something?" Monroe asks. "Can't really picture her slumming it in the communal bedroom. To be honest, I'm surprised *you're* down here."

Reid blinks, taking a second to register she's talking to him, his fingers already tearing into a third bag. "They have different procedures for her."

I glance at him sideways, thinking back to our conversation at the art studio. I'd thought he'd been exaggerating when he'd said the queen probably found him expendable —but her leaving him down here with the rest of us suggests there was more truth to his words than I'd realized.

Because surely, wherever she is, there would've been enough room for him too if she'd wanted him there. My chest feels a little heavier at the thought, and I quickly look away before he can catch me watching him.

"If we're *group one*, I can only imagine what the accommodations are like for everyone else," Monroe mutters.

Reid shifts, and his leg presses against mine. A jolt of electricity goes through me, and I sit up a little straighter, now hyperaware of him. He doesn't move away. In fact, he slides his hand beneath the table and lightly skims it along my thigh before resting halfway up, his fingers pressing into my skin. Monroe leans over, saying something else to Nathan, but I can't hear it. Heat pools low in my stomach at the contact, and I'm entirely consumed with the way his body had felt pressed against mine last night. How his voice had sounded when he'd said my name. How his mouth had felt against my skin.

How much I want to do it again.

His thumb slowly strokes up and down my thigh, and I pull in a deep breath through my nose, trying not to combust on the spot.

"I wonder where all of the Marionettes went," Monroe says, nudging me under the table. I blink back to the room around us, and Monroe narrows her eyes at me. She nods toward the group of vampires currently picking through the blood bags on the counter. "Half of their partners are gone." She turns her narrowed eyes on Reid. "You don't know what's going on and you're just choosing not to say anything, are you?"

Before he can respond, a stampede of footsteps echoes in the tunnel, drawing closer. I glance up as three older Marionettes hurry into the room, their heads whipping back and forth. A tall blonde woman is closest to us, and her eyes light up as they land on Reid beside me.

"Your Highness," she says, coming to stand beside our table. "We need you to come with us."

"What's this about?" he asks.

"We're evacuating the royal family," she says. "And the representatives. Your mother sent me specifically to find you."

"What's going on?" Nathan demands from across the table. "If they're being evacuated, we should go too." He waves a finger between him and Monroe. "Do you know who I am?"

The woman barely spares him a glance. "Your Highness, we really need to hurry. There's a plane waiting."

Reid glances at me, his brow furrowed. "Okay, we'll just—"

"Just you," she cuts him off.

Reid pauses, his hand tightening on my leg. "I'm not leaving without my partner. What reason could you possibly have to take me but not her?"

The woman shakes her head. "I just have my orders. All of the Marionettes who are still of student age are supposed to stay down here and protect everyone else left."

"You already have dozens down here," he says. "Surely you could spare one person. She's my partner. She stays with me."

"I'm sorry, but there's only a spot for you."

The other two Marionettes have joined her by our table now, looking like they're going to take him whether he's willing or not. The weight of her words settles like a rock in the center of my chest.

Reid tenses.

"Why are you evacuating them?" I demand.

The woman sighs. "I'm not at liberty to discuss that."

"Are we not safe down here?" Monroe asks.

"You're perfectly safe—"

"Then why are you evacuating?" Nathan cuts in. "And why aren't we on the list?"

The woman slams her hand down on the table, exposing a small glass vial full of a thick silver substance.

Alchemist.

She slowly meets each of our eyes. "Either the prince can leave with me peacefully, or I can knock all of you unconscious for the next twelve hours. Either way, he's coming with us, and the three of you are staying here. Understood?"

Reid's hand on my leg tightens so much it almost hurts as he flicks his eyes from the container to my face, probably weighing his options. If they want to take him and leave me here, he won't be able to stop them. There's more of them, sure, but the second she opens that vial, we'd probably all be knocked unconscious.

I stare back at him, my heart beating faster in my chest. How much longer are they planning on keeping us down here? Without him to help me feed, I won't make it through another day before I snap.

When no one says anything, she wraps her hand around Reid's arm and pulls until he rises from his seat. He doesn't look at me again, but the bond warms between us, and his voice appears faintly in the back of my mind.

It'll be okay.

The three Marionettes lead him toward the tunnels again, and my throat tightens, which brings my attention back to the hunger already building there.

Reid meets my eyes right before he disappears behind the wall.

Valerie, I'm going to have to ask you to do something. I'll come back as soon as I can, but it probably won't be soon enough.

Reid—

I need you to glamour someone to let you drink from them. Just for tonight.

My heart drops into my stomach. *Reid, I can't do that.*

You have to.

Reid—

I'm sorry. The bond goes quiet for several moments, and I can almost *feel* his sigh. *But you don't have a choice.*

CHAPTER TWENTY-SEVEN

THE ANXIETY and restless energy in the air is palpable. Besides the remaining student-aged witches and their partners, none of the Marionettes have been around since they came to take Reid. What is going on up there? Where are they taking the people they evacuated? Sitting here waiting and doing nothing is excruciating. The absence of distractions leaves me with nothing to focus on but the growing hunger inside of me. It beats like a drum, the rhythm slowly getting faster and faster.

Monroe offered to help, but at this rate, I'm not sure I'll make it until everyone goes to sleep. Maybe we could sneak off somewhere, but with everyone awake and roaming around freely, what if someone sees us? Or hears us? Or *smells* us? This place is crawling with vampires with senses even stronger than mine are.

The bond has been quiet since Reid left, and I don't know if it's intentional or if he's too far away now.

"Watch where you're going."

A shoulder smacks into mine, and I stumble to a stop, blinking back to the hallway in front of me.

Adrienne walks past without looking back and turns the corner into the kitchen. I should try to talk to her again, but while I'm fighting back the urge to rip out her throat is probably not the best time.

I need to find Monroe…I'd even take Daniel right now.

But Monroe and Nathan disappeared a few hours ago to explore the rest of the tunnels down here, apparently unconcerned about what happened earlier, and I don't trust myself to be around everyone else to go look for them. The hall branching off from the kitchen leads to the rest of the rooms, but I haven't ventured down there. The sleeping room and kitchen are empty, so everyone else must be down that way. Maybe if there's enough distance between me and everyone else, I can manage to keep my fangs to myself.

I slump into the same table we'd been sitting at earlier and eye the blood bags on the counter. I can smell them from here—rotting and sour.

Despite everything else going on, all I can think about is Reid. Is he okay? When is he coming back?

Is he coming back at all?

"There you are!" Monroe ducks her head into the kitchen. *Oh thank God.* "Come on! They've got some old games and stuff back here to pass the time. I'm kicking Nathan's ass in pool."

I shake my head, then gesture for her to come closer.

Frowning, she steps the rest of the way into the room and comes to sit across from me. "Is this about them taking—"

"I'm starving," I whisper. Even just having her this close

makes the hunger flare inside of me. "So, it's probably best I'm not...close by."

"Val, God, why didn't you say anything? What can I do? You want to go somewhere?"

I dig my nails into my palms and inhale through my nose, my control already starting to slip. My body vibrates with need.

"Okay, okay." She stands up and slowly comes to my side. "You and I are going to go to the bathroom, okay?"

I manage a nod.

Monroe's pulse ticks up as we trek through the hall back to the sleeping quarters. I count the beats in my head. *Bum-bum, bum-bum, bum-bum.* Eighty beats per minute, maybe ninety now.

My vision blurs at the edges, Monroe's hand on my arm the only thing keeping me moving forward. She speaks lowly under her breath, but I can't hear her.

We pass rows of empty beds, heading for the bathroom door in the back. We're alone, Monroe's pulse still the only one thundering in my ears. I grab the handle with a shaky hand. Just a few more steps, then I'll be able to think again. Just a few more—

"Macavei."

The Marionette who'd taken Reid earlier steps into the room and waves her hand impatiently. "*There* you are. I need you to come with me."

"What? Why?" Monroe demands.

The girl tilts her head to the side like she's listening to something in an earpiece. "I don't know. They've requested all of the skinwalkers. Maybe for a patrol or something." She waves her hand. "Come on. You're the last one."

"Okay. Okay. I just need to go to the bathroom first."

Her eyes flicker from Monroe to me. "Look, I don't have time for whatever this is. You can use one upstairs. Let's go." Before Monroe can respond, the girl flicks her wrist, and the floor beneath Monroe's feet shoves her toward the door. Monroe stumbles, and the girl does it again, forcing her from the room. She turns around and meets my eyes, panic coating her face, as the girl grabs her arm and yanks her down the hall.

UNSURPRISINGLY, drinking my own blood doesn't quench my thirst. I sit on the ground in the bathroom and lick at a slice in my wrist. My throat stops burning for a second, but the ache comes back stronger than before a moment later, probably increasing as my body expends energy trying to heal itself.

If they took all of the skinwalkers, that means Daniel's gone too. Not that I would have wanted to go to him, but he could've been a last resort. Now I have…no one.

I think back to what Reid said. *Glamour someone.*

Panic squeezes my chest, and I curse myself for refusing to practice it with Reid before. I never learned how. I have no idea how to do it properly. One wrong move down here, and all of the wrong people will find out about me.

That's it then. I have to get out of here. Better I get in trouble for trying to escape than slaughtering everyone.

Propping myself up on the bathroom sink, I force my vision to focus as I stare at my reflection. Her eyes are red, bloodshot. "Just keep your shit together for a few more minutes," I whisper.

I open the bathroom door, expecting the room to still be empty, but people are flooding inside.

"Come on, people. Move along," calls a voice from the hallway.

The sound of pulsing blood fills my head, layering more and more with each person who enters the room.

"What's going on?" I ask to no one in particular.

"Lockdown," a deep voice says to my right. "A breach on the property or something. They're locking us in here until they resolve it."

Locking us in?

My eyes dart to the red salt lining the walls. If they close that door, I'm not getting out.

I don't think. I just move.

I shove my way through the incoming crowd, the hunger growing louder and louder in my head with each warm body I pass. I just need to get to the hall. I should be able to teleport from there—to where, who cares? I just need to get out.

Shoulders bump into me as I plunge forward. Buzzing builds in my ears. Each breath I pull in is shorter than the last.

"Nope, sorry." A hand presses directly into my chest, pushing me back as I reach the door. "No one out."

"Get out of my way," I say lowly.

I can't see their face. I can't see anything. I can't breathe. I can't—

—something tugs on my arm from behind—

—and something inside of me—
—snaps.

CHAPTER TWENTY-EIGHT

FOR THE FIRST time in a while, something is louder than the blood.

The screams.

Warmth coats my skin as blood pours down my front and explodes in my mouth. No matter how much I drink, the hunger screams for more. A body falls to my feet, so I grab another, still working my way toward the door as I tear into the throat.

Hands grab at me. Gusts of wind pull at my hair. Someone tries to pry the body away from my hands, and I snarl, yanking it with me into the hall. A glint of light catches my eye—something in a glass container. My vision clears, just a bit, bringing me back from the haze. I may only have seconds before they immobilize me.

With how much blood is soaking every inch of my skin, I probably won't even need my own. I mutter the incantation under my breath, visualizing myself breaking down to the core of my being, the barest trace of a particle, then I drop the body, and I'm gone.

I WAKE on my back in the grass, a starless night sky staring down at me. I roll my head to the side, a splitting headache cutting down the center of my forehead. The estate looms in the distance. I'm still on the grounds.

The silence is chilling.

No one else is around, but also, the surrounding trees are silent. No birds, no insects. Just the wind rustling the leaves.

I push myself to my feet, frowning. I vaguely remember someone saying there was a breech on the property, and that's why they were locking everyone in. But as far as I can tell, the grounds are deserted.

The breeze brings the scent of blood to my nose, and my head involuntarily falls back with a moan. Unfortunately, I realize, the smell is coming from me. My clothes are drenched in it. When I look down at my hands, I can barely see my skin through the streaks of blood.

My gums burn, my throat aching for more. I run my tongue along the backs of my fingers. The dried blood flakes in my mouth, bitter and unsatisfying.

But I keep going. I lick every inch of my hand until it's clean. Hot shame coats me, but I can't stop.

Something moves behind me.

I whip around as figures emerge from the tree line. Three at first, but I know there are more, if my last experience with them is any indication.

Black cloaks hang loosely over their bodies, though the antlers from the animal skulls covering their faces and their jagged claws are still visible.

A memory takes hold of me—from another life, it feels like. A similar stance, them approaching me. Their claws digging into my chest. The searing pain that consumed me, and everything that's come after.

But here, now, as I watch them glide across the grass, inching closer, the fear I'd expected to feel in my chest isn't there. I just watch, waiting.

What more could they possibly take from me?

The one in the center, slightly shorter than the others, slowly tilts its head to the side, as if also studying me. The surrounding darkness seems to cling to it, wrapping around us like fog. More drift from the edges of the trees, coming closer, circling me. An endless number, one after the other, they slink from the shadows.

I keep my eyes on the shorter one. Somehow, I know it is the leader. It stops a foot away, and though it's shorter than the rest, it still towers over me, and I have to crane my neck back. Its head lifts again, as if sniffing the air. Sniffing *me*.

A buzzing builds in the air around us, as if I can *hear* the energy coming off them in waves. It raises the hairs on my arms.

And yet, still, I can't seem to muster any fear.

Where are they all coming from? How did James Westcott find them? And why are these creatures doing what he wants? What power could he possibly hold over them?

The wendigo bends down, bringing its face inches away.

My breath hitches in my throat as its eyes stare into mine—strikingly blue and…human.

Then just as quickly, it rises back to its full height and…

Drifts away.

The others follow, slithering across the grass like smoke, heading for the estate. Darkness descends over the grounds as they move, pulling it with them.

They're no longer interested in me.

I suppose they already got what they wanted.

I've fed now. I should probably go back inside and help the others. Warn them. Do *something*.

But I turn and walk the other way.

I COULD WALK FOREVER. With all of this blood pumping through my system, no matter how far I go, my legs don't tire. So, I keep moving. The streets are quiet, even once I make it to the city. Did they put some kind of lockdown into effect out here too?

I don't know where my legs are taking me, but I don't question it. By the time I reach the Brooklyn Bridge, the hunger has already set back in.

Slowly, I sink onto a bench, my clothes now stiff from the dried blood. The haze from earlier seems to be wearing off. I could go back to the estate. Get my herbs. Try to pull it together again. But what would be the point? Whatever happened in that bunker is a blur. I don't even know whose blood this is.

They all know about me now, so I wouldn't be welcomed back. And they're better off without me.

According to Reid, that bunker is the safest place for him. The only thing threatening them was *me*.

And according to Quinn's professor friend, the herbs won't keep working forever. Judging by how more and more frequently I've needed them, I know she's right.

Since the night of the attack at the academy, I've been a ticking time bomb.

And I think the time is here.

James Westcott could be anywhere. He's been alive for God knows how long, and if he doesn't want to be found, he won't be. The only remaining variable is how many people I'm going to take down with me.

Going back would be the selfish thing to do. To keep letting myself find comfort in the delusion that there's a way out of this. That I'm not just as screwed as every other vampire or witch the wendigos have targeted. Why did I believe I would get to be any different?

A tear runs down my face.

It should've been you.

I guess she'll get what she wanted after all.

I'm suddenly so, so tired. A wave of exhaustion washes over me, and I curl into a ball on the bench, watching the water lap against the rocks below.

"Maybe I'll get to see you soon, Calla," I whisper, then wait for sleep to take me.

RED SEEPS into my dreams like blood. I can tell I'm asleep, but the dreams never fully form. Colors and sounds blur past, none quite concrete enough to grasp. Screams play over and over again like a background track. Maybe that's how the people in the bunker had sounded. I can't remember anything, but I may have subconsciously held on to the memory.

Not that it's one I want to get back.

"Hello?"

The colors around me shift from red to yellow, the screams growing more and more distant.

"Are you all right?"

Something presses into my side, and my eyes fly open. Blood pulses somewhere nearby, the heart rate picking up as I rise from the bench. I sniff the air—a witch.

God, she smells good.

My gums burn, and I force myself to take a step back. My vision blurs around me, vaguely registering the water and bridge in the distance. A figure stands in front of me, but I can't make out her features.

"You need to get back," I grit out through my teeth.

"I called for—"

"Now," I growl. "*Run.*"

She hesitates.

At least, I think she does. She's still in front of me. Which means it takes me about half a second to cross the distance between us and sink my fangs into the side of her throat. She lets out a choked scream, but it quickly dies off. I drop her body when I'm done, her blood hot on my skin. I lick the remaining drops from my lips, moaning as the taste fills my mouth again, but it doesn't relieve the ache in the back of my throat this time.

I need more.

I sniff the air for another scent and start walking toward the street. In a city like this, it shouldn't be hard to find.

A sniffle sounds to my right.

I freeze on the sidewalk and glance back at the alley I passed. Voices chatter on the next street. My gaze darts from the alley to the corner, and I inhale deeply.

Humans one street over.

But whatever is in this alley is *not*. The smell is strong enough for me to pick up even past the rotting garbage in the dumpster. Silence greets me as I venture farther down. Someone is in here. I stop once I reach the middle of the alley, listening. To my left, a small, elevated heart rate, growing faster by the second.

I take a step closer, and metal clangs behind the dumpster. Two trashcan lids are propped up against the brick wall, shielding whatever's back there. I grab one and toss it aside. The shriek of metal on pavement fills the space around us as a small, dirty face peers at me from behind the dumpster. Light from a window above us falls on half of his face—he can't be older than ten. Tears stain his cheeks, and he looks from me to the way I'd come with wide eyes.

The woman, I realize. The one by the bench. Maybe that had been his mom.

My stomach twists, and I stumble back a step, breathing hard. The boy flinches as my foot hits the metal lid, and it scrapes against the ground. His hands fly up to cover his ears, exposing a long gash on his forearm, fresh blood still seeping out. The scent hits me a second later, and a low growl tears from my throat.

The boy cries out and shoves himself back, trying to get out the other side. I leap on top of the dumpster, my teeth bared, my breaths coming in hard and fast. Reaching down, I seize the boy by the back of his shirt before he has a chance to scramble to his feet. He lets out a choked cry as I haul him up beside me and slam him onto the lid.

"Please," he whimpers, fingernails digging into my arms as he tries to wrestle himself free.

My teeth cut into his throat all too easily. His blood fills my mouth, and I moan.

It doesn't take long for him to stop struggling.

———

I WAKE to the sun shining in my eyes. Groaning, I roll over, damp grass greeting my arms, then push myself into a seated position. My clothes are stiff and itchy, and my skin tingles from the sunlight—not quite painful, but definitely not pleasant. I squint and shield my eyes.

Central Park, it seems. How I got here, I don't know. The air is still cool enough that it must be early morning. The paths are empty.

I glance down at the dried blood coating my clothes. I can't keep walking around like this. It's under my nails, crusted against my skin. I'm willing to bet it's in my hair too.

Honestly, I'd bathe in the lake at this point.

My head pounds with each step as I walk. I need to get out of this sun. It's just going to make the hunger come back faster. I groan, my feet blindly leading the way. The Bethesda Fountain looms straight ahead, and I quicken my steps, kicking off my shoes as I get close. I'm about to climb inside when I pause, looking around.

It's completely deserted. Not just not-as-busy-as-it-is-at-night deserted. There's not a single other soul here.

I frown but climb in anyway, letting out a soft sigh as the cold water hits my skin. I sink down and lie on my back, tilting my head to let the water run over my hair. When I squint an eye open, the fountain's angel stares down at me, the sun reflecting off its wings.

I close my eyes again.

The sounds muffle around me as I push my head underwater. The hunger doesn't feel as immediate under here, or maybe holding my breath is enough of a distraction for my body. I scrub at my skin, my nails, my hair, trying to wash it all away, not letting myself think of where it came from.

Not letting myself think of anything at all.

When I can't hold my breath any longer, I let my face float to the top, but keep the rest of myself submerged. The moment the air hits my face, the burning in my throat creeps back in.

I squeeze my eyes tighter, ordering myself not to cry. It never stops. It just never goes away.

"Stop. *Stop.*"

I jerk out of the water at the sound of voices. Four figures are heading toward me, one holding her arms up to stop the others as she takes the lead. I squint, willing my vision to focus, but their forms remain blurry.

"Just let me talk to her," says the girl. "One minute."

I recognize that voice. Why do I know that voice?

She slows as she gets closer, then stops a few paces from the fountain. "Valerie?"

Her heart rate picks up, beating faster each moment I

don't respond. I swallow hard against the ache growing in the back of my throat.

"Valerie," she repeats. "It's okay. It's okay, we're just here to help."

I look from the girl to the three people waiting behind her.

"It's me, Val," she says, drawing my attention back to her. "It's Monroe."

My chest rises and falls with my quickening breaths, and I push myself farther back in the fountain. "Stay back," I warn, my voice hoarse. "I can't—"

"I know. It's okay—"

"It's not okay," I snap.

"All right. All right." She holds up her palms, and the others inch a little closer. "But we're going to take you home, okay? And we're going to get everything figured out."

"There's nothing to figure out," I snap. "There's nothing you can do, so *leave.*"

"Valerie—"

"Get the fuck out of here!" I push myself out of the water and flatten my back against the center of the fountain. "I don't want to hurt you."

"I'm not leaving you here," she says, her voice firm, then extends her arm. "So, you can either take my hand and come with me willingly, or the four of us will drag you back."

The rest of her group joins her by the fountain's edge now. One of them is Daniel, I realize. My stomach drops, and I shake my head.

"You can't come any closer. I can't—"

"We brought a sedative," she says.

I look between each of their faces again, every muscle in my body coiled tight, trying to weigh my options through the haze in my mind. I could die out here, alone—and take who knows how many unwitting victims with me—or I could die at home, surrounded by the people who know me.

People who probably won't love me anymore once they see the extent of what I've done.

"Valerie, please," Monroe whispers.

Her face finally comes into focus, and she stares at me with sad, pleading eyes. How long have they been out here looking for me? How long have *I* been out here?

How many bodies have I left along the way?

I won't let one of them be next.

I can't.

"Throw me the sedative," I squeeze out through the lump in my throat.

Monroe and Daniel exchange a look.

"Give it to me," I order.

After another moment of hesitation, Monroe fishes a syringe out of her pocket and tosses it to me. I catch it in one hand, the glass cool against my palm. All four of them stare at me as I remove the needle from its case, and with a deep breath, plunge it into my neck.

CHAPTER TWENTY-NINE

I GUESS I was wrong about not being affected by the cold anymore. Everything about this cell is cold—the air, the stone beneath my back, the metal bars standing between me and the narrow hallway. A single bulb dangles outside of my cell, buzzing on and off intermittently. At first, it's a good way to pass the time. Counting how many times it goes off, how many seconds between each flicker.

After however many hours of doing this, the noise starts to get under my skin.

I curl into a ball on the slab of concrete they call a bed, hoping if I make myself small enough, I'll be able to preserve some of my body heat. I don't know which is worse at this point, the hunger or the cold. My body vibrates with the need for blood, my gums hot and throbbing until my entire jaw aches.

I don't know how long I've been down here. The last thing I remember is sticking that sedative in my neck, then I woke up here, and I haven't seen anyone else since.

Maybe I never will.

Does anyone even know I'm down here? Are they coming back? Do they have a plan?

Is the plan to just let me rot?

I suppose that's probably what I deserve. There's still so much blood caked under my fingernails, and I have no idea where it came from.

Who it came from.

A metal door clangs, and I sit up, hugging my arms to myself. Slowly, footsteps make their way toward me, clicking lightly against the cement. She stops directly under the light outside of my cell.

"Mom." I swing my legs over the edge of the bed to stand. I don't think I've ever been more relieved to see her in my life. Tears prick my eyes. "I—"

"No."

I pause at the coldness in her voice, then realize how far away she's standing from the bars. Her back is practically pressed against the opposite wall.

I wipe under my nose with the back of my hand and shake my head. "I won't—I can't—"

"*No*," she repeats, louder this time. She stands with her arms crossed, her chin held high in the air as she looks down at me over her nose. "This not a social visit, Valerie."

"Mom—"

"You have lost the right to call me that."

My next words die in my throat.

She paces forward, slowly, and leans so her face is right up against the bars. When she speaks again, her voice is so low, it raises the hairs on the backs of my arms. "As far as I'm concerned, you are no longer a Darkmore."

I swallow hard, a lump rising to the back of my throat. "Mom—"

"You are so damn lucky, do you know that? You are so damn lucky your sister pulled through, because if she hadn't, I'd be in that cell right now to finish you off myself."

Pulled through…?

I stumble back a step and sink onto the slab of concrete. *No.* My heart stops in my chest. "Adrienne," I whisper.

"Don't you dare say her name," my mother spits.

I cover my mouth with my hand, desperately searching through my memory of the bunker, but there are only flashes of blood and bodies and screams. A body I'd dropped to the floor once I was finished with it…

It couldn't have been—

I couldn't have—

"I just needed to see you down here for myself," she continues. "But you won't be seeing me again." She turns to head back the way she'd come.

I jump up from the bed and wrap my hands around the bars, the tears flowing freely down my cheeks now. She can't leave. She can't just leave me down here, not until I can explain. "Mom, please. I'm so, so sorry. I didn't mean to. You have to understand—"

The metal door slams shut behind her.

The following silence is so heavy I feel like I'm choking on it. My legs fold beneath me, and I slide down the bars to the floor, resting the side of my face against the cold metal. I gasp, trying to pull air into my lungs, but my chest is so tight I can't breathe. The worst part is how fully I believe her.

She won't be coming back.

"For what it's worth," says a deep voice, "your mother sounds like a total bitch."

I jump, my breath getting caught in my throat. "Who's there?"

"Ah, sorry. You lose your manners down here. The name's Marcus. Guess we're neighbors now."

Marcus. Of course Marcus is still down here. I don't think reminding him I'm the one who put him here is going to do me any favors. But he'd seemed so far gone in the park that night—no trace of the person he used to be left inside of him.

Now he sounds...normal.

"Valerie," I say quietly.

"Darkmore," he finishes for me. "Yeah, got that. Sounds like you and I got dealt the same card, huh?"

I pull my knees into my chest and curl myself around them. "Have they been treating you down here or anything?"

He snorts. "You're the first person I've seen come down here. But the...*haze* from the hunger goes in and out. I think they're waiting us out."

What little hope had started to build in my chest deflates. "Oh," I say, because there's nothing else to say.

Apparently there's nothing else to do at all.

"You remember much?" he asks.

I shake my head, then realize he can't see me, and utter a soft "No."

He sighs, and something shifts on his side of the wall.

"Maybe you'll get lucky, and it'll stay that way. The memories have been coming back for me. Slowly. The people I killed."

A shiver runs up my spine. I hate having blocks of time completely missing from my memory, but maybe getting them back would be worse.

I rest my forehead against my knees and squeeze my eyes shut. It doesn't make any sense. What was the *point*? Why would James Westcott—or whoever he is—go through all of this trouble to do this just for us to end up rotting in these cells?

"No offense," says Marcus. "But you being down here is quite the bummer."

I let out an incredulous laugh. "Am I intruding on your alone time?"

"Nah, see, I'm no one. Them leaving me down here wasn't all that surprising. But *you*? You're kind of a big deal around here, aren't you? The *Golden Darkmore Child* or whatever the hell they call you. If they threw *you* down here, then there really is no hope for us, is there?"

"That's great, Marcus. Thanks."

"I just call it like it is."

"Do you know anyone else?" I ask. "Who this happened to?"

He hesitates a moment before responding. "Anyone in particular, no. But there have to be others. The bodies piling up around the city, they weren't all me."

"More have popped up since you came down here. Apparently it's been happening near the other estates too."

"And here I was, thinking I was special," he muses.

I grit my teeth, the light quality of his voice grating on my nerves. "How can you be joking right now?"

"Oh, I'm sorry, would you rather I cry? Scream? Lament about the unfairness of it all? Hate to break it to you, Darkmore, but we're both going to die down here. Me probably before you. And nothing's going to change that. It's just the way it is. If *you* want to spend your last days crying about it, by all means, have at it."

"So that's it?" I demand. "You've just given up?"

"If you have a better plan, I'm all ears, Golden Child." His voice dips low, the amusement suddenly gone. "All I know is, when I was out there, I killed my entire family. At least behind these bars, other people are safe."

"There could be a cure," I say.

He doesn't respond for such a long time, I think he's not going to at all. But then, barely audible, he says, "But they would still be dead."

———

MARCUS and I don't talk anymore after that. I go back to counting the seconds between light flickers, until eventually, the names of numbers don't make sense anymore. It's an endless cycle of sleep, wake, count, sleep. Even though I know it won't help, I sink my teeth into my wrist and fill my mouth with blood.

Maybe it'll speed up the process.

After a while, I get too afraid to call out to Marcus in case he doesn't answer.

Even after my mother's visit, I still held on to the smallest shred of hope someone would come for me. I don't know how long ago that was. It was before my body started to shut down.

My legs are stiff, and I don't think I could move them if I tried. It's a battle to open my eyes. My blood feels like it's coagulating, cementing my insides together. My body is deteriorating and eating away at itself to the point where I can no longer feel the hunger.

I can no longer feel anything at all.

MY WORLD IS MADE of only sounds, though they stopped carrying meanings long ago. Everything is dark, numb.

A groan of metal somewhere in the distance. Voices, though I don't understand what they're saying. One is deeper and getting louder with each word. Yelling. Angry. It sounds angry. Two of them? Yes, there are two. One shakes around the words. More metal screeches, this time closer. Tapping. Footsteps, those are footsteps.

Something brushes my skin—soft, heavy. It wraps around my shoulders. I can't move. My eyelids stopped working a while ago. I want to speak, but my mouth isn't functioning either.

Skin presses against mine, on my face, my neck. My head falls back as my shoulders lift. Something warm replaces the cold stone that had been under me a moment ago.

That voice again, deep and rumbling. The thing beneath me vibrates with the sound of it.

Something brushes my face again, pushing my hair

away. Pressure on my chin, my jaw, pulling my mouth open. My muscles give no resistance.

Hot liquid hits my face—my lips, my tongue, my cheek. More pours into my mouth, down my throat. Slowly, it works its way through my body.

And so does the pain.

It rips through me. My chest fills with heat, stretching and pulling and *tearing*.

But I can't move.

My muscles tighten and expand, fighting against my dry veins. My bones feel like they're breaking apart.

I gasp, my breaths coming in short and fast, and try to pull away from the liquid falling into my mouth, but my head barely moves. Whatever is around me tightens, holding me in place.

Arms. They're arms, I realize.

"I know. I know. It's okay."

I let out a small whimper as my body tries to claw its way back to life, the repairing somehow hurting more than the breaking down did.

"Shh. You're okay. I've got you."

The taste of blood finally registers. I try to pull away again, swallowing hard. "No," I whisper.

"Valerie? Valerie, I know it hurts, but I need you to keep drinking."

"No."

He shifts behind me and twists me to face him. I still can't open my eyes, but I can smell him.

"Valerie." His hand cups the side of my face. "Can you hear me? I need you to keep drinking."

I lick my dry lips, his blood still coursing through my veins, trying to repair all of the breakage inside of me.

"No," I whisper.

I pry my eyes open. It takes a minute for my vision to focus on Reid's face, inches from mine. His eyes are wide, and he brings his hands to my cheeks.

"You need more blood. I need you to keep drinking."

I shake my head, and his gaze sweeps my face, the furrow between his brows deepening.

He's right. If I want to live, I need more blood.

If I want to live.

Being stuck down here has given me nothing but time to think. To remember. To comb through the muddled memories from when I was in the haze, to piece everything together.

Still, I can't.

There are hours, maybe days, missing.

But there are flashes.

A scream in the bunker, black hair bunched in my fist. A child begging for his life behind a dumpster. A body split in half left beneath a car. Blood turning the water of a fountain red.

The three witches I killed in the field.

It should've stopped there. *I* should've been stopped there.

If Reid brings me back, it'll just go on. More bodies, more death, more chasing away the hunger just for it to come right back. I can't take another minute of it.

Reid stares at me, his jaw hard. At first, I think it's anger. Disgust, like I'd seen on my mother. I wouldn't blame him. But his eyes keep flickering over my face, his hands holding me almost too tightly, like he's afraid I'm going to slip through his fingers.

"I can't," I whisper.

"Valerie." His voice cracks.

"Do you know how many people I killed?"

Understanding softens his features, but his grip is still just as firm. "Valerie."

"Do you know how many?" I repeat.

Slowly, he shakes his head.

"Me neither," I rasp. Maybe I would laugh if I could. "Seems like it shouldn't be a hard question to answer, right? But I don't know."

"Valerie."

I close my eyes. "Please just go, Reid. I don't—I don't want to hurt anyone else."

"Valerie—"

"Please, Reid."

"Look at me." I don't move. He tightens his hold on me. "Look at me," he repeats through his teeth.

His mouth is set in a firm line as he looks from my eyes to mouth and back again. The bond had been early to go when my body started shutting down, but I can feel it now, a thin, tight line burning from him to me, humming and vibrating like a string on my violin. So many emotions are pouring through it I can't make any of them out.

"Do you know how many people I've killed?" he asks, his voice suddenly hard.

"Reid—"

"Do you know?"

I shake my head.

He doesn't blink. "One hundred and thirty-seven."

I pull in a shaky breath.

"Do you know how many of those were unintentional?"

I wait, and his eyes bore into mine, expression unchanging.

"Three. Alison Luo, Taamir Yang, and Malee Patel."

"Reid," I whisper.

"When I was first sent to Suksai when I was thirteen, I'd refused to feed from humans up until that point, but Suksai doesn't believe in blood bags. And I didn't know how to feed properly. I didn't know when to stop. So three humans who didn't have to die died because of me."

My breath hitches, and he rubs his thumb against my cheek.

"I know what you're feeling," he says. "And I wouldn't wish it on anyone. But you can't give up on me now. I found the specialist from Auclair. He's here at the estate. He says he can help you, and I believe him, Valerie. I believe that he can."

I shake my head. "It doesn't matter, Reid. I snapped down in that bunker. Everyone knows—"

He smooths his hand over my hair. "I already took care of it. They're under the impression it was just the psychosis —and those who weren't, I glamoured. With you still walking in the sun and everything, no one has reason to suspect this has anything to do with that."

A tear trails down the side of my face, and I press my lips together to keep more from spilling out. "You don't understand," I whisper, and my voice hitches in the middle. I drop my eyes again. "One of them was Adrienne."

His hands slide to the back of my head and pull me

against his chest. The tears cloud my vision, and I bury my face in his shirt.

"I'm sorry," he murmurs against my hair. "I'm so sorry I didn't get back sooner. I'm—" He stops, his chest rising and falling rapidly with his breath. "Valerie, I'm not going to lose you over this. I won't. Let me help you now."

"Where were you?" I whisper.

His arms tighten around me. "They sent us to Auclair since they'd already survived one of these attacks. But the border shut down shortly after we got there, and no planes were willing to come back this way until the lockdown was resolved. I swear to you, I tried everything I could to get back. Valerie, I'm so—"

"I know."

Neither of us says anything for a minute, and I focus on his heart beating under my ear.

"Giving up won't bring any of them back," he whispers. "But I promise you I won't let it happen again, okay?"

A tear runs down my cheek. I'm about to refuse again when he adds, his voice raw and barely louder than a whisper, "*Please.*"

The sound of it cuts straight through me. I squeeze my eyes shut as tight as they can go. The bond pulls again, desperate, pleading.

"Please," he says again, and his voice shakes around the word.

"Okay," I whisper. "Okay."

He pulls back an inch to search my face, then nods. He repositions himself so his chest is against my back, his arms bracketing me. His jacket is around my shoulders. That must have been what I felt when he first came in.

He lets out a slow breath and rests his chin back on the top of my head. "Valerie…this is going to…"

"Hurt? I know."

I close my eyes as he bites his wrist and brings it back to my mouth, every muscle in my body tensing and preparing for that splintering, devastating pain to fill me again. At first there's just the blood—the warmth in my mouth, the relief in the back of my throat. Then it starts to filter into my system, repairing my body piece by piece.

Reid's body tenses around me, and I hold on to his arms, digging in as my breathing quickens and sweat breaks out on my skin. The pain starts in my chest, the blood accumulating around my organs first before branching out to my arms, my legs. It's like expanding fire, burning and stretching at the same time.

A low moan escapes my throat as my body goes stiff in Reid's arms. He holds me tighter, murmuring something I can't hear over the blood pounding in my ears.

My heart beats like it's trying to break out of my chest, and spots creep into my vision. I try to hold on, but it isn't long before the wave of black crashes into me and pulls me under.

CHAPTER THIRTY

NOTHING'S CHANGED when I wake up. I'm in the same position, Reid's arms holding me against him. I must have not been out for long. He loosens his grip as I stir, but still doesn't let me go.

"How are you feeling?" he asks.

I stretch my fingers out, then slowly curl my hands into fists, testing. My joint function had been the first thing to shut down, but my fingers move with ease now.

"Okay, I think."

His hands glide up and down my arms, a small, unconscious movement. The bond pulses between us as if strengthened by how much of his blood I ingested.

It occurs to me how much blood he just *lost.*

"Are *you* okay?" I ask.

He nods. "I'll be all right."

"Reid…"

He squeezes my shoulders. "I'll feed when I go up. And if you're ready, I can bring the specialist down to see you."

My chest tightens. Of course I want him to bring him down, but if this doesn't work? This might be my last chance. My *only* chance. And then what? I start the agonizing decomposition process all over again?

Hopefully, Reid would at least be merciful enough to put me out of my misery.

"Okay," I whisper.

Reid extracts himself from behind me but doesn't head for the door right away. He kneels beside my head, and his throat bobs as he swallows.

"I'll be right back. I promise."

I nod. He still doesn't move. The bond tightens again as he leans forward and presses his forehead against mine. I don't blink. I don't breathe. I just watch him as his eyes take in every inch of my face, a harsh line carved down the center of his forehead.

His lips brush mine, lightly at first. Just the barest hint of contact. Then his hand comes up to the side of my head, his fingers twisting in my hair, and the kiss deepens like he's still trying to breathe life back into me.

A small seed of hope grows in my chest that maybe I will make it out of this cell after all. I don't know where my friends are, Connor doesn't give a shit about me anymore, and my family has disowned me, but maybe I have one person still in my corner. I have one person who cares about what happens to me.

At some point I start crying, and he shifts, his lips coming to my jaw, my cheeks, brushing away tear after tear. When he pulls back, his hands grip the sides of my face, holding me in place to look at him, and I see my own desperation reflected back.

"I'll be right back," he repeats.

I nod and wrap his jacket tighter around myself as he stands to leave. The cell feels much colder now as his footsteps disappear down the hall, or my body is functioning enough to feel cold again.

I push myself up to a seated position, testing my other joints—wrists, elbows, ankles. A lump rises in my chest as everything moves the way it's supposed to. Something I will never take for granted again. Just because I'd accepted what was happening hadn't made it any easier.

Footsteps patter outside my cell, but the sound is much softer this time. A mouse scurries beneath the pocket of light, and I let out a surprised squeal and curl my legs in toward my chest.

Then the air whistles.

The mouse shifts, quickly rising until there's a man in a suit standing in front of me. My breath catches as he leans his face between the bars of my cell and peers in.

He's older—old enough for his age to show in the lines of his face, though his hair is perfectly blond. I've never seen him before, but based on the way his eyes light up, he knows who I am.

He straightens back to his full height and puts his hands in his pockets, smiling at me. "Hello, Valerie Darkmore."

I push myself as far away from the man as the cell allows, my heart pounding in my chest. "Who are you?"

He rolls up his sleeves. "Honestly, Valerie, I thought you'd be happier to see me." He meets my eyes again, still smiling, still the perfect picture of calm. "I heard you were looking for me."

I stare at him. *Looking for him…?*

No.

"How did you get in here?" I ask, my voice coming out as little more than a whisper.

He quirks an eyebrow, as if I already know the answer to my question. "Your friend Reid let me in. I believe he thinks I'm some sort of wendigo specialist. How long do you think he'll look around up there before he gives up?" He waves a hand vaguely in the direction of the stairs. "It was very helpful of him to welcome me into the estate though, I must say. Certainly made my job easier."

Heat floods every inch of my skin, but I can't pinpoint the exact emotion filling me. My heart pounds, and my hands shake with it. "You're the one who did this to me."

He nods his head to the side. "Yes and no. I gave the order."

"You're James Westcott."

His smile widens into something wicked. "Yes and no."

Then he shifts again. His build remains mostly the same, though his shoulders are now a little less broad, his hair darker—the exact shade I see on myself in the mirror. A thick scar cuts down his face from one corner of his mouth to the opposite eyebrow.

I don't even have time to dwell on a skinwalker who can shift multiple forms—*human forms*—because my heart stumbles to a complete stop in my chest as a deluge of memories comes rushing back. When I speak again, my voice comes out breathy and barely audible.

"Dad?"

CHAPTER THIRTY-ONE

"We don't have a lot of time, so let's just get right to it. I can cure you, and all of this goes away."

I stand, arms crossed over my chest, but keep the same amount of distance between us. Half of his face is still hidden in shadow, and I can't read his expression at all. It's been fifteen years since I've seen him, but it's clear this is not meant to be a heartfelt reunion.

I'd stopped waiting for that a long time ago, but still, the utter lack of emotion in his eyes makes my breath hitch in my chest. I flex my jaw and tighten my arms, hoping it doesn't show on my face. I'm not going to play the role of the desperate, sobbing daughter for a man who didn't want her.

A man who did *this* to her.

"You said you gave the order for this to happen to me in the first place," I bite out, hoping the shake in my voice comes across as anger. "Why undo that by curing me then?"

He straightens the sleeves of his suit like this is some sort of business meeting. Like I'm a colleague. A stranger. "I'd want something in return, of course." His voice comes out smooth, calm. Had it always sounded like that? Was the warmth in the interactions I'd clung to in my memories just something my subconscious invented? "I cure you, but you'll have to come with me."

"I—" I shake my head and blink several times. "Come with you where? Why?"

He sighs as if my questions exhaust him and glances over his shoulder. "I'm afraid we don't have a lot of time for chatting. I think you and I both know if you want a cure, this is your only option. But it's up to you. If you'd rather, I can leave you here and be on my way."

I don't—can't—respond, still trying to process his words. Still trying to process *him*. A man I'd never thought I'd see again. But I guess a small part of me had held out the barest sliver of hope that if I ever did, he'd be the same one who'd gotten down on his knee to give me the violin. The one who had hugged me so tightly I could barely breathe. He'd be full of apologies and reasonable explanations as to why he's been gone all of this time.

But instead, he's *this*.

Instead, he's asking me to…leave with him.

My stomach roils, and a wave of dizziness crashes into me. "I can't—I can't just *leave*. And why? Go where?" My voice rises with each word, coming out higher and thinner each time. "And Reid—" My voice breaks around his name. "He'd—"

He sighs again and waves his hand. "Come after you, yes, that would be a problem. And in case anyone else around here gets the same idea, it wouldn't be too complicated to fake your death."

I stare at him.

"And your bond, another issue," he continues. "It'll have to be broken for it to be believable, of course."

Broken? Break my bond with Reid, so he and everyone else thinks I'm *dead?* My attention locks on to it, and my hand subconsciously comes up to rest on my stomach. The warm, comforting presence had been slightly annoying at first, but now, I can't imagine not having it. The thought of it being gone...of Reid...of *everyone* thinking I'm dead. Monroe, Kirby. Adrienne.

I can't just—he can't be serious.

He takes a knife from his pocket and slowly brings it across his palm, filling the air with the irony tang of his blood. He holds it out to me, as if offering a handshake.

My entire body goes cold.

A blood deal.

It's one of the first things we're taught about, the dangers of them. The implications. They're not to be taken lightly because once you're in one, there's no getting out.

But what does it matter if the other option is lying in here and waiting until I rot? No specialist is coming. My only hope had been finding James Westcott...

And he's standing right here.

When I don't respond, he shrugs, closes his fist, and turns for the door. His footsteps fill the silence, and I picture everything that would come next. The breakdown of my body starting all over again. The pain. The cold. The hunger eating away at my insides. No longer being able to speak, to move.

All of this, *all of this*, would have been for nothing.

His footsteps grow quieter as he nears the end of the hall, his hand reaching for the door.

I rush forward and press my face against the bars.

"Wait. *Wait.*"

He looks at me over his shoulder, a hint of amusement pulling at the corners of his mouth.

Everything inside of my body screams at me not to, begs me to step away, to let him go.

But instead, I say, "You have a deal."

SEE WHAT HAPPENS NEXT & A BONUS SCENE

Thank you so much for reading *Wicked Souls,* and thank you for your reviews! It's appreciated so much and really helps the books.

Continue with Valerie's story in the third book in the series, *Bloodless Ties,* coming 2022, now up for preorder.

Can't wait until then? Good news! I have a bonus scene **from Reid's point of view**, available through my newsletter. Find out why Valerie and Reid were *really* paired together in book one.

Download it for free here:
https://BookHip.com/FNRVCLZ

ACKNOWLEDGMENTS

I don't always write acknowledgements for my books, but there are so many people I want to thank this time around.

I've been living and breathing this series for the past year trying to get these first two books out, and so many amazing people helped bring this story to life...and keep me sane.

So in no particular order, thank you so much to Stef, my cover designer, for capturing the vibe of the series perfectly. To Beth, my proofreader extraordinaire, for cleaning this book up when I was too tired to read it again for the thousandth time. My beta readers Lydia and Naemi for always being supportive even after I sent them very rough drafts (and you have them to thank for the addition of *many* scenes in this book). To Stef, the amazing narrator who brought Valerie's voice to life via audiobook. I couldn't have found a better voice for her. My best friend Paige for listening to my complaints and frustrations over FaceTime. My mom for always being excited to read the next book. And my community over on YouTube for following along with the entire process with my vlogs and live writing sprints. Writing can be such a solitary career, but you make it feel like I have an entire village behind me. I feel incredibly privileged to know you.

And to my readers who've followed Valerie, Reid, and the others this far into the series, I'm so glad we have the same weird taste in books. I can't wait for you to see what else I have in store. *evil laugh*

ABOUT THE AUTHOR

Katie Wismer is a die-hard pig lover, semi-obsessive gym rat, and longtime sucker for a well-written book. She studied creative writing and sociology at Roanoke College and now works as a freelance editor in Colorado with her cats Max and Dean.

When she's not writing, reading, or wrangling the cats, you can find her on her YouTube channel Katesbookdate.

You can sign up for her newsletter at katiewismer.com, or check out her instructional videos on writing and publishing on Patreon.

patreon.com/katiewismer

instagram.com/katesbookdate

goodreads.com/katesbookdate

bookbub.com/authors/katie-wismer

facebook.com/authorkatiewismer

amazon.com/author/katiewismer

twitter.com/katesbookdate

CPSIA information can be obtained
at www.ICGtesting.com
Printed in the USA
LVHW092149090122
708156LV00020B/250